Wallace Family Affairs
Volume IV
Look Beyond Your Eyes

Carey Anderson

ISBN:069224364X
ISBN-13:9780692243640

DEDICATION

I would like to dedicate this story to all of my Rough Riders. Thank you for all of your continued support and constant request for more stories. My imagination gets to run wild with you, as you inspire me to create more.

Cover design: Cover Couture

Join me on Facebook –
www.facebook.com/careythewriteranderson

Twitter - @CareyTheWriter

Blog - http://careyanderson.blogspot.com

Website –
http://www.careythewriteranderson.webs.com

ACKNOWLEDGMENTS

I would like to thank my baby-girl who is my life's ultimate expression of a dream realized. Thank you for sacrificing mommy time so that I could have the time to work some things out on paper.

I would like to thank my Soul Sistah #1 who has been my captivated audience since middle school. Without your love, support, encouragement, and FIRE I never would've completed Volume I or II, etc. Thank you for bringing me laughter when I couldn't get outside of my head.

I would like to thank my Sister-In-Law for taking time out of your busy family life to humor me with a read through of my latest thoughts and expressions. (SS1 & SIL THANK YOU for the trip to St. Helena where we spent the day lost in my imagination. I will never forget it, and it was exactly what I needed. THANK YOU!)

I would like to thank my dear cousin for reassuring me that my little hobby was relatable and entertaining. You are definitely a speed-reader, thank you for taking time out of your busy life to be entertained by my imagination.

I would like to thank last but not least Mrs. Laverne Dyes! Mrs. Dyes the day that you read my short story to my class changed my life. Thank you for giving me a positive outlet for all the angst going on in my life. You have forever changed my life, I am so thankful to have ever known you.

Chapter 1

"Get to the point Henry!" I said swinging in my chair and drumming my pen impatiently. Sometimes I SWEAR he is too detailed about the things I don't care about. "I need high level reporting." I tried to soften my tone. "It's good that you have your information together, because I will ask questions and I won't want you to search for the answer. You should be able to speak to everything I ask of you. However, let me ask. When I ask about customer satisfaction, tell me our final scores. Highlight areas of improvement and challenges. If I ask why, then you better know." I smiled

"Ok" Henry said deflating and not standing up for himself. He lets me run all over him so I do. It's not my fault.

I exhaled and looked at Thea, "how are we doing on time?"

"But I wasn't finished," Henry said kind of sheepishly

I blew air, and sat back in my chair. "How much more do you have?"

"Promotions, and circulations" he said

"Nope," I said shaking my head. "We got that covered, no need to discuss."

"Yes, but..."

I cut him off, "Promotions and circulations have been handled by the same firm for years. We're not changing it." My Cousin Gwen's firm handles all of that and she's done an excellent job. She even cuts us a deal on pricing and Malcolm loves her work, so there's no point in discussing it.

"But we've gotten lower bids, if you would just look..."

I cut him off again, "NO! What don't you understand the N or the O? Let me know which one it is and I'll break it down for you if you like."

Thea tried her hardest to pull back her laughter. "I was just trying to do my job." He said looking at the floor.

"Henry you do an excellent job! I know where to find you when I need you. But I want to give you back," I looked at the clock. "Thirty minutes to your day. I'm sure Richard needs some numbers or something from you." I said as I stood up to let him know this meeting was over.

He exhaled, glanced twice at my breast and exhaled again as he grabbed his papers. "Ok, but next time I'm on your calendar I'm gonna need my full hour."

"You got it buddy!" I said giving a thumbs up as I walked to my door and opened it to let him see his way out. When I

closed it behind him, Thea covered her mouth and laughed.
"He is pathetic!" I said walking back to my desk.
"I feel so bad for him. He seems so docile and loving. He just
wants to love you Sasha, why do you have to be so mean to
him?"
I gagged, "PAH-LEASE GURL! I ain't worried about no
Henry!" Henry was a major dork he wore the same three
blazers to work every week. He'd switch up the slacks from
time to time, but sometimes I swore he got dressed in the dark.
I haven't thought of a nice way to introduce him to, his should
be best friends Head & Shoulders. You look at his shoulders
and say is it snowing in LA? In addition, he's always
scratching. Yuck! He's single and the way he looks at me you
know, he sets his sights too high. I would make him cry for his
momma on a regular basis. You need more game than he could
imagine to step to me so, nope not doing it. I think it's sweet
that he looks at me period but it's not gonna happen.
I pulled up my calendar; I was relieved to see the rest of the
day was clear. I blocked off the rest of my calendar. I was
taking the rest of the day off. As soon as I finished my phone
rang. I saw the 212 area code and I grinned. It was my soon to
be New York office counterpart. "WHAT?" I said with a smile
as I answered my phone.
"I was trying to set up a meeting with you this afternoon and
then your availability changed!" I loved the sound of his heavy
voice mixed with his accent. How could someone sound this
fine and not be?
"Sorry, I'm a hot commodity! If you snooze you lose." Thea
stood up and waved bye. I locked my door when she walked
out, and I put him on speaker.
He laughed, "I guess! I wanted to show what I had so far."
"I'm sure it can wait until Monday," I said looking through the
glass panel on the door of my office out onto the floor. The
staff was busy at work making us the outstanding company we
are today.
He exhaled, "it'll have to wait until Tuesday then. I guess that's
better anyways."
"El, you worry too much. I'm sure it will be fine." Mitigated
Staffing Solutions was moving out East. Juan structured the
East coast to follow under our West Coast jurisdiction, but
everything still rolled up to San Francisco and Oakland. El was
going to be head of the East Coast division. I haven't met him
in person, but I've been on numerous conference calls with
him. He's smart and knows his stuff. When my cousin Derrick

met with him I asked him what El looked like, you know how voices sometimes can be deceiving. Derrick looked at me and said he looked "married." I played it off like that wasn't the reason I was asking, but Derrick knew better. It figured that he'd be married though; he sounds too smart not to be. I was just curious to know what he looked like is all.

I could hear the smile in his voice, "right. Well, I'll let you go. According to your calendar you're busy right now."

"Right I am, so stop bugging me." I laughed, "I dismissed Henry early."

"Enough said." His voice smiled, "enjoy your weekend Sasha."

"Thanks El, you do the same."

Then he hung up. I looked out the window again. The coast seemed clear. I shut down my computer, and I packed it in my bag. I grabbed my purse and I locked my office door on the way out. I put my head up and walked. I could feel people watching me. They were mad because no matter how hard they tried, they would never be me. Some people think I get away with murder, but I don't ask people for their opinion about what I do around here. I was not hired to work here because I'm related to the owner. I don't tell people that I'm related to anyone around here. I was hired because I'm good at what I do. It's not my fault it takes others ten hours in one day to do what I can get done in four. I'm good at everything that I do. I know most of the people around here watch me, but I'm easy to look at so go figure.

When I got to the lobby I heard my name, I sighed. "Where are you going?"

"What do you need Richard?" I rolled my eyes

"Where are you going?" He repeated his question

"Out!" I said irritated

"When are you coming back?" He looked irritated

"Monday!"

"Monday? It's barely eleven am." He said looking at his watch.

"Your point?" I pointed to my bag, "I'll log in from home later."

"This is a business, you can't keep doing this." He said

"I have an appointment; I'll be online later on this afternoon." I said then I turned on my heels. I started to walk away and he grabbed my arm. "I know you aren't crazy!"

"You sure about that? I'm getting tired of you disregarding me!" He said through clinched teeth

"You mean like you disregarded me?" I said snatching my arm from him. "Don't play concerned dad. Just be Richard, ok?" I took my shades out of my purse put them on an walked out of the building into the parking garage.

"Sasha!" He said as he stepped into the garage. "We need to clear the air."

"About what? You are who you are Richard there's no shame in that." I said as if I was disconnected from the whole scene.

"I'm sorry for leaving you hanging the other night."

"I don't care! It's not like I believed we were really going to go out to dinner. It's not like anyone believes you're my father until they look us directly in the face anyways. I ruin your sorry excuse for game. I get it!"

"Sasha!"

"It's fine Richard! I have to go!" I left him standing there. I put my laptop bag in my trunk. Then I got in the car. I screamed at myself for feeling anything. All he ever does is let me down. All I keep hearing is, "I was only fifteen Sasha. I don't know how to be a father!" It doesn't change the fact that I need one. My mother's boyfriend tried, and as much as I love him and accept his attempts, it's just not the same as when it comes from the person who caused your birth. He makes me so angry! In addition, I know I'm only angry because he hurt my feelings. I hit the Bluetooth on my ear. "Call momma!"

Her line rang twice, "hey baby girl how's it going?"

"Ok, I'm calling to see how you're doing." I said trying to keep emotion out of my tone.

She heard it anyways. "What's wrong?"

"Nothing," I sighed

"What did he do now?"

"Nothing new, he wants to play daddy when he feels like it. I'm over it!"

"Sounds like you're in the car?"

"Yeah, I'm going to get my hair done, I got a date tonight." I smiled

"With who?"

"Nobody you know. It's still new. I'm still checking him out." I said

"Whatever happened to that other guy?"

I sighed, "nothing momma I still see Dennis from time to time, but we're not exclusive."

"That doesn't sound right." She said

This is coming from the woman who has spent her life running after my father no matter who she was with. I've known Dennis since college. His family owns a vineyard and winery out in Calistoga. We've met each other's families the whole deal. However, after graduation he got a job offer in Minneapolis, I needed to stay here in LA to work on my Master's, and then my cousin Malcolm offered me my current job at Mitigated. He worked around my school schedule and now I still get to run things. Besides, it wasn't like Dennis was asking me to come with him. He gave me the whole speech about he loved me but he's too young to settle down crap. In addition, how could he ask me to change everything about my life without a proposal? Yeah, I was devastated at first, but I got over it. Especially since business travels bring him, back out here about once a month at the least. So I still see him but nothing like it used to be. "How so momma?"

"Why date other people if Dennis is who you want?"

"Seriously momma?"

She started laughing. "Don't follow in my footsteps baby."

"I thought I already bypassed that. No babies for me and I'm out of college."

"Technically yes, but holding on to a man when he's not gonna hold you back is a waste of time."

"He is holding me momma. But tonight I'm going out with someone else."

"I hope he's worth it." She said tisking at me.

I pulled up to the valet in front of the salon. "I'm going to enjoy myself. It makes no sense to sit here and patiently wait on Dennis when heaven only knows what he does when he's home."

She sighed, "True. Who am I to talk anyways?" I smiled because at least she acknowledged her own weakness for my father and didn't pretend like it wasn't there. Both of them shared the same love and weakness for each other. Frankly, I don't understand why they broke up other than he wanted to move out here and she refused to follow him. It's not like she was hurting for money. She owns two very successful restaurants in the Bay Area. Aside from that, my family has MONEY; most of them are pretty successful. But you know there's always a black sheep here and there. Even though both of my parents have moved on, they keep coming back to each other.

"I love you momma, I'll call you back because I'm walking inside."

"Ok love you. Call me back."

It was a lovely day outside, and the air conditioning kissed my skin as I walked in the doors. "Hello Sasha how are you today?" The receptionist asked me.

"Wonderful as usual! How are you today?" I said
"I'm good. Brea will be out to greet you in just a moment.
Please have a seat."
The main lobby was very chic, modern art on the walls. There
was a monitor that ran their commercials constantly.
Everything in here was set to put you at ease and help you
relax. I sat for all of twenty seconds when Brea emerged from
the back. That quickly as I was watching the water fountain,
the sound of the bubbling brook started to release a lot of the
stress I felt. Brea placed my purse at Ava's station. As she
pulled a robe out of the closet for me, she asked what I was
doing this evening. I looked at my nails. "I got a date tonight; I
need a color change on both, a good massage, a wash and
diffuse." I said
"You're letting your curls hang out tonight." She smiled.
I smiled; Shawn was nice enough like I told my momma. I met
him at the coffee shop a block away from the office. I caught
his reaction all over his face the first time he saw me. He was
stuck, and I frowned. Shawn didn't strike me as my type at first
glance, so I kept moving. I go in that shop every day, it varies
according to my schedule what time I go though. On the
occasions that I saw Shawn there, I kept it moving. If all he
was gonna do, was look I didn't have to pay attention for that.
One day I walked in and the cashier has a big smile as he
hands me my coffee. I was confused, he told me it was paid for
and had been timed to be ready when I came in. Then he
pointed at Shawn, who was sitting in the corner reading. He
raised his cup to me and then went back to his reading. I
thanked him for the coffee and I kept it moving. After a week
of this I went over to his table and thanked him for the coffee,
but I told him this was going to have to stop. I told him I was
capable of paying for my own coffee. He smiled and said it
was the least he could do. He asked me to sit, but I couldn't I
had to go. So he kept buying my coffee, I started to feel bad so
one day to his surprise I sat with him. His conversation was
nicer than I expected. Shawn wasn't much to look at, but he
had the gift of game. Talking to him, I forgot he was kind of....
I won't say *ugly*. I'll say *not my type*. So when he asked for my
number I didn't object. I still wasn't assigning him high priority
on my list of important people in my life. After a couple of
rounds of phone tag, he finally reached me. We made plans for
our first date, I wasn't expecting much. Shawn worked for the
coffee shop's Franchise office and it was his job to make sure
that each location remained within the franchise standards. So

he wasn't rolling in money, but at least he was employed. We actually had a nice time. Dinner was nice and we saw a nice movie. He fumbled through the kiss though, but who could blame him for being nervous. Tonight will be our fifth date and he hasn't brought sex up. But come on dinner and a concert, doesn't that sound like he's setting the stage? I don't know that I want to sleep with him tonight, but I guess I could if he sets the mood just right. I'd rather be prepared than caught slipping.

Janet dug into me working out all of my knots while we laughed about her crazy kids. Janet had two small boys who were two small bundles of pure energy. She playfully complains about how crazy they make her. She said I was really tense and instantly I thought of Richard, which made my body temp go up. She tapped me and told me to relax. I took a deep breath and told myself not to think about him.

Brea had my hands soaking while she gave me a pedicure. I was in heaven. The vibration of my chair was lulling me to sleep. Brea asked about my date tonight. So I gave her general information, nice guy, fifth date, dinner, and concert. Brea's eyes got so wide as if I was giving her the goods. Brea has had the same boyfriend since high school. They lived together and acted like an old married couple and she's only a few years younger than me. She told me she lives through me. I told her to make her man take her out. But she'd only ever sigh and shake her head at the thought of exerting herself.

Once my nails were dry, Brea sat me in a chair in front of the washbowl. I closed my eyes preparing myself for my final amazing massage.

I could smell her floral perfume I smiled. "Hello doll face!" I said not opening my eyes.

She snapped her fingers. "One of these days! I'm gonna successfully sneak up on you."

"Not as long as your perfume keeps giving you away."

"Is that what it is? Next time I see you on the books I'll have to change it up."

"I don't think that will save you, but you can try." I laughed

She turned on the water and lowered my chair. This was my favorite part of the whole experience. I LOVE her scalp massages. When I moved out here, a lot of people suggested this place around the corner from her old location. It tried to be as nice but it missed the mark on so many levels. No one there knew how to do my hair. Crunchy hair one time, and straw feeling hair another, I was done. As I was walking away completely disgusted I saw Ava. She had such a warm and bubbly smile. But I was looking at her hair. She wore hers straight and that's what I had been looking for. I asked her who did her hair. Her smile got bigger and she said she did it herself. I was impressed but saddened, until I realized she was giving me her card. She told me she recently stepped out on her own and she was trying to build her clientele. I took her card but I hesitated for a minute, I wanted the whole salon experience. But I told her I'd call to book an appointment. She was really friendly, not like a lot of these snobs out here so I figured if I didn't like her, it would be back to the drawing board. Back then, her space looked more like a shop, but she was just getting started so ok. WHEN I SAT IN HER CHAIR! After that first shampoo! I was hooked! She understands my hair, and I love the way she works with it. I had my momma and my cousin Amber check her out too. I was telling everyone at school about her place and her clientele was slowly building. Then I convinced my cousin Gwen to come in. Ava pulled out the red carpet for Gwen and by the time her hair was being styled they worked out a deal. My cousin Gwen, who has similar hair to mine, even though she's not black, was in love with her curly hair, which was now bone straight. Gwen agreed to handle promotions. Amber endorsed Ava's place, and some of Amber's high profile clients got on board as well. Ava and I became fast friends. She said giving me her business card changed her life. Now she has this luxurious spa and salon, "The Hair Salon on Rodeo" in a prime location. I told her taking her card changed my life as well. She's taken my hair from ok, to oh my goodness look at her hair. Not only that, I had another friend, and I don't have very many of those so I cherish the ones I have.

"So what's new?"

"I'm going out with Shawn tonight." I peeked at her.

Ava smiled, "be nice to him."

I laughed, "I have been nice."

"Yes, but you know how you can chew him up. Be nice, remember he has feelings too."

I faked surprise at her statement, "I'm the sweetest person he'll ever meet."

"Until you get tired of him or Dennis comes into town."

I sucked my teeth, "I'm bad news huh?"

She shrugged. "I think it depends on the guy." Then she changed the subject. "So what look are you going for tonight?"

I described my dress options to her. She has seen all of them before. We narrowed it down to three dresses. She moved me to her styling station. I said hello to her staff and their customers along the way to her chair. She brought headbands and gorgeous barrettes. We picked four, then she gave me style ideas. I liked the idea of a semi up-do. Then we selected a headband and she put the other accessories back. I sipped on champagne while she pinned my curls. Turns out, we were going to the same concert. I couldn't tell Ava where we were sitting since Shawn set the evening up. I was hoping for good seats, but I know better than to set my hopes high on his pockets. Our dates so far have been nice, but I still can't gauge what I should expect. Ava always has prime seats when she goes to concerts. So at the very least, I know I can look to the stage to see her and her friends sitting front row.

Under the dryer, I took out my blackberry to review and respond to emails from work. In a two-hour space, I had over twenty emails. I rolled my eyes, as some of them were just feelers to see if I was coming back in the office. Nosey people should worry about their task and leave my business to me. I admired my hair in the mirror. I did the happy dance while Ava beamed with pride. I thanked her for her work while everyone watched me go on and on about my hair. She told me how to preserve it tonight and that it *should* last until Sunday if I'm gentle with it. Then she smiled at me. I raised my eyebrows at her and told her we shall see. I drove home to the apartment I used to share with my Uncle JoJo when he was in school out here. Although he still comes out here on a regular basis, this place is basically mine. He still has his key and he comes and goes as needed. He said he wanted to keep me on my toes, whatever that's supposed to mean. I constantly remind him that he's my uncle, not my father. Although he felt more like a father when I moved out here than Richard ever did. In a good way though, every time I bumped heads with Richard; JoJo was there to smooth it out for me. I walked in the door, music was playing, and I could smell food being cooked.

"JoJo?" I said as I closed the door.

"Nope it's me." My cousin Darryl called out from the kitchen.

I laughed. "Did JoJo give you a key?"

He popped his head out the kitchen, "come on now." He had a big grin. "You know better than that. You hungry?"

"I could eat a little but I got a date tonight."

Darryl sucked his teeth, "who's the loser?"

I walked into the kitchen as Darryl flipped the homemade burger patties over. It smelled delicious, and the fact that he was cleaning as he cooked meant I wouldn't have a dirty kitchen in the end, I smiled with approval. "It smells delicious in here!" I said as my mouth watered. Darryl cleared his throat waiting for an answer to his question. "He's just a guy I can't say whether he's awesome or not yet."

"Ok..." He said rolling his hands

Ok so, growing up with all these men was nice at points; but their overly protective nature sometimes was too much. Darryl is younger than me. He was my baby, and now he's standing here questioning me as if he's a father figure. My momma would always tell me to take it as a sign of love. She said her cousins would do the same thing to her. I try but sometimes I wish they would back off. If I would've known moving to Southern California wasn't far enough to avoid incidents like this I might've stayed in The Bay and went to Berkeley with my twin cousin Andrew and my best friend slash twin sister Tanisha. But if I stayed I would've had to deal with Toya's DRAMA, etc. Toya is Andrew's on again off again girlfriend. If there was ever somebody who seemed to miss the point and make you put hands on them that would be her. But I don't want to think about her even now. I'm relaxed and I want to stay that way.

I told Darryl about Shawn. He looked at me out the corner of his eye. Then he called Amber his momma my cousin slash aunty slash second momma and asked her if she could get him tickets to the concert. I could hear Amber laughing through the phone as I begged her not to. She told Darryl she would have to see. Darryl frowned at me. "I see how it is. The girls gonna stick together. There's more than one way to skin a cat. I'm going and that's final!" He said like he was putting his foot down.

"Fine!" I said knowing Amber had my back. "JoJo said this place was secure." I said then I took a bite of my burger.

"It is secure." Then he took a bite of his burger. He shot up out of his seat, punched the air, and then he swallowed. "I'm AMAZING!" He yelled. I covered my mouth while I laughed at him. "Sasha now you know you've never had a better burger than this! Maybe I should be a chef." He argued with himself. Saying it was selfish to hold back his gifts from the world. Then he shook his head, "Naw! I don't have the patience."

I was cracking up, Darryl was born hilarious. The complete opposite of his big brother Derrick. Somewhere in the middle of Darryl and Derrick, there was Andrew, as far as temperaments. "I'm glad you worked that out. So back to my peace of mind." I said redirecting the conversation back to my previous statement.

"Sasha, now you know! There's not a lock that can keep me out." He said giving me a knowing look.

"Ok, but if you can get in, then someone else can too is my point."

"I doubt it. JoJo has you pretty secure. Don't worry about it. I'm the exception, you're good." He said dismissing my fear and taking another bite. "Admit it, best burger!"

"Yes Darryl, this burger is the Atomic bomb!"

"Thank you, now try my fries!" He said holding out the plate. I slapped the table asking for mercy. Everything was delicious. "Now you can order a salad and pretend like you eat like a bird."

"He's seen me eat."

Darryl faked surprise, "and he invited you out again? He must really like you."

"You are so crazy!" I said laughing, but also finding my exit to go log in for a bit and then get ready.

I logged in and responded to more emails. Before I knew it two hours flew by. Darryl was looking over my shoulder while I answered emails. He had an off the wall answer for every inquiry. Most of them were hilarious. However, some of them I found myself wishing I could use. When it was time to get ready, I shooed Darryl out of my room and then I took my shower and began my process. I heard Darryl on the phone while I was getting dressed, but I assumed he was talking to his momma trying to convince her to go against me. When I opened my door Darryl looked angry. "Just because you got a body doesn't mean you have to show it off Sasha!" Then he shook his head. "NO! I don't like that dress! Go put a different one on!"

"That must mean I look really good!" I said rolling my eyes

"Not any way I want my sister-cousin walking outside to be with some guy I don't know." He said angrily

"Calm down Darryl. If this guy was going to attack me he would've done it already. I'll be fine."

"See! That's exactly what he wants you to think and then BAM! He's got you right where he wants you. Out in the open and vulnerable. I think you should fake a cold and then hang out with me. I've got woman troubles Sasha! I need help! I don't want to hurt nobody!" He said throwing up his hands in frustration.

"Right Darryl! Like that will be happening." I walked over to him and put my hand on his shoulder. I couldn't believe my once upon a time baby, that Tanisha and I used to carry around everywhere, was now taller than me and looking down at me. "Look, Darryl, I know you mean well. But please trust me when I say that I will be fine." I got on my tiptoes and kissed his cheek. "I appreciate the fuss, but I'm a big girl. I can handle this guy. If you come back tomorrow, we can talk until there's no more talking needed."

"Whatever," he said in defeat.

When Shawn arrived Darryl answered the door. He wasn't going to let Shawn in. But I brought him in and then I introduced them properly. "Nice to meet you." Shawn said to Darryl.

Darryl looked at his hand then he looked at me. "Seriously Sasha! He's hiding something. Look at him!"

Shawn looked at me without a reaction. "Darryl is my over protective little-brother-cousin." I explained

"Little?" Shawn said looking up at Darryl.

"Yeah! That's right! And I'm the one who's going to be coming at you when your time is up!" Then Darryl said, "Naw! I take that back. You better hope it's just me." Then Darryl pleaded, "Just look at him Sasha you can see it."

When I looked at Shawn I saw it. That uncertainty in the corner of his eye. "Bye Darryl!" I said grabbing my purse and sweater. Didn't matter what he was hiding. I was going to the Maxwell concert and I didn't have to pay for the tickets. I was going to enjoy myself.

We walked out of my building together and to the curb where Shawn and Darryl were parked. Darryl was driving his momma's rental car while she was at work. I knew Darryl wouldn't leave without threatening Shawn. Shawn didn't look scared or anything. He accepted Darryl's behavior and kept it moving.

Dinner was fine, but now since Darryl pointed it out, all I could see in his eyes was that he was holding something back. Shawn took us to a hole in the wall spot for dinner. Thus far we've only gone to random places for dinner, but he said he likes authentic verses the commercial and over processed. I told myself to shrug it off. It's not like I was going to fall in love with Shawn. Let's face it; quite simply he isn't fine enough to hold my attention.

When we got to the concert, we weren't front row like Ava and her friends. But they were decent seats. I called Ava and I told her where we were sitting. She stood up, looked around until she saw me. Then she waved. She gave me a thumbs up when I modeled my dress. I think Shawn thought we were talking about him cause he sat there blushing. People were quieting down when I saw Darryl walk over to Ava. I looked in disbelief, he had to have found another way there, because I knew Amber didn't betray me and send him here. Ava pointed me out. Darryl put his hand up to his eyes and then he pointed at us. I knew he already knew where we were sitting, and he said something to Ava so that we would see him. Maxwell's performance was smooth and sultry, I sang along and swayed to the music. Maxwell put me in a lovey-dovey, sappy, sentimental, and missing Dennis kind of a mood. I started to feel alone and sad, and then Shawn put his arm around my shoulders as he swayed to the music. I laid my head on his shoulder, even if it wasn't Dennis I guess his touch would do. Darryl shook his head at me. When the concert was over, Darryl was at the end of my row waiting. I sucked my teeth, I asked Shawn to stay put while I went to talk to my little cousin. I waited for the people exiting the row in front of me to move out the way. I asked Darryl to sit down; I knew his heart was in the right place. He didn't understand that he needed to back up and give me some space. We had a quick heart to heart. Darryl was pulling all of the understanding he could out of the air. He couldn't understand why I would want to go on a date or go home with someone who was hiding something. I told him Shawn was just the guy on my arm tonight. Darryl didn't like it, and then he told me he'd see me back at my place loud enough for Shawn to hear, and then he walked away.

"How did he get here?" Shawn asked looking a little annoyed

"My cousin Gwen has connections. She got him a ticket, when I asked his momma not to." I smiled

We stood there awkwardly staring at each other for a minute, "so." He said

"So," I said debating with myself whether I wanted to invite him back to my place.

"So miss Sasha what would you like to do now?" He said watching my eyes.

I told myself, whether I invited him back to my place, depends on if he did anything inspirational. I yawned and stretched, "I could go home if you can't think of anything else."

He grabbed my hand and led me through the crowd and to his car. He put on Maxwell's music in the car. I smiled and looked out the window as I thought, "Nicely played," as I leaned back and relaxed.

Chapter 2

No matter how hard I try to find a happy place or think about something pleasant I can't seem to get any act right. When I'm mad at Richard I can't seem to find joy in anything else. SIGH! I don't want to do anything or go anywhere tomorrow. I was laying in my bed staring at the ceiling trying to fall asleep when my house phone rang. I looked at the caller ID and instantly happiness spread all over me. I quickly picked up the phone, the sound of his voice made my heart pound out of my chest. All I said was hello and Dennis could tell I was upset about something. He asked me what was wrong, but
I didn't want to spend our call talking about Richard. I tried to change the subject but he wouldn't let me. I sighed deeply and then I told him about Richard standing me up. I got angry with myself when I surprised myself and cried. It was something about talking to Dennis that made me release like that. One thing that irritated me, but I guess it should've made me happy; Richard and Dennis got along very well. They got a long too well if you ask me, sometimes it seemed like they shared a bond that I didn't like. Dennis could talk to me in a way that Richard couldn't, so it was nice to hear about my father from a different slant. I didn't want to but Dennis had a way of making me forgive my father even when I didn't want to. When I tired of talking about Richard, I asked: "When are you coming to see me?"
"What do you mean when?" I could hear the smile in his voice. I popped up, my heart started fluttering. "Are you here already?"
"Oh I don't know, have you made up with your father?"
"I'm not a little kid Dennis!" I said still smiling
"I know, but you'll always be my little girl."
"Answer the question!"
"I want to see you but not until you and Richard have resolved your disagreement."
"WHAT??"
"Sasha, you know how it goes. If you're mad at Richard, we're going to end up arguing and I want our time together to be good. So if it means I have to go this visit without seeing you then so be it."
I rolled my eyes. "Are you here or not?"

"Not yet, you have a day to work it out." I sucked my teeth, "and don't try to lie to me and say you've worked it out when you haven't. Remember I know you."

"Fine Dennis! Fine! What's the plan?"

"I'll come in Friday afternoon. Saturday Morning we'll fly out to Napa. We'll come back Sunday. I have meetings Monday and Tuesday, and I fly out Wednesday."

My heart started pounding. "I can't wait to see you."

"Make up with Richard and you will. Otherwise I can change my itinerary and keep going." He was putting his foot down.

"I don't want to make up with Richard! He should be trying to make up with me. He's the one who did me wrong!"

"But you're the bigger person Sasha, do this for us."

"Fine! I love you!" I said in defeat

"I love you. Now…" He exhaled like he was getting comfortable. "What do you want to do to me when you see me?"

"I want to kiss you." I said feeling like a teenager.

"Un huh, and what else?"

"I want to hug you."

'What else?"

"I want your hands all over my body."

"Where do you want me to touch you?" He said his voice got heavy.

"My face, my hands, my back, my stomach, my butt, my breast, everywhere!"

"How do you want me to touch you?"

"Like a man!"

"How does a man touch you?" He asked

"Strong and deliberately."

By the time we were finished my mental orgasm had me seeing double. Dennis breathlessly told me he loved me and he couldn't wait to see me. I said the same, "bet you, you can fall asleep now."

"Yes baby, I'm tired now."

"Good! Now be a good girl and make sure everything is right for us."

"Ok, love you can't wait to see you."

"Ditto" then we got off the phone.

In the morning, I headed straight over to Richard's office. He was on the phone when I came in, he gestured for me to have a seat. He was on the phone with a potential client. This company had a bunch of hoops they needed us to jump through in order to work with us. Richard was good at smoothing out the bumps and making Mitigated look really good. Once he could get the HR rep to agree to go to lunch to discuss our services it was pretty much a wrap, the vendor would be begging us to fill their staffing needs, he got the contract. I did admire that aspect of my father, his charm was undeniable… when he wanted to use it that is. When he hung up the phone his eyes smiled at me, "how you doing Sassy baby?" He smiled.

I rolled my eyes, "seriously Richard? Here?"

He straightened up mocking my demeanor, "I'm sorry how can I help you?"

"I'm coming over tonight!" I said standing up

He frowned, "Um, I got a date tonight." He said standing

I stared at him, "who's more important? Me or her?"

"Sasha!"

"Richard!"

"You are such a spoiled brat!" He said shaking his head.

"If you never would've stood me up we wouldn't have this issue right now. DON'T STAND ME UP!" I said walking to the door and I blew him a kiss.

When I went back in my office I got an email from Juan. He and Malcolm were coming out Wednesday. My heart sped up when I saw that we were going to discuss a meeting with all senior management over video conferencing. FINALLY! I've been suggesting a video conference since curiosity has been plaguing me about El's appearance. I looked at my calendar and the meeting was already setup for 11am. I immediately called "The Salon" I needed the earliest appointment Ava could give me. I couldn't look ordinary the first time El saw me. But I also didn't want it to look like I was trying too hard. 6am appointment with Ava, check! When my phone rang and I saw the 212 area code I smiled. "Hello" I said with a smile

"It's El," he said as if I wouldn't know.

"Hello" I said

"I'm looking at the calendar and trying to grab a few dates for our meeting. Did you see Juan's email?" He said getting straight to business

"I did, what did you have in mind?"

"I'm looking at the calendar and I have dates selected for the next three months. Surely one of these date spaces will do." His English accent laced his words

"So what's the dilemma?"

He sighed, "Once we have the meeting we'll have to make a decision on the office space... I guess it's not a dilemma really. You're going to have to spend some time out here. Do you prefer corporate housing or a hotel?"

"I like having access to a kitchen. So I'd say corporate housing."

"You know they have hostiles with kitchens."

I smiled, "I know, but corporate will do." I said

"Suit yourself. But it would be easier if everyone stayed centralized." He said thinking about it. "So if the majority votes against you, I'll try to find a location with a kitchen just for you."

"Oh El you take such good care of me."

"Un huh, right! Ok so, that's all I wanted. I'm taking the wife on holiday so I won't talk to you until the meeting."

I rolled my eyes, "oh really? Where you going?"

"To visit her family." Then he sighed, "the things you do for love right?"

"Right!" I said, "is everything ok?" I asked hoping he'd spill it.

"Of course," he said catching himself from sharing with me. "I'll see you next week Sasha, take care."

"Bye El." I said snapping my fingers when he hung up.

Then I texted Shawn and cancelled our date for this Saturday night. I didn't offer an explanation, I told him I couldn't make it. I refused to feel bad about it either. I wasn't canceling at the last minute and it's not like he wowed me when we spent the night together. It was ok at best. He wasn't horrible, but if I had to grade him I'd give him a C-, he was very average almost to a fault. He tried to call me but I let him rollover to voicemail, if he left me a begging and pleading message that was it for him. I waited five minutes then I listened to his message, "Hey Sasha, it's Shawn. I was hoping we could reschedule for another time. I know you're really busy so, you let me know when you're available and we can go from there." Not exactly begging borderline soft, I rolled my eyes.

I knocked on Richard's door at seven. Nothing and no one was going to get in my way of enjoying my time with Dennis. Richard brought home take out from my favorite Thai food spot. When I walked in the door he looked at my face like he was reading me. "Uh oh my Sassy baby is going to go hard on me. Let me bust out the Hennessy." He said walking to his bar. We sat at his table eating in silence; I kept cutting my eyes at him whenever he looked at me. He seemed to be so tickled by my attitude. "You remind me so much of your mother."

"The problem is that you seem to think that I will respond to you like my name is Sophia. You forget my name is Sasha and my heart doesn't skip a beat just because you say my name!" I said with fire in my eyes.

He motioned for me to join him in the living room. Richard exhaled, "go ahead. Get it out!" Then he reclined in his chair and took another drink of his cognac.

"What's the point? You're never gonna change. You and my momma are retarded."

He frowned, I knew my comment was pushing it, but I didn't care. "Why are we retarded?"

"Why aren't you together?" A question I never ask.

"For one your mother is playing house with the white guy."

"His name is Travis, and they're more than quote unquote playing house; they're in love. But there would be no Travis if you guys would've gotten it together. So again I ask you, why aren't you together?" My momma said that she and Travis were over, but if she didn't tell Richard, I wasn't gonna be the one to tell him either.

"Ask your mother." He huffed

"Seriously Richard! I'm here, and I'm asking you."

He stirred in his seat. "Sasha!" He stirred some more like I was asking too much of him. I gave him my sad eyes. He got up almost filled his glass, and then he poured a little more in my glass. He took a big chug of his drink. It was smooth but strong, I imagined him screaming in his head. He sat down stirred and stirred in his seat. He started by saying that he loves my mother very much. He went all the way back to the beginning; when they met in middle school. He said he's loved her since he was a child. As I saw the alcohol take its affect he relaxed more and more. He was more open than I've ever experienced. He said when my mother told him she thought she was pregnant he freaked out. He said immediately he knew his momma was gonna kill him. He told her she couldn't be. They argued and he ran away like a coward. He said their relationship wasn't cold before she was dating and then marrying my stepfather. He said the night before her wedding they had a long talk, he didn't want her to get married. However, he wasn't ready to step up either. He said he felt horrible because he was the only one hiding while Malcolm was standing by Amber, and then Ben came to his senses and stood by Rosalind. He said he was going to let my mother go but she wasn't happy in her marriage. Honestly, what fifteen year old is going to be happily married? He felt responsible for

22

her unhappiness. The pregnancy was his fault, he was the one who forgot the condom, convinced her that pulling out would work, and then laid there shooting his seed all over her soil. He said it was one of those moments he could never forget. He said the moment he laid eyes on me he knew I was his even though he tried to convince himself that I could've been my stepfather's child. The tricky and most fear inspiring part was telling my Dan-Dan, his mother. He said he didn't know what to do, so he invited my mother and I over when I was a few months old. The doorbell rang and he pretended like he had to use the bathroom. Dan-Dan opened the door then he heard her screaming his name. She was holding me and crying. They came clean about everything, even about my momma being married to someone else who thought I was their child. My momma said she gave me her maiden name cause she felt like giving me my stepfather's last name was going too far. Plus it wasn't like he was there when she signed my birth certificate. My birth certificate has Richard's name listed as my father. My momma said it wasn't like my stepfather would be involved in anything that officially listed my name so it wasn't a problem. Dan-Dan cursed Richard out so badly that his ears still bleed to this day. He said watching my momma handle herself against his momma made him love her more. Dan-Dan asked my momma if she was black and didn't know it. My momma said sometimes she wondered the same thing. So even though Dan-Dan hated the situation she quickly fell in love with me. Any who, Richard said the hardest thing was watching my momma play house with my stepfather. When my momma and stepfather broke up my parents came clean to my grandparents who said they already figured it out and were waiting for them to come to them. My granddaddy was so angry with my father for being a coward and running from us. Eventually he came around but it took him a while to do that. My grand momma was more or less on the understanding side; she told my momma she wished they would've been honest in the first place. No one seemed to really like my stepfather except for me. Richard said he wanted to marry my momma; she kept reminding him that she was married. When my stepfather died she had no excuse but she kept holding back. I think she was still hurt that he ran from her in the first place. At the time, I thought Richard was only my momma's boyfriend and that my stepfather was my real father. I'll never forget it; we were on a family vacation and my great-grandparents Poppa and Nana were showing pictures of everyone over the years. They showed pictures of my momma and my stepfather and I, and they were nice. But there was this one picture of my momma, Richard, and I. My hair was wet and pulled back and I was sitting between my momma and Richard. I looked like a lighter skinned version of Richard. I looked at my momma with so many questions. My momma tried to shrug me off like I was being ridiculous, but I asked poppa if I could see the pictures again after the slideshow, and I kept wondering why? Why I never looked like my stepfather, why? On the car ride home my momma was in tears and Richard lowered the boom. I HATED them for lying to me. My mother lost so many cool points with me that day. She always stressed honesty but she had been lying to me my entire life. And just when I was FINALLY coming to terms with losing my daddy, then they tell me this. Oh but then the catcher… "RICHARD WAS MOVING AWAY!" He was leaving us again! Richard said he wanted to get away from the madness of my family and let them figure out who they were going to be as a couple together. He honestly thought my mother would always ride with him no matter what. When she told him no, he couldn't believe it. So he rehashed this whole long story to tell me that they broke up because she chose her family over him.

"You could've said that." I said rolling my eyes.

"I love your mother very much! I've never loved anyone like I love her. At the time I thought we needed some space from your family."

I frowned, "what's wrong with my family?"

He was feeling his drink; "they can be a bit much at times." He looked from right to left, "Wallace's everywhere you turn!" He exhaled, "I wanted to be my own man. I got that job out here, I wanted you guys to come, and then we'd have a few more babies. I wanted us to have our own."

"Just for you to end up working at Mitigated!" I said rolling my eyes

He shrugged, "that company going under had nothing to do with me. Malcolm came to me, as I was about to take another job. He understood why I moved out here."

"Please explain why all of this justifies why I continue to get the short end of the stick with you."

He exhaled, "I'm sorry Sassy. I don't intentionally try to hurt you." He exhaled, "I was only fifteen when you were born."

"SO WHAT! YOU'RE NOT FIFTEEN NOW! WHY DOES YOUR AGE WHEN I WAS BORN SEEM TO MAKE YOU THINK THIS TYPE OF BEHAVIOR TODAY IS OK! IF

YOU'RE GOING TO BE MY FATHER THEN BE MY FATHER! IF NOT, LET ME KNOW SO I CAN MOVE ON WITH MY LIFE!"

"I know Sassy, I'm sorry. You're right, you're not Sophia. I need to step up. I just can't believe that you came out here to be with me and not her." Richard looked like he wanted to cry but no tears fell.

"Do you mean that? Or is that the Hennessy talking?" My heart wanted to believe him. I know how hard he's taken my momma's relationship. He was never happy about my momma and Travis dating. But then, you should've seen it. I came out here to LA to spend time with my father during my break from school. When he asked me nonchalantly how my momma was doing I smiled at him. He frowned at my smile and asked me what the smile was for as he walked towards the kitchen. I held onto my smile and I said she was pregnant. He stopped in his tracks; it looked like I shot him. He lost color and turned to face me. He asked me to say it again. So I said, "she's pregnant," again. So many emotions flashed across my father's face. Lastly he landed on jealousy, which he didn't try to hide. He hit me with rapid-fire questions. Every answer seemed to hit him harder than the one before it. I smiled as I watched him lose his bearings. When he couldn't take my smiles to his questions any more. He picked up the phone and called my mother. He didn't try to pretend like he was calling for any other reason than to give her a hard time about her new life. He was so angry the vein in his forehead was pulsating. He was screaming at my mother and I could tell she was calm. We knew he was going to be hurt when he found out. She said he responded exactly the way she thought he would. He was a complete grump the rest of my visit. But the pure joy of his pain was reward enough for me. No matter how hard he tried, he couldn't pull it together. I imagined my mother completely lost and as hurt if the shoe were on the other foot. She told me she let him get it out, she didn't know what else to do. She said she wasn't expecting him to respond so harshly. At that point they hadn't spoken for quite some time. She was still mad at him for leaving us.

At my high school graduation party I held my baby sister in my arms then I kind of followed him around with her. I guess he thought I'd back off if he stood next to my Dan-Dan. She looked at us and asked who I was holding. Richard didn't tell his mother about my baby sister. Dan-Dan said Sabrina looked just like my momma and me, while Richard stood there looking like the sight of Sabrina was breaking his heart. But I stayed in his face; I knew he couldn't resist her cuteness. Eventually he reached out to touch her. Sabrina reached for Richard and that quickly they were best friends. I knew it probably hurt, but he had to get over it at some point. Sabrina was done with me and enjoying Richard's company. Richard couldn't be cordial with Travis but at least Sabrina was separate from their foolishness.

Richard poured out his heart to me telling me everything he felt for my mother. I had never seen him like this, but then again I asked. By the end of the night he promised to be better and to stop putting his relationship woes off on me. I wasn't sure that I believed him, but at least I could honestly tell Dennis I tried.

****

I stood by the escalator with butterflies in my stomach. Dennis was here and I couldn't be happier. He was standing in his GQ stance as he descended. He looked good enough to eat! His light almond kissed complexion and straight dark brown almost black hair was cut in a nice corporate approved style. Dennis was a little taller than me, and when I wore heels we were the same height. His white button up and dark blue jeans looked extremely comfortable, he had his blazer draped over his shoulder. He smiled at me and my heart melted. "Hello Gorgeous!" He said picking me up.

"Hello Handsome!" I said kissing his lips. Dennis looked polished even when he was relaxing and I loved that about him.

"Somebody's been a good girl I see." He used his dark brown eyes to search mine.

"What?" I said bashfully

"Daddy knows his little girl." He said kissing me again.

"I have to go back to the office for a bit then we can go have dinner."

"That's fine."

He grabbed his garment bag and his suitcase. Put them in my trunk and then he drove my car to the office. He set up his laptop in my office and then he went to see Richard. I finished up my day then I went to Richard's office, but it was empty.

"So I see Dennis is here." Thea said

"Where did you see him?"

"They're in the break room I'll walk with you."

Sure enough they were in the break room laughing about who knows what. "Hey Sassy!"

26

I rolled my eyes, no matter how many times I say don't call me that at work, it's like Richard can't help it or he doesn't care. "I invited your father to dinner with us." Dennis said

"Seriously? I was looking forward to spending time just me and you."

"We'll still have our time, but I'm not ready to say bye to this man yet."

"How did I end up as the third wheel on my own date? You guys are going to be talking about stuff that doesn't interest me, I'm gonna be bored stiff!" I whined

"Thea will you come and keep her company?"

I put my hands on my hips. "It's not even a date anymore. Tonight might as well be a kick back! Besides Thea could have a date or plans."

Dennis looked at Thea, "do you?"

"No, I'd love to come if it's ok with you Sasha."

Dennis smiled a knowing smile. "Fine! Whatever! Can we go?" I huffed

"Where you wanna go?" Dennis asked Richard.

"Is there a game on tonight?" Richard asked searching his mental Rolodex.

"Oh heck no! If I have to endure the two of you together I demand to go somewhere nice!"

Richard looked at Dennis with a smile. Dennis smiled at Richard, stinking guy code! "Let's go shut down our computers and we'll meet in the lobby." Richard said. But I knew that was code for, get your woman in check and then let's roll.

Dennis shut the door behind him when we went in my office. "I can't believe you! Are you here to see him or me?"

He packed up his laptop. "Of course I'm here to see you. What do you think?"

"Then why are Richard and Thea coming with us? I want to spend time just me and you!"

"We're going to have our time together. I don't get a chance to talk to Richard nearly as much as I talk to you. I wanna catch up with the man."

"I don't care! You could go have a drink with him on Monday after we come back, why do you have to see him tonight?"

"You're blowing this way out of proportion. Monday night I'm snuggling up to you."

"That's what you say now. But you're gonna be watching football." He turned a little red. "Seriously Dennis! You gotta choose Richard or Monday Night football."

"Come on Sasha!"

"I'm not playing! Choose!" I crossed my arms.

He stood there thinking, "um!"

"It amazes me how you could ever consider yourself a lawyer!"

He put his arms around me. "Of course I choose Richard. But I need you to act like you're happy about it."

"I might go along with it, but trust! I'm not happy about it! I don't like sharing!"

He kissed me, "I know. What you won't do, do for love." He grinned.

"Stop trying to act like you know something about my music."

"Your music? You don't own the rights to R&B!"

"My people do Rhythm & Blues, my people. You ain't got no Rhythm!" I teased

He laughed, "I may not know how to dance. But I got Rhythm!" He gave me a knowing look.

I wanted to tear his clothes off. "Prove it!"

He turned red, "here? Somebody could walk in, or look through the glass."

"They won't see us if we're up against the door." Dennis smiled a devilish grin, but then he hesitated. "You scared?" I said walking to the door and locking it.

Dennis pulled out a condom and served me nicely in front of the door. Nothing like a power nap to get you through the night. I was now relaxed and able to sit through dinner at a semi sports bar environment. Thea and I had our own conversation going while they thoroughly enjoyed their guy talk. When it was time to go, Dennis hugged Thea and gave Richard a pound. I said bye and I excitedly walked away with my man. As we waited for my car, a couple of guys walked by us. One of the guys did a double take when he saw me. Great! Just what we need, I thought to myself. The guy said something to his friend and the friend looked at Dennis and I. They came back and I sucked my teeth.

"This your girl?" The guy asked Dennis.

Dennis wasn't paying the guy any attention so the question caught him off guard. "She's with me isn't she." He said with his eyes bouncing between the two of them.

"What you know about dating a black woman?" The second guy spit at him.

"It's none of your business!" I spit at them.

"Don't you know it's disrespectful for you to date him!" He spit back

"It's disrespectful for you to come at us with any of your foolishness! If you're smart you'd walk away!" I said wiggling my neck.

The other guy laughed, "Oh I get it. She's his protector!"

"Sasha!" Dennis snapped at me. "No, I'm her protector. If you're smart you'll keep walking." Dennis said raising his arms.

Richard and Thea walked out of the restaurant, Richard's face turned serious. "What we got going on over here?" Richard said as he calmly strolled over.

"These guys got their panties in a bunch cause I'm with Dennis! I'm so tired of ignorant guys like you! I can date whomever I want. And even if I wasn't with him I wouldn't be with an idiot like you!"

"Who you talking to?" The first guy said.

"Why are you yelling? No one's yelling at you." The second guy said as they moved closer.

"Hey! Hey! I suggest you guys keep walking, continue on to wherever you were heading. You don't wanna do this." Richard warned.

"Who asked you?" The first guy said, "This white boy needs to learn."

Richard shook his head. He took out his phone and made a call. I'm so tired of this scene, stupid guys, being upset because I'm with Dennis. What they don't know is, his momma is creole. She's very fair skinned, but creole all the same. Technically he is a black man even if he doesn't look it. But it's none of anybody's business. Dennis took off his jacket and gave it to me. I handed his jacket, my jacket, and my purse to Thea. "What are you doing?" Dennis looked at me.

"Whatever Dennis!" I said disregarding him.

"Hold on Sasha!" Richard said cause he knew I was about to fire on whoever was closest to me.

"Your woman always fights your battles?" The second guy said.

I swung at the guy and Richard pulled me back right before I made contact with the second guy's chin. His eyes got big when my wind gushed past his face. "Sasha calm yourself down!"

"She wanna fight a man! Let her go!" The guy said squaring off.

Richard pushed me behind him and threw his arms up, Dennis moved in front of Richard squaring off. Then two guys came out of the darkness of the night. They walked directly up to the scene and stood to the side. I recognized the stance, our backup has arrived. "No Richard move!" I said moving around him. "You decided to walk up on the wrong one tonight!" I said squaring off.

"Sasha come on, come back here, and let the men handle this." Thea said holding our stuff.

I ran around Dennis and I hit the second guy, he wasn't expecting me to connect with him as hard as I did. The guy's face showed shock and surprise as he stumbled backwards. I shook my hand cause yeah his face felt like wood. Dennis shot me daggers and he followed up with a 1, 2, 3 punch knocking him down. His friend started to charge as Dennis had the guy on the ground. Richard motioned to the backup, and the other guy was on the ground before he knew what was happening. "Next time you see a couple enjoying their evening, leave them alone!"

The manager ran out of the restaurant, "what's going on?"

"Toby these men came to assault us. We're going home. Call the police." Richard said casually strolling up to his car that was now at the curb behind my car. "Thea, you coming?" He said walking to his car.

She reluctantly handed me our jackets and my purse. My hand was throbbing as I got in the driver's seat. Dennis was fuming and not speaking in the car all the way to my house. When we walked in the door as soon as the door closed Dennis spun on his heels. "I'M TIRED OF THIS!"

I went to the kitchen and put ice in a paper towel. "Dennis please! You act like this every time!"

"YOU NEED TO LET ME HANDLE THE SITUATION! YOU ACT LIKE I CAN'T HANDLE MYSELF! I HAD IT!"

"I had your back!"

"AND NOW YOUR HAND IS BUSTED! WHEN ARE YOU GOING TO LEARN! STUFF LIKE THIS IS EXACTLY WHY WE ARE NOT TOGETHER!"

"Who gets mad at their woman for having their back? What you want me to do? Shake in my boots like Thea? I'm not just a decoration!"

"Sasha you need to learn how to let a man be a man!"

"I let you be a man! You finished him!" I said

"You should've stood back." He exhaled, "how's your hand?" He said looking at me.

I pouted, "it hurts!"

"You want me to kiss it?"

"Yes" I said giving him my hand. He kissed my hand, "what about the rest?" I pouted

****

"Look Sasha! Look!" Jim said as he jumped in the pool.

"Very good Jim!" I said clapping for him.

"Did you see me? I jumped up in the air, I was really high. Then I just jumped right in, and I made a big splash! It was big huh!" He said excitedly.

"It was so big you almost knocked me out of the water." I exaggerated

Jim laughed, "Watch me swim over there. Watch me!"

"Ok, I'm watching." I said

Dennis jumped in the water and swam up to me. When he came up he picked me up then he kissed me. "Sasha! You weren't watching!" Jim said

"That's because I'm here now." Dennis said

"So, I was here first!" Jim said getting angry.

"Chill out little man, she's here with me."

"Is Sasha your girlfriend?"

Dennis looked at Jim in disbelief, "why does it matter?"

"Because if she's available she should be my girlfriend."

"You're only six, you wouldn't know what to do with all that." Dennis laughed.

Jim frowned at Dennis like he was planning to drown him.

"Don't tease him, Jim you can be my boyfriend. Your uncle plays too many games." I said swimming away from Dennis.

"Like that Sasha?" Dennis put his hands up.

"Come on boyfriend lets go in the Jacuzzi." Jim grabbed my hand and then he stuck his tongue at Dennis. When we sat in the Jacuzzi Jim had the goofiest grin on his face. "What?"

"How long should we be boyfriend and girlfriend before we get married?"

I laughed so hard I thought I was going to pass out. "I think you should graduate college before we get married. Besides you might change your mind about me."

"Nope, I've wanted to be your husband since I was little."

I smiled, "let's wait and see. But I can still hang out with your uncle until we get married?" I asked

"Until you get married?" Lawrence asked, walking out into the backyard.

"Yes, your son, and I are getting married as soon as he graduates from college."

Lawrence gave us a goofy look. "Son you can't marry Sasha."

Dennis got out of the pool and walked up on his big brother. "Aren't you supposed to be at work?" He was completely annoyed.

"Yeah, but I heard Sasha was here in a bikini, so I had to take a lunch break." Lawrence was very handsome in his own right. If you didn't know him you might even think he was as handsome if not more than my man. He was taller, a little darker (thanks to Napa sunshine), and his hair slightly curled when he let it grow long enough. Lawrence's features were more pronounced than Dennis's, but once you got to know him none of that mattered.

"Where's your wife?"

"At the winery working like she's supposed to be. Sasha when you gonna leave this loser for me?"

"For you?" Jim asked protectively, "She's my girlfriend!"

"Boy please! You wouldn't know what to do with all that!"

"Like you would?" Dennis glared at his brother.

"Better than you do. Why haven't you married her?"

"Don't worry about my life! You need to focus on your own. Take your wife for a walk or something. Find out why being married to you makes her so miserable."

Jim's faced turned sad. I took him in my arms and rubbed his head. He rested his head on my chest. "Can you guys change the subject?" I hissed. Then I looked at Jim's sad face. "Let's get dressed and then we'll go say hi to your momma. Would you like that?" Jim shook his head yes and then we hurried out of the Jacuzzi. Lawrence got quiet when I followed his son. I didn't look back until I heard the big splash. Dennis pushed him in the pool. Lawrence started cursing and yelling cause he was fully dressed. His pagers, etc. were in his pockets. Dennis followed me in the bedroom he was going off about his brother. He told me I couldn't wear my bikini anymore. So then we argued because it didn't matter what I wore his brother was still going to break his neck to come over their parent's house to look at me.

His wife Kelsey is a pretty woman, but she gained a lot of weight when she had Jim. She lost a lot of it but not all of it, and Lawrence is such a horn dog and so disrespectful. She loves him to a fault. Dennis's momma is always defending Kelsey but she looks at me like I do something to provoke Lawrence. She doesn't care for me all that much, and even though I try not to think that way, I know it's because I'm black. She doesn't like the fact that she is black and she tries to run from it rather than embrace it. Where I love everything

about myself! I love the richness of both of the cultures that combine to make me who I am. I am a black woman, I know this, and I embrace it. I also know that I am a white woman, I know this, and I embrace it as well. I don't understand being confused about who I am, but that may have a lot to do with the fact that when you look at me there's no question about me. You know I'm black. My caramel skin and curly dark brown hair are complete giveaways. Mrs. Barbeau doesn't look black just like Amber wouldn't if she didn't carry herself like a black woman. My momma said Mrs. Barbeau isn't comfortable in her own skin, and that she wouldn't like me for being comfortable in mine. If my momma wasn't telling the truth! She tolerates me to a point, where Mr. B loves me! But he's the sweetest guy. Mr. B's family is from France; a lot of them are still there. Barbeau's Vineyard and winery are affiliates of the even larger Barbeau's vineyards his family owns out there. Mr. B's grandfather began his vineyards with roots from the family vines in France. Although Mr. B is American, his family raised him with the same values from back home. So I guess that's why it was easy for him to fall in love with a black woman in the early seventies when interracial marriages and dating weren't all that popular. Mr. B is as tall as Lawrence but his kind spirit and long black hair pulled back into a tasteful ponytail, give him a more relaxed and pleasing appearance. I come out here to be with Mr. B, Kelsey (hoping she's in a good mood), and Jim. I normally have a ball with them although this is the first time Jim has ever been bold enough to ask me out. "Dennis I'm not gonna cover up because your brother doesn't know how to control himself. You were fine with my bikini until he came around. I didn't bring another suit so I guess I won't get back in the water."
"At least not here. You can do whatever you want at the hotel." Then he sucked his teeth. "He's acting like that in front of Jim. I hope he doesn't think that's how you're supposed to treat your wife."
I didn't know how to take his comment. Dennis genuinely liked Kelsey and I know he felt bad for her too, but he always seemed nicer and more emphatic towards her life than he ever was with mine. I try not to be jealous about such little stuff but sometimes I can't help it.
"I guess whenever you take a wife you'll show him how it's supposed to go." I spit at him.
Dennis frowned, "why you gotta say it like that?"

"You're so worried about how Lawrence treats Kelsey. What about how you treat me? At least they're together."

"If you call that together."

"It's better than what's happening here."

"Why are you trying to pick a fight?"

I didn't respond. I put on my clothes, slicked my hair back in a bun, and then I walked out of the door. Jim was patiently waiting while his dad was in the kitchen on the phone cursing like a sailor about both of his pagers, personal, and business, being ruined. I took Jim by the hand and we walked out to the rental car and waited for Dennis.

The winery was buzzing with tons of people. We walked around the tasting floor looking for a glimpse of Kelsey. People were packed in spots at the counters. Dennis spotted his father and he left us. Someone walked up behind me, "you got too much booty to be walking around here." She said as she smacked my butt. I gave Kelsey a hug then she hugged Jim who informed her that he was my new boyfriend. "Well, I always hoped you would find a nice girl to marry. How did uncle Dennis take it?"

"She said I gotta graduate college first, but I'm only in the first grade." Jim put his hands up like my requirement was ridiculous.

"That's actually a good timeframe. No weddings until you graduate from college." Then she looked at me with sad eyes.

"So my husband went swimming?" She blushed.

"You know Dennis." I didn't know what else to say.

"Yes I do." She said trying to shake off her mood. "Come taste some wine." She took me over to the side; she poured a glass of Riesling for me. We sat over to the side talking about the customers and staff on the floor. Who thought they were slick, hooking up with each other when they thought no one was watching. Then Mrs. Barbeau glided onto the floor like royalty. She walked around the floor greeting customers and smiling at the employees. Irritation flashed across her face when her eyes landed on me. She threw her nose in the air and went in the other direction. Kelsey and I laughed and continued to drink. As six o'clock rolled around, the customers cleared out and the staff cleaned up the floor.

"There's my girl! Why haven't you come to say hello to me?" Mr. B said walking over with his arms extended.

"Brad!" Mrs. Barbeau said sternly

Mr. B ignored her and wrapped his arms around me. He kissed my cheek, and then he hugged Kelsey the same way. "I always

wanted a daughter. Instead I got these knuckle head boys."
Lawrence was still brewing about his stuff. He kept giving
Dennis evil eyes, and Dennis gave him his award-winning
smile. "Kelsey you pick the restaurant tonight."
Kelsey clapped her hands together very excitedly. She picked
up the phone and made reservations. Mrs. Barbeau came over
and fussed at Mr. B for ignoring her. He picked her up in a
very romantic fashion and then he kissed her ever so gently.
Although I'm sure she's used to Mr. B's charms it appears that
he still knocks her socks off. It looked like she forgot what she
was fussing about. We stood there smiling at her as she tried to
remember what she was saying. Frustrated she walked away.
Her mood softened, but she still wasn't happy about me.
Kelsey, Mr. B, Jim, Dennis, and I sat close to each other while
Mrs. Barbeau and Lawrence sat close to each other on the
other end of the table and enjoyed each other's company. When
we went back to our hotel I asked Dennis why we weren't
together. He got all huffy and accused me of trying to pick a
fight. Then he drilled me about my conversation with Richard.
In the morning, we checked out of the hotel then we went back
to his parent's house to say goodbye. Jim told me he was going
to make a ring for me when I came back. Mr. B made me
promise to say hello to my family for him, and to come back
soon. I tried my best not to be annoyed by Dennis and Kelsey's
sidebar conversation. I could tell he was more than likely
doing the usual apology to her because his brother is a jerk
song and dance. It just felt like Dennis was all over the place
on this trip over. I was ready for Sasha time and I was tired of
sharing. In true Lawrence style he couldn't let Dennis leave
without some sort of retaliation. When we walked out to the
rental car the driver's side window was busted out. Lawrence
stood there belly laughing while Dennis changed colors.
Dennis walked back inside and then Kelsey came running out.
She yelled at Lawrence for being so childish. He completely
ignored her. Mr. B was not amused either. I held the paper bag
while Dennis and Kelsey swept out the glass.
"When are you going to come see me?" Lawrence said in my
ear but he wasn't whispering.
"You are so disrespectful! What on earth would make you
think that I would ever be interested in my man's brother,
Kelsey's husband, or a married man period!" I didn't whisper
either. Dennis and Kelsey stopped what they were doing and
looked at us.

"The fact that it's me of course!" He said with a smile not caring about our audience.

"Lawrence!" Kelsey sounded like she was about to cry.

"What?" He shrugged. "Since Dennis cares so much about your feelings I propose that we do a wife swap. What do you say Dennis? You can have the wife and kid and I'll take your spicy little number."

Dennis and Kelsey turned red. Dennis dropped his broom and stood up. "Dennis he's stupid. Let's just go!" I said handing the paper bag to Kelsey who also made her way around the car. She looked like she wanted to say something but Dennis turned his attention to her. "He's stupid and bitter. You deserve so much better." Dennis said hugging Kelsey.

Lawrence looked at me. "You see this!" He gestured with his hands. "Stuff like this is exactly what I'm talking about. He's always running behind her. You've always wanted her, you can have her. I'm tired of looking at her."

It did annoy me watching them embrace. Then Mr. B came out. He had a blanket in his hands. "Send me the bill for the window, it'll come out of his check."

"WHAT?" Lawrence said livid. "What about my stuff that he ruined yesterday?"

"He settled the bill for your work stuff with me yesterday. You guys get going before you miss your flight." Then he put the blanket over Dennis's chair.

Lawrence still proceeded to go off like he was being done some huge injustice. Dennis was quiet the rest of the night. I gave him his space until it was time to go to bed. I was ready for more Dennis loving and he was trying to go to sleep. I complained until he gave in, but all I got was a quickie. I was not happy.

Chapter 3

"You do know I only come in this early for you." Ava said yawning.

"Thank you, we have a video conference today, and I want to look good for it."

"You mean for the guy who sounds good over the phone?"

"Yes." I smiled, "he's married so it's just a curiosity really. But! In my defense I didn't know he was married when my obsession began. I've calmed down a lot. Now it's just a confirmation that I was right."

"And dragging me out of my bed this early would be?"

I laughed, "vanity! I always gotta look my best!"

"You're a mess, how come Thea isn't here? She's on the call too?"

"She had to go take care of her momma suddenly. She won't be back until tomorrow."

Ava frowned, "since when are they close? I thought she hated her stepmom?"

Ava had a point, Thea's mother died when she was young and her dad remarried. She didn't like her stepmom. "I don't know maybe they made up or something. That's what she said." I said thinking about it. Now that she pointed it out it didn't make sense. She probably snuck away to spend time with that lowlife Rodell. Thea definitely had a thing for stupid thugs. I didn't mind a thug, but he better be smart and have a good and steady hustle. Rodell was stupid and wreaking havoc on her life. It was to the point that she was embarrassed to acknowledge that she was still seeing him from time to time. She was smart and hardworking; she needed someone better than that.

"So guess what," she said changing the subject. I looked at her in the mirror. "I need a vacation how about you?" I blew air shaking my head yes. "Let's use my timeshare. Let's go somewhere warm."

My mouth watered, "when?"

"As soon as we can. I can call, get the dates, and call you later. Let's compare calendars."

"Sounds like a plan!" I said feeling good already. I couldn't wait to get away. This entire visit with Dennis was disappointing. As if that quickie was bad enough, he said he was too tired Monday night. And he tried to claim tired last night, then he gave me three fourths of a salute. Anger stirred in my stomach as I remembered that. I was ready for him to go home. I refused to feel sad about his nonchalant response to me. Doesn't he know who I am? Men fall all over their selves to be with me, and he has the nerve to sit up here and act like I wasn't a big deal.

Ava turned me to face the mirror while she handed me a small hand held mirror. She straightened my hair and it was long and shiny. I lightly shook my head and my hair moved with each movement. I sang her praises while Ava smiled and accepted my praise. Dennis was gonna die when he saw me, he loved when I straightened my hair. Too bad for him he would only see me while I was on my way to drop him to the airport.

As soon as I hit the lobby people were looking at me. "Good morning Sasha." Henry said staring at me. "You look really nice."

"Thank you Henry, it's good to see you as well."

As others entered the elevator their eyes darted to me, some looked away while others stared.

I could hear the rumble of Malcolm's voice as I approached Richard's office. I looked at my watch and it was two minutes to eight. If Malcolm says he's going to be somewhere at a certain time, you should come an hour earlier and then still hope you get there before he does. I waved as I walked past the office. My office door was open, I rolled my eyes. Why don't my cousins respect locks? Derrick was at the small table I used to meet with people at sometimes. He had his laptop open and all you heard was the click of his typing. "You couldn't wait for me to unlock the door?"

Derrick looked at me with no smile, "no." Then he returned his attention to his laptop.

What did I expect from little Malcolm. "Good morning big head!"

He got up to give me a hug, "good morning." Derrick was a little taller than Darryl. Derrick was more solid than Darryl; you definitely didn't disregard him as a lightweight when you saw him. The fact that his facial expressions rarely held a welcoming tone could be off putting, since I've known him all his life I've learned that he actually has a warm and gentle core, but you gotta get deep to get there. He was the most like Malcolm out of all three of his little soldiers as we used to call them. Neither one of them smiled very much. But I can make Derrick laugh and smile. Malcolm on the other hand, I don't even try. I know I'm not the only one who wonders how in the world Amber ever ended up with a guy like him. But then his softer side comes to light when he deals with Amber. When I realized that whether they were together or not as long as Amber was on my side Malcolm would come around, I had power. Derrick was like that with his childhood sweetheart Brooklyn. Whatever Brooklyn wanted she got, she was a little older than him but you'd never know it. Derrick always carried himself in a more mature manner. He was devastated when her family moved away. He became extremely cynical and over the whole idea of love. He dated another girl seriously, but he didn't have her around me much and they broke up eventually, I guess he'll be a mature bachelor like his father. He looked at me. "I thought we were going out to dinner."

"We are," I said not understanding where the comment was coming from.

"You just got your hair done." He said trying to read my eyes. "How do you know I just got my hair done?" He blank stared at me. "I always get my hair done. Don't act like this is something new. "

"Un huh. Let's go get coffee." He said changing the subject. Everybody on the floor was moving at a hurried and nervous pace. Upper management knew Malcolm, Juan, and Derrick were coming. But we didn't tell the worker bees. Wendy slowed down when she saw Derrick. The corners of her mouth turned up. She stopped walking in our path, "good morning Sasha. Who's this?"

"This is your boss Derrick." I said sternly.

"Nice to meet you Derrick, I'm Wendy."

Derrick's face showed no reaction. "What do you do here?"

"I'm a recruiter." She said with a smile

"Get back to work," he said as he continued to walk past her. I thought Wendy's feelings would be hurt, but she stood there openly drooling. I shook my head and followed Derrick into Richard's office. He told them we were going for coffee and he asked if there were any takers. Juan said he'd come along. Malcolm asked for drip coffee black, simple enough. Richard rattled off a fancy and very specific order. I reached for a pen and paper. Derrick told me he had it. As we strolled down the street I asked Juan about his family. He whipped out a picture of his granddaughter as he smiled with pride. Juan said his wife Gloria constantly spoils their granddaughter. His daughter decided to go back to college and get her act together, so the baby spent her days with her grandmother. He said things have been a lot better since Juanita moved back home and away from her boyfriend. Derrick held the door open for us. I immediately spotted Shawn. As soon as Derrick stood next to me, "who is he?"

There was no point in playing dumb. "We've gone out a few times, it's not serious."

"Doesn't look that way on his end." Derrick said staring Shawn down.

We ordered our coffees and then Shawn came over. I guess he figured he was entitled to approach us since I spent the night with him. Derrick could've been anyone, this was strike two.

"Hello sir, I'm Shawn a friend of your daughter's." Shawn said to Juan.

Juan's face was stone, "no you're not."

Now he looks dumb, when did I say my father was Latin? I frowned, "Shawn."

"You haven't mentioned me?" He looked at me.

I opened my mouth to respond, but Derrick spoke first. "Do you know who I am?" A few customers looked over due to the low rumble from Derrick's voice

"No I don't."

"Exactly! Go walk back over there to your corner. You should've stayed there." Derrick said

The store manager came out from the back. "Shawn is there a problem?"

"You work here?" Juan asked even though it didn't sound like a question.

"Not specifically here, but for the company."

Juan frowned, "you dated this guy?" He said pointing at him. "Why Sasha?"

"Let's go." I said completely embarrassed.

"Coffee's not finished." Derrick pointed with his eyes.

"I apologize for interrupting." Shawn said

"And yet you're still standing there." Derrick said sounding irritated.

"You know you can't date him anymore." Juan said

"She's grown!" Shawn said

"Yes daddy," I smiled at Juan.

"Like that Sasha?"

"You heard him." I said

"You have to be embarrassed. It's only going to get worse from here. You should go." Derrick said shooing him away. This was his last chance to flee peacefully. Derrick has no patience. Shawn swallowed air, and then he walked away. Juan laughed at me saying he expected more from me. I felt the need to explain that I was passing time with Shawn and that he wasn't anyone I was serious about. Juan told me I better be happy he was with me and not Malcolm. I cringed at the thought.

At ten-thirty I couldn't work anymore. I kept talking to Derrick until he stopped working and looked up at me. "Shawn Pender huh?"

I should've known he was going to look him up. "Should I go prying into your love life?"

"That life is on pause for me. We're talking about you."

"Pause? What does that mean?"

Derrick stared at me for a minute. "Are we really going to have a battle of the wills right now? You always pick the wrong guys."

"Your paused love life would suggest that you have the same problem."

"It doesn't suggest anything other than a pause."

"Whatever. Are we going out after dinner?" I said changing the subject.

"Of course, where's your friend?" He asked referring to Thea.

I smiled, "you checking for Thea?"

He huffed, "no. I'm her boss. I was just asking. I have a specific taste, and I don't check for chicks."

"Thea's pretty." I said defending her.

"Didn't say she wasn't. Pretty isn't enough. If you're seriously looking at someone you gotta look past your eyes. Pretty isn't gonna fulfill anything past superficial."

"Yeah, but ugly doesn't get a second look."

"That's your problem. You always go for the pretty wrapping. When do you think about the gift inside?"

"I do."

He smiled, "I know you don't."

"Yes I do, and no you don't."

"You just spent the weekend with Dennis, I know you don't."

"Dennis has a gift inside!" I barked

"He may, but he isn't giving it to you. If he was you wouldn't date outside of that no matter where he lives."

"Please! I'd be stupid to think he's not dating when he's home. I'm not going to waste my time waiting for him."

"Yeah, but it should be someone worth your time."

I had no come back for that. I got up and took my notepad and pen into the conference room. Betty was running around making sure everything was setup correctly. She was testing the system with the East Coast office Admin. "Amelia this is Sasha; she's head of our Servicing and Placement Division. Amelia is the me over there."

"Nice to meet you. Everyone on their way?" I asked
"Just about. I can't wait to meet you guys in person." Amelia
said showing excitement.
We laughed and people started filling into both conference
rooms. I watched to see if I could pick El out without hearing
him speak. None of the guys taking their seats fit my mental
description, I was thankful that some of the seats were still
open. Derrick sat next to me; he smiled at me like he was
reading my mind. As Malcolm and Juan walked in our room
two guys walked in. I leaned back, now which one? At ten
fifty-seven Malcolm told them to shut the door. Anyone not in
the room by then was late and would be dealt with. Malcolm
didn't introduce himself I guess because he didn't need an
introduction. He welcomed the skeleton crew on the East
Coast. It was hard not to pay attention when Malcolm spoke, it
was like you held on to each word in anticipation for the next.
My heart sped up when he said he wanted everyone to
introduce their selves. Since East Coast was the newest
addition he said we'd start with them. Each person stood, and
introduced their selves. At this point I was hoping the other
possible guy was not El and not married cause it would be nice
to have someone to flirt with while I was out there. The first
guy stepped up, "Alonzo Thompson Assistant Director or
Servicing and Placement Division East Coast."
Well hello Alonzo I thought to myself, I held back my smile
cause I knew Derrick was listening for it. Alonzo was average
height, a little browner than me but still light skinned, black
curly hair, all around nice features.
"El Parsons Director of Servicing and Placement Division East
Coast." I felt a sense of accomplishment since I picked him out
without hearing him. El was every bit as FINE as I imagined.
Can Sasha pick them out or could Sasha pick them out! El was
average tall deep cocoa brown skin with a well-groomed and
slight beard. His eyes showed that he was focused and always
thinking. His hair was cut very low, and his grey suit, crisp
white shirt, and grey tie looked like they were made with him
in them. His handkerchief in his lapel was white with the
initials EP embroidered in grey. I saw the wedding band,
simple and not flashy. Even though I know he has a cellphone
he had a nice watch on. It wasn't flashy but it was simply nice.
I instantly felt disappointed to be right. BUT Alonzo didn't
appear to be a bad consolation prize. Provided he's single, and
I got an extremely single and playboy vibe from him. The sub-
East Coast side in Florida introduced their selves, the Mid-

West, North West, San Francisco, and then our Office. They started next to Malcolm. "Richard Cardell Acquisitions and Special Services Southern California" the others in my room introduced their selves. This was it, my big reveal! "Mary Keiths Branding" it was my turn I stood up, "Sasha Wallace Servicing and Placement Division West Coast, which also covers everything except East Coast." I instantly felt disappointed when El's expression nor demeanor appeared to be affected by me, but then again he is married so it's not like he could really afford to have one. I told myself to get a grip. The rest of the meeting was fine but I kind of felt like I was over it. El went over the plans of the five suitable options that he felt good about. Derrick eliminated two locations based on building codes and zoning. El shot out dates for our trip out East, now more than ever I needed to get away. I hoped Ava called with dates before my trip out east happened. Malcolm advised that it would be a while before the East Coast Division would be completely up and running but we were on the right track and he thanked all of us for all of our hard work and efforts. Malcolm dismissed most of us while he asked a few to stay behind. I felt disappointed that I didn't see even a glimmer of appreciation for my appearance. I told myself to shrug it off; he's married and obviously a good guy. My phone rang and I didn't look at the caller ID.

"This is Sasha." I said dryly

"Hey, how's it going? You sound the way I feel." Tanisha said

"Hey girl! Dennis is leaving today, this visit will not go down in the history books." I sighed, "I got a ton of work but all I can think about are the dates Ava's gonna call me with for our impromptu trip."

"Sounds like fun, where you going?";

"Don't know yet, she's gonna check with her timeshare. What's going on with you? How's a day in the life of officer Seaver?"

"Nothing much, I was actually calling to make sure you were going to be in town cause I'm looking to get away myself."

"Everything ok?" I said picking up on her tone.

"I need a break from here. I met someone but it's still new. I can't even deal with my momma, and my father's mother keeps calling."

"Why?"

"He's coming out and they're begging me to come." Her voice started to sound angry. "He should be reaching out to me, but no... They seem to think I should initiate any form of interaction and I'm not going to do that."

I smiled, "how's...."
"Sasha! Don't go there with me!"
My smile got bigger, "why can't I ask about him?"
"Yussef is my brother, it's just nasty to me. We discussed this already." She was irritated
"Yeah but..."
"But is what you get beat on! There's no if ands or buts about it."
"Yes ma'am! I guess you have spoken. Has he asked you about me at least?"
Tanisha sucked her teeth, "you're not helping my irritation. That moment you guys shared was years ago. You're family, cut it out!"
I rolled my eyes, "you're such a hypocrite."
"What? How?" She said about to blast me.
"Drew!" I said with a smile.
Tanisha hissed at me. "I hate you!"
"So you were saying? I'm your sister, and he's your brother?" I said laughing.
"We were kids, that's not fair." She whined
"Doesn't matter, it's the same thing. But I know Yussef isn't checking for me. If he wanted me he knows where to find me." I exhaled, in that moment I didn't feel very pretty. If I was so pretty why didn't Yussef ever react or respond to me? I started thinking about what Derrick said earlier.
Then one of the recruiters came in with a list of questions so I told Tanisha I'd call her back. When my meeting was over Ava called me. I was on the phone with her when Derrick came in the office. His fingers moved lightning fast on the keyboard. The soonest date Ava had was for Puerto Vallarta. I asked her if she would mind if I invited Tanisha, she laughed and said she was thinking of inviting one of her friends. She said this all-inclusive resort had two bedroom condos. I told her it sounded heavenly. I blocked off my calendar for that week and I started rescheduling the few meetings I had. Ava and I booked our flights while we were on the phone. I was starting to feel better already. I called Tanisha back very excited with the details. She thanked me for the energy cause she needed it. She booked her flight while we were on the phone. Derrick pointed his eyes at me then he shook his head at all of our excited chatter. When I got off the phone I told Derrick about my trip as if he didn't hear.
Dennis stood in the doorway frowning. "You're leaving?"

"Yep, what are you doing here? I was supposed to pick you up."

"I can make my way here." He said

"Why couldn't you make your way all the way to the airport then?" Derrick said not amused.

"Hey Derrick how you doing?" Dennis said realizing Derrick was there as he walked completely inside. Derrick nodded at him and then he turned his attention back to his computer.

"You didn't tell me the family was coming."

"Oh," I didn't have to report to him all the events in my family.

"You're gonna go see your boyfriend Richard right?"

Dennis put his bags on the chair then he walked out the door. Derrick chuckled, "you can't treat him like that."

"Like what?" I asked not knowing what he was talking about

"You can't treat a man like he's less than a man and expect him to honor you as his woman." I blank stared at Derrick, "look at me crazy if you want to. But we both know how you can be sometimes."

"No I don't! How can I be?" I said completely defensive.

"Let him handle things, stop trying to fix everything for him. Most importantly, let him be a man."

"I do!"

"Fine Sasha, you do." He turned his attention back to his computer.

Then my line rang, "this is Sasha."

"Sasha, Alonzo." He paused like I was supposed to have a reaction.

"Hello Alonzo," I said as dryly as I answered the phone.

He was quiet for a minute. I irritably waited for him to speak.

"I wanted to confirm your travel arrangements for your trip out."

"I haven't booked anything out yet. Has anyone else booked yet?"

"You were my first call. I guess I'll send out an email blast instead, that way people can confirm as they make their arrangements." The confidence in his voice wavered.

"That sounds like a good idea. I'll respond to your email when I'm ready. Talk to you later." I said as I reached for the hang up button.

"Later Sasha." Now if only that would've been El, I might've perked up a bit.

When I stepped back on the floor the watchers were too busy working to pay me any attention. Malcolm and Juan were in their offices. It's very rare that Derrick and Malcolm come out at the same time. Normally Derrick works in Malcolm's office when he's here. He knows that I don't mind him crashing in the office with me when he needs to. I walked to Richard's office and I watched Richard and Dennis talk. It didn't take long to realize that Dennis was talking about his brother and the foolishness over the weekend. They talked for a while then when Dennis realized the time he stood up, and realized I was standing there. "You never make noise when you walk. You love sneaking up on me." He smiled and I released some of my tension.

"Are you ready to go?" He said his goodbyes to Richard and then we walked back to my office. Malcolm watched us walk, you could never tell anything by the expression on his face half the time. Dennis and Derrick said goodbye and then we left for the airport. "Do you know when you will be back?"

"The Firm is moving my case load around, they have a client out here they want me to work with. A lot of our interaction will be over the phone, but I can imagine coming out here a little more often to hold the client's hand." I sighed loud.

"What Sasha?"

"I was just thinking, that if each visit is going to be like this I could pass on seeing you altogether."

I offended him, but I wasn't going to pretend like we had a good visit when we didn't. "Maybe I won't see you then."

"Maybe you won't. Normally I can count on you to make me feel loved even if we aren't technically together. These past five days you have succeeded in making me feel like an afterthought. I don't know what you thought you were doing last night, but it was weak. And…. if I'm not crazy did you serve me after serving someone else?"

"What? Sasha!"

I waited and when he didn't say anything else. "That wasn't an answer Dennis. Don't forget I KNOW the difference between first and second. How many females you got out here?" He opened his mouth to speak. "You know what it doesn't matter. I come first! Pun intended! If you can't get with the program delete my name and everything. I will move right along to the next man with no problem."

"You've got a wild imagination!"

I looked at him taking my eyes completely off the road. "Don't play on words with me! Remember I don't fall for those games!"

"Sasha watch the road!"

"Is today a good day to die Dennis? Don't play with me!"

"Ok Sasha! Ok! Watch the road!"

"Ok what?" I said staring at him.

"YOU COME FIRST! I GOT IT!" He turned completely red.

"You are so guilty!" I looked at his face, and then I turned my attention back to the road.

"And you are CRAZY!"

"Officially 51/50, and you better not forget it! When you come, you put me first; or don't come back at all!"

"Guess I'm not coming back then!" He said mad that he showed me fear.

"PSSSHHHH! You're coming back! I'm not worried about that, but when you do, you better come correct!"

"I'm not coming back! You treat me like this and you expect me to come running back?"

"YES! Yes I do! There's only one me! Whoever she or they may be, they will never be me! You'll try to hold true to your word, but after a while your body will be screaming for Sasha! I am not a decoration, and you will not toss me to the side like sloppy seconds will ever do! Don't come at me at all if you can't come correct. I'm not playing with you Dennis, you know me!"

Dennis didn't say anything he sat there brewing, he was still beet red! "Park your car!" He told me when we got to the airport. So I went to the garage and parked my car in the corner in the back. He grabbed his things. "I'll be right back." He calmly walked to the airport. I was checking emails on my phone when he came back to the car. He was looking around the parking lot as he approached the car. I knew that look. I put my phone down. He snatched my driver's side door open, and pulled me out of the car in a smooth glide. I slapped him as he pulled me out the car. Still holding onto my shirt he kissed me passionately and deeply. This was my man, and this is what I had been waiting for. I tried to take his hands off of my shirt but he had a firm grip on me. "You wanna act crazy! I'll show you crazy!" He said throwing my back against the car as he kissed me again. He pressed his body up against mine. Then he looked at me, "Get in the back!"

"No!" I felt like he was asking me.

He moved me out the way unlocked the doors. He opened the back door and threw me in. "How you gonna straighten your hair and then act like this? WHO'S YOUR DADDY?" He demanded to know as he worked me over. I couldn't respond in any complete wording, my body was enjoying this on a whole other level. Two condoms and a double orgasm later I didn't want him to leave. My rage was gone, and I was mild and meek Sasha again. "Who came first?" He asked as he breathlessly kissed me.

"Sasha did!" I said with the biggest smile.

"I like your hair, it looks good. But you always look good." He said smiling at me while he fixed his clothes.

"Thank you, I know!" I laughed, if only he knew this hair wasn't for him.

****

"This is the best idea you've had thus far!" I said raising my fruit drink to Ava.

"Thank you! Thank you! I think I'll give myself a pat on the back for this one as well." She said taking a sip of her drink.

"Ahem!" Someone cleared their throat from behind us. We turned around and Ava got up very excitedly to hug her friend. "Sasha this is my friend Kai, Kai this is Sasha." Then she pointed across the pool to the swim up bar. "And that's Sasha's sister Tanisha at the bar. Tanisha turned around when she heard her name and waved. "I'll help you with your things up to the room. Sasha we'll be back."

I waved bye to them and then I relaxed on my lounge chair. Tanisha walked over with her drink. "Her friend is pretty." Tanisha said

"Isn't she, Ava said she's really nice." I said, "she just broke up with her boyfriend so she needed to get away."

"I'm not mad at it. Poor thing suffering from a breakup." Tanisha took another drink on her straw.

"How are things up North? How's the new place?"

"They're fine, my momma is fine. I have a few more interviews, it looks like I'll be at the Oakland PD."

"What's wrong with working for Oakland?"

"All the people I will know, your uncles and cousins; I don't need that."

"Drew's not still acting out?"

"He's been a lot calmer lately. But he's gotta make better choices. He needs to let Toya go. Drew keeps saying he's done, but he keeps going back to her. Sometimes I swear she's setting some of these fools up just for the fun of it."

"He still letting that girl lead him to drama." I said shaking my head.

"I don't know why he holds on to her so tight. Let her go!"

"You know why he holds onto her." I said with an evil grin. Tanisha rolled her eyes, "quit it!"

"He's waiting for you to come back to him." Tanisha faked disgust. "Come on, you know you miss my cousin."

"Miss him for what? I saw him every day when we stayed in the same building. Him and all his women! You know I don't swing that way anymore."

"That's what you say, but I know you. You still love Drew, I can tell."

"I love him like a brother, that's it."

"Who sleeps with their brother?"

Tanisha rolled her eyes so hard it looked like she was going to fall asleep. "LOOK! I HATE that I ever let you figure that out. I don't want to talk about it." She said turning in her chair.

"Do you ever miss him?" I asked trying to imagine what it would be like not to have a man in my life.

"I'm a girl, of course I do. But it's never serious enough to go back there with him."

I knew that had to be the alcohol talking Tanisha wouldn't normally admit to missing him. "What do you miss most about him?"

"He was always very sweet, he had a way of making me feel like...." She searched for words. "Drew was always good to me."

"Do you guys ever talk about what happened?"

"One time."

"How long ago?" I couldn't believe it. I sat up to listen to her answer. "Why didn't you tell me?"

"When he and Jennay broke up. Amber was so done with him. He was double heartbroken, but that was by far the dumbest thing he's ever done." She laughed

"He has genius moments I know, but get to the part I want to hear about."

"I went by to check on him, cause he was losing it. He told me the whole story and I sat there shaking my head. He actually got mad at me and told me he wouldn't have been going through any of that if I wasn't confused about what team I was playing for. I couldn't believe he was trying to pin it on me. I told him I wouldn't have put my foot down if he would've sent Toya packing in the first place. She was always lurking. The fact that they got together at all just proves my point. I just don't know if they began after we broke up or before." She exhaled, "we argued about it. I held on to I'm not interested in men like that. He said he's not just a man, but I told him this is who I am. We went back and forth for a long time. But in the end I think he finally understood."

"Understood that you need more time."

"Whatever. When Toya sees us talking she swears we're hooking up though."

"Toya would accuse me of hooking up with Drew if I was out there. She's ridiculous!"

"True," Tanisha said sitting back in her chair and taking another sip of her drink. "Last thing I wanna do is sit here and think about Toya's dumb behind. Let's swim, you need to fix your tan anyways. Instead of technically swimming we lounged in the water in inner tubes while making our way to the bar every time our drinks got low. Eventually Kai and Ava joined us in the pool. Kai was plus sized and beautiful, she had more confidence than even I had. I didn't think anyone could be more confident than me without being in love with their self, but Kai had it down to a science. She seemed more in love with her body than any person I've ever met. Kai was a breath of fresh air.

When we got dressed to go out Tanisha wore a baby blue button up with brown pants. She had this brown fedora that looked really good on her. I put on a soft yellow dress that hugged my body perfectly. Ava wore an orange dress that kissed her tan and made her skin glow. Kai put on this turquoise dress that made her stand out as the knock out she already was. This club was packed with vacationing Americans, etc. We found a table then we went to the bar, bought drinks, drank, and then we hit the dance floor. Kai was the woman of the night, she barely danced with us cause she had them lined up she couldn't get a break. A few guys approached Tanisha and each time I was surprised when she agreed to dance with them. Clearly she was on vacation from everything. Ava couldn't believe that Tanisha appeared to be enjoying herself, I was a little surprised myself. I was getting my groove on with this CUTE guy who had rhythm, when I thought I saw Dennis out the corner of my eye. The crowd on the dance floor shifted and I couldn't see. The vibe changed, my eyes landed on Ava. When she rolled her eyes at me, that confirmed that he was there. I danced harder with my partner, I was angry. When I couldn't dance anymore I sat down completely drenched in sweat. "Surprise!" Dennis said as he sat down. I stared at him, "I missed you." He said kissing my lips.

"I'm here with my friends and sister, how rude are you?" I barked

"I've been feeling uneasy about the way we left each other." I stared at him, "I mean the icing was fine. But I wanted to apologize for ignoring you on that trip."

"You could've called me, sent me jewelry, or made it up when you came back." I looked around, "this made it worse. Who does this? Who are you? What did you do with Dennis?" Tanisha came back to the table catching her breath. "How you doing brother in-law?" She said reaching out for his hand. Dennis was being extra sweet, but I was annoyed beyond belief. Dennis walked us back to our resort, and then he took a cab to his hotel. In our room Tanisha asked me why I seemed surprised that he showed up. She said whenever I act distant towards him, he always comes running. When I tried to argue my point she gave me case-by-case example of times in the past when he's popped up, maybe I was tired of the game.

Chapter 4

"There we are." Mary said pointing at the man holding the Mitigated sign. Our driver had airport assistants ready with luggage carts to escort us to our ride. I had mixed emotions I wanted to go site see, but I was tired from my flight. Why does sitting on an airplane make you tired?

"So Sassy, it's gonna be me, you, and Thea for dinner?" Richard asked

"Sure why not." I said unenthusiastically

"What? You wanna sneak away together?" He leaned in.

"No cause she'll ask me, and I don't wanna lie. I'll invite her once we get checked in." I mean who cares that she's sleeping with Rodell? But she's been acting so weird; it's starting to get on my nerves. Thea is nearing her expiration though. For whatever reason I tend to get along with a female for about two years. If we're still cool after two years then we're good to go. Thea and I are on the cusp of two years and sure enough she's acting weird. When I asked about her mother she was real short saying she was fine. We've cried together about her family drama. When her sister was missing cause she ran away, I had her found and returned home. True she didn't know I was connected to that, but I was right there holding her hand through it all. I have my own issues I don't have time. The hotel was nice and sure enough I had a kitchen in my one bedroom unit, so I was pleased. I called Thea and invited her to dinner, but she declined sighting that she was tired and going to call it a night. Richard and I had a blast! It's kind of hard to take him seriously, as an authoritative parent when, we're growing up together. My momma can seem like a girlfriend sometimes, but I never forget she's my momma. Richard gets real comfortable and sometimes it's like I'm talking to Drew or Derrick. I have a more fatherly regard for JoJo than I do Richard. And JoJo is only a year older than me. Richard told me he and Juan were going to do some screening for Special Services staff while they were out here. Which meant they would be disappearing and then reappearing suddenly. I have to admit that his job seemed cool to me in that regard. Richard is normally real chill and laid back, but watch out for his temper. If you push him to the point of flashing, watch out! I smile every time I think about that. My momma is the only person he runs from. I liken him to Malcolm in that regard, they run stuff and yield to their women. Is it weird that when

I'm with Richard I don't need male attention? I hate to admit that my attachment to Dennis could be related to daddy issues. But when Dennis is good to me he's good.

In the morning I woke up refreshed and ready for my day. Thea called me when she was ready to go and I was putting on my big puffy coat since it was freezing outside. She laughed at my big coat, hat, and gloves until we opened the lobby door. I told her LA attire didn't work out here. We loaded on the shuttle and then we drove in the snow to the office space occupied by the New York skeleton crew. Malcolm, Derrick, and Juan were already there. Malcolm and Richard were reviewing the proposed client list for this location and the recruiting strategy to locate our staff, etc. Derrick told me he gave Alonzo a list of morning coffee orders and it would be here shortly. Since there was limited space in this office we sat in the conference room working from our laptops. "Finally!" Malcolm said as he reached for his coffee cup. Alonzo's eyes kept darting between Thea and I. "Hello? Pay attention!" Malcolm said to Alonzo.

"Sorry Malcolm." Alonzo was embarrassed and Malcolm looked annoyed. Alonzo and Amelia walked around the table passing out coffees. When Alonzo got to Thea he stopped. "You weren't on the call."

Thea blushed, "no I wasn't."

Then he turned his attention to me. "Hello miss Sasha!" His eyes filled with appreciation for my appearance.

"Hello Alonzo, thank you for the coffee." I said taking my cup. I glanced at Malcolm who was watching us, but so were Derrick and Richard.

"You're a little bit too eager." Derrick said

Alonzo laughed Derrick's comment off. I was embarrassed for him. Malcolm stared at me for a minute like he was thinking about something then he went back to his computer. THEN! El walked in, no he glided in. The butterflies that only surface for Dennis banged around in my stomach. His eyes toured the room and he nodded at those looking at him. Again I felt disappointed when there was nothing special or different in his reaction to me verses anyone else in the room. He said something to Malcolm and then Malcolm stood up and followed him. "Who is that?" Thea leaned over.

"El girl! Ain't he FINE!" I whispered back.

I got up to go to the bathroom and I stopped as I passed Malcolm's laptop. Pictures of Amber were appearing and disappearing in his screen. When I leaned in I could hear

Michael singing, "there'll be no darkness tonight. Lady our love will shine, lighting the night..." I smiled really big while Derrick shook his head at me. I wondered if Dennis was this sprung off of me. As I washed my hands I checked my reflection in the mirror. Why didn't he notice me, I look as good today as any other day? I sighed oh well. As I walked to the conference room Alonzo and El were talking in the middle of the floor looking at a report. "Sasha," I loved the sound of my name on his lips. "Welcome to New York, how was your first night?" El focused on my eyes only.

"It was nice, thank you." I gave him direct eye contact.

"That's good. Tell me something, how do you approach fourth quarter forecasting?"

"Where's your computer?"

"Right this way." El led the way. I watched his slightly bow legged walk with appreciation. Alonzo walked next to me clearly checking me out.

I used my log in to show him prior numbers and projected numbers. Alonzo was so busy drooling I think he missed some of the things I showed him. El on the other hand was taking it all in and asking questions along the way. He was all business and it was kind of nice. He didn't have any pictures of his wife or kids up. He never mentioned kids, but that didn't mean he didn't have any.

"Miss Sasha knows her stuff." Alonzo said smiling.

"Thanks" I said frowning.

"Are you ready?" Malcolm's voice rumbled off the walls like the roar of a lion Alonzo and I jumped.

"Ready?"

"Site tours," El said to me reaching for folders. "Let's go." When I got my coat I didn't see Juan or Richard. "Richard?" I said to Derrick.

"In the field." Derrick said holding the door open for me.

On the shuttle Alonzo made sure he sat in front of Thea and I. El addressed the team with the specifics about each location as we approached them. Since most of our clients are acquired on the West Coast our office space would be bigger and would have more staff. But we wanted to make sure that the East Coast was equally as nice, and efficient. Derrick didn't like something in the structure that he pointed out to Malcolm. It was like they were speaking a different language. Meanwhile Alonzo kept making small talk with Thea and I. I stopped entertaining his conversation when I noticed that every time I looked up Malcolm was looking. I couldn't say he looked mad cause Malcolm always looked intolerant, but the fact that he was looking was a sign to me to shape up. Why Alonzo or Thea for that matter weren't getting it was beyond me. I separated myself from them and Malcolm's glances in my direction lessened, but as soon as they got close to me again he was watching. Ok so I got it, Alonzo needed to back away from me. I guess he felt compelled to watch over me since Richard wasn't here. Guess he didn't realize that guys assume Richard is my brother and approach me in front of him. Richard was always cool about it. However, for my cousins and uncles, no one was good enough.

The last two places were equally liked. Malcolm gave El and I instructions on how he wanted projected budgeting. El was all over it, but he needed information from me. I loved the idea of talking to him more even if it was only business. When Alonzo asked Malcolm if he should be a part of that meeting. Malcolm stared at him for a minute, and then he told him he could remain as entertainment until he tired of him. Alonzo swallowed air, but I think he got the point. He stopped flirting and started paying attention. Once he put his business hat on I then understood why Malcolm hired him. For a minute I was wondering though. At first I didn't understand why El needed an assistant to do my job on a lesser scale. But after being here I realized that he was being groomed to run the office. Around the evening time we were starting to get tired. We had been talking all day and bouncing ideas off of each other. "What's for dinner?" Thea asked Richard.

"Sassy what you feel like?" He asked me then Thea looked like "oh yeah you too."

"I don't think I was included in that invitation." I said looking at Thea to let her know I saw her.

"Of course you are. Don't be ridiculous."

Thea was starting to look fake and plastic to me. "I think I'll go to the grocery store and cook something in my room."

"I'm coming!" Derrick said

"Seriously Sasha, you were included." She said

"Aaaaa I want some of that action if you are cooking." Richard said

"No hard feelings. You go ahead and do your thing." I said returning my attention to my computer to start shutting it down.

"Sasha you cook?" Mary said like she was shocked.

"My momma is the best cook I know. People come from everywhere to eat at her restaurant. She taught me a few things."

"If your room is as small as mine I know you don't have a lot of space. But you've sparked my curiosity, you gotta cook for us one of these days."

Alonzo walked in the room at the end of her statement. "Cook? Who cooks?"

"Apparently Sasha can cook." Mary said

Alonzo chuckled, "of course she does."

"Uh oh Sassy, that sounds like a challenge." Richard said instigating

"How big is your kitchen?" I asked

"My place is good sized."

"Big enough to accommodate everyone here?"

Alonzo glanced around the room. "Easily."

"Friday or Saturday work for you?"

"Friday, and I don't want no spaghetti."

"Dietary limits?"

"What?" Alonzo looked confused.

I looked at Derrick, "she means are you allergic to anything?"

"Oh, Naw! I'm good. Bring it!"

Malcolm and El walked in the room. "Are you guys coming? I need a head count so I can plan." Although inside I was begging El to say yes.

"Where?" El asked, so I gave him a rundown of the challenge. "Can I bring Zoila?" El asked Alonzo.

Zoila? I wondered what she looked like. Based upon her name I couldn't tell. Alonzo said of course and then El agreed to come. "Decline." Malcolm said flatly. "But you're going right?" He said pointing his eyes between Richard and Derrick.

"Where are you going?" Thea asked Malcolm feeling too comfortable.

Malcolm's eyes burned her. "Minding my business!" Thea sat up straight and turned away from Malcolm. I wanted to laugh at her, but Derrick's smile was satisfaction enough.

"No diet food either! Bring it!" Alonzo said smiling. Malcolm stared at Alonzo again. If I was Alonzo I'd start looking for a plan B.

The rest of the week, I spent most of my time with El and it was heavenly. He never made a pass at me, and his eyes never traveled around my body. When I asked him about his wife I did see sadness in the back of his eyes. All he talked about is how much he loved her; they have been married for three years, dated for two. He said they met on a blind date, and he loved her from the moment he set eyes on her. His love for her was undeniable, something that is rarely highlighted anymore in men. I told him how impressive that was, and in that conversation I realized my crush was stupid. I told myself to look at him like he was a cousin and nothing more. Once I did that I relaxed a lot and my time seemed to fly by. Alonzo was excited about our dinner, and the fact that we were coming over period. Thursday night Dennis called me while I was going over my grocery list that I was giving to Amelia to give to the personal shopper. Everything was going to be at Alonzo's when we got there. I told him about Alonzo's challenge, Dennis didn't like it. He tried to tell me I couldn't do it. I laughed at him and told him to get real. Then he asked me who was gonna be there he relaxed when I said Derrick and Richard were going. He asked me if I wanted him to come out for the weekend and I told him no. I told him to plan for the next weekend. He agreed but not happily. Dennis is used to me jumping at any opportunity to be with him. I'm not feeling the love right now so I could go without.

Malcolm told us to knock off work around eleven, no one was complaining. Malcolm and Juan would be back on Monday at some point. We went back to our hotel to change, etc. Derrick and I were going to Alonzo's early while everyone else was coming around dinnertime. Derrick made us sandwiches while I changed. "I don't understand women." He said like he was surrendering.

"I thought you were on pause?"

"I am!" He snapped.

"So the problem?"

"We're no different, except for some hormonal differences." He looked at me with pain in his eyes. "I miss her."

"Who?"

He shook his head, "doesn't matter. We're over." He took a big angry bite of his sandwich.

"Brooklyn?"

He made a face, "no! She's not even the same person anymore."

"How's she different?"

"Her legs spread too fast for my liking."

"You turned her out. What do you expect?" I said.

"A measure of loyalty I guess." He took another big bite and then he chewed angrily.

"Who is she?"

"I thought we'd be back together by now." He blew irritated air. "Drew's back with Toya did he tell you?"

"Tanisha told me."

"Are you going to Hubby's wedding?" He asked watching my eyes.

I frowned, "No!" Andrew's best friend Hubby had the biggest crush on me, but I found his even bigger crush on Amber off putting. So, where I wanted to indulge him and return his advances I hesitated for good reason. THEN when he appears to be ready for me and over Amber we start dating. I never told Andrew that Hubby was my first. We swore each other to absolute secrecy! I would've felt bad about it if I didn't figure out that Andrew and Tanisha dated. And since he's never felt the need to come clean about that, I don't feel the need to share, and I KNOW Hubby is not crazy enough to tell anyone, so our secret is safe. When I left for school we agreed to an open relationship. Ok fine, everything is going good then he meets his soon to be bride. Separated by miles and school I didn't care at first but I come first, and he was acting sprung on her after just a little bit of time. I told him I didn't want to have to cut him so I called everything off. He could've married me; he could be in love with me! I still feel jilted! Why would I go watch him be excited about someone else like I support his choice or something? "You know I'm not going. You going?" He chuckled, "you're jealous!"

"So! I'm human. And at least I'm honest. I'm not gonna pretend it's ok with me that he's marrying someone else." Now I took an irritated bite. "Good sandwich." I said

"Thanks." He said lost in his thoughts. Then he looked at me, "that's what you're wearing?"

I had on a tank top and jeans. "While I'm cooking, yes. It's gonna be hot." I smiled.

"You're such a tease."

On the shuttle ride over to Alonzo's, Derrick and I admired the architecture along the way. Alonzo's house was a beautiful Brownstone that he recently had completely remodeled. He opened the door with so much pride as he welcomed us in. His eyes went straight to my breast when I took my coat off. Derrick mumbled something to himself to keep his cool. He explained that his mother grew up here, and his grandfather left it to him when he passed away. He said it needed a lot of work. He showed us each room in his house. The hardwood floors were beautiful. I asked him why he didn't have carpet in his bedrooms at least. He said they weren't practical. The house was decorated so nicely I asked him if he picked everything out and he said no. He said it was a collaboration between his brother and cousin. He put on music then we went in the kitchen. He looked at Derrick funny when he washed his hands to help me. I told him to roll up his sleeves and wash his hands as well. It was quite comical while we were prepping things. Derrick and I seemed like we were racing to chop our veggies first. We were chopping like pro's, Alonzo asked how long we've known each other. I told him we were cousins, Alonzo looked relieved he said he was starting to think we were involved. Alonzo told Derrick he was going to have some friends swing by. He raised his eyebrows; Derrick didn't say anything but he didn't look intrigued either. I made a marinade for my steaks and set them to the side to put on last, then I made a salad, steamed vegetables, and dill salmon. Then I made a citrus scented chicken with roasted potatoes and more vegetables, I made a risotto, then I made a trifle for dessert. Alonzo said his house had never smelled so good. I changed my top then we set the table. Alonzo's friends, three girls and a guy arrived. They were pretty girls, and although they appeared to all be in to Derrick, he didn't appear to be interested. They were nice enough towards me, but their glances let me know we'd never be friends. Their fake smiles and insecurities were all over their faces. Everyone else seemed to arrive together. El's wife was pretty,) but she was hiding something. I could see it in her face, and where his glances were glances of love. Hers were secrets and something…. "I bet she's cheating on him." I said to myself. Why would she ever cheat on El? Was he soft behind closed doors? Or maybe he wasn't putting it down in the bedroom. I don't take him for a little man, but could he be "lacking" and she's bored stupid? My mind kept flipping over the possibilities. "Zoila this is Sasha, Sasha Zoila." El said taking a drink.

"Nice to finally meet you. He talks about you all the time." I said

She looked me up and down, "she wants you! El, I don't have time for this!"

El looked like he was going to choke, I guess the thought never crossed his mind. I don't know why but that insulted me. "Your husband is very handsome, but he's your husband." I stood there waiting for her to say something else. I guess I was

supposed to shrink away to a corner because she read me.
"Who cares!" I said to myself.
"Zoila! I work with her, can't you even be cordial?"
"Why be cordial, the only reason we're here is so she can see
what she's up against. It's been a long week and I'm tired."
El was mad; he grabbed Zoila by her arm and yanked her so
hard. I did my best to pull back my smile. El's got that put her
in her place spice. I couldn't hear what he was saying but the
way he was handling her was sweet. Derrick walked over,
"you wrecking marriages now?"
"Not intentionally of course." I smiled at him. "You carve the
chicken?"
Dinner was buffet style and people stood around talking as
much as they could while all you heard was everyone singing
my praises. "SASHA!" Mary dramatically said, cause she had
been drinking as well. "I WILL NEVER! NEVER EVER
NEVER! DOUBT YOU AGAIN! EVERYTHING IS..." she
sucked on each finger. "DELICIOUS!"
"I'm glad you like it."
"There's no limit to your talents. You're a powerhouse at work,
you're gorgeous, you cook, and I bet you're a tom-cat in the
sack." She said
I looked at Mary, "are you hitting on me?"
"Only if you're interested. Otherwise I've had too much to
drink."
"You've had too much to drink then. I didn't know you swung
that way Mary. I guess you're not as up tight as I thought."
Mary always wore her hair in a neat short haircut, but that
short style is all the rave right now. I thought she was being
trendy.
"Sasha doesn't wanna play?" She said touching my hair.
My mouth started to water like I was gonna throw up. I walked
away from her. Derrick and Richard were laughing at me.
They were watching from across the room. That woman
needed a club and quick. As if he was reading my mind,
Alonzo turned up the music on his stereo system. Alonzo's guy
friend and Mary started dancing. Then I watched Thea
convince Richard to dance with her. Slowly but surely
everyone started dancing in the Living Room. I sat on the
couch watching El and his wife interact. I wondered what their
story was. How they ended up where they were today.
Eventually Alonzo came over to talk to me. He asked me to
dance, but I told him I was tired. We spent the rest of the night
laughing and talking. When I felt eyes on me I looked around

the room casually. When my eyes met El's I felt confused. He didn't turn his eyes away or act like he wasn't looking at me. It was the first time he actually looked at me. I felt nervous and unsure. Nothing told me whether he appreciated the privilege to look at me. He was unlike any guy I've known, in a long time. I couldn't read him, and that was so unusual.

****

Ok so this week has been interesting. It was business as usual on Monday, nothing extra in El's glances in my direction. When we met he was normal. Then Wednesday we were alone in his office planning and strategizing. He actually looked at me and he apologized for his wife's behavior. I told him he didn't need to apologize and it was perfectly ok. He asked me why it was ok for a stranger to treat me that way. Which made me back pedal, so I said I was used to that type of behavior. Then he asked why would that make it ok just because I was used to it. His eyes were focused on me and although I wanted him to look at me all this time when he's actually doing it all I wanted was to run and hide. His eyes felt intense, I couldn't tell if he was disapproving of me or telling me to accept his apology. So I told him it wasn't ok and I thanked him for apologizing. His eyes stayed on me. "What do you think of yourself?" He asked me.

I frowned, "what do you mean?"

"I'm wondering about who you are. It's obvious that you understand that you're beautiful..." OH MY GOODNESS!! He thinks I'm beautiful! "But my question is whether you understand what makes you beautiful? Good skin yes, but what else?"

"Are you saying I'm vapid?"

He smiled, "no. I'm saying that when someone like you dismisses disrespect from someone else on the grounds of usual behavior, it makes you seem tolerant of things that should be beneath you."

"You're scolding me for accepting your apology?"

"Kind of." He smiled again.

"Don't get it twisted. I grew up in Oakland! I know how to stand up for myself. Your wife on the other hand." I searched for a nice way to put it. "Seemed threatened. I was being peaceable by saying it was ok. She only got that pass because she's your wife."

"Oh I see." He said sarcastically.

"Anyways, you can return the favor when my man comes in Friday."

61

"What's Friday?"

"Alonzo is trying to get everyone together for our last Friday out here. We're gonna have dinner and whatever. I thought you were going."

"I'm going now!" He laughed. I liked his laugh. "I wanna see what kind of taste you got."

"Why do you care what kind of taste I got?"

"Sasha there's a difference between caring and wanting to see."

"Which is?"

"The levels of curiosity."

I smiled, "I'm not gonna chase you through that maze. Hope to see you on Friday. I'm heading back to the conference room." I walked away feeling his eyes on me. After that everything went back to business as usual.

****

"Meet us at 4515 Waters street. Then we can link up for dinner and then we can figure out what we wanna do from there." Alonzo said as I headed for the door.

"See you tonight Sasha." El said returning to his computer.

"Tonight." I said walking out the door. Ok, so I was actually excited to see Dennis. He's been very attentive since his pop up, but that could have something to do with my nonchalant response to him. I didn't give him any while we were in Puerto Vallarta, and I didn't invite him when we went out. He got the message loud and clear. When I watched him descend on the escalator, the butterflies were back. It was at that moment that I noticed the difference between El's butterflies and Dennis's. El's butterflies were for the unknown things with him. Like did he intentionally insult me after he complimented me to cover his tracks? I only wanted acknowledgment that he noticed me, nothing more. He's a married man whether he's happily married or not. Dennis swept me up in a romantic fashion and kissed me deeply. Dennis was staying with me and flying back to California with me. He told me I was going to get sick of seeing him. I was up for the challenge.

In the car service to my hotel we talked fast and loud. You'd swear we were just old friends catching up. Richard saw us in the lobby, I sighed, as they got lost in conversation. Richard came up to my room, but unlike last time Dennis kept his attention on me. As we were leaving we saw Derrick and Mary in the lobby. They were leaving tonight; Derrick was staying at Malcolm's townhouse. Since I wasn't leaving until later I stayed with the group at the hotel.

Dennis and I were building anticipation for our return to my room later. When Thea joined us she said an awkward hello generally. I stood there studying her face and demeanor. Dennis squeezed my hand to pull me out of my trance. Richard and Thea held their own private conversation in the car. Is she pushing up on Richard? That would be dumb, and there's no way I could approve of that. "Next Saturday lets go out to Napa." He said

"Are you crazy? Every time we go out your brother gets worse and worse."

Dennis smiled, "Lulu's gonna be there!" He gave me a knowing look.

"You're kidding!" I said leaning in to hear more.

"My mom doesn't know of course. But she told me she's going and she wants to see you." Lulu is Dennis's grandmother, his mother's mother. I love that woman. How she ever had a daughter like Mrs. Barbeau is beyond me.

"Of course I'll go to see her." I said happily.

When we arrived at the address Alonzo gave me, he was standing next to his car freezing. He motioned for us to continue following. We drove for a while then we stopped at a restaurant. Alonzo's smile dropped when he saw Dennis. I introduced Dennis to Alonzo's friends from last week. I could see the pheromones rising off their heads as they said hello. Dennis said a respectful hello, and then he returned his attention to me. We were shown to our table and I noticed the two empty chairs. Just when I thought El wasn't coming I saw him gliding across the floor. Zoila had the same uninterested look on her face until she spotted Dennis. I could tell she was curious. I introduced Dennis to them and both of them had curious looks on their faces. They sat directly across from us. Zoila spent most of the night checking me out but I was doing the same to her. Her face was kind of flat and her big brown eyes almost slanted a little, high cheekbones, clear skin, almost full lips, button nose, small bosom, no butt, her waistline suggested that her stomach should be flat, maybe she had one too many beers since El's never mentioned kids. She made sure her makeup highlighted her eyes. Her skin was mocha brown colored. Her hair was just past her shoulders and permed straight. She had an innocent baby face that could turn evil in the flicker of an eye. I watched her eyes glide over my features as well. She watched Dennis and I's interaction. I guess she was checking to see if Dennis was here as a ruse. Alonzo asked Richard if he was married, he said no but he has a daughter. Alonzo asked him what parenthood was like. I saw pain flash all over Zoila's face, and El's eyes saddened. Richard said he wasn't a good father. He said at the time he was very immature. Obviously no one at the table besides Thea, Dennis, Richard, and I knew he was talking about me.

"As our only resident married couple, do you plan on having children or do you have any?" Dennis asked Zoila and El.

El looked away like he was gathering himself. Zoila took a big gulp of her drink. "Funny you should ask." She painfully smiled. El told her she didn't have to talk about it but she shrugged him off. "We lost our little girl." Stress lines appeared across El's face.

"I'm sorry, I didn't know." Dennis said feeling guilty for asking the question.

"It's ok! How could you know? He acts like nothing happened." She said slurring her words. El left the table. I guess that sobered her up enough to make her realize what she just said to his coworkers who are mostly strangers. She huffed, made for movie tears streamed out of her eyes then she looked at me. "I can't do this anymore. You can have him!" Then she got up, and walked away. Neither one of them came back to the table.

We sat there quiet for a few minutes. Then Alonzo's friend told us about an off Broadway play, that sounded pretty interesting. The play was pretty good and then Richard, Thea, Dennis, and I made our way back to the hotel.

"Why did his wife say you could have him?" Thea asked like the question had been bugging her all night.

Dennis looked at me, "I was gonna ask you the same thing." Richard smiled at me. "She thinks I want him."

"Do you?" Dennis asked watching my eyes.

"I don't know him to want him. He's handsome, smart, stuff like that. But I don't know him to want him." I bucked my eyes at Dennis cause he was still staring. "Like you've never noticed someone at work before."

"I've never had someone's husband throw in the towel and tell me I could have their wife either."

"That was probably the liquor talking. I doubt their marriage is over." I said dismissively.

As soon as we got in the room Dennis went into prosecution mode. He asked me question after question about El. So I started objecting to some of his questions cause he was trying to lead me to say that something has happened between El and I. I told him nothing had happened and I reminded him that I don't do married men. Fueled by his jealousy Dennis and I had a night for the history books.

That weekend was nice, but his constant need to include Richard and by default Thea in our outings was getting annoying. I told him how she's been acting weird lately and he said she's probably going through something. He told me to cut her some slack and that she'd come around. I rolled my eyes at the thought of it.

****

Sunday night I had a dream about my stepfather. I usually only dream of him when something's out of whack with me. During midterms Dennis would sleep on the couch or go home.

Dennis was looking at me when I woke up. I went in the bathroom and splashed cold water on my face. "What's wrong Sasha?"

"Nothing!" Dennis stared at me. "I don't know!"

"Is this the first one?"

"Yes." Then I went and sat on the bed.

"When are you going to talk to your mom? Maybe these dreams will go away once that chapter is closed in your life."

"You don't think I've tried. We end up arguing about the same old stuff. Maybe I should try someone else."

"Like who?"

"My Poppa maybe? I don't know." I thought about it. "Maybe I can swing by and see my grandparents on our way back."

"You know he doesn't like me."

"No more than your mother likes me. What's your point?"

He exhaled, "can't I go with you on a different weekend. I told you Lulu's gonna be in Napa. That's gonna be emotionally draining enough. I don't know how much energy I'm gonna have left to deal with them too."

"Fine! Then I'll go by myself! Tell Lulu I'll catch her on her next trip out!" I said throwing myself in the bed.

"Sasha! I already told her you were coming and she's excited."

"Sucks to be you then. Tell her you lied! Good night!" I said throwing the covers over my shoulder.

Dennis got in the bed all huffy. I grabbed my work phone and I looked at my calendar for Thursday and Friday. I crammed everything into Thursday morning and then I blocked my calendar for Thursday afternoon and all day Friday, and Monday. My alarm went off while I was laying there in my thoughts. I got up making as much noise as I could. I made breakfast for myself and I slammed the door as I left. In the lobby we were missing one person, so I went to Thea's room.

Her room was completely dark, she had over slept. She said she would meet us at the office. Richard kept asking me what's wrong, and when I said nothing he continued to sit there and read me.

When we stepped in the office Alonzo said Malcolm called a meeting at 8a.m. I wondered if he ever sleeps that's five California time. El and the rest of the office staff filled into the office. El didn't look at me directly; it wasn't like he was avoiding my glance. But he didn't appear to be in the mood for nonsense either. Malcolm got straight to business. He assigned task and he wanted results by the end of our day. When he spoke to Thea I felt bad for her. She was nowhere to be found.

"Malcolm she's running a little late, I can give...."

He cut me off, "she will be dealt with moving on!"

I looked at Richard and he shrugged. I needed to meet with El directly after the meeting. He told me to come to his office. He got straight to business and no small talk, and he didn't look at me unless he had to. If I didn't know better I would've thought he was mad at me. But I didn't do anything? Besides bring Dennis who asked the wrong question. Thea's eyes were red when she knocked on the door. I could tell she had talked to Malcolm. She asked me for some reports and then she left. When we finished I asked El if he was ok. He said he was fine, without paying me any attention. On my way back to my seat in the conference room I wondered if my dream was a sympathy pain for El and Zoila. Maybe she isn't cheating on him, maybe their relationship is too painful, and I feel sorry for them. I don't know. I looked at my cellphone and Dennis had been calling all morning. I looked at the clock; it was almost time for lunch. I knew he was going to pop up at any moment. At a quarter to one Amelia came and said I had a visitor. Richard told me to stay close by. Dennis was in the lobby looking relaxed and unaffected by my irritation with him. We had lunch at this little restaurant a block away. "I'm leaving Thursday afternoon. I'm gonna book my flight this afternoon."

"To your grandparents?"

"Yes!"

"Good then you can still go with me to see Lulu."

"I'm not going with you if you aren't coming with me."

He leaned forward, "yes you are." He said lowly.

"No I'm not!" I said getting loud. "Test me if you want. I'm not going with you if you don't come with me. I deal with your mother and your brother out of love for you. If you can't give me the same, then I'm not going."

Dennis got angry, "I promise Sasha! If you stand my grandmother up, make me look like a fool then I'm done with you!"

That hurt, "then I guess it's up to you. If you don't come with me, I guess we have nothing else to talk about. You can take one of your Sasha stand-ins." I don't know why he insists on testing me. He knows I won't back down, and he knows he can only go so long without talking to me. I wasn't worried about what he was gonna do, he fears disappointing Lulu more than his mom. So it was only a matter of time before he saw things my way. In the lobby El saw us saying goodbye. As he approached us I tried to read his face.

"How are you doing Dennis?" He said putting his hand out for a shake.

"I'm good, you?" Dennis said matching his stance.

El apologized for leaving so abruptly the other night; he said the conversation got heavy too fast. Then he asked what we did with the rest of our night. So Dennis started talking about the play we saw. It was this old married couple and the drama with their kids. "So when are you two going to have any?" There was no emotion in El's face when he asked the question, it felt like a setup.

Dennis shrugged, "I don't think children are in the plans for us."

I frowned at Dennis, "speak for yourself. They may not be in the plans for you, but I will have at least two kids with or without you."

Dennis's head looked like it was gonna fly off when he whipped his head around so fast. "You can't change your mind now!"

Satisfied with himself, El excused himself and walked away. "I can't have this conversation right now. I'll see you this evening!" I said walking away. I couldn't believe he was holding the past against me. I was a freshman and he was a senior when we met. Moving too fast I was in complete panic when my period didn't come like it was supposed to. Dennis assured me that we would be fine and he'd get a job while in school to support us. I flipped out told him I didn't want to end up like my mother. I told him I didn't want to have his baby. How was I supposed to know we'd still be together today? Well not technically together. I got my period two weeks later and we never discussed children again. I guess I figured we'd discuss it when we got married, but I guess I was wrong. If we aren't technically together then I guess there's nothing to discuss.

El and I kept our distance the rest of the day. Guess he wanted to show us how it felt to have someone meddle in your business. I guess it was a point worth making. I guess!

Dennis took me out to dinner and tried to reason with me. But I wasn't budging, in defeat he agreed to come with me, but he wasn't happy about it. I gave him a knowing smile.

****

"POPPA!" I ran to him and put him in a bear hug.

He kissed my forehead, "how's my Sassy doing?"

"I'm good now that I see you! I miss you! When are you gonna come see me?" I said

"When you learn to keep better company. Dennis!" He said glaring at Dennis.

"Mr. Wallace," Dennis said matching Poppa's stance.

"You're staying with us too?"

"Yes sir," Dennis said

My Poppa huffed, "let's get your bags." He said to me, "your momma got here this morning. They're at the house cooking up a storm. But somebody just HAD to come with me."

I started jumping around clapping, "where is she?" Poppa pointed by the carousel and my BEAUTIFUL Sabrina was shyly standing waiting for me to notice her. I ran and picked her up. My baby was getting so big. "Did you miss me?" I said kissing her face all over.

"YES!" She said giggling and squeezing me back.

"You remember Dennis?" I said pointing to him.

"Yes, hello." She said waving hi to him but not letting me go.

"You are the best surprise EVER!" I said to my little sister, I could see her inner light glow. Dennis and Poppa got our bags then Dennis got his rental car. He followed the three of us in Poppa's car to his house. Poppa lives in Natomas a suburb of Sacramento. His neighborhood had a huge gate in front. Poppa's house was the biggest house in the development. It was towards the back and kind of off to itself. My Poppa's brother Dale is an architect and he told my Poppa about the real estate gold mine out here. He told him that the housing market was going to take off, and if he wanted in he could tell him about a few projects. When he told us they were moving all the way out here it made me sad; my family had always been centralized in Oakland. At that point Momma and I were living in Concord already though, but Concord to Oakland still wasn't much of a drive, Sacramento was about an hour away.

"Your house is still beautiful Poppa."

"Thank you baby girl, when are you going to buy a house?"

"You think I should?" I hadn't thought of it.

"Don't you need the tax break?"

"Yes!" I blew air thinking about the money I pay in taxes each year.

"I don't see why you would wait." Then he glanced in Dennis' direction. "It's not like you've met anyone worthy of considering to marry." Dennis huffed.

"Come on Sabrina. We'll leave you two to get the bags." I said walking towards the door.

"Nope! He got the bags! I'm coming with ya'll." My Poppa said

"She's here!" I heard my Nana's voice. "SASHA! MY BABY!" She said giving me the biggest hug. My Nana always smelled like baby powder no matter what. I missed that smell. "Is that Dennis with you?"

"Yes," I said still hugging her.

"He's still handsome I see."

"Sasha!" My Momma said, and I ran to hug her.

"Hi Momma!"

"How have you been?" She said standing back to take a good look at me.

"Good, I've missed you guys so much."

We ate dinner in the dining room. All dinner I kept shooting Poppa looks. When my Uncle Jeff walked in his eyes went straight to Dennis then he smiled at my Poppa. We were up really late talking and being silly. Dennis went to bed first. Momma asked me how things were going with him. I know that she was hoping that I would say that we were exclusive. But I told her nothing has changed. Sabrina told me about the classes she takes at North Star, Amber's school for performing arts. Momma said this summer they were going to come out for a visit. I stared at her for a minute cause I knew Richard had a lot to do with her visit. I told her that Poppa suggested that I buy a house. Momma got excited at the idea. We were talking when the doorbell rang; Jeff came back with my cousin Andrew in tow. Every time I saw someone I realized how much I missed them. Since Derrick and I work for Mitigated I see him the most. Darryl comes out with Amber quite often, in between his classes, even if I don't see her I see him. But Andrew is working for a financial company so it's rare that I see him. We were like twins growing up. For the longest time it was only the four of us, my Uncles Jeff, JoJo, Andrew, and I. Since our momma's were more like sisters than cousins we were like brother and sister. Only months apart in age, we did everything together. Our momma's were only fifteen when we were born. I don't know about Andrew but I always felt like my momma and I were growing up together. Andrew would always remind me that our mothers had choices; we didn't have to be born. He would remind me to go easy on my momma when I would get extremely frustrated with her. He's always been my sounding board. I jumped on him hugging and kissing him. I told him I missed him and he needed to come see me. The night got sillier and louder once Andrew was there. Jeff told Andrew that Dennis was there. Then they teased me about crushes I tried to have while we were growing up. My stomach was sore from laughing so hard. Jeff assured Sabrina that no man would be good enough for her either. Everybody was staying; I couldn't have been more excited. In the morning, Andrew, Sabrina, and I made breakfast. "So..." I said eyeballing Andrew.

He smiled unleashing his dimples. "So..."

"Toya? Really?"

He laughed while he exhaled. "I know!"

"Why Drew?" I really didn't understand.

"I messed up huh?" Then he exhaled, "I was seeing someone else, it was going pretty well too."

"Then why are you with Toya?"

"I thought she was really gonna change this time."

"Toya change?"

"You can judge me until it's your turn then you'll understand. It's not easy to walk away from someone you have a lot of history with."

"If you say so."

Then he smiled at me, "Hubby wants to know if you're coming to his wedding." I rolled my eyes. "I told him you weren't coming."

"Why would he even ask you? He should know better."

"Don't get mad at me, I'm just the messenger." Then my momma called Sabrina. Drew moved in close. "What's wrong?"

He knows me too well. "I had a dream about my dad again."

"Ok... So what's going on?"

"I wanna talk to Poppa, I need answers."

"We know what happened." He said with sad eyes.

"We don't know why. First they said David did it, and then it's unsolved. Somebody knows." I swallowed, "he was my dad. Don't I deserve to know something? Don't you have questions?"

He shook his head, "not like you. I know what happened. The questions I got the only person who could answer them isn't here." His whole demeanor changed.

"Sorry, I'm not trying to bum you out. I just...." Tears flooded my eyes. "Even if no one else liked him, I loved him! He was my dad!"

Andrew hugged me, "I know." He said rubbing my back. "I understand, you know I do."

"Will you come with me to talk to my Poppa?"

He stopped hugging me. "WHY I GOTTA GO?" He frowned.

"PLEASE DREW!" I said putting my hands together to stress my plea.

"I came out here to visit with your biscuit head. Not to get caught up in emotional conversations."

"Please Drew! I'll breakup with Toya for you this time."

He laughed, "what makes you think I'm breaking up with her this time? This could be it."

"I talked to your momma she's forbidden you to marry that girl! It's only a matter of time before she crosses the line again. Was this girl that bad?"

He exhaled, "no. She was great actually, it scared me. I miss her like crazy, but I blew it. As usual, at least this time there wasn't a dramatic scene. If I run into her, I can hold my head high when I see her."

I eyed him, "you wanna slide backwards don't you?"

"I messed up, if she'll have me I won't let her go ever again."

I leaned against the counter, "what makes her special? I mean..." I tried to figure out how to phrase my question.

"Derrick said I'm always looking for shiny wrapping or something like that, and I don't look for the gift inside. Does this girl have a gift inside?"

"I think so. I happened to think she's very beautiful, but beauty is in the eyes of the beholder. She stood out to me because her demeanor was very reserved. She didn't stomp around like everyone or anyone really had to notice her."

"You mean she's not like me." I frowned at him.

"You're used to being the center of attention. We spoiled you." He pinched my cheek. "Tracy is cool and laid back. We could sit in her living room and she was content. We didn't always have to be running the streets or seen in public. She's not about status or labels or all that superficial stuff. She was perfectly ok with letting me run things. She let me be a man, and I didn't have to prove anything with her. I could go on and on, but to sum it up. Everything that Toya is, she isn't. She has a cool little job, got her own thing going on."

"Outside of working, she sounds like the opposite of me too. Why aren't you together?"

"I MESSED UP!" He looked at the ceiling dramatically. I laughed. "How do I fix this? I think she's seeing someone."

"Would she cheat?"

"I don't think so, but I guess there's only one way to find out. You sure you won't come to the wedding. You could help me if I can't figure this out before then."

"What wedding?" Dennis said walking in the kitchen.

A tolerant look came over Andrew. "My best friend's, you wanna go?"

Dennis looked at me, "do I?"

"No," I said looking away.

"Go where?" JoJo asked walking in the kitchen.

"Hubby's wedding, you're going right?"

"I guess, I'll check my calendar when I get the invite." Jeff said, "breakfast ready?"

While we ate breakfast my Poppa kept looking at me. He was reading me; as soon as I finished he announced that we were going for a walk. I told him Drew was coming with us. Drew faked a scared face. My Poppa held my hand as we walked out the door. He asked what was up? I looked at Drew hoping he would know how to phrase my thoughts. Drew explained my dreams and that they weren't necessarily nightmares, but they felt like it. He said talking to my momma hasn't helped me. My Poppa looked me in my eyes and asked me what my question was. The question stumped me. Andrew couldn't answer for me. "Why is my dad gone? I know you didn't like him, but why is he gone?"

"He was weak, and he was in the wrong place at the wrong time." Poppa said point blank. "Sassy you gotta let him go! Let him rest in peace. I know it can be hard to understand, but he was barely a dad to you. Richard has always been a part of your life and more of a father to you than Charles ever was."

"That doesn't say much!" I rolled my eyes.

"Why do you act like that with Richard?"

"He's a coward! He ran from me before I was born, then he announces he's my father and runs again! He's goofy; nothing like I see a dad being."

"Sassy, everybody can't be me, but it's unfair for you to compare him." We laughed. "Your parents were kids playing with "grownup" fire. But Richard has always been there for you. The moment you realize the differences between them the better off you will be. Charles didn't care about your family. He didn't provide for you. Anything you guys had was because your mother made it happen despite him. There's more to being a dad than telling a child you are their dad. You have to ask why he hung around. He had to know you weren't his child. When your mother kicked him out how often did you see him? Did you know his family? Don't assign him honor Sassy. There was nothing honorable about him." He did have a point, I hadn't seen or heard from my dad for months before the night he died. I would call him crying cause I missed him or he didn't show up to get me like he said he was going to. Now I felt more confused. "It sounds like whenever you feel unsure, you relate that to Charles and then you dream about him. But your emotions aren't about him."

"You're right, but I don't know why."

"Maybe it's that fool who's sitting in my house."

"You don't like Dennis?" Drew asked laughing. My Poppa shot Drew a look, which made him laugh harder.

"Poppa I love him, please be nice to him for me. It's bad enough that his mother doesn't like me. I need my family to be the standard of measure."

I could see Poppa's anger, "why doesn't she like you?"

"Cause I'm black is the only thing I could put a finger on."

"I WILL SHUT DOWN THEIR SHACK OF A STORE!"

"Poppa I love Mr. B, if it wasn't for him I wouldn't care."

"HE NEEDS TO CHECK HIS WIFE THEN!"

I looked at Andrew, "you can take the man out of Oakland..." My Poppa always has my back. "He does Poppa. It's ok cause Mrs. Barbeau's mother is coming tomorrow and she loves me. I'm going to visit with her and then I'll drive back here. Drew you wanna come with me?" I asked him in front of Poppa so he'd have to say yes.

Drew squinted his eyes at me. "You aren't slick!" Then he looked away.

"It'll be good to see you put in some detail work. Stay up on your skills nephew." My Poppa smiled.

He exhaled in defeat, "any girls gonna be there?"

"No, and that's a good thing, huh? You have a girlfriend." I smiled

"It's only Toya."

"YOURE BACK WITH HER?" Andrew smiled an embarrassed smile. "You like learning things the hard way." My poppa said

When we got back to the house Sabrina, Momma, Jeff, and Dennis were playing dominos. Andrew said he and I got winners. I sat next to my Nana on the couch. She had her photo albums out. When we were all very little Nana kept all of us. We would have so much fun together every day. She took pictures of us regularly. Sometimes on the weekends Amber would keep us and then Tanisha would come. I would be so happy to have another girl with me. Our moms would try to sell the idea that we were triplets; just because they were the same age and all pregnant like they caught it from each other. People would always think that all four of us belonged to my Nana, my uncles, Drew, and I. People's eyes would get really big when she would say I was her granddaughter. They'd ask her how does she have a child old enough to give her grandchildren? And she would say she didn't. One day she said it and I understood it for the first time, it made me sad. She never said it again; she would smile and hug me. I looked at the pictures of my childhood with fondness. My Poppa named me Sassy, Sassy Sasha. No explanation needed.

"So, what are you going to look for, a condo, townhouse, or house?" My momma asked.

"I don't know yet." Then I asked Andrew, "when are you going to buy?"

He shrugged, "not worried about it right now."

"I'll come out and we can go over your options." Poppa said

I got excited, "is everybody going to come? Let me know when."

"We'll plan it." Nana said

****

Andrew kept talking to Dennis until he relaxed. I know he's worried about everything happening today. We drove all the way to Oakland to pick Lulu up from the airport. Dennis said that's where we were supposed to come in originally. Lulu glided down the escalator like royalty. Her eyes were locked on me and she had the biggest smile. "COME HERE SASHA BABY!" She said at the top of her voice. "Dennis I know I say this every time, but she's beautiful!" She hugged me again.

"I'm so happy to see you. Why have you been away so long?" I pointed my head towards Dennis.

"No! No Sasha! Don't play!" Dennis said not wanting the lecture.

"Doesn't matter, you're on my list anyways. I don't understand you young people, why aren't Sasha and I related by now?"

"Hi Lulu, I love you too." Dennis said in defeat.

Lulu was average height, creole, and about my complexion. We have been in love from the moment we met. Dennis brought me home with him on winter break to meet his family. Lawrence and Kelsey were happily engaged then. Now that I think about it, he's been this monster since Jim was about a year or so. Before that he had his moments, but he wasn't like the monster we know today. When Dennis walked in the door with me Mrs. Barbeau gasped and everyone else was excited to meet me. Lulu especially, she took me in a separate room and we talked for hours. She said I was a breath of fresh air. Immediately Mrs. Barbeau did not like the connection between her mother and I. From the moment I walked in, I was on her bad list. But Lulu gave me the nod, and shortly after Mr. B gave me the nod as well.

When we walked out of the airport with Dennis carrying Lulu's bags, Andrew was just circling again and he pulled up to the curb and got out the car. "OH MY! Who's this handsome chunk of manliness?" She said looking Andrew up and down.

"I'm Andrew ma'am." He said blushing.

"Ma'am? I'm not that old. Call me Lulu.." She said going in for a hug.

"Lulu this is my cousin." I said

"Oh, your family has good genes I see. Whew! You feel so… MANLY!" Lulu said exaggerating a shiver.

Andrew gave a bashful laugh; I could tell he didn't know what to do. "Come on Lulu, we gotta get on the road if we're gonna do this right." Dennis said opening the front passenger seat for her.

Andrew whispered to me that he had no idea that Dennis was black. I told him after our family he should know better than to be surprised by anyone's family tree. He nodded in agreement. Our drive to Napa was nice and sweet; there wasn't too much traffic out that way. In the winter months people didn't come out as much for wine tasting. Most customers came to stock up for parties and get-togethers.

Kelsey was pulling up to the winery at the same time as us. She was completely shocked to see Lulu; she came over and hugged her. Lulu tolerated her hug and then she kept it moving while Kelsey said her hellos to the rest of us. I introduced her to Andrew; she told me that Jim has replaced me with a little girl at school. She said he's besides himself trying to think of how to break the news to me. We laughed and then I asked Kelsey if she had time to give Andrew and I a brief tour. I knew Mrs. Barbeau was gonna need a moment to gather herself once she saw her mother and Andrew didn't need to see all of that. I told Dennis we were going to go with Kelsey and he said a relieved ok. I put my arm under Andrew's arm while we waited outside for Kelsey to come back. Andrew asked me why my bags were in the car if we were going back to Sacramento tonight. I didn't know Dennis put my bags back in the car. I guessed he was staying. Andrew said he would call for a ride back to his car in Sac since I was staying. I told him I was going with him, but I appreciated the help if he could get us a ride. That way we could slip out hopefully before any fireworks. Kelsey looked frustrated when she walked out and then Lawrence was right on her heels. His smile dropped when he saw Andrew standing next to me. Andrew was talking to someone on the phone. "Is this your brother?"

"Almost, this is my cousin Andrew. Andrew this is Lawrence, Dennis' older brother."

"Hey how you doing?" Andrew said reading Lawrence's demeanor.

"I'm good, nice to meet you. I knew something about Kelsey's story wasn't adding up. I didn't understand why she was giving Sasha a tour. This must be your first time out here?"

"Yep, I've heard about you guys for years. But I've never been here."

"Cool, I'll join you guys."

Kelsey swallowed, "don't you have something to do inside?"

"IT'S SLOW!" He barked at her.

Andrew looked at me and I squeezed his arm tighter. Lawrence turned out to be a lot of fun on our tour. Kelsey was doing her standard tour details, and Lawrence would interject hilarious comments. That didn't stop Andrew from noticing Lawrence's constant attention in my direction even in front of his wife. Lawrence was in no way as bad as he normally is, but he saw it anyways. When we completed our tour we walked on the sales floor and the background music was higher than normal, but I could hear Lulu and Mrs. Barbeau arguing in the manager's office. Mr. B hurried over and introduced himself to Andrew. I think he wanted to think about anything other than those two. Then Mr. B asked Kelsey to have food catered to the house for dinner. Normally we went out to dinner, but I know he said catered because of Lulu and Mrs. Barbeau. Lulu rode with Lawrence to go pick up Jim from his friend's house.

When we got to the Barbeau House, Mrs. Barbeau was in Dennis' face for bringing her mother out there without at least, giving her a heads up that she was coming. Dennis told her he hated being in the middle of them. "It's bad enough I have to deal with her- little Miss Oakland!" Andrew grabbed my arm so I wouldn't react. "Then you bring the Bad News Queen in here! I'm your mother Dennis, your loyalty is supposed to be to me first!"

"Naomi, calm down. Apologize to Sasha!" Mr. B said

"CALM DOWN? APOLOGIZE! I WILL NOT! I should not feel attacked in my own home or my place of business. Brad defend me!"

Mr. B's eyes turned to fire. "You heard me! You should be mad at your mother for putting your son in the middle. Sasha has NEVER done anything to you. The issue is not with her, APOLOGIZE to her now! Or we will have WORDS later!"

I smiled, and I waited for my apology. Mrs. Barbeau rolled her eyes, "I apologize!" She said with as much attitude as she could muster. Then she stormed away, Dennis was looking at Andrew's hand on my arm. I could tell he was taking in the fact that I listened to Andrew's nonverbal queue. When we sat down at dinner Jim sat next to me, and Andrew sat on the other side of me. When Jim finished eating he ran upstairs to watch TV. Lulu dove right in on Mrs. Barbeau, asking her why she tries to separate herself from everything that says that she's a black woman. Mrs. Barbeau said in an exhausted voice that she knew who she was and she didn't have to prove who she was to anyone. Lulu accused her of hiding all the way out here in Napa. She said she knew Mrs. Barbeau couldn't have been happier when Lawrence came home with Kelsey. A cute little blonde white girl. She said she bet that Lawrence used to try to convince himself that he loved Kelsey because it made his momma so happy. I looked at Lawrence and he had a guilty look like Lulu was reading his mind. Lulu told Lawrence he behaves so badly because he's hiding and he needed to come clean. Lawrence looked confused, he told her he didn't know what she was talking about. Lulu looked at Lawrence and told him she knew him better than he knew himself. Lawrence wiggled in his seat but he didn't say anything. When Lulu turned her attention to Dennis, I leaned in. Maybe she would finally explain why instead of moving forward, we moved backwards. Lulu probably got two sentences in when Mrs. Barbeau jumped in to save her baby. She wouldn't let Lulu talk. Andrew looked at his phone and then he told me that our ride was here. "Mr. B, Lulu I want to tell the two of you that it was a pleasure to meet you, and I hope to see the two of you again soon." Then he looked at me, "Sasha you aren't allowed to come out here unassisted again."

"What? Andrew!" I said

"What does that mean, unassisted?" Dennis asked

"She knows, that's all that matters." Then he stood up, "Sasha let's go."

"Go? Where are you going?" Dennis said looking at me like his patience was growing thin.

"I told my Poppa I was coming home to him tonight. I didn't know why you packed my luggage without talking to me."

"The whole point of this trip was for you to spend time with Lulu, you added your family at the last minute. Why wouldn't I think you were staying here with me?"

"Dennis this is just a miscommunication, call me when you get back to Minneapolis." I leaned in to kiss him and he backed away.

He shook his head, "you always do this. How you gonna choose your family over me?"

My anger boiled, "since you wanna do this in front of your family FINE! You were supposed to be spending this weekend with me in LA. This week together was supposed to be about us reconnecting, but did I complain when you threw Lulu in the mix? I was happy to come see her and your father. You throw a fit when I added mine! I don't need this Dennis!"

"And I don't need a female who listens more to her cousin than she does to her man. All Drew has to do is touch your arm and you stand down? But I tell you I got a situation and you still can't let me handle it."

"Maybe if you were a man she'd treat you like one!" Andrew said, his voice rumbling the table.

Dennis stood up, "Drew this is between me and her."

"But you're doing this in front of me. You can't think I'd let you talk to the closest thing I have to a sister like you've lost your mind. You need to come clean about your stuff and stop hiding. Your brother is over here looking at any brown female that walks past him, but he's married to the whitest white girl. You're...." Andrew looked at Kelsey, then he looked at Lawrence, then he looked at Lulu. She was shaking her head like she was reading his thoughts. "Sasha there's a lot of drama in this family. Say goodbye to Lulu and Mr. B, you're not coming back."

"What?" I looked at Kelsey and Lawrence who were completely red. "What is it Drew? Is it something I need to know?"

"Dennis you know I love you, but you need to come clean." Lulu said

"Come clean?" I looked up at Dennis, "about what?"

"Lulu?" Dennis looked at her like he had no clue as to what she was talking about.

"It's time to come clean honey." Lulu said

"Lulu, I told you in confidence." Lawrence said

"Told her what?" Mrs. Barbeau said

Lulu sat back and smiled at Lawrence. He pushed his chair away from the table. "Kelsey, I know." She swallowed and looked at him waiting for him to continue. "I know Jim is not my son." Dennis sat back down.

"He is..."

Lawrence cut Kelsey off, "DON'T LIE TO ME! YOU'VE BEEN LYING THIS WHOLE TIME! I JUST WANNA KNOW WHEN YOU GUYS BEGAN?"

"Lawrence, why do we have to do this in front of everyone?" Kelsey said

"You never came to me. Jim is six almost seven, and you've never come clean."

"Lawrence how could you accuse your wife, of being like... other people." It was no doubt Mrs. Barbeau was talking about me. Andrew glared at her.

"Mom, the problem is that you put Kelsey up on this pedestal, and you've never looked at her for who she is." He exhaled, "it was my fault for wanting my mother's approval so badly that I actually convinced myself that Kelsey and I could work." He sat back in his chair. "It's no secret that I've always cheated on you. I should've never married you. But hey, hind sight is always twenty-twenty." He took a gulp of his drink. "My girlfriend since high school wanted to have a baby. I figured my wife was pregnant, it should be easy." He looked at Kelsey, "I'm sterile! There's no way Jim is my son." Dennis turned red, and Kelsey started crying. "I wondered how my son could definitely be a Barbeau man and not be my son. Everyone was on trial." Lawrence said looking at his father. "I wondered about you for a long time." Mr. B looked at Lawrence like he was crazy but he said nothing. "I know we've always flirted with each other's woman, but how could you? My wife?" Dennis said nothing.

"You're the father?" I needed Dennis to admit it. Dennis looked embarrassed. "This is why isn't it? You try to make it seem like it's something I've done."

"No! The reason why is because you've got too much attitude!" Mrs. Barbeau said

Andrew looked at Mr. B, "with all due respect to you and Lulu. She got one more time to talk sideways to Sasha!"

"And then what?" She said wiggling her neck, something I never see her do.

"And then I'm on you. You knew about this whole thing a long time ago and you said nothing." Andrew said

She blew air, "little boy! You don't know what you're talking about!"

"Mr. B is shocked, Lulu is the one speaking up. Lawrence is hurt; Kelsey and Dennis have busted looks. But you... you sit over there unfazed and not even surprised. You knew and said nothing! You are a cold piece of work, and yet you give Sasha a hard time for actually loving your son. If the shoe were on the other foot, you would've busted Lawrence out as soon as you knew."

"THANK YOU!" Lawrence said, "Mom you knew about this?"

"I saw them once, but I didn't want to get involved so I didn't say anything."

Lawrence shot out of his chair, "my feelings, my heart, my life means NOTHING to you!"

"You act too much like my father I can't deal with you." She said dismissing him.

"I act too black? Dennis brings home the black girl, and you still act like I'm the one reminding you of who you are!" He looked at Kelsey. "I want a divorce! I'm marrying Marika; I'm done with this! Sue him for child support!" Then Lawrence walked out of the door.

"Dennis," my brain was going crazy trying to pinpoint when they began. "You cheated on me with your brother's wife, are you guys still hooking up?"

"Sometimes," he said nonchalantly.

"You want to be with her? I mean you have a son that you've lied about."

"I didn't know he was mine, she didn't know."

"You're in love with Kelsey?"

He looked at me, "no." Kelsey got up crying and she ran away.

"I felt sorry for her. I liked her, Lawrence is such a jerk. But I've only been in love with you."

"So you bring me out here to endure all this knowing everything? You couldn't be with me whole-souled cause you're not whole. Is there anybody else I need to know about?" I looked in his eyes.

He was debating whether to lie to me and or come clean. He huffed, "yes." I waited for him to say. He turned real red; he started to speak and then would pull it back.

I slapped him as hard as I could. Lulu's eyes got big and she almost smiled, "see this is what happens when you hide your children's dirt. They start thinking they're invincible and they always go too far!"

Dennis started pulling at my shirt with his head down. He couldn't argue his way out of this. As if Kelsey wasn't bad enough, you know what I was gonna roll with him on it. He crossed an undeniable line. I waited for him to confirm my suspicion. "Sasha, we can work this out, please!"

I started crying, "say it!"

"Sasha! Please!"

"You are not a man! You can't even look at me!"

"I'm sorry!" He said with his head down.

"You're the reason she ran late on Monday!' I said wanting to hit him again. "My friend, really Dennis? You are not a man!"

"Let's go Sasha!" Andrew said

Mr. B was completely embarrassed; Mrs. Barbeau seemed pleased to know her son was sleeping with my so-called friend. Lulu was shaking her head, "if you would stop hiding maybe your kids could get some act right." They started arguing again. Mr. B pushed away from the table and walked upstairs more than likely to be with his grandson away from the noise.

"Forget you ever knew me!" I said to Dennis with tears streaming down my face. Then I took Drew's hand.

When we walked outside the trunk to Dennis's rental car was open and a car was parked behind it. My heart sank when Yussef's head popped around the corner. "I figured your bags were the girly bags. Did I miss anything?" I looked in the trunk and shook my head no. Yussef saw my tears but he didn't say anything. Drew got in the back with me and comforted me all the way back to Sacramento. I cried at first but then I pulled it together. Yussef and Andrew kept talking about silly stuff the whole ride until I found myself laughing. "Yussef, you never called me!" I pouted

He looked at me in the rear view mirror. "I didn't think it was a good idea."

"Why?"

"You're Andrew's cousin, that's a little bit too close for me."
He said giving me a look.
"But we aren't related, that's not fair!" I said
"Well from the sound of things, you weren't emotionally ready
for me anyways. So let's call it even. I don't want to be one of
your conquest."
What could I say to that? I looked at Drew who was watching
my face. "Lulu wanted you there so that you would know once
and for all."
I sighed, "I know."
"What are you going to do when he comes back begging and
pleading?"
"Whatever!" I sighed
"I need you to do something for me." I looked at him.
"Remember this evening and our conversation when you guys
get back together." I gasped, "then you'll understand how I'm
back with Toya now."
"That's never gonna happen!" I said feeling insulted.
"Sasha, in relationships never say what you will NEVER do.
It's easier to save face."

Chapter 5

When I got home, I was so happy JoJo was there. He greeted me with a big smile, but he quickly dropped it when he saw my face. I fell into his arms crying my eyes out. I told him everything that happened, he rubbed my back and told me I needed to take a timeout. Figure out if I like the way I present myself in relationships and see where I felt my relationship IQ needed tweaking. I listened to him, but my heart was telling me I needed the caress of a man to feel better about myself. I cried all night. I envisioned myself beating Thea up so many different ways. Ten minutes before my alarm, I told myself to get up. I looked at my face in the mirror. Sleepless nights did not agree with me. My eyes were puffy and red. I told myself "be fabulous!" But I couldn't do it. I felt ugly, unloved, and pathetic. When I walked in my closet nothing made me feel pretty in there either, and if nothing else my clothes normally do it for me. I put on a black turtleneck sweater, grey slacks, black boots cause of the rain, and I pulled my hair back in a bun. I left my face naked, I hugged JoJo, and then I went to work. I got coffee before I went in. I found myself hoping I'd see Shawn. But he was nowhere to be found. When I stepped off the elevator Mary was stepping off a different one. She said her usual hello and we chatted like we normally do. When I pulled up my calendar, I saw that Malcolm had a meeting scheduled for Friday that he rescheduled for this morning. I had meeting after meeting all day on my calendar. I exhaled, "I DON'T WANT TO BE HERE!" I yelled to myself. I grabbed my pen and paper then I went to the conference room. Everyone piled into the room then Malcolm came on the line. I couldn't take my eyes off of Thea when she walked in the room. I didn't know if she had talked to Dennis or not, but I wanted to take off on her immediately. Malcolm told us there was going to be a change in our plan of attack on the East Coast. He said there would be broader information later, but he was calling the meeting to let upper management know that some of us were going to need to delegate our normal responsibilities to focus on this task. Then Malcolm sighed, he said there would be more details to come later but for now he was going to need the entire New York team, he named a few people from each of our other sites, a few people from ours; he named me as part of this task force. My work phone showed a meeting invite from him directly following this meeting. The others he named got the same invite. We stayed in the room while the others exited. Malcolm said instead of starting from the ground up we're going to acquire a similar company that has presence in New York already, that way we wouldn't have to build from scratch. He said he had a long list of companies, and he needed that list scrubbed to identify the companies that were closely matched to ours. Malcolm said this project was going to be huge and require a lot of late hours and travel. I embraced the idea of focusing on anything other than my stupid life. Malcolm said he wanted everyone to come to San Francisco next week. He told us to delegate everything we could.

When I got back to my desk, I felt deflated still. I had voicemail messages from Dennis on my work and personal phones. Since he just took a week off from work, I knew there was no chance of him popping up here unannounced.

When my personal cell phone rang, I stared at it for a minute. Shawn was calling and I knew I only wanted to answer because I wanted someone to be with. I heard myself say hello. Shawn was in all out charm mode, which was only right because he had forever to practice and get this moment down right in his head. I heard myself agree to go out with him. I told myself he only had two strikes against him so it was ok, right. I got off the phone with Shawn when I saw that El was calling. El informed me that he was coming out here Friday to see the LA office, and then we could fly out Friday night as a team. I said a very dry ok, he wasn't asking me. He was basically telling me.

****

"I'll be back tomorrow." I said as I popped my head in Richard's office.

"Sasha! Come here! Close the door." Richard said as he searched for the words to give me a hard time. I sat in the chair in front of his desk waiting for him to get to it so I could go already. "Sasha, you can't..."

I cut him off. "Richard save it. I have my laptop, I have a date tonight, and I need to get my hair done. I will log in when I get home." I said in my defeated tone.

Richard's eyes softened. "What's up Sassy? You've been lacking Sass all week."

Tears poured out of my eyes. "Dennis and I are done! He has a kid, and he was sleeping with Thea."

Richard's eyes turned to fire, I know he didn't expect me to unload like that but I was tired of holding back. "WHAT?"

"Lulu put it all out on the table. She didn't know about Thea, but she wanted me to know about the rest."

Richard paced, "this is the ULTIMATE disrespect! Please tell me you're done with him." Then he looked at my face. Before I could respond he said, "don't be weak!"

"I'm not Richard! It hurts you know?" I said wiping my eyes. Richard hugged me and rubbed my back just like JoJo would do. This is the first time he's shown me affection like this. "I know you're hurting but you're gonna be ok. Hang in there. Both of them will be dealt with."

"I already delegated a lot of my grunt work to her. I know she hates that so I'm satisfied with that for now. This is California; I can't have her fired without a good reason. Believe me I looked it up. But I can force her to quit."

"No Sassy, you focus on Malcolm's project. I'll handle them." "Ok," I said not wanting to know exactly what that meant. I stood up.

"Which reminds me. Malcolm wasn't too happy about you being gone last week. I mean we just got back then you took time off. If Malcolm catches wind of how much you come and go I can't protect you from that."

"Ok," I said rolling my eyes.

My eyes didn't ask for permission any more, they leaked when they felt like it. I kept my shades on until I was at the shampoo bowl waiting for Ava. I leaned my head back and let my tears leak. Ava was trying to be real quiet; I actually smelled the slight hint of her perfume before I heard her calmed breaths.

"Hello doll face." I said faking enthusiasm.

"Still? I give up." She said laughing until she saw my face. "Sasha what's wrong?"

I told her everything while she washed my hair. I couldn't stop crying. Ava cried with me, then she called Brea, she told her to cancel Thea's appointment tomorrow. Then she told her not to allow her to reschedule. I told her she didn't have to do that. Ava ignored my comment and then we started piecing together the clues. Ava said the way I carry myself can be intimidating for a lot of females. I didn't understand why that translated to sleeping with my man.

I didn't want anything fancy, especially with the weather we've been having. Soft defined curls was the look for me right about now. Ava put a pretty barrette to dress it up a bit. I didn't even have the energy to fake excitement. I wanted attention that was the purpose Shawn was serving this evening.

I logged on when I got home, nothing too eventful at work. I wrote a few letters, searched a few company performances then I got ready for my date. I lethargically sat on the couch waiting for Shawn. When I opened the door his smile got completely big. He asked to use the restroom after he kissed me and told me how beautiful I looked. I had to take his word for it, cause I didn't feel beautiful right now. I was standing in the middle of the room when he came out of the bathroom. His eyes danced all over me and then he kissed me again. When the kiss kept going I realized we weren't going anywhere right away. I wasn't enthusiastic about this part but I played a long. I guess in his mind he thought he was going to blow my mind. But let's check it, unless your name is Dennis foreplay is IMPORTANT! I guess kissing on my neck and breast was supposed to count, and barely that. I was dry as the desert when he entered me; strike three and you're out! Instead of helping me out, he relied on the lubrication on the condom. He was gone from the moment of contact. He was so gone he didn't realize this wasn't a shared experience. I laid there looking at him, I could've been sleep, and he would still be carrying on like I was working him over. I will never do this again! This experience felt worse than before.

At least before I could say that it was new, etc. This is pathetic; I could fall asleep from boredom. He had the nerve to finish like he really put in work. When he collapsed on top of me I wanted him off of me. He rolled over with a huge smile like he just did something major. His smile faded when he looked at my face. He was quiet for a while, and then he proceeded to eat dessert. He was actually really good at it, why didn't he at least start with this? The rotation for this still left me frustrated, but at least I got some kind of release. He wanted me to cook but I refused, especially since he didn't know whether I could or not. At dinner I couldn't help it, I kept looking at him like he was weak. I was never going to do this again. It wasn't hard to read my mood so although I know he wanted to take me, home he asked me to go dancing. If his bedroom skills were any indication of how he dances I wanted to pass. But I wasn't in a hurry to go home to cry myself to sleep yet again, so I agreed to go.

On the dance floor I was pleasantly surprised. He could actually dance. Why didn't he start the evening this way? Dancing, then he could've had dessert, and then at least both of us would be feeling some sense of calm and release. Shawn and I were breaking it down in our own world when I started to hear commotion coming from behind me. All I saw was blonde hair charging in my direction. I moved out of the way just in time. She slid across the floor like a bowling ball knocking down all the unsuspecting pins of people. "Shawn!" She screamed when she got up.

Shawn had a busted look on his face as he went to help her up. "Marsha let me explain!"

I clinched my teeth, I DON'T NEED THIS! "Explain what?" I said as calm as I could.

"That I'm his wife! Who are you?"

STRIKE FOUR! I put my hands up, "I didn't know he was married."

"How could you not know?" She said moving closer to me. This trick thinks she's gonna fight me in this club! I shifted my weight as I waited for her to get closer. "He doesn't wear a ring, and he never mentioned you." I looked at Shawn, "you betta come get her!"

Shawn reached for her and she started charging again. I hopped out my shoes and popped her in her face. As she went down, I hit her in the middle of her back. I needed her to stay down. I picked up my shoes and walked away as Shawn ran to his wife.

****

"You can work in here for the day. This is Juan's office. Malcolm's is next door." El put his briefcase on the desk. I gave him a tour of the office space. It seemed like every female was batting her eyes at him. He didn't respond to any of that. I did notice that he wasn't wearing his ring, but I wasn't asking if he wasn't telling. His eyes glided over everything in my office. It seemed like he was looking for something.

"Who's this lovely young lady?" He asked pointing to a picture of Sabrina.

"My little sister."

"Nice. Nice office."

"Thanks" I said glancing at an email that just arrived.

"Where can I get a decent cup of coffee?" I rolled my eyes.

"What?" His sudden smile was pleasant to look at.

"Nothing, you just reminded me that I need to find a new coffee spot."

"There has to be more than one in walking distance from here."

"There is but LA is not like New York, we don't walk everywhere down here."

I invited Richard to go with us, even though an interesting look flashed across El's face when I did it. Richard had a call in a

87

few minutes so he couldn't leave. When we stepped back out of the office Henry stopped walking and stood by us. El looked at me and I shot him a look. "Can I help you?"

"Oh I thought I was talking." Henry said shaking his head letting snowflakes fall. El's mouth literally fell open at the site of it. "Can I come with you, I need coffee too?"

I thought about telling the two of them to go together and to bring my coffee back. But I imagined Henry insisting on carrying my coffee and then letting his snowflakes fall on my lid. I looked at El, letting him know it was up to him. "Why don't you give me your drink order, and we'll bring it back. We need to discuss some pretty classified information for the big project."

Henry huffed in defeat. He wrote his order down then we left. El said he hoped Henry would be better in person than he was over the phone. We walked about a block in the opposite direction. El looked at me with a smirk. Then he asked me who the guy was that we were avoiding. I gave him a none of your business look and I didn't dignify the question with an answer. I hadn't packed anything yet, and our flight left tonight. I didn't feel like packing. I just unpacked four days ago. My momma called me all excited cause she was looking at properties online. She asked if I had done anything yet. I told her my week had been too busy to wrap my mind around it. She deflated, and then she told me to snap out of it. She said Dennis was a nasty dog, and good riddance. She was on my case real bad. She wouldn't let up until I got mad, then she told me to go handle my business and not to let a worthless guy steal my joy. I was trying to explain how much it hurt me that Dennis would sink so low. Billions of females on this earth and he had to have the one I called a friend. I felt like he took my self-esteem and then that whole display with Shawn didn't help me. I've been seeing "unknown" calls on my phone all day. Before I took one more step, I deleted Shawn's number and I called and changed my number. I refused to spend the weekend being harassed by a female who couldn't handle her man. I packed a few things, but I was going shopping with my momma anyways so it didn't matter. El was sitting at the gate reading something when I walked up. "What's up Sasha?" He said waiting for an answer.

"What do you mean?"

"You're upset about something, you're not as carefree as you normally are." Then he mimicked what I guess is supposed to be me flipping my hair.

"I don't look like that!" I smiled

He chuckled, "yes you do. You walk around like you know everybody is jocking you."

"I do?" I could hear the way Andrew explained that girl in my head. She was nothing like me except the working part. "I carry myself like I think that way?"

"You know you do, don't act surprised."

I sunk in my seat, "I'm that bad huh?"

"Who says confidence is a bad thing?" He adjusted to face me. "There's a thin line between confidence and conceitedness. The trick is to straddle that line until it's gone. Now my turn, do you think I'm full of myself?"

"I don't know, I guess not."

He smiled, "I'm completely aware of the affect I have on women. It's perfectly natural to be attracted to someone upon first glance. But that gets old fast and then you're on to the next. Beauty is only skin deep."

"Yeah, but you can't talk. Your wife is gorgeous!"

I knocked the wind out of him. He slumped a little, "yeah." He said getting quiet.

I sat there not knowing what I said to provoke such a response from him. "You ok?" He nodded his head yes. When they announced boarding for our flight, I looked around. I asked him where the rest of our team was; he said they were coming Monday morning while he stayed lost in his thoughts. I frowned at him, I could've used two extra days to pack and get myself together. "So tell me." I said rolling my hands once we were seated on the plane.

"Tell you what?"

"Why the sudden change?"

"You share first."

"No." I said backing up into my seat.

"Fine, then I'm not sharing."

"El, come on. You know you wanna tell me, so go ahead."

"Not until you do."

"You promise you'll go next? I'm trusting you," I raised my fist. "This is something I don't normally do."

"Promise," he said smiling.

"Dennis and I are over." It felt good to say it. "I've loved him for so long, I don't know how to feel without feeling love for him. As long as I had Dennis in some kind of way in my life other guys didn't matter as much. Now I don't know how to feel about anything. I feel lost, and so unsure." I wanted to cry, but I told myself not to release one tear. "Your turn!" I said trying to shake off the feeling of crying.

"I'm sorry to hear that." He said faking a sad face.

"No you're not! Stop lying!"

He smiled, "I'm really not. Who asks such a personal question in mixed company? If you ask me he was sizing me up."

"Why would he be sizing you up?"

"The same reason Zoila was sizing you up. They see our unbelievably attractive coworkers and they feel threatened."

"Was that a backwards compliment?"

"It is what it is." He said looking at me.

"Your turn, spill it." I said

"Zoila wants a divorce." Pain showed immediately in his eyes.

"And you don't?"

"I didn't get married to get divorced. Everything else is nonsense to me. I just want my wife. But what can you do if she doesn't want you anymore?" He exhaled and leaned back.

"Why doesn't she want you?"

He exhaled and patted my hands. "We need drinks to get that deep."

"Hotel bar?" I asked

"Just say when." He said sighing and leaning back in his chair. We chatted here and there during the flight and along the way to the hotel. I checked-in first, I told him I was in room 529 and to call me when he was ready. In the elevator I frowned, what if he ends up getting back with his wife as soon as he goes home. I told myself not to get caught up. Twenty minutes later he called my room and asked me to join him at the bar. I changed into sweat pants, a T-shirt, and thong slippers. When I walked into the bar he started laughing. He said he never would've thought I owned sweats or that I'd be seen in public in them. I told him they were absolutely comfortable and I love to relax in a good pair of extremely baggy sweats. Then he told me he was happy I was letting my hair down. El was drinking something brown. The bartender asked what I wanted. I asked for a fuzzy navel with a double shot of grey goose floating. When my drink came I smiled and told the bartender to bring another whenever El had his second. Then I looked at him while I enjoyed my drink.

El sighed again, he signaled for another round while he finished his drink. Then he told me the story, throughout their courtship El made it clear that he wanted a wife and family. A few months before their wedding they decided to go for it and start their family right away. Six months after they were married they went to the doctor to make sure everything was ok. Zoila just knew that the reason why their family hadn't began was going to be El's fault. She was devastated when they learned that she was the reason. After multiple rounds of IVF therapy they were finally pregnant. But Zoila's body did not respond well to being pregnant and during her last trimester of pregnancy she was bedridden. Then they were blessed with a beautiful baby girl Zohra Elise. Life was good and they didn't care about everything they went through, they were happy. When Zohra was four months, Zoila put her down for bed as usual. El said he was alarmed when Zohra didn't wake up like she normally does. He said when he touched her, she was cold. The doctors listed her cause of death as SIDS (Sudden Infant Death Syndrome). Zoila is convinced that El needs to start over and that he can still have the family and everything. El tells her that he wants her and he doesn't need the rest. My drink was getting to me and I was already sad, so I gave way to tears. El's eyes glazed over, but I was crying so hard. He stopped and stared at me like I was crazy. I told him not to look at me like that. "I grew up with all boys, I know how to read between the lines. So what happened, you pulled away from her?" I asked him. He said he did the opposite, she became his everything, and the closer he drew to her the more she pulled back. He said even his mother-in-law, who could be a piece of work at times, has been on his side. He said Zoila has shut down on him, she's pulling away from him, and it hurts because this is when they need each other the most. He sat back to chew back his emotions which were getting hard to keep at bay with all the alcohol. I told him the whole story of Dennis and I. How we met, how we fell in love, our pregnancy scares, our family dynamics, when he started pulling away, and how that made me feel. I told him how my father was very fond of Dennis; I left out the part that Richard is my father just because we didn't run around the office broadcasting it. I told him how I expected my father to defend Dennis in some sort of way cause they were buddies. My father to my surprise, had my complete back. I told him that has never happened, but I've never let my father in when I've been hurting either.

We sat in the bar area talking until the last call. In a moment of clarity I looked at El who was completely heartbroken over his wife. He looked like a wounded puppy. I asked him for his key card, and then I walked him to his room. I opened his door for him and then I sat him on his bed. He looked at me and then he looked around the room. I grabbed all the sobriety I could in that moment to realize this was not where I wanted to be. I put his card on the dresser, and I told him to call me when he was ready for breakfast. He didn't say anything he just watched me as I walked out.

****

My momma and Sabrina came out to the city to hang with us on Saturday. Even Sabrina was blushing cause she thought El was cute. We took El to all the tourist spots in the city. Fisherman's Wharf, Lombard Street (the crookedest street in the world), Golden Gate Park, and then we took him for a walk across the Golden Gate Bridge. My momma and Sabrina were spending the night so we hung out in my room playing cards and relaxing. Around midnight New York time Zoila called and proceeded to pick a fight over the phone. I wondered if Dennis would've done the same if I hadn't changed my number. I'm learning El's expressions enough to know that he was happy to hear from her initially, and when she started arguing with him he was disappointed. He said he was going to his room. As soon as he left my momma started drilling me. I told her he was married and he and his wife just separated, the wound was still fresh. I told her he was in love with his wife. Then she said, while he liked me. I told her it didn't matter if he did, he's married and very in love with his wife.

In the morning we were starving and ready for breakfast. I called El's room and he didn't answer. I told my momma and Sabrina to go ahead downstairs and I would go check on El. When I got to his room I knocked on the door and he didn't answer. I told the housekeeper I forgot my key when I went downstairs. She opened the door and then I heard the shower turn off. It didn't dawn on me that he could've been in the shower, but I called earlier. "El?" I called out from the door. "Sasha? What are you doing in here?" He peeked his head around the door.

"You weren't answering the phone, so I came to make sure you are ok."

He smiled and came out of the bathroom in only a towel. "You came to see if you could see anything good."

I smiled, "that too. My momma and Sabrina are downstairs. Are you gonna join us for breakfast?"

He stood in front of me; I read the tattoo on his heart "Zohra Elise." He watched my eyes. "Ok, I'll be down in a minute." Then he turned and walked towards his bed. He looked back at me, "you better go before you end up in trouble." He didn't smile, he watched my eyes.

92

I nodded ok, and then I slowly backed out the room. I kept smacking myself upside the head. Get it together Sasha! He's married and in love with his wife! When I got to the table my momma smiled a knowing smile and asked me why I looked all flushed. I told her I would tell her later. When El glided towards our table I turned my eyes. He looked good, even my momma said "oh boy!" When El asked us what was the plan for today, all three of us said, "SHOPPING!" El smiled and said he needed to get a few things himself. I don't know why I expected him to be sad and sulking today. Maybe it was because of the way he left my room last night. But he was in good spirits. He loved the look inside the Union Square mall. He said it reminded him of the New York malls. We went our separate ways in the mall and we said we'd meet up once we were exhausted.

My momma insists that he likes me. I told her he misses his wife, and I'd be a fool to go for it. She said if his wife continues on like this, she's gonna lose him forever. She said there's only so much you can push a person away before they leave.

I expected El to be bored and ready to go first. When I called him he was at the cash register and he told me he'd meet us at the bottom of the mall. We were standing with our many bags. To all of our surprise he came down with almost as many bags as we had. On the way back to our hotel my momma pointed out the Mitigated office in downtown, it wasn't far from the hotel. My momma told El it was nice to meet him and then they hugged and kissed us goodbye. I told her we would be out here at least for the week, so we had to come to Sophia's, her restaurant, at least once.

El and I put our bags in his room, since his room was on the third floor and mine was up on the fifth. Then the concierge gave us information for a few local restaurants.

We walked a few blocks over in the crispy San Francisco air to our restaurant. It was a nice but dimly lit place. I felt a little under dressed; no one said anything about a dress code so I figured we were fine.

As soon as we sat down we ordered our drinks. He ordered a dirty martini and I ordered a lemon drop. El apologized, and then he said my mother had to be very young when she had me. I told him she was almost sixteen when I was born. I told him about my uncles who are my age and all the fun we had growing up. He kept his eyes on me the entire time I was talking. The women were definitely noticing him; he wasn't paying any of them any attention. It was like I was the only woman here as far as he was concerned. Then he said, "you are really pretty."

I blushed, "come on El are you just now noticing?"

He smiled, "no. But I am seeing it for the first time right now."

"I don't get what you mean."

"When you look around you will see attractive people everywhere you look. All of them wanting and some demanding to be acknowledged for it. The thing is there's always someone better right around the corner as far as appearance goes. You can't look at people based on face value. There has to be more. So, now that you're acting like a person, I can see what makes you."

"I wasn't acting like a person?"

"No," he smiled at me.

"Forget you! Neither were you then." I said laughing.

He laughed, "you're just being spiteful."

"Whatever! You tried to act like your eyes didn't like what you were seeing. I know you were as curious to see me, as I was you. Then you sit there like you had no reaction. You should've fell out of your chair." I smiled

"Ok, ok like you weren't swimming in your panties when you saw me." He gave me a knowing look.

I crossed my legs under the table; butterflies were dancing around my stomach. "Like you said, you know the affect you have on women." Then I looked him in his eyes, "but you love your wife." He turned his eyes. "So is this what we're gonna do? We're gonna flirt with each other dance around the fire, but never touch it?"

He finished his drink, and signaled for another. "What do you want?"

"I don't handle being teased too well. I know you love your wife. I'm guessing I'm out here with you to distract you from your thoughts. This whole thing is different. I'm used to being used, but never in such a mild manner. I guess my body radiates sex cause that's what most men come for."

"So that's what you learned to accept?"

"From men in general yes, but Dennis was supposed to love me."

"So as long as he loved you, the rest didn't matter?"

"Right. It's been years since I've been out here all alone."

"So if I wanted to kiss you right now?" He asked

"You could, but why would you? If Z called you right now you would go running back."

"What if Dennis called you?"

"He can't, I changed my number."

"But if he came back begging and pleading, promising you the world. You wouldn't take him back?"

"Actions speak louder than words. But in order for me to see his actions I have to see him, and I'm blind to him. The difference between you and me is that I don't want him anymore. You're the one who got dumped in yours. I'm done with Dennis, but you're still in love with Zoila."

He sighed and gulped his drink, and signaled for another. "I apologize. I needed to get away and I didn't want to spend the weekend alone."

"It's fine El, I needed to get away too."

We left the restaurant very tipsy but alert. In the elevator he reminded me that my bags were in his room. I looked at him, why didn't I see this setup earlier? In his room he was quiet, he held my bags, but he didn't move. "Sasha..." His voice was low and aching. I looked at him and there was a mixture of pain and confusion in his eyes. "Can I kiss you?"

I felt bad for him, and it wasn't like I didn't want to kiss him. I put my bag down and I walked up to him and I kissed him. There wasn't any passion behind his kiss, and I could feel his heart pounding in his chest. He misses his wife; I'd be a fool to think this kiss was about me. When we stopped kissing I hugged him tight. Then I picked up my bags. We went to my room in silence. He picked up my extra room card key on the dresser and replaced it with his additional card. He said I was his in case of emergency person on this trip. He hugged me and then he left. I took a shower and then I set my alarm clock, drank water, and then I crawled in bed. I was almost completely sleep when the phone in the room rang. "Hello?" I said with sleep in my voice.

"Sasha."

"Yes El? What's wrong?"

"Can I sleep with you?"

I frowned, "what?"

"Can't sleep, can I sleep with you?"

"Whatever! Don't call, just come." I said irritated then I hung up. Not even a minute later I heard him coming in the room. "Where did you call from?"

"Hallway phone."

He put his robe across my dresser. Then he scooted up to me and spooned me. He put his hand between my breasts then he relaxed. Within minutes he was sleep, I guess he really only wanted to sleep.

****

"Chantel, they're a part of the East Coast Project." The receptionist said to Chantel.

I recognized her immediately. She smiled, "hello Sasha."

"Hello." I said putting all the pieces together in my head. Is this who Derrick was talking about? "Good to see you again. This is El, he should be on the list as well."

"Nice to meet you," El said extending his hand for a shake.

"You as well, I'll show you to the conference room." She said unaffected by El in the slightest way. Chantel was tall and thin, pretty in her own way. I met her at Derrick's graduation party. I guess this is who he was whining about. She showed us to the conference room, which also had hot breakfast waiting for us. El and I were the first to arrive. I took my jacket off and then Chantel came back. She asked me to come with her; her tone was professional so this wasn't a chatting request. Then she led me to Malcolm's office, she closed the door when I stepped in.

"Have a seat." Malcolm said clicking away on his computer. I looked around at the pictures of Amber, him and Amber, and then my cousins. Everything was specifically placed and very neat. He stopped typing and looked at me. "Where is your head?"

I frowned, "what?"

"Is your head in the game? What are you doing? I set up a meeting to launch this project and you're not in the office! I know you weren't lacking work. Is your personal plate overshadowing business? People on the ground are telling me you come and go as you please." His eyes were serious and his tone was matter of fact. "Do you belong on this team? Let me know now, if you can't handle it I need to know."

"I can handle it. I'm on board."

"Since it's been noticed on the floor that you tend to leave you need to ping me whenever you leave early or take a day off. What are your office hours?"

"Malcolm, I run that whole office. They don't know what I leave for..."

He cut me off, "and neither do I. You're not special services. Is there some reason I don't know about what takes you away from the office?"

"No," I said still giving him eye contact.

"You're right, you run that office. But you gotta be there to run it. I'm not saying the occasional knock off early isn't ok. But

you're abusing that privilege." He waited for me to disagree.
"Now that that's out the way, what's going on with Althea?"
I frowned, "she complained about me?"
"If she will stab you in the back over a guy, why don't you
think she'll do it over her job?" He waited for me to connect
the dots.
"She told on me because she got scolded for being late in New
York?" I watched Malcolm's face but it didn't change. "How
do you know about Dennis?"
"I'm watching over everything."
"Richard didn't know though."
"You told him?" Malcolm smirked
"Yes."
Malcolm picked up his phone, dialed someone on speed dial.
He asked the person to send him the orders under Dennis
Barbeau and Althea Hannigan. He waved me over as he pulled
up orders for them. There were a lot of painful events
scheduled for them past and present. Like Thea's car windows
were all busted out Friday night while I was on the plane, same
thing with Dennis. Malcolm chuckled then he called Richard
and put him on speaker. "Yo M-head!" Malcolm frowned at
the phone. As if Richard could see his reaction he laughed.
"I have your baby girl in my office."
"Hey Sassy baby, Daddy loves you." He said with a smile in
his voice.
"I see!"
"I pulled up your orders. Don't you think this is a bit juvenile?"
Malcolm said
"Yep!" Then he laughed. "I LOVE YOU SASSY!" He quietly
yelled into the phone.
"You need help!" Malcolm said almost smiling.
"What did you find on this other guy?" Richard said changing
up.
"She filed for divorce Thursday." Malcolm said looking at me.
Richard sounded like he was thinking. "I get it, but that's my
baby girl."
"Me what?"
"You have fun this weekend?" Richard asked, I couldn't decide
for his demeanor.
"Lots, why is that any of your business?"
Malcolm looked at me, but he waited for Richard to respond.
"You are my business! Malcolm, I'll talk to you later." Then
Richard hung up.
"Why would you talk to your father like that?"

"He only cares about me to get to my momma." I huffed
Malcolm shook his head. "I can't tell you how to feel about
your father, but you really need to step back and examine that.
When Althea pushed up on him, his primary reason amongst
others for turning her down was you. You guys are going to
make me put a code of conduct in writing about interoffice
dating."
"El and I aren't dating."
"Dinners, family outings with your mom, do I need to go on?
Looks like dating to me."
"We're just friends."
"Right," Malcolm said nodding his head.
Curiosity wouldn't let me let it go. "Zoila filed for divorce?"
Malcolm typed something in the computer, "irreconcilable
differences." The document had her signature, she wasn't
asking for support. She simply wanted the marriage dissolved.
"You think he'll sign?"
"He loves her, I doubt it!" Malcolm said again watching my
face. "You sure you wanna be involved with this?"
"We're just friends!"

****

I've been sitting on the fence. Talking to El all the time was
fine. Sleeping with him was nice when we traveled together.
But we weren't "sleeping" together. I ask myself why the only
way I can know and understand that a man wants me is if he
expresses it in some kind of sexual manner? What's wrong
with me that I can't respect the fact that El was taking his time
with me? Probably because I still kind of felt like he was
passing time with me more than he was taking his time. I know
his wife still has his heart on a string like a puppet. He still
wanted his wife back and she was the one saying no, even
though he was spending a lot of time with me on this merger.
"Are you going to be ok going to Minneapolis without me?" El
asked.
"I know my job, remember I've been doing it a lot longer than
you have. I got this!" I said
"That's cute, however you know what I'm talking about."
"Does it even matter?"
"It does matter Sasha!" El said in a frustrated tone.
"It shouldn't!" I shook my foot. The flight attendant
announced First Class boarding. "Look I gotta board the plane.
I'm going to handle business then I'm going home."
"You could come here after you finish business."

"For what?" I waited, he didn't say anything. "I'll talk to you when I get back." I had no intentions of seeing Dennis. But as far as I'm concerned the fact that he would be wondering served me well.

I checked into the Marquette Hotel in downtown Minneapolis. Lindsey came and got me in the morning. We walked through the Skywalk tunnels that connected all the downtown buildings so you didn't have to brave the freezing cold weather outside. Shopping definitely was in order as we walked past all these shops and stands. I breezed through my meetings for the day, and I told them I would be back tomorrow. I knew I had gone completely crazy when I had a bunch of silk scarves in my hand. I liked scarves yes, but I was trying to fill the void with this gigantic retail therapy session. I put most of the things back that I picked and I made myself only purchase the things that I felt were super cute. I told myself I would need to buy another bag to fly home with all the things I had before. As I walked back through the skyway I spotted Lindsey and her friends before she saw me. She got really excited when she saw me, and she introduced me to her friends as the girl from California. They looked me up and down with smiles as if I fit the description of what they imagined a girl from California looking like. Lindsey asked what I was about to do, and I told her I was going to order room service and get ready for my day tomorrow. She begged me to come out with them. Well she didn't have to beg all that much cause I was down to go out. Lindsey and her friends waited downstairs as I showered, dressed, and fixed my hair.

To me I had on a simple top, jeans, and heels. Lindsey and her friends acted like I was completely done up. When I asked where we were going they said in unison, "The Shout House!" There was a big, I guess he was supposed to be scary looking guy at the door. He asked each person for their ID before they could enter. The place looked like a pub. There was a full bar, small tables for parties to squeeze into, and a stage with two pianos facing each other. We ordered shots, and then we took them together. We did this a few times before we ordered drinks. I blinked my eyes to make sure I was seeing straight when I saw Dennis and what looked like a colleague walk in together. Dennis was loosening his tie while he smiled at the waitress who followed him and his friend to their seat. He hadn't seen me yet; I could've walked out of there and went back to my room. Or I could lay low and then escape when I felt the timing was better. I hadn't laid eyes on him in a minute and I was upset with my eyes and heart for betraying me and longing for him. I was in my own world battling with myself about the whole thing, as I watched the two guys come out and open their show. They played a song then they encouraged the audience to request songs they wanted to hear. Dennis was talking to his colleague when I heard one of the pianist call out my name. "Sasha where are you?" The guy said using his hand held spotlight to search the crowd. Lindsey and her friends ratted me out, and they called me to the stage. Dennis heard them call my name but he wasn't paying all that much attention until I stepped on the stage. "Well HELLO there pretty lady! Why are you acting so shy?" I put my hand over my face as I laughed. "Do you need more courage juice?" I shook my head yes. "Please get this beautiful woman a shot of whatever she was drinking so we can get her to loosen up," he said. When the waitress brought me my shot, he played a melody that the regulars knew, and they all sang along as I took my shot. "There, there! Now do you feel ready?" My body was tingling so I said yes. The pianist explained that my friends chose a song for me so I needed to dance to the song while they played it. I started laughing hard as I heard the music, "I'm too sexy…"I did my muted version of a dance, and invisible strip tease around the stage. The other pianist forgot he was supposed to be performing as he watched me move. Dennis's eyes were glued to me when I walked off the stage. I could tell he was trying to gauge how drunk I was before he approached. Was I drunk enough to be open to him, or so drunk that I would fight him? I ignored him and acted like I didn't know he was there. To my surprise he didn't approach the table, but somehow a "secret admirer" paid our bill, which I knew wasn't cheap cause we were throwing our drinks back. The girls walked me back to my hotel and then they caught a cab home. I waited in the lobby, when Dennis walked in. His eyes pleaded with me to talk to him. I sprayed insecticide on the butterflies that thought they were going to move around my stomach. I stared at his face waiting for him to say something. He asked me if he could talk to me. I told him we weren't going to my room. He took out his phone and made a couple calls, then he reached for my hand. I snatched it before he touched me. He put his hands up to say he was sorry then he asked me to come with him. I walked behind him out of the door, into the courtyard of the offices and stores that occupied this section of the skyway. He held the door open for me to the IBS building. The security guard asked if he was Mr. Barbeau, when he said yes she asked for his ID. She made a note and then she turned on the elevator for us to go up in the elevators on the side that went up to the top. Dennis pressed the button for us to go up to the fifth floor. When we stepped off the elevator the cleaning crew was finishing up. Dennis took me to the conference room at the end of the hallway. He walked to the window, and said we could see all of Downtown Minneapolis. I looked at him for a minute, and then I eventually walked to the window. He pointed out the Metro Dome, and other spots in downtown. It looked so pretty from up here. "I can't believe you're here!" I looked at him. "Sasha, there's so much I wanna say to you. I don't know where to begin."

"Doesn't matter what you say, you will never be special to me again!"

"NO! Please Sasha! I'll do whatever it takes. I messed up."

"Admitting that you messed up doesn't take away what you've done to me. I feel so ugly and ordinary."

"You could never be ugly or ordinary."

"Like your compliments matter to me anymore!" I said wrapping my arms around myself.

Dennis started rambling about when we first met, and how quickly he fell for me. He was going on and on about how amazing I am, and how much he loves me. My drinks were hitting me, and I didn't react when he stepped closer to me. He kept talking and then he moved closer. Pretty soon our shoulders were touching. When I had no reaction he stepped behind me and put his arms around me. Our reflection in the window was so beautiful. My beautiful man looking at me with so much love for me in his eyes. He kissed my neck and my body got excited, he wasn't waiting for me to say no. He kissed me like it was killing him not to. When I turned to face him he picked me up and kissed me with everything in him. He kept saying my name and then kissing me again. When my back hit the cold glass window, the reality of what was happening shocked me. I could hear Drew's voice telling me that he told me this was going to happen. The coldness shot through my whole body. I made Dennis put me down and then I put my arms back around myself as I started walking out. Dennis called after me, his voice even whimpered like a wounded puppy. I pressed the button for the elevator, when Dennis came and kissed me again. He was begging me not to leave him. I had to literally put my fingers in my ears, I had no business being up here with him. I had a screaming match with myself. I couldn't allow myself to give in to Dennis, no matter how much my bleeding heart wanted me to. Dennis was familiar and all I've really known. No one else mattered to me cause in my heart I knew I was going to end up with Dennis and that was all that mattered. "Sasha, please! I'll do whatever it takes!" He pleaded

"Whatever, as in anything?" I asked

"Yes," he watched my eyes.

"Drop dead!"

"What?" He looked confused.

"The only time I will feel anything else for you is when you die. I may come to your funeral. I'm done Dennis, I can't be with you ever again. Leave me alone!" I said hurrying out of the elevator, out the door, and across the courtyard.

"Sasha!" Dennis said grabbing my shoulder.

"Dennis, she wants to go to her room." The guy I had never seen before said.

I could tell he was Mitigated staff, most likely sent out by

Richard. "Who are you?"

"I've got family everywhere. I gotta go." I said hurrying past the guy into the hotel. Dennis looked devastated. He was so close.

****

"Malcolm do you need anything else from me? I need to meet with the realtor."

"These numbers can't be right!" Malcolm growled

"I told you worst case scenario they were going to try to fight back." I said drumming my fingers on my desk.

"We gotta fix this, you can go, but I need everyone on board tomorrow."

"But tomorrow is Saturday! I had plans!" Alonzo exclaimed

I looked at the speaker; I guess he thought he might as well go for it. I braced myself for Malcolm's response. "You're right! It is Saturday. How about when Monday rolls around you hit the unemployment line!"

"I was just saying," Alonzo said deflating.

"I had plans!" He was supposed to be going to Hubby's wedding. I knew Amber was going to hit the roof when he cancelled. "You know what..." Oh no here it comes. "Alonzo your contribution to this merger has been less than spectacular. I won't tolerate whining while I'm sacrificing as well. Turn in your badge to Amelia, I'll have her pack up your desk." You heard Alonzo gasp, but no one said anything. I heard Malcolm's fingers clicking over the keyboard. He was probably telling Amelia to get his badge. After a minute of silence and clicking Malcolm asked what time we were meeting. He said the earlier we meet the sooner we could knock off. Someone said nine and Malcolm made it so. I called Malcolm from the car, I was going to ask if I could call from home, but he picked up telling me he would be in the office by eight. So I asked him what he needed from me before the morning. I wrote it down then I packed up and I took off.

I met Carl at his office. He got really excited when he saw me. I promise you this whole thing has been dragging on for months because he likes spending time with me. I say I'm not interested in a condo or townhouse and he takes me to see condos and townhouses. "I hope you've got something good." I said

"I think so."

He opened his car door. "Wait! Wait a minute Carl." I should've asked before I left the office. "Let me see the list." I said sticking my hands out.

"You don't trust me?"

I sighed, "Carl! I am a high profile client. Did you see my pre-approval letter from the bank? You came highly recommended, but quite frankly I am not impressed with you as a businessman at all. Your little crush is pathetic, and..." In that moment I asked myself why. I started walking towards the office.

"Ok! Ok! Wait Sasha! I can do better!" He said running in front of me with his hands up.

I shook my head and kept walking. The office manager watched us walk back inside. "Everything ok?"

I grabbed my composure. "No!"

"Seriously Sasha please come with me." Carl said holding the door open.

"I would like to work with someone else. If that is beyond this office then I will take my business elsewhere."

"There is no one else. It's me or no one!" Carl said like he was talking to an idiot.

I picked up Carl's card from the table. I called Richard, when he answered I started talking. "Carl Weston, Western Coastal Realty, License number #6543..." I could hear Richard writing it down. Carl looked at me like I was no threat to him. "This man has been wasting my time for the past four months. I've asked to work with someone else, and he's informed me that there is no one else. Tell me who is his top competitor, I will take my business there." I could hear Richard typing.

The office manager picked up her phone and called someone. A woman came from the back office. "Is everything ok out here?"

"Who are you?" I said with the phone stuck to my ear waiting for Richard to answer me.

"I'm the Broker of this office."

"I got the information Sassy, I'll text it to you now. Assistance will be in the parking lot in thirty seconds. He will be handled, move on."

I took the phone off my ear, but I didn't hang up. "Mister Weston here just lost my commission. He's been wasting my time."

She looked at Carl. "Is this true?"

"She's been wasting mine so I went along with the game." He said

"What do you mean Carl?" She sounded annoyed.

He walked to his desk and pulled the file containing my pre-approval letter. "Look at her documents. Yeah right she makes this kind of money. She's running a scam!"

My blood boiled! I looked at the Broker, she looked extremely embarrassed. "Carl, before the bank issued this approval they did an employment verification. Her credit report supports her income. It's not your place to say who's legitimate and who isn't."

"If you wanna waste your time chasing a sale that will never happen that's on you." He said like he was doing her a favor.

"I'm so sorry," she looked down at the file. "Ms. Wallace, he does not speak for WC."

"That's fine, but you do understand I cannot do business with a company who employs such a person." I spit

"I understand." She said shooting Carl daggers.

"Now I'm on my way to," I looked at my phone at the text message screen. "To Wide World Realty, Susan is awaiting me."

Everyone's mouths dropped open. I walked out the door and I saw Bruce. He pointed to Carl's car with a question mark. I nodded to say yes. I got in my car and followed my navigation to the other office. When I walked in the door a woman came to me immediately. "How may I help you today?"

"My name is Sasha Wallace I'm here to meet with Susan."

She smiled real big, "that's me. Nice to meet you Sasha." I liked her already.

She made a copy of my copy of my approval letter. We went over the preliminary paperwork and I told her exactly what I was looking for. She pulled up six properties. Two of them she had to make appointments to view tomorrow afternoon. She said she'd make them for around four. I hoped we would be done working by then. Then we rode in her car to the first four listings. I immediately smiled at the single family home. The house was nice but it was on a busy street and it needed a lot of work. But I was so happy she understood the gist of what I was looking for. In between houses I told her about Carl and she couldn't believe he acted that way. She said he had to be a relative acting like that in a place of business. Then she said, "people look at us like we can't achieve anything." Susan had fair skin and brown curly hair. She didn't exactly have African American features, but they weren't exactly European either. I smiled, "right! Well he should've asked someone who I am, I'm not the one to be messed with."

The last house I really liked, but it needed a lot of work as well. But the location from the office was beautiful; it has a huge back and front yard. The house itself had an upstairs and downstairs, it was three bedrooms with one bathroom. On the way home El called me and asked what I wanted for dinner. I told him it was his turn to choose, I told him to call me when he was on his way to the hotel. I ran home, showered, packed an overnight bag and as I was walking out of the door El called and said he was on his way to the hotel. I looked out the window and I saw Marsha and one of her friends trying to figure out how to get into the building. I rolled my eyes and pulled out my phone, I texted Bruce. I told him "the troll was circling." Then I went down to the garage. Next time I talk to my Poppa I'm gonna tell him he could charge more for these apartments if he put security gates in, etc.

El and I are just friends outside of the feels he cops on me when we sleep, the kisses he asks for when he's missing his wife. At most, he doesn't look at me as more than a friend. Meanwhile I've been trying to turn down my sass a lot. I mean I can't turn it off completely. I was born this way, but my need to be the center of attention, I've been working on it. Taking the backseat to someone who's in love with someone who doesn't want them is a hard pill to swallow. El is a great guy and so in love with that woman I don't understand how she could walk away from him. Dennis has sent flowers, cards, letters, himself, and anything he can think of. I've never gone this long without talking to him. I missed certain things about him, but for the most part my friendship with El filled that void. When I walked in the room El was setting up our dinner at the table. He had gone down and picked up fried catfish from this food truck that parks a few blocks from our office. For everyone to be so health conscious out here the line was always long at this truck. I told El about the fixer-upper. I told him that it had character, but it would need a lot of work before it would be up to my standards. Then I called my Poppa, I told him about Carl, and he said he knew already. I gave him the MLS number of the fixer-upper. I told him I was going to look at two more properties tomorrow. He told me to keep him posted on what I found. El and I ate while going over our information for the morning with Malcolm. It's been a minute since I've gotten my feet wet. I tried not to look at El too hard or too long. I thought men were supposed to cave first. But I don't think he's looking for a bed buddy. Well not like I mean. "Hey sexy," I said climbing in the bed

"Hey yourself."

"You wanna go out dancing tomorrow night? I think we need to burn off some steam."

"A club?"

"Yeah, what, you don't dance?"

He smiled, "what are you up to?"

"Why do I have to be up to something?" He stared at me. "Ok, ok! I need to burn off some steam. I'm feeling pent up."

He started belly laughing. He got in the bed and laid on his back. "You are funny."

I laid my head on his chest, "an old friend of mine is getting married tomorrow. I can't believe it."

He rubbed my back, "who is he?"

"Conrad, he was my first." I said out loud for the first time ever.

"What happened?"

"I thought we would be in love forever and that he would marry me. He asked me not to go so far away to school. But I thought we would be fine. When he was professing his love and how much he missed me, I couldn't handle the emotion. So I told him that we needed to see other people. He started seeing her, and now they're getting married tomorrow."

El rubbed my back, "I'm sorry. You want to go dancing, how is that gonna make you feel better?"

"I need to blow off some steam, maybe meet someone."

His hand stopped moving. "Meet someone?"

"Yeah, men have some use sometimes."

"Do we?"

"Don't you miss sex?"

"When I allow myself to think about it. But I don't really think about it until I think of Zoila."

"Oh come on, you know I make you horny." I said putting my leg across his.

"You know you give me fever." He laughed

I exhaled, "but?"

"I think I'm using you more than I should already."

"El?"

"Yeah?"

"Do you think any man will ever take me seriously? Tell me the truth. If not, I don't see why I shouldn't go back to my old ways. I see too many women holding on to false hope."

"Men will take you as seriously as you make them. Unfortunately that doesn't mean the right one for you will be one of them. But why would you settle?"

"Because I need a man!" I laughed, he didn't.

"Lowering your standards only leads to more frustration down the line."

"Frustration now or frustration later? I'd rather feel release right now."

"Maybe that's your problem."

"I don't have a problem!" I said trying to pull back.

"Focus on...."

"Why don't you focus on the fact that I'm here right now! I need sex, and we're both here."

El looked down at me. "Stop playing." He started laughing and rubbing my back again.

I kissed him, I kissed him deeply he was lost in my kiss. I pulled at his clothes. Then I stopped and turned on my side with my back to him. He spooned me and put his hand between my breasts as usual, but he put his leg up on my hip. He fell asleep, early in the morning I wiggled my butt in El's crouch. His breathing got heavier but he was still sleeping. His hand came alive as he groped me. I turned around and threw my leg around him as I kissed his neck. He pulled in closer, when I worked my way up to his lips his eyes opened and his body deflated EVERYWHERE! He put his forehead on mine, and then he got up and went to the bathroom. When I heard the shower turn on I cursed at the ceiling! I got dressed and I left. I kept gripping the steering wheel the whole way to the office. Over these past few months we've done everything together. I flew to New York and helped him pack his things. Zoila took the few things she had and left the place they bought. El didn't want to sell it so he rented it out. He put just about everything in storage and got an apartment. I helped him decorate; I cooked numerous meals for him in that kitchen. We're always traveling together which helps me to get away as well. Dennis seems to have the worst timing and comes by the office whenever I'm out. Richard has had him thrown out so many times, you would think he'd stop showing up. But that was one of the things I used to love about Dennis, when he set his mind to something watch out. It's almost impossible to stop him and I guess he feels he can win me back, but I refuse to deal with him. Althea is still here; she's wearing wigs now and looking rough. Mysteriously when she tried a new hairdresser the lady ended up burning her hair out. I imagine she has bald spots in her head. Every time she gets her car fixed somehow it gets messed up all over again, oh my. I think she's on public transit these days when Rodell doesn't bring her in his busted jalopy.

El and I play it cool at work. We arrive separately and we're not overly conversational while we're there. When we travel, we have dinner as a group with whomever is with us. Before bed El comes to my room, he leaves early enough to be ready to go on time. Aren't men supposed to move on faster than women? Aren't men supposed to have needs? If so, how come I'm the only one complaining?

I sat at my desk at a quarter to seven; I couldn't believe I was here this early on a Saturday. Twenty minutes later Malcolm, Derrick, and Juan walked on the floor. Juan looked upset, and Malcolm, well he always looks like that. They said good morning then they went in their offices. Derrick set up in one of the cubicles on the floor. Malcolm came over with the information El and I worked on last night. He was almost smiling; he told me this was better. We were going over something when El arrived he looked whooped as he said good morning. Malcolm said good morning but you could tell he was reading El. When El left he looked at me with serious eyes. He told me to stop pushing him. I got up and closed my door. "What do you mean?"

"I told you that he's in love with his wife."

I got irritated, "he's in love with someone who doesn't want him. I want him."

"Doesn't matter. You're not his wife. If you're ever going to have him, even if it's temporary, you can't push him."

"Why does it have to be temporary?"

Malcolm looked at me, "stop trying to play hard. I know today is hard on you."

I stared at Malcolm, "why do you know about that?"

"I know about most things. I don't know why you kids thought you were getting over. We're barely older than you, we know what's happening."

"How did Amber take you canceling on her?" I gave him a knowing look.

"She's not happy," he looked around the room. "I think we can finish early. It's better to be late then to not show up at all."

"How do I not push him? He's fighting the divorce."

"That means he's not ready for you. He's still fighting for her, holding out for her. I think you should let it go altogether."

Then he looked at me, "but you like to learn the hard way."

Everyone showed up to the meeting with their game faces on. We worked hard and got everything together for our somewhat hostile takeover of a smaller, in comparison, company. Malcolm would tell us to go one way and Derrick would run down the counter moves. In the end we had everything sured up and they had no way out of this deal. I couldn't tell if Malcolm was more excited about the deal or being done by noon. Juan booked their flights out and then they invited those of us who wanted to come to lunch at the airport. El agreed and then I agreed, everyone else ran out to get to their families. I rode with Malcolm and Juan to the airport, Derrick and El rode together. I could tell Malcolm was anxious to get home, but he was trying to be cool. At the restaurant he looked at his phone and sunk in his seat. I asked him what was wrong and he said Amber sent him a picture. He got real anxious after that. El kept looking at me, but he had no expression. Derrick was looking at me too, which made me wonder what they talked about. Juan entertained us with stories about his granddaughter. Malcolm popped up when he looked at his watch. He said bye and he walked determined towards the security checkpoint. I hugged Juan and Derrick good-bye then I walked with El.

"Sasha about this morning," he paused. "I'm sorry."

"Ok," he didn't really have anything to say. So why make him say more right?

I called Susan and I told her my meeting was over early. She asked me to come to the office. El was quiet the whole car ride. Susan's eyes got big when she saw El, but she was respectful. She showed me two other properties in addition to the ones she wanted to show me in the area. I liked the first and third ones out of the four. The fixer-upper kept coming to mind. So I asked Susan to take us there. I called my Poppa and I told him I liked two of the houses I saw today, but I couldn't stop thinking about the possibilities of the fixer upper. He said he talked to my Uncle Dale about the property and he said there are so many possibilities. He told me to decide if I wanted to keep looking. And if not, we could dig in on the fixer-upper, he said when it was all said, and done I would basically have a brand-new house. I didn't need to hear anymore, I wanted it. I told him I would make an offer, and he told me what to offer stating that I was buying it with the intention of fixing the place up. When I got off the phone with him I told Susan that I wanted to make an offer on this place. She looked at me with the most confused look. El didn't say anything, he stood there listening. She drew up the paperwork and I made my offer. I asked El if he was gonna stay in tonight or if he was going to go with me. He thought about it and then he said he didn't know. He said he'd go get his clothes in case he decided to go, and he'd come over my house. I felt a little tired when I got home. When El came, I snuggled into him and I fell asleep on his chest. Who needs Dennis when El is around? I woke up because Ava was calling my phone. It's like we were in sync. She wanted to know if I wanted to go out tonight. I told her El may come with me, she was excited to finally meet him. She said Kai was with her. When I sat up I was straddling El, he was looking at my face. "When was the last time you spoke to Zoila?"

"Wednesday."

"You still want your wife?"

"Yes."

"Why would you wait for someone who doesn't want you?"

He exhaled, "she wants me. She wouldn't have married me if she didn't want me. She's going through a tough time right now. I'm trying to wait on her like I'd want her to do for me."

"I see," I said searching his eyes. "What about me?" Immediately confusion settled in them. "I care about you Sasha. You've been such a good friend to me."

"I don't want to be your friend any more El. I have needs too. I deserve love too."

"You're right."

"Do you love me at all?"

His eyes said yes, but his mouth said, "like a really good friend."

"Well, I love you."

He sunk in the couch, "not like you love Dennis."

"Dennis? Forget Dennis!"

"You're still in love with him. At least I'm honest."

"I AM NOT!" His comment made me angry.

"Whenever he comes up you are emotional."

"I have emotions about him not for him. There is a difference."

"You are just as stuck as I am."

"If you say so, none of that stops me from wanting you."

"You think I don't want you?" He said watching me.

"No I don't."

"I'm with you all the time!"

"While you're fighting for her. You can't hold on to someone who wants to leave. Let her go!"

"She's going to come back though!"

"El, I want you. I'm here!" His face looked stressed. "Fine." I said getting up.

I got in the shower then I got dressed. El got in the shower, he
was dressed, I told myself not to respond, but he looked
GOOD! I told him he looked nice, he told me the same, but his
eyes stayed glued to my breast. He told me twice that he liked
my dress. We went to club Fire in Hollywood. We met Ava
and Kai at the table, El took our drink order and then he went
to the bar. Ava started fanning herself and Kai melted in her
chair. Ava said I understated how FINE he is. He brought our
drinks to the table then he stepped away to take a call. It was
nine o'clock, midnight on the East Coast; it didn't take a genius
to figure out who was on the phone. Otherwise, I don't think he
would've answered if it was anyone other than Zoila. A guy
asked me to dance and I was gone. This guy and I were
dancing for a minute, and then I noticed that El and Kai were
dancing. I hadn't seen him dance before so my head was
turning. El was ok, he wasn't a phenomenal dancer, but he was
cool. I asked the guy to switch me for Kai, he got the biggest
smile. He spun Kai around and they were off. El danced closer
to me. A slow song came on and we were so close I could feel
his heartbeat. My hands roamed his body and he kept looking
at me. When he kissed me there was passion for the first time.
My toes curled, that kiss was intense, and if I wouldn't have
pulled away it would still be going. Normally he touches me
and holds me. Tonight he grabbed me and held me with strong
hands. Instantly my body was on fire, I was going to be
disappointed if this led nowhere. When the next song came on
El looked me in my eyes with passion in his. He asked me how
much longer I wanted to stay. I walked away from him as fast
as I could to Ava on the other side of the floor. I told her I was
leaving then I ran back to El grabbed his hand and tried to run
out of the club. As he drove us I kissed and touched him all
over. When we pulled into the garage I got annoyed when I
saw JoJo's car. I asked him if he had condoms in his room, and
of course he didn't. I sat there trying to decide what to do next.
I didn't want to chance that the gift shop was still open or run
around all over the place looking for condoms. I didn't want to
go upstairs unless I was staying. El turned off the car before I
was convinced that going upstairs was what I wanted to do. He
opened my door and held my hand as we walked up the stairs.
To my delight the apartment was empty. I closed my door so
hard it slammed. We laughed then I turned on music. I was
READY but El needed a minute. So we danced some more. I
undressed him like I was unwrapping a present. His body was
beautiful, and he watched me as I took in every inch of him

with appreciation. He was at attention when I got to his shorts; the butterflies in my stomach were going crazy in anticipation of this moment. He grabbed my hands and he pulled me up to kiss him. He took my dress off, he told me I was beautiful, I don't know why that made me blush, but it did. I know this is his first time outside of Zoila so I wasn't expecting him to knock my socks off. But I was happy to be moving in this direction. When we were naked I looked at him and smiled, I couldn't wait to feel him. I reached in my nightstand and handed him a condom, I saw the look on his face, and he started deflating. I took the condom from him then I massaged him back to full salute. Then quickly I slid the condom on him, and then I mounted him. I moaned with the completion this was happening and he felt good inside of me. I've never seen someone so conflicted about being with me. Pleasure and Pain were all over his face. I tried not to get distracted by it, but I couldn't help it. When he picked up on my slacking enthusiasm he stepped up. He flipped us over and took charge. When my body left me for the second time I couldn't believe it. I looked at my ceiling asking myself if this was real? Could he really be this good? I always thought sex with El would be good, but this was over the top. He finished hard as he said my name in a painful outcry. Even though I laid there completely spent I wondered if he was thinking about Zoila. Because in that moment all I could see was Dennis.

Chapter 6

After falling asleep very satisfied, I woke up a few hours later my stomach was in knots. I wondered if I pushed him too hard? Was he going to shy away from me now? Normally I would tell myself it was the guy's loss and tell myself not to worry about it. But everything with El is different, for him being pretty isn't enough. There have been times where I doubted that we'd ever make it this far. With the way he looks at people, he's had me doubting whether I measured up to his standards. Like when he tells me I'm pretty, I know he means it in a way no one else ever has. I don't have to be Sasha the vixen with him. He doesn't respond to me when I act like that either, which is why I was surprised that last night even happened. I was definitely acting like a spoiled brat! His arm was around me like normal, so I pretended to be sleep and I turned over. I wanted to watch him sleep for a bit, and take him in while he's resting. I used to love to watch Dennis sleep, and he was a hard sleeper so I could stroke his hair. Kiss him, and tell him how much I loved him without him being the wiser. When I turned over I counted to ten and then I slowly opened my eyes. Even though it was pitch black in my room I could see El staring at me. I jumped really hard and I quietly screamed! El said he didn't mean to scare me. I wanted to roll back over and pretend to go back to bed, but I was busted there was no way around it. I started apologizing right away. He rubbed my stomach and told me it was ok, then he told me to go back to sleep. I laid there and tried to go back to sleep, but it bothered me that he was awake. I tried to fall asleep for what felt like forever, and then I opened my eyes again. He was looking at me still. He smiled and said I was hard headed. I told him I was worried about him. I asked him if he was ok. He slowly moved his head to say yes. I told him I didn't believe him. He exhaled and told me he was taking everything in, but that he'd be ok. It was my turn to draw him out. I pulled his face to mine and I gently kissed him. Then I asked him to talk to me. He said he was in a little shock cause he honestly believed Zoila would be the last person he slept with. I smiled and said, then in walks Sasha. He laughed a little; I was relieved that he understood that I was joking. I told him it was ok if he wasn't ready to do it again, and that I understood. He kissed me passionately and then he said, "thank you for understanding when I need understanding the most right now." Then he told me to go back to sleep so he could think in peace. He smiled at me and I thought I'd lay there awake, but I fell asleep. And I fell asleep hard!

****

"I'm so happy you're here!" I said giving Drew a big hug
"I'M VERY HAPPY TO BE HERE!" He said faking an African accent
We had a good chuckle behind that one. He took his bag into JoJo's room. "So spill it! How was the wedding? Were there any mishaps?"
He plopped on the couch next to me, his phone rang, and he sent the caller to voicemail. "The wedding was cool. Hubby is happy, his wife is happy. Everybody's HAPPY!" He said with a face full of disgust
"Uh oh! What happened?" I sat on the couch and got ready for a good story.
"That girl I was telling you about, Tracy. She was Nicole's maid of honor. Sasha when I saw her..." He shook his head while his eyes took him back to the memory. "Sasha she was beautiful. And then I was there with Toya!" He put his hands up to gesture his disgust. "Nicole's friend Sonya had Tracy's ear the entire wedding so who knows what she told her about me. That girl got a big mouth! Anyways, her eyes said she wanted me, but she kept telling me no."
"Was she alone?"
"No, she came with her boyfriend. But he don't got nothing on me. That girl did everything she could to steer clear of me. She even ran from me."
"Literally?"
"Yes, I was calling her and she tried to act like she didn't hear me and ran. "
I frowned, "We're grown Andrew why would she run from you?"
"Cause I was chasing her." He laughed, "Don't matter, I'm gonna give mister can't get right a chance to mess up and then I'm claiming her again. Once I got her I'm not letting her go!"
"What if she doesn't want to be with you."
He smiled, "How she gonna not want me? Do you know who I am?"
"Does she?"
He deflated, "No!" We laughed. "But that's the beauty of it. I'm just Andrew with her. She don't know about the Drew files, unless big mouth Sonya told her. But I doubt it, cause she's not scared of me."

"I hear you, isn't it funny how you say your name to someone in Oakland and they know exactly what that means. But then you venture outside of that and people are like who is that? What does that mean? Sometimes it's refreshing."

"Yeah, but our family didn't really represent at the wedding. Malcolm got there at the end of the night, so I'm told. My momma was there; Derrick and Darryl didn't make it. Yussef didn't even come. When I get married everybody better be breaking their necks to get there."

"I wouldn't come if it was Toya. But then again your momma forbid you so yeah sure I'll be at your wedding. Shoot, I know I'm in that bad boy! That'll be twenty years from now of course. "

"What about you? You know as soon as you take Dennis back he's gonna pop the question."

I frowned again, "What?"

"He's probably telling you how sorry he is now. He's gonna have to work hard to get in good. He'll even try to tap that nerve, blow your back out! And when your head is still spinning he'll ask you to marry him. He does love you in his own way. He has one heck of a way of showing it though."

"You think I should get back with Dennis?"

"Don't make me curse you out. NO! He should've kept that junk outside of your inner circle. That's worse than what my Momma deals with, with Malcolm. Malcolm would never smash your mom or Rosalind."

"I know, right. The ultimate disrespect! But I'm seeing someone else." I felt nervous to talk about him.

"Name?"

"El."

"El?"

"Eldridge, but he goes by El for short."

"Like that light skinned cat who sings?"

"I guess, but not important."

"Good guy?"

"The best! It's still kind of new, but I'm majorly digging him."

"When do we meet?"

"Any minute now, he went to get dinner."

Drew's phone rang again, and he sent it to voicemail. "Ok cool, so what's the plan for tonight?"

"Dinner here then we'll go out for drinks."

He shook his head, "that works. They got anything like EA out here?"

EA or Elegant Affairs is the nightclub that he owns in Oakland. It's an awesome place, the vibe is very mature inside, and it's still a club. But it's a nice one. "Not that I've seen, you got the market cornered on that one cousin." We high-fived. "Do I need to change or can I go like this?" He said turning around in front of me. He had on jeans, a button up shirt, and boots.

"You're fine. I'm gonna wear jeans."

His phone rang again, "some people don't know how to take a hint."

"Who is it? They're blowing you up!"

"Toya," then he sat up straight with a smile. "I broke up with her right after the wedding. That was a long drive home, she was carrying on like she does, and I told her..." He put his hand up to show me how he was holding the steering wheel while he was talking to her. "Toya! I'm done with this. I'm tired of all your games and nonsense. We both know you're only with me cause you couldn't seem to catch a bigger fish and you were mad that somebody had me. I don't see the point of this anymore. I told her when she got out of my car I was done with her. She tried to argue, but it didn't matter what she said. When we got back to Oakland, I dropped her off at her mom's house she was speechless. She's been calling me, and trying to pop up everywhere ever since. I mean it this time. I've seen the light and her name is Tracy. I've been trying to come up with a manly way to put myself back in her life."

"How sweet!" I pinched his cheek. "Andy is in love!"

"Quit it!" He said blushing.

"I hope she's worth it."

"She is."

Then El walked in the door carrying bags of food and groceries. "How are you doing, I'm El."

"Drew," he said rising to help him with his bags.

They went in the kitchen and I went to my room to give them a moment to size each other up. When I walked in the kitchen they were drinking beers and talking about cars. Andrew asked where El was from and he said the east coast. Then Andrew pointed out his slight accent, and he said his family was British. They moved state side when he was eight. El said his accent gets heavier when he talks to his family. I could tell Andrew liked him when he kept talking to him and he showed his silly side. After we ate, I got dressed, jeans and heels. And we went to Lucy's Lounge. Every once in a while celebrities and athletes descend upon this place. But it was a nice spot to

relax and chill. We were sitting at a table over to the side sipping on our drinks. "So El you like my little cousin."
"You are only four months older than me." I protested
Andrew waved me off. "Yes, we're pretty close." El said
"But there's something, my question is, does she know about it?" Andrew asked
"She knows everything, but what do you mean by something?"
"There's hesitation in your eyes. You're holding back. I don't need to know what it is but she should."
"I know about it Drew!" I rolled my eyes and huffed.
El frowned at me, "why would you act like that with your cousin who's only trying to protect you?"
"Because I can take care of myself!" I said slightly embarrassed.
"Don't do your cousin like that. He could not care about what happens to you. Appreciate the fact that he cares."
"Yeah Sasha!" Andrew smiled, "you heard the man!" Then he and El bumped fist. When I didn't throw attitude or say anything, Andrew touched my forehead like he was feeling for a fever. "El!" He fist bumped him again. "This is the first time a man not related has checked Sasha and she didn't react. I'm telling everybody!"
"Shut up Drew!" I smiled an embarrassed smile.
Andrew was completely relaxed and having a good time even though his phone kept ringing. Finally he picked up the phone. "Toya! I told you to lose my n..." He turned a little red, "what?" He said in a low rumble. His face was angry. "Are you sure?" He hung up the phone swearing at the top of his voice. Then he looked at me, "she just said she's pregnant!"
"Whoa Drew! Is it yours?" I asked
"If she really is then yes. I have proof that she was behaving at least in that regard." Andrew cursed again.
"Let's go back to your place. You can relax and I can get ready for my flight in the morning."
"You don't have to leave." I said to El not wanting him to go.
"I'm gonna be on the phone blowing my brains out anyways." Andrew said sounding defeated.
El paid our bill even though he and Andrew fussed back and forth about who was paying. El drove my car while Andrew sat in the back whining and complaining about Toya. I noticed the sadness El was trying to mask. I asked him if he was ok, he exhaled. "Aaa Drew, I know it's none of my business and from your reaction the situation doesn't sound ideal. Just remember that every child is a blessing and should be celebrated. For

every unplanned pregnancy, there's probably two or three couples asking God why they can't have children. Provided that everything goes well, there's gonna be a piece of you here living on. Cherish your child man, everyone isn't so fortunate."
"You're right! I'll try to find the grateful part. I'm disappointed in myself! I guess I gotta let Tracy go. I've made my bed." Andrew said staring out the window.

When we got to the apartment, Andrew went in JoJo's room and shut the door. I took El into mine, I turned on music, and then I asked him if he was ok. He said yes but I could tell Andrew's experience triggered something in him. I kissed him, he accepted my kiss, but he wasn't enthusiastic about it. "Talk to me" I begged him.

He shook his head, "there are no words." He took a deep breath. "I don't want to spoil your evening."

I kissed him again, "as long as I'm with you it's all good. Talk to me, it's ok."

He shook his head, and then he kissed me instead. I tried to hold out to talk about it. But he put powerhouse kisses on me. My body responded to him even though my mind wanted to help him. When he reached for a condom I knew we weren't talking for a while. In between my eyes crossing, I watched his face. He was sad; I knew he was thinking about his baby. He was trying to serve me, I found the strength to downshift on him and put him on his back. He came slow but hard! He dozed off for a second and then he woke up. I was staring at him. He exhaled and then he talked to me. He said it kills him that Zoila blames herself for everything. She told him one day he was going to get angry and she'd rather leave before she saw it in his eyes. He admitted he was angry about the situation, but he would never be angry with her. She did everything in her power to try to make it happen. She risked her life to give him their daughter, how could he ever be mad at her? He said now that he's not fighting the divorce his mother-in-law calls him regularly to check on him. He poured out his heart to me, and I listened while rubbing his back. Then he thanked me for listening to him and letting him talk it out. "You are so beautiful!" He said stroking my hair. Then he gently kissed ME! Then he made LOVE to ME! Saying my name and looking me in my eyes.

****

"Now Sasha you know I love you." Ava said lacing her words with sugar. "You know I'm not judging you, and I understand." I exhaled, "yes."

119

"You do realize you're sleeping with a married man?"
I sunk in my seat. "I know, but he's not fighting the divorce anymore. We've been counting down the days."
"Ok, I just wanted to keep things real with you." We were quiet for a few minutes. "Let's change the subject. What's happening with the house?"
"My cousin Sharon submitted the plans to the city. Once they're approved, my great uncle's gonna have his company come do the work. They're going to gut everything. Five bedrooms, three and a half bathrooms, three car garage, pool, living room, dining room, huge kitchen, family room! Oh Ava it's going to be beautiful!"
"That's a lot of house for one person."
I blew air, "my momma promises to come visit more since she'll have her own room. With as much as my family comes out here I'll have moments alone actually." I clapped my hands excitedly. "I can't wait!"
I was getting my hair done cause I was on my way to New York. El and I were going to go tour the main offices of Accessed Staffing the company we took over. I was excited to be with El on his turf. He's still holding back, but so am I. Dennis sent me the most beautiful love letter that actually moved me to tears. It was like the old Dennis, the Dennis I fell in love with was pleading with me. I thought about what Andrew said and it gave me chills. The Dennis I fell in love with could've been my husband easy, with no regrets. The heartless monster that felt entitled to sleep with my friend was deserving of death. I put the letter in my nightstand, and then I had a passionate night with El. Ava said it was pointless to straighten my hair anymore. As soon as El and I were together I'd sweat it out.
I called El from the gate and I gave him my flight number. He excitedly told me he couldn't wait to see me. I told him the same then I shut down my phone. "Sasha?"
I turned around to see Lawrence. He looked a lot calmer and happier. "Hi Lawrence!" I said not knowing whether it was safe to hug him or not.
"I wanna introduce you to my fiancée Marika."
Marika was browner than me but light brown, long black hair, and a few freckles. "Nice to meet you. So when's the big day?"
"As soon as the nightmare is over we're going to Vegas. How's Dennis?"
"I've only seen him once since that night."
Lawrence's eyes got big, "really? Why?"

I forgot he left before me. "His shenanigans didn't stop at your wife."

"Oh, I'm sorry to hear that." It was awkward silence for a minute. "Jim still asks about you." He smiled

I chuckled, "I thought I was replaced?"

"Yeah, but when we sat him down to explain everything to him. At first he thought we were saying you were his real mother. He gets it the best a seven year old can understand."

"Lawrence I gotta ask, are you sure there's no way you're the father?"

"Before they told Jim they got DNA test done to be sure. Dennis has a 99.99% chance of being his father where Lawrence only had a 23% chance." Marika said

"I see, you asked for the test?" I asked her.

"Yes, everyone needed closure and no what ifs."

"Right, good thinking. Are you going to New York or connecting?"

"It's been a long day. We're on our way to Florida. What about you?" She said

"Vacation?"

"Yes"

"I've got work, and I'm spinning time with my boyfriend." Marika smiled Lawrence's eyes got big. "I guess the beautiful ones don't stay single."

Marika cut her eyes at him. "What? You haven't been single since junior high school!" She continued to stare at him.

"I'm sorry. Jesus!" He chuckled

"Don't make me cut you!" She said still staring at him.

"I'm sorry, I was out of line." He surrendered.

I fell out laughing, "oh my goodness Lawrence! The difference is like night and day." Lawrence smiled real big.

I told Marika how horrible he acted with Kelsey. I didn't put emphasis on the things he said to me of course, but I told her how he stopped caring. She still huffed and said there was no way she'd let him get away with that.

On the plane Marika and I ended up sitting next to each other so that a mother could sit with her son, while Lawrence sat a row up and over from us. I really liked her; she was down to earth, and way more assertive than Kelsey ever was. No offense to Kelsey, cause I know she loved Lawrence and tried her best to make it work. But! Marika and Lawrence appeared to be a better fit in personality, temperament, even in their sense of humor. Kelsey never got our jokes. She always courtesy laughed, but never cracked up. Plus Kelsey never

really said anything; she let Lawrence walk all over her. But she did have the last laugh by having his brother's child.
I asked how she got a long with Mrs. Barbeau. She huffed and said they didn't get along. She loves Mr. B though.
We talked the entire plane ride; she showed me a picture of her dress for their wedding. Her dress was sexy but simple, she told me about her accessories. She said she's been waiting a long time for this. I asked her how she tolerated Lawrence's marriage. She said it wasn't easy for sure, but she knew he was making a mistake and getting married for all the wrong reasons. She said it took a lot of patience, and the reason he reached out to Lulu was because she wasn't dealing with him anymore, the nonsense had gone on long enough. She asked me if my boyfriend and I were going to get married. I told her it was too new to know, although we've known each other we were still a new couple. Then she asked me if he was the marrying kind. I told her he was, and then I explained that he was at the end of his own divorce. I told her I doubted that he would want to dive right back in. She said a man who has been married is more likely to remarry and right away. Again I thought about Dennis and then it felt like someone turned on the heat. I changed the subject. As we pulled up to the gate Marika told me she liked me and missed me already. I smiled and told her the same.
I waved goodbye to Lawrence and then I made my way to baggage claim where El was happily waiting for me. He gave me a big kiss hello and then we got my bags. He asked me if I was hungry and I told him I wasn't. Just as I realized how quiet I was being he asked me what was wrong. I didn't know how to explain what I felt without coming off like a jerk. So I said I was tired from the flight. He said we needed to go to bed early because we had to get up early and drive an hour upstate to Access's processing center. That was fine with me cause I didn't feel much like talking.
I checked into my hotel as planned. Whenever either of us came out we checked-in even if we didn't sleep at the hotel otherwise it would raise questions. Tonight however, we were staying in my hotel though. El watched my face at first, he didn't say anything, then he got angry. I didn't understand his mood change so I threw an attitude right back. We went to bed pissy but that didn't stop him from putting his arm around me, and his hand between my breasts as he fell asleep. In the morning I was still funky but a lot of that had to do with the time difference. About fifteen minutes into the drive El turned

off the radio. "What is it Sasha?" I opened my mouth to say nothing, but he cut me off. "And before you open your mouth to say nothing or something about being tired let me stop you from lying to me and really pissing me off. I know your face. Whatever it is, it has something to do with Dennis. Dennis is written all over you. If you don't want to talk about it fine! But don't ask me to share with you, if you can't do the same!" He growled.

I sat there feeling dumb, so I dumped everything. How I met Marika, how different Lawrence was with her, I was truly amazed. El listened patiently and quietly. Then I told him how seeing them made me reminisce. Then I told him about the letter I got from Dennis and what Andrew told me. He looked like he was taking it all in. Then he asked what I wanted to do. I shrugged cause I didn't know. I told him my father would have a cow if he thought I felt anything other than disgust for Dennis. That made him even quieter. I didn't know how he was internalizing any of this. If I was explaining it right or what, so I rambled for a minute trying to explain more. Sensing my nervousness he patted my hand to calm me and then we rode in silence. When we walked in the door to the lobby, Bruce, of all people was there. His expression told me to be cool. I said hello to the receptionist and she said the rest of our party was inside and Bruce followed us. She took us to a conference room and another guy I didn't recognize was there. As soon as the receptionist left, the big guy said that we were all clear to Malcolm who was on the phone. Malcolm introduced Bruce, and Kirk. He said they were Mitigated staff as well and they were going to accompany us on the tour of the facility today. I looked at El; he looked like he was trying to get a read on Bruce and Kirk. If Malcolm sent Special Services out here something had to be up. Malcolm told us to get acquainted and that he wanted a full report at the end of the day. When Malcolm hung up, Bruce gave me a hug and shook El's hand. I had never met Kirk before so I introduced myself and El did the same. El asked what division they were from. Bruce told him he was with the Acquisitions & Special Services team. When he put it that way it didn't sound so bad. El nodded in agreement and threw in that they reported up to Richard. Kirk said exactly. We chatted a little longer and a couple of guys came to the conference room, I guess they run the facility. Moss and Farmer, then Farmer said, "look Moss it's three guys and a little lady." He started cracking up while Moss watched our reaction. All of us stood there looking at him like he was

an idiot. Farmer didn't care he was a jerk and that was final.
Moss was a jerk as well, but at least he was quieter about it. I
did most of the talking, Farmer tried to hint at weakness within
Mitigated because a woman was doing most of the talking. I
told him we were strong enough to take over, so if there was
any weakness to be had, I blamed Access for hiring those two
clowns. I advised Farmer to stick to the tour and to keep his
side comments to himself. I glanced at my men and they were
smirking. I noticed that Bruce and Kirk were very touchy
feely. They touched everything the clowns showed us.
Although I could've had a V8, instead the clowns took us out
to lunch. I guess they thought they would talk above our heads
as if we wouldn't notice.
"How long have you been with Mitigated?" Farmer asked El.
"Almost three years." El said matter of factly.
"Do you have a degree in anything, or are you guys the visual
muscle behind the little lady?"
I started to say something and El touched my hand like
Andrew, Derrick, or JoJo would. "I wasn't under the
impression that I was interviewing today." Farmer chuckled.
"Instead of these childish and thinly veiled stabs at your
bosses, you might wanna start asking yourself, or each other,
whichever works best for you; whether you'll have a job this
time next week based solely on your performance today."
Farmer didn't laugh for the first time. "As far as I can see this
place is a lawsuit waiting to happen. If this is the way you
conduct yourself with your superiors I can only imagine the
hostile environment you provide for the staff here."
Farmer blew air, "you're not my superior!"
"Oh yes! I'm the Head Nigga In Charge! You report up to me!
And quite frankly I know someone else could come in here and
do a far better job." Farmer and Moss sat there changing
colors, you could tell their dumb behinds didn't consider that
we were their bosses. I wanted to jump on El right then and
there. I crossed my legs and tried to calm the butterflies that
were dancing in my stomach. "Now! Let's play your game,
how long have you been with Access? Is this the only position
you've held with the company? Moss you go first because
Farmer needs a minute to pull his foot out of his mouth." Then
El took out his notepad and pen and jotted down their
comments. Kirk and Bruce smiled at El. As Moss was talking,
Bruce and Kirk interjected comments and questions. I sat back
quietly and enjoyed watching them squirm.

When we got back to the office, Farmer excused himself and we knew it was to go look at the Mitigated employee catalog to verify our claims of authority. Bruce got a text message; he smiled and showed it to Kirk. When Farmer came back he had somewhat of a permanent red tan it appeared. Moss turned red when he saw his expression. When they finished showing us around, El told them bluntly that he didn't understand the purpose of their facility. He said it was a processing center an hour away from all of their offices. They squirmed trying to explain what they had already said. El let them finish and then he restated his point. Then he pointed out the areas that he wanted to see that were not covered in our tour. They were trying to explain to him why they couldn't show them. El wasn't letting them slide or wiggle their way out of it. He told them we weren't leaving until we saw them. When they stood there deadlocked in a staring match El took out his phone and called Malcolm. He explained the situation. Then Malcolm had him put him on speakerphone. "Who do you boys report to?" Malcolm's voice boomed through the phone.

"Phineas Cobbs," Farmer said like he just gave the biggest name ever.

"Go to the conference room and await further instruction!" He said

"Uh! No disrespect, but who are you?" Moss said as smart as he could.

"This is Malcolm Latour!"

"And you are?" Farmer said

I could feel Malcolm's glare through the phone. "Go to the conference room and you will find out!" Then Malcolm hung up the phone.

Farmer rolled his eyes and told us to come on. "I mean really, I don't care how important you think you are, you don't have clearance to access those rooms. I don't understand why that's so hard for you people to understand!"

"What do you mean by you people?" I put my hand on my hip.

"Mitigated people. Your friend would have to be God himself to give clearance!" Moss said

"Prepare to meet our Father!" Kirk said as we walked into the room.

Then the receptionist came in the room. She was moving fast with nervous energy, she told Moss and Farmer that the last of the staff had gone home for the day. She set up the camera and the projector. Then she connected the phone line. We were looking at the projection of ourselves until the line rang. Moss answered the call, and Malcolm and Juan came up on the screen. Both of the guys jumped when they saw Malcolm, a big black guy and Juan, a Mexican. Malcolm didn't speak, but he glared at Farmer and Moss. We waited five minutes in silence then the second line on the phone rang, Moss pressed the button and a conference room, full of Access staff as they filled in, came up. "This is Phineas Cobbs who do we have on from Access in your location?" A very poised older white gentleman said.

"Mr. Cobbs sir, my name is Frederick Farmer, and this is Robert Moss."

"Is the San Francisco office on the line?" Cobbs said

"Yes they're on the other line."

"Great, conference us in." Cobbs said. Moss hit the conference button and there were now two screens side by side. "This is Phineas Cobbs."

"This is Juan Ramirez"

"And I'm Malcolm Latour!"

"Mr. Latour, it is nice to finally meet you. I look forward to meeting you in person." Cobbs said, the woman next to him very nervously handed him papers. "We weren't aware that you would need a thorough tour of the facilities today. Otherwise we would've prepared high security clearance for your employees. Unfortunately…."

"Let me stop you right there!" Malcolm said taking control of the situation. "Unless you're opening your mouth to tell me that your boys over there are opening the doors for my team, I don't want to hear it!" Cobbs was visibly upset. "I want access to everything now!"

"But Mr. Cobbs, Bill has gone home for the day." Farmer said

"Bill?" Malcolm said folding his hands

"The security guard who processes the clearance to access the rooms. Mr. Latour we have a process in order, if you would've discussed your plan with me prior to now we could've had everything set up for your team when they arrived. Unfortunately, we cannot allow your team access at this time."

Malcolm looked at Juan, Juan chuckled. "Ok so it appears you don't understand. We're going in and we're going in now. Kirk do what you have to do! Phineas if I were you, I'd tell your folks to stay out of the way."

Kirk stood up, "YOU CAN'T DO THIS!" Cobbs shouted while he was visibly upset.

"I own this company! If there's anything illegal happening, I need to know about it. Sit down and shut up! It's happening." Malcolm said waiting for results. We heard two pops of gunfire. Farmer and Moss hit the floor, El looked at me like he didn't understand everything that was happening, but he was reading me at the same time. "Bruce, that's one door, go sweep the room! Sasha and Eldridge stay put!" I nodded. We heard more gunfire. The receptionist came running in the room.

"Who's that?" Malcolm asked.

"The receptionist," I said nonchalantly

"Have a seat!" Juan said

Everyone in the Access conference room looked horrified but like they couldn't turn their eyes away. "What's going on? Why is he shooting?" The receptionist said hysterically.

"Ruth, have a seat. Everything's going to be ok." One of the women from the conference room said.

"Malcolm all the doors are open." Kirk said standing in the doorway.

"Good, Sasha and Eldridge go collect data." Malcolm commanded.

I stood up, "Mr. Latour the police are on their way. Your team will be arrested." Cobbs said still looking distraught.

Malcolm waved his hand, he picked up his phone. "This is Malcolm Latour." Then he waited, "how are you today? Yes, it appears that I'm having a bit of a problem with my employees… Yes my team is there already… That would be the alarm trigger you're seeing right now…" He looked at the camera, "he did! You don't say… Well, my team is going to go over everything first and then we'll get back to you… I will keep you posted! Thanks again…" Malcolm laughed, "there are a lot of nice golf courses out here, but I can come and visit your grounds the next time I'm in town. Ok now… Oh and don't forget to give Phineas Cobbs a call for me when we hang up, apparently he needs someone else to tell him who I am… Alright now! Alright!" Malcolm hung up the phone then he glared at the screen. Cobbs turned red and then his face flushed as he answered his phone. When El and I got to the doorway, Yussef was walking in the conference room with Malcolm with a laptop that he was connecting, and Cobbs plopped into his seat with his phone on his ear. When we walked out of the room, El was watching my face, but he wasn't saying anything. In each of the three rooms there were computers and file cabinets. Bruce brought the computers up and then he kept touching everything like he had done during our tour. I realized there was a certain way he was touching everything. When I looked closer I realized he was placing bugs everywhere. Bruce was talking into his earpiece and reading information from the computer screens. That's when I realized he was talking to someone, I wondered if he was talking to Malcolm. I wouldn't doubt that he was talking to either him or Juan or Yussef. Once he said complete, the computer would shut down like he turned the switch off or something. I asked for boxes, and I placed report folders that looked interesting for whatever reason in them in order by date. When I went back in the room, Yussef was clicking away on his computer. He would turn his screen to Malcolm every so often to show him something. Kirk and Bruce stood over Farmer and Moss who now looked like scared little girls shaking in their boots. Malcolm asked us if we had everything that looked interesting. And when we said yes he told Ruth to print shipping labels for the boxes. Bruce left and came back with packing tape. He just about laminated each box with tape to secure their closure, and then he stacked the boxes on a cart. Malcolm told us we were done, and to follow Bruce and Kirk out of the office. Then he turned his attention to Phineas Cobbs, he told him that the security guard could arrange to have the doors repaired or whatever they needed to do. He told him this will never happen again! If he sends staff, whether Phineas cleared it or not he needed to know everything that was happening within this company. He said this site stands out as a liability and this little situation right here has called more questions to mind regarding the true ethics of this company. Then he told Phineas to never deny him again or there would be consequences worse than today. When we walked out of the door two guys in a van were out front. Kirk took pictures of their badges and when he received confirmation that they were valid Mitigated Staff they loaded up the boxes. New shipping labels were placed on the boxes. Kirk sent information about each box to Malcolm directly. Kirk told Malcolm he should have the boxes by tomorrow afternoon.

Then I waved goodbye to Bruce and Kirk as they got in their car. El was quiet the whole way back to the city. When we pulled into his garage, he parked and then he turned to face me. He asked me why I wasn't scared back there. I frowned, and then I asked him what was there to be scared about? He asked me why the guns didn't scare me. I told him I grew up in Oakland; guns were a part of everyday life out there. He asked why I wasn't alarmed that Bruce and Kirk had them, he said it was as if I expected that they had them. I shrugged; I really didn't know what to tell him. I told him that situation was unlike any situation I've ever dealt with in my professional career, but it didn't surprise me that Malcolm was prepare for anything to happen. When that didn't satisfy him I told him my Poppa taught Tanisha and I how to shoot, while my cousin Malachi, and sometimes my Uncle Tim taught the boys. All the boys started carrying guns around the age of thirteen, it was never a big deal. I told him I'm used to guns and I have a few of my own at home. His eyes got big, when he said, "you do, why?" I laughed and told him I did, and that I knew how to use them too. I told him I live alone for the most part, it made everyone more comfortable knowing that I could handle anything that came up if I needed to. El said he wasn't expecting the guns, he thought big ole Kirk was gonna knock the doors down by ramming into them. I told him Kirk was using his thinking cap, why possibly hurt himself when he could shoot it. That made El smile. I stroked his face, and then I told him watching him check those punks made me so horny. He laughed and said he could tell, and then I asked him why he didn't want me to get after them? He said he liked the way I handled myself with them, but when it became time to check them as I called it, that needed a man's touch. Then he kissed me and thanked me for letting him handle it. Again I felt bad cause I thought about Dennis and how I never let him handle things. Then he called me on it. "See! You just thought about Dennis!"

I exhaled, "he said we weren't together because I wouldn't let him handle things. I would always tell him I wasn't just a decoration. I told him I wouldn't sit by idly when I could help. And then today with your non-verbal queue to let you handle it, I quietly sat back and watched you handle those fools. Why does that make me feel guilty?" I asked him.

El said that we should go up. He got my bag out the trunk and then we went up to his apartment, he called a Chinese take out place that delivers. Then we sat on the couch. "Don't beat yourself up about that. I tend to be able to say the things to you that I couldn't find the words to express to Zoila until it was too late cause we were in a fight by then." He remembered something and he smiled, "I gotta show you something, but it's a surprise." He said smiling really big. I smiled big, closed my eyes, and put my hands out. He dropped paper in my hands, "ok now open them!"

It was a white envelope that had been opened. I opened the letter and it was a court-recorded dissolution of marriage document. "Does this mean?"

"Yes, I'm divorced!" He said with a tortured smile.

"Are you ok?"

"It came yesterday. I'm free!" He faked excitement.

"That wasn't an answer."

"I didn't get married to end up divorced." He swallowed, "nothing about being single again feels right."

"You're not single!"

"Yes, but you're not my wife."

"But I'm here El." I said

"I'm not saying this right." He said, "you were right, there's no point in fighting for someone who wants to leave. Besides that night at the club." Pain appeared in his eyes, "she assured me she didn't love me, and she didn't want me. I told her that was just her pain talking, but she went on and on about how much she didn't love me and she needed me to let her go. Then she told me she met someone and there was no point in me fighting for something that would never be, ever again." I grabbed his hands, "why didn't you tell me?"

He looked at me, "I just did."

****

"Taste my sauce," I said holding a spoon up to El's mouth. He tasted my sauce and then he rolled his eyes in his head.

"That is SO GOOD!"

"Thank you," I said kissing his cheek.

I was cooking in his kitchen in my bra, panties, and apron. El was in his boxers, it was a lazy Saturday. Early morning sex, mid-morning make out session, afternoon make out session, pre-dinner foreplay, I was making dinner and then for dessert, ME! I poured my sauce over the chicken, covered it with mozzarella, and then I stuck it in the oven. El sat me on the counter he held my face and he kissed me. We were in the middle of kissing when his intercom buzzed. The doorman was on the monitor, "Hello Mr. Parsons, your mother Ester Parsons is here to see you, and she says your father will be following shortly. Shall I send her up?"

El's eyes were big, "yes of course. And for future reference my parents do not need authorization, send them up."

"Yes sir," the doorman said.

We ran to his room and threw clothes on. I put my sweats and T-shirt on. I asked him very nervously if I looked ok. I personally would've preferred that I was dressed up and wearing something fabulous the first time I met his mother. It was going to take too long to get dressed according to my standards of first impression. And I had no idea of how that would be received. There was a knock at the door a lot sooner than I wanted it to happen. I grabbed my wild hair and smoothed it as much as I could into a ponytail. I exhaled, no matter what his mother was going to know I've been in here screwing her son all day. I exhaled again and prepared myself for this woman to hate me. I stood in the hallway while El opened the door. He smiled really big.

"Mum!" Instantly his accent was there and heavy.

"Eldridge baby!" I saw her arms wrap around his neck. "It smells delicious in here. Did you suddenly learn how to cook?"

"Come in, come in." He told his momma as he reached out for me to come over. My heart was pounding I was scared. "I want you to meet Sasha."

"Sasha's here? Why didn't you tell me?" She said sounding surprised.

I loved the sound of my name on her lips, and the fact that this moment was not the first time she was hearing about me.

"Hello Mrs. Parsons, it's nice to finely meet you."

She opened her mouth real wide, "Eldridge she's even prettier than you said. Hello sweetheart. Wait until your dad sees her!" Then she hugged me. I felt like I wanted to cry, El noticed my face. I knew he was going to ask me about it later.

When Mr. Parsons walked in the door he was not what I expected to see. He was a lot shorter than El, and... well... He looked nothing like him. El looked a lot like his momma. His parents were working class people and they were great! Fortunately, I was making enough food for leftovers the next day so we had enough for everyone. Mrs. Parsons was very loving with her son. She asked him how he's been doing, and if he was sleeping well. He told her he's been doing better, and he sleeps well whenever I'm with him. With love in her eyes for her son she thanked me for being here for him. I told her I should be thanking her for raising such a wonderful man. Mr. Parsons and El watched us with the biggest smiles while we discussed El like he wasn't sitting there. Mrs. Parsons asked me if I met her daughter Brielis yet. She said we had to meet, and then she gave me her number. She told me to call her and let her know the next time I was coming out so we could plan for me to meet their family. I looked at El and he was watching me for a reaction, and I couldn't read his. When we finished eating we continued to sit at his table and talk for hours. Mr.

Parsons is funny and you could tell he's really proud of his son. Mr. Parsons doesn't have an accent; there was definitely a story.

When his parents left after two in the morning we kept staring at each other. He was trying to read me, and I him. He hadn't mentioned anything about me meeting his family yet. So I didn't know how he truly felt about the evening. I stripped down to nothing and climbed in the bed. El kissed me deeply then he asked me why I held pain on my face all evening. He said his parents didn't notice. I asked him what his read was on his mother's reaction to me. He told me she loved me, which made tears come to my eyes. He asked me why I was always prepared for people not to like me? I told him it was what I was used to. I hated thinking a person would give me a chance like anyone else when I knew better. Everybody isn't always going to like you, and sometimes they didn't need a reason. So I chose to blame it on the fact that I'm pretty. At least I could understand it in that regards. El smiled then he said I should try to think more of people. Some people know how to look at the person and not get caught up in their appearance, so much that they can't see who the person is.

****

"Sassy..." He adjusted in his seat like he was trying to find the words. I waited for him to get there. "I'm happy for you, the house sounds amazing. But why didn't the thought cross your mind to include me in the process? I might've wanted to help."

I smiled, "Richard you wanna pay for something?"

"Yes! I'm your father and I can pitch in. And while I have your ear, why hasn't El said anything to me?"

I swallowed, "that's my fault. I haven't mentioned that you're the father that I talk about."

Richard's eyes looked angry, "why?"

"I don't know honestly. Outside of Dennis I haven't introduced you to anyone I've dated."

Richard thought about it, "true. But let's start something new."

"Like what?"

"Let's start with how we talk to each other. You talk to me the way you want me to talk to you."

"Ok," I said with my eyes dancing around the room.

"I know things have been less than ideal between us in the past. But I've been trying to be better."

I smiled, "I've noticed."

He smiled, "so I would like a fatherly invite to be properly introduced to your boyfriend."

I smiled, "ok." I couldn't put my finger on why his request tickled me, but it did. I wondered how El would respond to knowing that Richard was my father. I wondered if he'd feel like I was holding back or something.

Then he cleared his throat, "now about your house. I don't appreciate being an afterthought but what's left?"

"My Poppa is paying for the remodel. But there's still the landscaping and then furnishing the house. Pick your poison." I smiled

"Either way, I can see that I'm gonna be broke." He smiled

"You better believe it! I want a salt-water pool instead of the typical chlorine pool. I want a circular driveway, and a fountain in the center."

"Security on the premises?"

I frowned, "why would I need security?"

"Your family gonna come out from time to time?"

"You know they are. My momma said she'll come out more often now that she will have her own room."

He frowned at me; I could tell he was trying to move past the comment. He sat back in his chair, he blew out air. "Anyways! I'm gonna let that go. If your family comes, especially Uncle Frank for example, you'll need security on the premises. I guess I'll take care of the landscaping. How do you feel about puppies?"

I huffed, "Richard I travel a lot. I don't have time to care for dogs."

"I'm not talking about flea market dogs. I'm talking about dogs from Uncle Frank. The more I think about it the better it sounds."

"Oh yeah, if it sounds so good why don't you have any?" I snapped

He cut his eyes at me, "listen here little girl you should know better than anybody you can't see with your eyes." He stood up and walked to his sliding door. He tapped on his window, first one BIG dog appeared, and slowly three more appeared. He commanded them to sit, and they did. He opened the door and he told the big one to come say hi to me. The dog approached me with caution like he was reading me. I told him to sit when he got to my seat, I let him smell me, and then I petted him.

"That's Bruno." Richard said. Then he told the other dogs to come to me. They came and sat as well. I petted each dog, and then I told them to relax and immediately I had four puppies that were loving me up. Ok, ok. I wanted a puppy of my own now. Richard closed the screen, and then he told me that the dogs came from Uncle Frank's and they were fully trained. I started to tell him that I wanted the dogs but I got a text from El. He told me to go to the computer and look up the news for channel KWIK in New York. I told Richard and we went to his computer. The top news out there was the fire at the Access building we toured. The news said there was a raging fire. The reporter interviewed an employee who said that the fire started in one of the high security rooms. They thought they smelled smoke, but were told to get back to work. He said it wasn't until they saw black smoke coming from underneath a few doors that they evacuated the office. At this point the reporter said a few people were unaccounted for, and the local fire department was trying to get the fire under control. Then they showed violent flames pouring out of every opening in the building. Richard said a simple "Oh," when he saw the news. He explained that some major illegal activities were happening at that location. Richard said that fire was clearing the deck. I asked him how Malcolm knew about it, and he said when it was announced that Mitigated bought Access the chief of police in that city reached out to Malcolm. Malcolm told Richard that the chief was assuring him that they had his office covered and that everything would be business as usual. Malcolm said the staff in the know about his location wanted to buy it back from Malcolm, however Malcolm felt that was a set up. So after he got confirmation from the paperwork we sent and Yussef's review of all their internal information. Malcolm told Richard he was dismantling this office, and sending a message to those who thought he would roll over and take the fall for their illegal activities.

****

"Why do you need such a large mirror?" My momma said
"I like the idea of this mirror in the hallway. It will make everything seem bigger and create the idea of more open space." I said
"This mirror, this vase, this chaise lounge chair." Shasta was touching every piece in this furniture store that I wanted, and making arrangements to have them delivered and set up.
"I love this part!" Amber said clapping excitedly, and then she looked at her watch. "We got an hour before we need to get to the airport."
I looked at Amber, "you are more excited about this than I thought you'd be."
She shrugged, "it's done. I gotta make the best of it."

We were flying back to The Bay this morning for Toya's baby shower. "I can't believe you're going to be a Nana," my momma said to her

"Me neither! I'm not old enough to be a Nana. But that's not up to me, so here we are." Amber said

"What does Malcolm say about the baby?" My momma asked. "Nothing." Amber said walking away. She was annoyed and done with the direction of the conversation.

But my momma wasn't letting it go. "You guys still at odds?" Amber bucked her eyes at my momma like she wanted her to let it go. "Yes!"

"Amber!"

"Sophia!"

"Sasha!" I said trying to lighten the mood.

They smiled, "Sophia he broke my heart! I'm not over it! My therapist says I need space, so I'm doing that."

My momma exhaled, and then she turned her attention to me. "Guess who came by the restaurant the other day?" I frowned I had no idea. "Your buddy Hunter."

"Ooh!" I squealed clapping my hands together. "Please tell me he gave you his number?" She pulled out her phone, and then she gave me his number. "I can't believe you were out here for two days and you tell me this now."

I stepped out of the store and I called my good friend Hunter. In high school people always thought we were dating, but we were only ever good friends. He was my first friend when I moved out to the Concord and Walnut Creek area. And all throughout college we kept in contact, went on trips together, everything. Hunter sounded very excited to hear from me. He was starting to wonder if I was going to call him. I told him my momma just gave me his number a few minutes ago. Then I told him I was on my way out there for a baby shower and then I could swing by wherever he was and we could go get a drink and get caught up. He told me I was on and he wanted me to call him when I was ready. I was so excited to see my friend I couldn't wait to tell him about El, and my new house. All new beginnings for me.

When we got to the apartment complex we followed the balloons to the recreation room. There were single "it's a boy" balloons outside, but ok fine why waste the balloons for outside right? When we walked in the door the recreation room was really small. I expected to see balloons, flowers, and baby decorations. You know a baby shower theme. There was one more balloon just inside the door, and that was it for decorations. I can count on one hand how many females were there. They looked us up and down when we walked in. A girl said an unenthusiastic hello and didn't wait for our response. I was ready to go as soon as I walked in the door. Amber put her gift basket on the gift table next to the other two gifts, and my momma and I put our gift bags there as well. I heard one of the girls ask another girl who we were as we took seats at the table. When the girl said Drew's family, the first girl said she didn't know he was white. Then the second girl said we were probably all cousins. As I rolled my eyes, I looked at my momma and Amber and they were doing the same thing. Everyone was sitting around waiting for Toya to show up. A woman came in the door with a foil tin pan. She said a happy hello to everyone and then she went in the kitchen. Everyone followed her, and opened the pan as soon as she sat it down. It was full of chicken wings and everyone was piling as many as they could on their plates and then sitting down. We stayed frozen in our seats. I kept saying ghetto! The woman went back out and she came back with a Pyrex dish full of cupcakes. Again they swarmed. The woman came over and introduced herself as Patty she said she was Toya's auntie, and then she asked who we were. Patty was trying to be nice, but you could tell she had that same ghetto twang like the rest of her people. When Amber said she was Andrew's mother, Patty made a big deal about it. She said she would've never guessed that Amber was Drew's mother. We didn't play any games and the music was too loud and ridiculous. We might as well had been at someone's house for all of this nonsense. Toya finally showed up an hour late. Her face was a little full, but she was really all stomach. Her chocolate skin was glowing and her hair looked like she had gotten it freshly done. Toya was pretty and you thought so until you got to know her, and then she was completely YUCK! She said hi to everyone then she came over and put her stomach in my face. "Hi Sasha!"

"Hello," after all it was her baby shower.

Everyone was looking at us. "You got any kids yet?"

"No, not yet." I said shaking my head.

"What's wrong with you? What are you waiting for?" A couple of the girls snickered.

"Nothing's wrong with me. I know better than to be stupid enough to think that a baby guarantees me a man." Then I smiled, "but I'm sure you've learned that lesson by now."

"No she didn't!" One girl said.

Toya rolled her eyes and walked to the gift table. "Oh you guys! Everything looks so nice!"

I frowned at my momma and Amber. Amber looked like she was ready to go. Toya moved Amber's basket around like she was looking for more than the baby trinkets inside. Amber's basket was full of stuff she would need, but no big-ticket items. Toya sucked her teeth like she wasn't impressed. She opened my gift bag; I had the baby's first photo album with the silver plated label that could be engraved with the baby's information on the front. There was a gift certificate in the bag for the engraving. My momma bought the baby an outfit, but honestly none of us were breaking the bank on anything that Toya was going to keep. The baby's nursery at Amber's house was decked out though. And I spent over four hundred on the stuff I bought for his room. Everything there was state of the art and nice, but for her shower we were doing good just to be here. I mean I flew out here for crying out loud. When Toya frowned at our gifts without saying a word we stood up and walked out. I called Drew and I went off, then I put him on speakerphone and he had to listen to the three of us go off about how tacky and whack Toya's shower was. I told him you could tell they threw that sorry excuse for a shower together thinking we would come through with big ticket items. She probably would've sold it anyways cause we all knew Drew was going to furnish her nursery. Andrew thanked us for going and he said he was sorry it was such a waste of time. I told him I would catch up with him later.

My momma and Amber were now hungry and wanted to know where Hunter and I were going to eat and if they could tag along. I called Hunter and he asked us to meet him at the bar in Claim Jumpers in Concord. Hunter had a table in the bar area for us. I got so excited when I saw him, we hugged. He said I was still beautiful! My momma was so happy to see him too, he remembered Amber, but she didn't remember him. The four of us sat and Hunter and I reminisced about high school and even some of the trips we took once we were in college. When he mentioned Dennis, I flinched. He saw me flinch, and then he smiled. "Guess who reached out to me recently?" Hunter said raising his eyebrows. I sat there in disbelief as I waited for him to spill it. Grinning from ear to ear Hunter explained that Dennis came to his job and made plans to have lunch with him. He said Dennis poured his heart out and said that he was at his whit's end and he didn't know what to do. I told Hunter there was nothing Dennis could do, he hurt me beyond

comprehension. I told him he needs to encourage Dennis to move on and to never hurt the next one like he hurt me. "Come on Sasha! I was there; I know how much you love that man. I know what he did was wrong, but he regrets it like you wouldn't believe. What could he do to win you back?"
I frowned, "how much is he paying you?"
Hunter smiled really big, "A LOT!" we laughed. "I got so much to have this conversation with you. I get a bonus if I can convince you to meet up with him."
"At least he's honest." Amber said
"Sorry Hunter, I've got a man!"
"Nobody replaces Dennis though. I know how much you love him."
"Loved!"
"So who's the new guy?"
"Hunter, you're working for the enemy. Let's talk when you're not on the clock. And it's a shame I had so much to share with you."
He smiled, "I have news." He took a deep breath, "I'm getting married."
I screamed, "CONGRATULATIONS! Who is she? When are you getting married? Where are you getting married? Give me details!" I said bouncing in my chair until I saw his eyes glance at my bouncing breast.
"Her name is Lisa. We just got engaged a month ago. We're shooting for next year. You know you're in the wedding right?"
I clapped my hands, "really? I'm honored." I said excited.
"Wait a minute!" My momma said putting her hands out.
"How are you gonna invite Sasha into your wife's bridal party? They've never met, what if they hate each other?"
"Trust me, they're going to get a long really well. Lisa knows all about Sasha, she's the one who suggested it."
My momma and Amber exchanged looks. "And the whole time you're going to be talking up Dennis right?" My momma said
"Hunter I don't care how much money he pays you, your loyalty should be to me. Can I trust you?"
His eyes bounced around, then he said yes.
****
"If we follow this schedule the Mitigated brand should be up and going in these offices by end of quarter." Stacy said
Henry raised his hand, "but from a year end budget perspective I think your plan is too aggressive."

I smiled at Henry for asserting himself. Stacy shot Henry daggers; "if we cut a few corners we can make it within budget."

"Really? Like what?" I asked

Stacy exhaled then she wrote on the whiteboard. Then Henry spoke up again, telling her that she was cutting funding for needed operating cost. I told Stacy that her plan looked very good on paper, but there were too many risks involved to move at her suggested pace. Stacy was beyond frustrated, and it wasn't necessary to be that upset. I could tell she was pent up and needed to get some. I laughed to myself. El told her to come back to the table so we could start over from scratch. Stacy was angry but she sat down. During the course of our meeting Stacy kept looking at El. He paid her no attention other than he had to. When I saw her look at Henry I knew she was desperate. But I thought about how good this could be for Henry. I looked at the time; I leaned over and asked El if he wanted to break for lunch. He studied my face for a minute then he reluctantly agreed. I asked if there was any place nearby that delivered or that we could go to for lunch. She said she'd have the receptionist order pizzas. Not what I was thinking, but ok. I told her to order enough for the entire office. Stacy moves too fast, she's very optimistic but a little reckless. Henry moves slow and is very cautious; I could see them balancing each other out. As long as Stacy was willing to upgrade him. When the pizzas came I pushed back from the table. I got everyone to chat, Stacy and Henry shared that they were single. Stacy looked at Henry again especially when El said he was not single. After work I asked Stacy to pick out a restaurant for dinner since we didn't know our way around Seattle. As we walked into the restaurant I walked behind El and I kept grabbing his butt. I was having my own fun; he shot me a look that said cut it out. I knew I was playing with fire, but I hadn't seen him in two weeks I was dying. Thomas told us he and his wife come to this restaurant all the time. So he gave us personal pointers on what to order. Stacy asked Henry if he's ever had oysters. He said a nonchalant yes. She ordered oysters and we ordered drinks. Stacy started flirting once the drinks came, and Henry's goofy behind wasn't picking up on the fact that Stacy was throwing herself at him. I asked El to help him out with my eyes and El shook his head no. Thankfully Thomas went to the bathroom behind Henry. I hoped he told him something.

"So mister El you have a girlfriend... Is she pretty?" Stacy asked

"Some people think so." He said

"What do you think?"

"What do you think pretty is?"

Stacy shook her head, she was tipsy. "Me!" Then she laughed. El debated whether to continue or not. "What makes you pretty?"

"Look at me! I'm pretty!" She said laughing.

"My girlfriend is very appealing visibly. But her appearance is not why I think she's pretty." I sat there listening like he wasn't talking about me, it was cute. "She's powerful, and very kind hearted."

Stacy looked at him as she tried to take the irritated look off her face. "She sounds ugly!" The words spilled out of her mouth. She slapped her mouth when she realized she said it out loud.

We laughed, "she does, doesn't she!" I chimed in.

"I'm sorry El!"

"Don't worry about it, as long as I'm happy with her it doesn't matter."

Henry came back from the bathroom dandruff falling, and feeling his drinks. Stacy didn't seem to notice, which was nice. Henry was not used to female attention for sure. He blushed a lot and he was awkward. It was almost sweet. When we finished dinner Stacy told Henry she wanted to take him to a place to hear music. She didn't invite the rest of us. I was happy she didn't, I wanted to get El in the room. Thomas walked with us to the parking lot cause Stacy and Henry were long gone. We chatted with Thomas for a while then we got in the rental car. We laughed back to the hotel about Stacy and Henry. I wanted to kiss him, but just because I did that someone would see us. So I went to my room and impatiently waited for him to come. He barely made it in the door before I was all over him.

"I missed you!" I said touching his face.

"I see! You were trying to give me a heart attack!" Then he chuckled, "my mum wants to know when you're coming back."

"Your mum," I giggled. "If I'm coming before the weekend we have to have a business need for me to come out. I still have to report to Malcolm my comings and goings." I exhaled, "do you think we'll still be together when this acquisition is all said and done?"

El frowned, "why wouldn't we be?"

I shrugged, "I was just asking cause I can see the distance taking its toll on us when it's all said and done."

"We can make it work."

"My father wants to have dinner with you the next time you're in town."

"Good, I was going to ask to meet him next trip out."

Then I remembered Hunter. "Oh baby, I saw my old friend from high school. He's getting married and he wants me to be in his wedding."

"That's nice."

I laughed, "Dennis paid him to tell me he wants me back."

El's head popped up, "what?" I repeated myself. "What kind of friend is that?"

"Hunter is a good guy, but I'm sure he needed the money especially with a wedding coming up. I'm not mad at him for taking the money. And he told me about it."

"Has he sent you anymore letters?"

"Why are you asking about the letter?" I said sitting up.

"I saw it, I was putting condoms in your drawer when I came across it. Why didn't you mention you kept it?" His eyes searched my face.

"Do you tell me everything that happens with Zoila?"

"The things worth telling you."

"Worth telling me? Ok so fine, I tell you the things worth telling you."

"Why did you keep the letter?"

"Cause I thought it was beautiful! You have a whole storage unit and house that you refuse to let go of because of her but you're questioning my letter?"

"This wedding is an excuse for you to get back with Dennis."

"How is someone else's wedding an excuse for me?"

"Sounds like Dennis is going to be there. You gonna get drunk so you can use liquor as the reason?"

"El," I searched his eyes. "You slept with Zoila?"

He didn't expect me to ask him. "No!"

"Then what?" I said with my eyes on his.

"What are we doing?"

I frowned, "it hasn't been a year. Why do we have to define us already?"

"I need to know if we're only helping each other through our rough patches or if we have a future. Zoila called me crying the other night. The way I thought I'd feel isn't how I felt at all."

"Why didn't you call me?"

"How can I tell you how I feel if I don't know?"

"Feel?" I tried to check myself, but this conversation was taking my good feeling away.

"You know what I mean."

"Maybe I don't. You're jealous about my ex, should I be jealous about yours?" I asked

"Jealous?" I stared at El. He made an exhausted sound. "I don't know Sasha! I'm not a jealous person, but your refusal to deal with your Dennis issues makes me feel...." He looked for words, "vulnerable. Your heart is still with him."

"And yours is still with her!"

"So......... Is this what we're gonna do? Exist on pause with each other? Cause that's not what I want."

"What do you want?"

"What do you want?" He asked me back.

"Eventually I want a family. Most important I want love in my life. What do you want?"

"I want a second shot at everything I lost." He said with pain in his voice.

"Do you think you can have that with me?"

He sat up straight, "sometimes. You're still in love with Dennis."

"You're still in love with Zoila! You still say her name in your sleep. Sometimes I wonder if you're sleeping with me or her. I've always come first, I can't believe I let you get away with this."

He halfway smiled, "you're wild! There's no way I could confuse sleeping with you with anyone else."

I smiled big, "I stand out for something?"

"I care about you Sasha."

"And I you," then I smiled wickedly. "Am I the best sex you've ever had?"

He gave me a wicked smile back, "YES! How do I rate on the good sex meter?"

"Strong ten." I smiled at him.

"You need to come to terms with your ex."

"That's the pot calling the kettle black." He kissed me then he went to the bathroom.

As if it was timed one of our phones was vibrating on the nightstand. I picked up both and it was a text from Zoila asking him if he could talk. So I kept him busy the rest of the night.

****

"Are you nervous?" El asked me

"Why would I be nervous?"

"I'm about to meet your father."
"No!" I said shaking my head. "You'll see why in a minute."
Of course Richard picked the fanciest restaurant for his big
reveal, talk about dramatic. My momma and Sabrina were here
as well; Richard picked them up from the airport. When we
walked around the corner Richard was sitting in the middle of
my momma and Sabrina looking like a King. I watched El's
eyes as he rounded the corner. "Hey Richard how are you
doing?" El said not connecting the dots yet. I slid in the booth
next to Sabrina and I hugged her. Sabrina said an excited hello
to El. My momma stood up and gave El a hug; she told him it
was good to see him again. El looked around, "he's not here?"
"Who?" Richard asked
"Her..." Then he looked at Richard then he looked at me. A
slight smile crept up on his face. "How come I didn't put that
together on my own?" Then El exhaled.
We were having a lovely dinner, but I could feel eyes on me. I
looked around for their source then I spotted Dennis. It looked
like he was on a date and his eyes were locked on me, and his
face was heartbroken. I dropped my eyes, and then I looked at
El who was thoroughly enjoying his conversation with my
parents. The waiter was explaining the dessert options when I
looked at Dennis's table again. He told me to come, and I
slightly shook my head no. Richard caught the pained look on
my face then he saw Dennis. It seemed like his eyes turned red.
He texted someone, then someone came to escort Dennis and
his date out. This was the first time I laid eyes on him in over a
year. El saw Dennis as he was walking out.

****

I did one last walk through of my apartment. This has been my
only home since I moved to LA. Here's to a new beginning!
It was weird driving away from my apartment for the last time.
But there were too many memories in that place anyways.
The sensor on my car opened the gate to my driveway as I
entered the cul-de-sac. There were trees along my property
line, so from the street you couldn't see my house or the
property really. There was a gate at the walkway and a gate at
the driveway; both of them had cameras and intercoms. The
houses along the street were all older homes but nice, and
nicely kept up. Most of them had been remodeled, but none
like mine. My house was the ugly duckling of this street, until.
I know that my house boosted everyone's property values.
During the remodel I came by regularly to see the progress and
to chat with my Great Uncle Dale and his daughter, my cousin

Sharon. My new neighbors would come out to say welcome to the neighborhood, etc. but we knew it was to be nosey. Their eyes would get big when I'd share the plans for my house with them. Yep this young black woman is moving in and upgrading you, you're welcome. I slowly drove up my driveway taking in my new home in its entirety. The lighting around the house and property made it seem like a palace. Yes, Queen Sasha is home.

I caught a glimpse of Champ standing by the trees watching me drive slowly. I loved the pillars that stood strong as part of the archway across the driveway to the front door. I parked under the archway since there were cars and the moving truck in front of the garages. The movers were moving the last of my things inside. The temps from Mitigated were unpacking the boxes according to Shasta and my momma's instructions. Richard was in the backyard with the dogs and special services staff. I'm sure he was making sure my security was set up to his liking. Smoke and Chubs were standing next to Richard as if they were waiting for instruction as well. When I stepped out Champ casually walked over. My Rottweiler's were huge and trained. Richard said Uncle Frank sent his more seasoned puppies to be with me.

I bumped Bruce and told him now that I moved we wouldn't have to deal with the troll stalking my apartment building anymore. Shawn's wife Marsha is a stupid somebody. You would think she would've learned from our introduction that she didn't want none. But no, she was determined to try to find out where I lived so she could confront me. So that had to mean that every time she came around my apartment she came with something, only a fool would come empty handed. Bruce smiled and said thank goodness for that.

I left to pick up El from the airport as the movers and extra people were leaving. I was so excited for El to see my house. El looked tensed, but I figured he was missing me. When I kissed him hello there was no passion behind his kiss. I looked him in his eyes and there was sadness in them. The room spun and I hugged him, I told him to tell me when he was ready. When we got to the house my momma and Richard were outside kissing by the pool.

"What's up Sasha!" Darryl said from my kitchen. "Who's that?" He said wiping his hands on the apron he was wearing.

"This is my boyfriend El, El this is my cousin Darryl. He's Drew's younger brother."

Darryl shook his hand and then he looked me up and down. "This is your man, and you're dressed like that?"
I frowned, "what's wrong with what I'm wearing?" I had on jeans and a T-shirt.
"Nothing, you normally dress up too much for my liking when there's a man involved. You look comfortable in your clothes and skin." Then he walked back to the kitchen.
I don't know why that comment embarrassed me, but it did. I gave El a tour of the house; he smiled whenever I looked at him. In my room I hugged him tight. "El, do I have to know? I'm perfectly ok with denial for today." I felt myself getting emotional. I hugged him and kissed him until he kissed me back. "I don't have to know. I don't want to know." I said kissing him.
"Baby it's not like me to not tell you. We can wait until we're alone."
"Kiss me!" I kissed him like my life depended on it. Then I hugged him putting my ear on his chest. His heart was pounding.
Darryl called up to us saying that dinner was ready. My parents were lost in each other. El asked where Sabrina was and my momma said she was with her father. Darryl engaged El in conversation, but he was holding back I could tell. Darryl would've normally had me in stitches by now. But tonight he was reading El. If he saw something he didn't like, I knew he wouldn't hold that back. I asked Darryl if he was staying with me and he said next time. For tonight he was going back to his mom's condo.
My parents were foaming at the mouth, and everywhere else, over each other. They left behind Darryl. El led me to the family room and sat me on the couch. He told me to calm down cause he was sure it was nothing like I was thinking. I took a deep breath then I looked at him. He told me he ran into Zoila. I figured that much, but I waited for him to tell me the part that would hurt me. Like they slept together, and he realized that Dennis was right and I could never be enough to hold any man's attention beyond ejaculation. He said they chatted for a while, and then she invited him to eat. He said they walked a block up and they sat down at a cafe. He said she told him she realized that she made a mistake and she wanted him back. I started crying, I wasn't ready to let him go. I needed him in my life, I needed him with me. El seemed surprised by my tears. "Sasha I paid the bill and I left. I'm changing my number tonight. I want to be with you. She left

me when I needed her the most. A quick apology and a salty lunch don't change how she hurt me." He put his cheek on mine. "I love you!"

"You love me?" I couldn't believe it.

"Yes! I can say it now."

"El I love you." I cried while hugging him.

"It's been just me and you right?" He said, "since we got tested."

"Yes, of course." I said not understanding where he was going with his question.

He kissed me again. When foreplay moved forward, I told him to go get a condom from upstairs. He looked me in my eyes and said no. He said we were moving forward. He watched my eyes as he entered me. It had been years since I've had sex without a barrier. He felt smooth and wonderful! I was on the pill and had been for years. But I knew I was lost in the moment when the thought occurred to me to stop taking them.

Chapter 7

"We're in the lobby," Hunter said
"Ok, I'll be down in a moment." I hung up and went to the bathroom brushed my teeth and then I made my way down. Since I had to fly out to meet with Malcolm, I asked Hunter if I could meet Lisa.

Their wedding was moving ahead in full swing. Hunter sent a picture of the dress I would be wearing in the wedding. They had me go to a specific dress shop in LA to have my measurements taken. I didn't mind, but it seemed odd to me not to have met his future wife and the wedding was coming up. Also, Andrew was driving over to the city with the baby since I hadn't met him yet. I couldn't wait to meet him. The pictures Andrew sent of little man, he looked just like Drew's baby pictures. He barely looked like Toya at all. I asked him to give me a couple of hours and then to come on over.

When I walked into the bar Hunter and Lisa were at the bar. Lisa tapped Hunter as I approached them. Hunter spun around with excitement; his smile dropped a little then he looked me up and down. As he hugged me, he asked what I was wearing. I frowned and said jeans and a T-shirt; I asked him what was wrong with what I was wearing. He said it wasn't my normal attire. Then he introduced me to Lisa who was very excited to finally meet me. She told me she's heard so much about me. Lisa was average height, brunette, her brown eyes seemed like they sparkled and she had the happiest and bubbliest personality. She was a talker, so immediately she dove in. She started telling me that she's heard so much about me and she was so happy that I agreed to be in the wedding. While she and I were talking Hunter kept scanning me up and down. I stopped my conversation with Lisa and I looked at Hunter, "WHAT?" He asked me what was up with me. He said I seemed off or just different. I was getting sick of hearing it. I still dress, and I'm not lacking confidence. But I don't look to be the center of attention these days. Even with El being so far away, I still felt like his attention was enough. As long as I had El I didn't need everyone else. And honestly, I was liking this way of existing, it was more relaxed. I waited for Hunter to put his adjective on his sentiments.

"You look like a soccer mom."
I felt like he shot me. "WHAT?"

"Comfortable jeans, form fitting T-shirt, ponytail, and sneakers!" He scoffed, "you're not even wearing earrings!"

"Hunter! She looks fine!" Lisa said

"I'm not saying she looks bad, I'm just saying you've changed. Normally you're...." He searched for another adjective. Then he snapped his fingers like the light bulb went off. "Normally when you walk into a room all eyes are on you. You get a kick out of watching the men drool and the women squirm, what happened to you? What happened to my friend?"

"Dennis happened!" I spit at him. "I'm not trying to be Sasha the vixen anymore. I have a good man, and I'm happy. You'll meet him at the wedding."

Lisa looked at Hunter, "um yeah! Sasha we weren't planning on giving you a plus one. We have limited space and seating."

That irritated me, "so you two will be the only ones that I will know at your wedding?"

"Not true, people from school will be there, and my family will be there."

"You're not even inviting my mother?"

"She has your sister. We figured she'd understand."

"Hunter tell me how much it will cost to add one or two more people. I'll pay for it."

"Come on Sasha. You're going to be busy doing bridesmaid's stuff. He would be sitting alone most of the time anyways. The day is going to move so fast you won't have time to worry about who's there and who isn't." I was beyond irritated with Hunter, but because it was their day, I was going to let it go. As if the bell saved me I spotted Andrew walking in holding the baby. I left my seat and ran over to hold the baby. He was so tiny looking at me with his daddy's face in miniature form. I'm not that girl, but I started crying looking at him. He was real; Andrew was a daddy, which blew my mind. I brought them to our table, while the little guy stared at my face like he was taking me in. Hunter introduced Andrew to Lisa. I frowned when I caught Lisa giving Andrew wanting eyes when Hunter wasn't looking. Andrew looked at me like what's going on. "How long have you two been together?"

"Off and on for five years. Why?" Hunter asked

"Why is your woman shooting my cousin quote-unquote do me eyes?"

Hunter gave Lisa a COME ON! Look. There was no doubt in his mind about the truth of my comment. He told Lisa to keep it together, at least in front of his friends. I leaned back in my chair and I frowned at Andrew. Hunter's reaction was dismissive at best. I couldn't stop frowning at him. Hunter exhaled, "different relationships are made up of different things. Lisa and I are swingers." I frowned again; Hunter explained that they encouraged each other's curiosity and exploration of other people.

"Eeewwllll Hunter!"

"More couples than you realize are into this lifestyle whether they admit it or not. Any person who sticks with their mate when they know they sleep around just isn't calling the situation what it is."

I guess that made Dennis and I swingers. That made me mad even more. "Well cut it out! We don't swing that way over here!" I said shaking my head at them.

We stayed in the lobby a little longer then Andrew, baby Andre, and I went up to my room. I kept looking at the baby, he was so precious. I told Andrew I couldn't believe he was a daddy. He sighed and said neither could he. Andrew sounded like he was suffering from postpartum depression. He said everything came down to money with Toya. He didn't feel like she cared about the baby at all. He said once it was clear to her that he wasn't going to marry her, she started acting up. He said he's had to keep a lawyer on retainer cause she's constantly taking him to court. My blood boiled! I told him she wasn't pregnant anymore and I could go handle her for him. He smiled, thanked me, and then he said he's had to hold his other cousins Pearla, Liz, and Paulette back on numerous occasions. He said he feels like that's where she tries to push him so she can use it against him. I hated seeing Andrew look so defeated. He was always Mr. On Top Of It! He had a comeback for everything, I understood the feeling though. When I found out about Dennis an Thea, it sucked the life right out of me. Andrew said there was no reason for his back pedal; he doesn't understand himself, why he went backwards. I asked him if he thought that girl was still an option. He sunk lower on the chair and said he really didn't know. Last he knew she was still with her boyfriend probably happy and enjoying the life they were supposed to have together. He said with everything Toya's putting him through, he could understand why his Momma was done with Malcolm. When I asked him how Malcolm responded to the baby he said he didn't tell him. When I asked why, he said his life was none of Malcolm's business. He didn't want to hear the judgment from someone who couldn't get their own stuff together. I kind of understood, but now that Richard and I have a better understanding of each other I couldn't imagine him not knowing or being there. But Andrew and Malcolm weren't your typical father and son, or maybe they were and I just didn't understand how this works. I got the baby to laugh and smile at me; I was in love with him already. The next morning I expected to see Chantel, but her cubical was empty when the receptionist took me to the conference room.

Malcolm and Juan came in with paperwork, Juan gave me a hug, and Malcolm sat down ready to get to business. Malcolm said the Access conversion was going really well and they were very impressed with how I managed it. I thanked them and told them the team they put together was top notch so it was a nod to them. Malcolm got quiet while Juan continued. He was staring at me, but not in a mean way. He smirked and asked me what was new. My eyes traveled around the room. Please not Malcolm too, I told him other than my house nothing much. He asked me what I thought of the baby. I was relieved that he wasn't making some off color remark about my appearance, although this morning when I did the last cursory glance in the mirror I knew I looked nice. I told him that Andre was precious and unbelievably tiny. I asked him when he was going to meet his grandson; he shrugged and went back to business. Malcolm said he asked me to come out cause they were thinking of moving some pieces around. He said it was kind of redundant to have El and I in the same position doing the same job. I swallowed cause I couldn't tell if he was firing El or me. I sunk in my seat; Malcolm said he wanted El to hold his position across the company. Then he said he wanted to promote me to work for Latour Enterprises. I waited for him to explain what he was saying. He said Mitigated Staffing Solutions is an affiliate of Latour Enterprises. He explained that I would still work in the same building in LA, but a different office. He said I would dabble in everything that he owns that included Mitigated, his recording studios, his restaurants, etc. He said I would still report to Derrick but in another capacity and with another level added to my annual salary. When Juan put my offer letter on the table my mouth watered. Malcolm said he appreciated how I stepped up during the conversion and everything else. He said my discretion in part played a big roll into this decision. I knew he meant El and the fact that we didn't let our relationship interfere with our job or broadcast our relationship either. I was very impressed with our discretion as well. The old me wouldn't have cared, and it would've been my right to brag that I was sleeping with El.

Malcolm told me to take the rest of the day off to think it through, and then come back in the morning. I didn't understand what I needed to think about but since he offered the day off with pay I needed to pick something worthwhile to do. I caught a cab to the airport then I rented a car. I called my momma on my way to Sabrina's school, I told her I was picking my baby up so that we could spend some much needed time alone together. My momma was fine with it, but I needed to discuss what time her father wanted her to his place cause it was his night to have dinner with her. She gave me Travis's number; I called him from the school parking lot. Travis got so excited to hear from me. I felt bad, with everything going on in my life my relationship with him got lost in the shuffle. Travis was always good to me and he looked out for me like a father should. He asked me if I would be willing to have dinner with them as well. He wanted me to meet his girlfriend. I agreed even though I knew Richard wouldn't like it. Richard could shower Sabrina with gifts that her working class father could not afford, but the moment he realized how fond I was of Travis he had a fit. That's annoying but I deal with it.

When I walked into the office a guy was talking to some of the students and he stopped talking mid-sentence when he saw me. I saw him and his reaction to me but I acted as if I didn't notice. I told the secretary I was there to pick up my sister. The secretary checked my ID against Sabrina's emergency card and then she picked up the phone. The guy stopped her and told her he would escort me to Sabrina's class. I said, "whatever!" Under my breath.

"How you doing, I'm Cleavon." He said extending his hand for a shake.

"Sasha" I said quickly and uninterested. He wasn't ugly, but he had nothing on El.

Then he looked at his watch, "school just started, and you're taking one of my students already." He revealed a beautiful smile

"What are you gonna do?" I shrugged not wanting to give him any information.

"Are you coming to our Fall Festival?"

"Hadn't heard of it." I said going through the door he held open for me.

"It's our annual fundraising event for the school. Families donate their time and services that we sell or offer on that day to raise money for things that we need for the school that aren't covered by the budget. More information will come out this week about it. We strongly encourage all families to come and to bring everyone they know. Like your husband or boyfriend should definitely come."

"Ok" is all I said, I wasn't gonna confirm or validate his fishing.

Cleavon opened the door and one of the kids in the class was giving the teacher the blues, he froze in place when he saw Cleavon. Sabrina screamed and ran out of her chair to me.

"Mr. Dajean, how may I help you?" The teacher said

"Hi," I said extending my hand. "I'm Sasha Wallace, I'm here to pick up this little lady." I said hugging Sabrina as tightly as she hugged me. "Can I have her make up work for the day, she's not coming back until tomorrow."

"Will you bring her in tomorrow?" Cleavon asked

"No" I said, "get your stuff baby." Sabrina was so excited she couldn't stop giggling.

"I don't think we've met. I'm Kelly Walters her teacher."

"I'm her big sister."

"Oh! I see, I was wondering." She said letting her mouth run away with her.

"Wondering what?" I said with a frown.

"I've met Sabrina's parents I didn't know where you fit in to the family picture." She said tiptoeing.

"You mean you didn't know where this black woman picking up Sabrina came from?" I cut my eyes at her.

"Ms. Walters you're out of line. Please return to your class." Then he gestured for me to follow him out. "I apologize for my staff, I will have a conversation with her later." He looked around, "they don't see very many of us out here who haven't been whitewashed."

"Is that an excuse to behave in that manor?"

He licked his lips, "not at all."

I shook my head at him, the old Sasha would've been digging this scene, but now I feel embarrassed that I ever thought so low of myself to go for something like this. When Sabrina came out the class she said goodbye to her principal and we were off. We went to the Concord mall and got manicures and pedicures. I got my makeup done at the makeup store, and they gave Sabrina some shiny lip-gloss. Then we shopped, stopped for lunch, and then we shopped some more. When we got to Travis's house he was pulling up at the same time. He hugged and kissed Sabrina, and then he gave me a BIG fatherly hug and kiss. He told me it was so good to see me and that he missed me so much. When his girlfriend showed up, I could immediately tell she was there to fill the void of my momma. It's as clear as day that he's still in love with my momma and he doesn't understand why they broke up. After dinner I went over to my momma's restaurant. She wanted to know what I thought of the girlfriend, and I told her I felt sorry for Travis. My momma lowered her eyes to look at her paperwork. I told her I might be a little biased on the second chance relationship front, I told her I was voting for Travis. She couldn't believe I was speaking against my father. I told her they would always have love for each other. After all they had me, but I was still cheering for Travis.

When I called El he said he was on the other line and he'd have to call me back. As soon as I answered the phone he said, "BABE! I just got off the phone with Malcolm!"

I smiled, "I know, I met with him this morning."

His voice squeaked, "you knew about this, this morning and you said nothing all day???"

I laughed so hard, he was completely excited. He told me he couldn't wait to see me and we needed to celebrate when I came out. My trip out there was two weeks away. Mrs. Parsons was so excited when I called her to tell her I was coming. My heart always flutters when El tells me he loves me, it's like I'm hearing it for the first time in life. I told El I would call him when I got to my room.

As I walked to the elevator I heard my name. The sound of his voice paralyzed me. I stared at the floor for a minute and I turned to face him. He was not confident at all; he looked like he was searching my face for permission to approach me. I wouldn't give him permission; in fact my curls should've come alive like snakes and turned him to stone. I wished I could've thrown a fireball at him and burnt him to a crisp in that lobby! I looked at Dennis like he was crazy for coming here. He clasped his hands together begging me to allow him to come closer to me. When he took the third step I took one backwards. He stopped moving; we stood there staring at each other. I felt like everything inside of me was burning up and then melting. I was sweating like crazy. I told him to leave and there was no point in him being here. He begged me to talk to him; I picked up the vase on the table against the wall next to me. It had beautiful flowers in it. I threw it at him and the vase shattered against the wall when he moved just in time to miss the impact. I looked for something else to throw cause I wasn't gonna miss a second time! He rushed me and hugged me; I stomped on his foot and hit his jaw. Dennis grabbed his face then he came in again for another hug and I backed up. A lady screamed that I was being attacked. Then I heard another familiar voice say that it was ok and I wasn't under attack. I hit Dennis again as I looked and saw Yussef. Hotel staff still came running to my rescue. The guy asked me if I wanted them to call the police. Yussef shrugged to say it was up to me. Dennis' lip was busted and his jaw was bruised. He stood there firm and unwavering. Yussef told me he wasn't leaving. I told the hotel staff I was ok, and then I told Dennis to pay for their broken vase. He gave them his card and told them to send him a bill without even looking at them. Dennis asked Yussef if he was my boyfriend. Yussef told him that was none of his business; I wish he would've just said yes. When Dennis started to walk up on Yussef I knew he was underestimating Yussef's ability to take him out. I put my hand out to Dennis as I grabbed Yussef's arm. His body was hard and ready for whatever. "Dennis leave! I don't want you here!"

"I need to talk to you! Apologize at the least! Please talk to me! I'm begging you!"

"Talking to you will only make you feel better! I have nothing to talk to you about!" I yelled. Yussef put his hands on my shoulders; I wished he would've pulled me in for a hug.

"You gotta go! This is too much." Yussef said too calmly. If I was Dennis the calmness of his voice would alarm me.

"Sasha! Please!" Dennis pleaded

"No! No Dennis! Go away! Leave me alone!"

"My love for you hasn't changed, I messed up! I want you back! Please baby I'm so sorry! I'll do anything!" He pleaded quickly, "no one will ever love you more than me! He doesn't know you like I do."

I looked at Yussef and he was in full protection mode. I grabbed his hand and I led him away. I didn't want to hear anymore. Dennis was pleading from the bottom of his heart. I didn't doubt his declaration of love. It was just too little too late. When we got to my room I put my head on Yussef's shoulder as I cried my eyes out. We stood in the doorway while I cried, Yussef rubbed my back like he understood the pain I was feeling. My phone started ringing in my pocket, it was El's ringtone. El could hear the tears in my voice from my simple hello. Yussef was still rubbing my back while I talked to El. I told him everything that happened, and that I was still on my way to my room. El asked me who Yussef was and I told him he was my sister's brother. El was breathing hard. He asked me if I was ok, he sound like he felt completely helpless.

I told him I was ok and I was happy he called. I told him I would call him back. Then I hugged Yussef smashing my ear into his chest, while he rubbed my back. I told Yussef the whole story, and then I asked him why he was there. He said Richard called him when he received notice that Dennis flew in. He said Dennis was flying out in the morning so I should be ok. He said Richard doesn't want Dennis sniffing in my direction. Then he smiled and asked me about my boyfriend. I rambled on and on about El, he smiled a courtesy smile. Then he told me he wished me the best, it was the way he said that, that made me feel weird. To change the subject, I asked Yussef how Dennis knew where I was. He opened the door and then he said Dennis put a tap on Hunter's phone. He said its amateur at best, and then he walked out.

****

"So I hold the stick like this?' I asked in a helpless voice. El looked at me like he was trying to figure out if I was playing him or if I was for real. This evening was kind of all over the place we had no real plan when we left the house other than we wanted to spend the evening doing something together, eventually we ended up in a pool hall. For whatever reason El assumed I didn't know how to play. He started to explain the game to me immediately. I decided to go along with him and not show how good I am at this game until the end. You know, teach him a lesson for underestimating me. Meanwhile, I was going to enjoy him being all over me as he showed me how to play. My form was all wrong as I waited for instruction.

"You should be used to holding big sticks by now." He smiled at me.

I smiled back, "this stick is smaller than the stick I usually hold."

He showed me how to hold the stick according to what worked for his game. We played the first game with him "taking it easy" on me. I amazed myself with how dingy and clumsy I was being. I didn't think El was completely buying my act, but he went along with it. I noticed the guys a few tables over who were watching us. More like watching me bend over. But I ignored them and continued on with my game with El. After the first game, El patronized me telling me how good I did. Then we played a second game and I still had no real game. He rubbed my back and told me it was ok, and that with practice I could get a lot better. He was acting so ugly I had to teach him a lesson. He suggested that we play one more time. I acted like I didn't want to. So he told me he'd make it worth my while to play. I protested saying I hate to lose, that was a truth so I didn't have to act that part out. So he decided to make it a win-win situation for me. "If you actually try to beat me this time, I'll rub your feet when we get home." Then he laughed, "if you actually beat me I'll give you a full body massage."

I put my hands up to my chest, "all of that for me? Can't I get the massage without playing this stupid game?"

"Nope, you've gotta work for it." He smiled at me like he was doing me a favor.

"Fine, but I want a full body massage in the hot tub." I huffed

He laughed, "sure Sasha. Anything you say." I asked him to show me how to set up the table. He was so tickled when I put the white ball in with the rest of the balls. Our audience continued to watch us. I pretended one more time that I didn't want to play. El told me he'd let me break just so I could know what it sounds like when I do it. I told him I was taking off the gloves I wanted that massage in the hot tub. He laughed at me like I was dreaming. My whole demeanor changed and I was now focused. I held the stick the way my Uncle Jeff showed me and then I broke. I told him he was stripes. His smiled dropped when I sunk four balls back to back. I didn't want him to go down without a fight so I scratched on purpose. Then I said, "darn" overly sarcastically. El actually played me, and he was really good. However, when I sunk the eight ball, I watched his eyes as he concentrated on what just happened to him. "And that my friend is game. I believe I won."

"You hustled me." He smiled at me.

"You assumed I couldn't play, you hustled yourself." Then I kissed him. "My massage is going to feel so good." I moaned at him.

He smiled, "I'll go close the tab. Then I guess I have no choice but to pay up."

I started collecting the balls from the pockets as the guys made their way over. I exhaled telling myself I hoped they were smart and walked away cause tonight was not the night. The one guy said the way I hustled my friend was beautiful. I thanked him shooting him an annoyed look. Then he asked me if El and I were in a committed relationship or if I could have friends. I didn't say anything; I let my expression speak for itself. Getting the hint, the guys congratulated me on a beautiful win and then they walked away. I took the balls to the counter. The bartender cut her eyes at me as she spoke to El. "This is your date?" She spit at him. Her tone must of suddenly changed cause El looked at her like he didn't understand. "Figures. Every time I turn around you got brothas dating these kinds of girls."

"What kinds of girls are you referring to?" El asked, but I knew exactly what she was talking about.

For some people it's not enough for them that I'm black. They gotta make it seem like I don't count cause my hair is curly or I'm not as dark as the next black person. Looking at me there's no denying that I am black but I guess because my skin wasn't like Malcolm's and my hair wasn't like wool, I wasn't black enough. Comments like that used to hurt me, they used to set me off. But now I feel sorry for those people. There are so many other more important things to care about in this world than about a man who has already chosen me. I know I'm beautiful but not because of my parent's backgrounds but because I simply refuse to be anything less. If my blank canvas was leaning towards the jacked up side I would be all over the makeup scene until I had the process down just right to make me feel as beautiful as I know I am. Now I never liked the guys who act like the reason to drool over me was anything more than that the fact that its me. I'm gorgeous because I carry myself that way. Now this female is average short height. From what I can see through her all black uniform she had a nice body as well. We were about the same complexion so go figure, but my hair is long and curly and hers is in an Afro. Had she not opened her mouth, spit her ignorance. I would've told her I liked her look, the headband she had on was too cute. But now she's on my nerves cause she's over here spouting some ignorant militant garbage because she doesn't approve of El's choice. In the end she's mad cause he chose me and not her. "It's ok, I know what she's talking about. This conversation is going to go nowhere fast, and it's only going to piss me off."

"I'm sick of seeing it." She spit at me.

"Then stop looking. No one here asked for your opinion about whom my man dates. Why would you worry about the choice of a man who has already made his choice? You don't know him or his preference, but you want to spread your ignorant complex to him. You're wasting your breath and furthering the divide amongst us." Then I leaned in, "and you're doing this on the clock. I could have your job. You don't know me, or what you're dealing with. Don't under estimate a stranger." I warned.

"All I'm saying is try a real Sistah next time." She said to El.

"There is no one realer than me. You're ignorant and the reason why black people struggle to get along."

"You think you're better than me!" She spit at me.

"First of all, you don't know me so you have no clue as to what I think. However, at this exact moment I KNOW I am better than you. You have a chip on your shoulder that's got you all hunched over like the Hunchback of Norte Dame."

"At least I'm a real Sistah!"

"What makes you real?"

"You're bougie and the poster child for mixed kids of America."

I scanned her face again, "your features are no blacker than mine. Those thin lips and that pointy nose. Just because someone made you feel less comfortable in your skin gives you no right to…"

She cut me off, "you mulatto looking…"

I don't know what she said next, all I know is she crossed the line and my fists connected with her mouth so fast, El jumped and pulled me by the waist out of there. "SASHA! What was that?" El said completely annoyed as he put me in the car.

"I'm sorry!" I said trying to grab a hold of my temper. "I shouldn't have let her push my buttons. But she took me back to a ugly place."

"Clearly, why did you even bother to be involved in such a juvenile conversation?" El said as he drove away.

"I don't know." I pouted.

"Who cares what one girl at a pool hall thinks!" El said

"It's not just one girl. You don't get it."

"You don't get it, you don't have to dignify anyone's comments about who you are. What if that girl calls the police? Will it be worth a night in jail?" He said

"Drop it El you don't get it. When has anyone called you Mulatto? Or any other derogatory name?"

"There's nothing wrong with the mulatto descriptor. It just means you're parents were black and white."

"The fact that I have to describe myself in any way is insulting. You really needed to pay attention during black history month when you were in school. EVERYTHING is wrong with that descriptor. I am not some hybrid race for manual labor. My parents were in love and I am a product of that. Mulatto is a slave term used to describe the child born from the rape of slaves. As if those children were a special breed of children. It's insulting! It's demeaning! It's! It's!....." I couldn't find the words so I screamed.

"Calm down Sasha!"

"You don't understand! You don't get it! You're not even American so how can you tell me how to feel about this!" I spit at him.

"Oh so now I'm different because of where I come from? What's the difference between what she just did and what you're doing now? My skin is brown. Kids teased me so badly when I came states side because I was different. My mum may not come from the tragedy that African Americans experience, but I am black and I do live in America. Honestly, no matter where you're from people are going to find a way to try to put you down so that they can appear superior. You have to rise above that. You can't beat up every person who uses a ugly term against you Sasha."

"I know, but she hit a sore spot. I know she was flirting with you, and then she got mad."

"Just like I saw those guys approach you. We're not children, we can do better than this Sasha." He said pulling into the garage.

I turned on the jets to heat the hot tub. I turned on the music, which also played softly outside. I grabbed two glasses and a bottle of wine. I stripped in front of the door and I went out and I sat myself down in the hot tub. When El came out to join me I apologized for letting that girl ruin our evening. Then the song came on, "Let me know! Let me know!" El said this song always makes him think of me. I sat there calming and blushing, he said at my best beyond my appearance I have a beautiful heart and that was why he fell in love with me. He said I was the positive motivating force within his life. I melted in his arms, naked under the stars.

****

"SSSHHHH! She's here! She's here!"

El and I smiled from ear to ear as we listened to everyone in his parent's house scramble to find their places.

I got up early so that I could obsess over what I was wearing. El couldn't believe I was up at five, which was two my time, getting ready. My makeup had to be right. I kept going over my options. El even took me shopping, something he never objects to, just so I would have more options in his closet. El has never seen me like this, but I couldn't look crazy the first time I met the rest of his family. And yeah Hunter's soccer mom comment still pains me. I could be a toned down vixen today. Not too sexy, but gorgeous enough so that his family doesn't ask him why he's with me. Moments like this I wished I could carry Ava in my back pocket. Since it was cold out here it didn't make sense to wear a dress. I ended up wearing my black boots, black pants, and claret red sweater, with gold accessories. I put my hair half up and half down. I used gold to highlight my eyes, but not overdone. When I finally had everything together the way I wanted it, he had the nerve to beg for "some." But I was firm in my NO! I told him he'd have to wait until we came home. I served him up good last night, he was being a snot. I wasn't going for it.

Mrs. Parsons opened the door with the biggest smile on her face. "Sasha! You're gorgeous honey! Come in! Come in!" She said extending her arm to hug me. The smell of a home cooked meal slapped me in the face. "This is my daughter Brielis," she said proudly.

Brielis was short, she had a short haircut. Her hair was sandy brown, and she had a few freckles. She was definitely Mr. Parsons' daughter. She was a little round in the middle, but I wasn't gonna ask if she was pregnant or not. It was none of my business.

Brielis looked me up and down, she smiled, but I was waiting to see if it was genuine. "It's nice to meet you, I've heard a lot about you." She said shaking my hand.

The rest of the people there were aunts, uncles, and cousins all on Mr. Parsons' side. They said we were waiting for Uncle Pete and then we could eat. Everyone was nice and stated how happy they were for El. But Brielis was watching me from across the room. Like she was trying to dissect everything about me. I was talking to one of the aunties and she asked where I lived. I saw Brielis' ears perk up when I said Southern California. The Auntie gasped and said that was far, she asked who was moving where if El and I continued. I told her El and I hadn't discussed it yet. Brielis sucked her teeth and walked out the room. I asked the auntie what was wrong with her. She faked like she didn't know. El was talking to a cousin, he looked over at me. I shrugged at him; he excused himself and came over. He asked what we were talking about. His sister stuck her head back in the doorway. His auntie repeated her question, and I repeated my answer. Then his sister planted herself next to me. "El you can't leave! Me and the baby are going to need you here."

El squinted, "what?"

"Why would you move all the way across the country just to be with her, when you have family that needs you here? Let her move out here!" She said like I wasn't standing there.

"I didn't say I was moving anywhere. Like Sasha said, we haven't discussed it."

"I know you El! You think you're in love and you change everything about you to make her happy. It didn't work for you last time and it's not gonna work this time. The only person you can trust to love you is your family. We will always be here for you. These females are a dime a dozen. And I don't even understand this one." She gestured in my direction. "She's too sadity, you don't like females like her. You said they're high maintenance!"

I looked at El, "Brie calm down! It was a simple question and you're overreacting." I frowned at him.

"Promise me you won't move away!" She yelled getting everyone's attention.

"Brie!" He said trying to calm himself cause she was pushing his buttons. "I'm not gonna do that. When Sasha and I decide that's it, and it's done!"

"El!" She yelled, "you're gonna let her move you to California, and then she's gonna break your heart just like the last one!" Her words wounded him. "Meanwhile, me and the baby will need you here!"

"Where's that baby's father?" His aunt asked her.

"Auntie Hazel I'm talking to El!" She said putting her hand up. Auntie Hazel spoke through clinched lips, "little girl! I don't care if you're pregnant or not. If you ever in your life think you're gonna disrespect me, I'll have to remind you of who I am! Leave your brother alone! You caused enough problems in his last relationship! I think he needs to get away from you more than anyone else in this room! You're brother has been through HELL and all you can worry about is how his happiness affects you! There's a reason why today is your first time meeting this girl. You are selfish and irresponsible! How dare you lay up and make a baby and then get mad when he doesn't assume responsibility for your family. He's been through enough! And all you're doing is thinking about yourself!"

"Aunt Hazel you know how he starts bending over backwards for these females who take him for granted! I'm tired of seeing him hurt like that!"

"SHUT UP BRIE! All you're caring about is yourself right now. Sasha hasn't done anything to your brother but accept him and love him for who he is. A good man with a beautiful heart! Sasha is not Zoila! Just because she lost sight of what she had doesn't mean Sasha will! Your brother is being way

more patient with you than I can bare to watch in this moment!
SAY ONE MORE THING!"

Mr. Parsons walked in the room, he looked angry. "What's
going on?"

"She started yelling at me for being honest with El!" Brielis
said crying

"Hazel, did I hear you threaten my child in my house?"

"If she's wrong it don't matter where we are!" Aunt Hazel said.

"No, no you don't! Come talk to me." He said walking out the
room.

Brielis smiled at me and walked away. I frowned at El and I
walked into the living room. I sat next to his mom who
apologized for her daughter's behavior.

As soon as the doors closed to the car, I told El to spill it. He
said there were a lot of compromises that he made while he
was married that his family didn't agree with. Like moving to
Brooklyn to be closer to Zoila's volunteer job, even though that
made his commute to work longer and harder. He left his last
job cause Zoila was upset about the women who had eyes for
El there. Even Mitigated has proven to be a step up, but at first
it looked shaky on his end. He admitted that he did bend over
backwards for Zoila and he spoiled her rotten, then he said I
haven't done even a tenth of the things she's done so his sister
was over reacting. I exhaled and I said she had one valid point.
I asked him what we were going to do about our living
situation. He kept his eyes on the road, and then he told me I
wasn't ready to be with him yet. That comment made me mad,
I asked him why he thinks that. He looked at me, "Dennis!"

****

Buzz! Buzz! "Open up Sasha! We're here!" Dan-Dan said into
the intercom.

"Sasha how come every time they come out here you gotta
have me around?" Darryl whined.

I buzzed the gate to let them in. "Darryl you know you're the
life of the party. You love it!" I teased

"Just because I love it doesn't mean you can use me for it.
Your cousin gonna be chasing me around. I keep telling her
I'm too sexy for her. You better tell her she don't want none.
I'm only flesh and blood Sasha!" Darryl said following me out
of the door.

Dan-Dan got out of the passenger side of my Uncle Phillip's
minivan. She was looking around with big eyes and a mile
wide grin. She told me she loved the house. Whitney got out
the back all smiles and admiring the house as well. She gave

me a big hug and she said the place was beautiful. Then she said a very eager hello to Darryl. He bucked his eyes at me and then he said hello. I told Whitney that she couldn't harass Darryl on this visit, and she said an unconvincing ok. Uncle Phillip's girlfriend got out the car and gave me a hug. Her son gave me a nod with his headphones on. I gave them a tour of the grounds while Darryl took care of the dogs. Then I showed them the inside of my house. Whitney asked me how much I paid for the house and I told her close to nothing. I told her the remodel was the most expensive part. I showed them pictures of what the house looked like when I bought it. My Dan-Dan was very proud of me; she said she brags about her grand baby all the time. Richard pulled up moments later. He got out of the car very proud and asked Dan-Dan how she liked the house. She said she loved it. Richard's family was out to do their tourist thing and visit all the amusement parks and shop. Since I was transitioning to my new role I couldn't take Thursday or Friday off but I was going to be with them over the weekend and Monday. I looked at the time and I told Dan-Dan that Ava was waiting for us. We were having an all-out pamper day at Ava's, just us girls. Janet was so happy to see Dan-Dan; the last time Dan-Dan came out, they hit it off. Dan-Dan said that Janet's massages were the best! Janet always tells Dan-Dan that she can't believe she's my grandmother cause she looks like she's only my mother and a relatively young mother at that. Like my momma, Dan-Dan got started young. She thought Uncle Phillip was going to make her a grandmother first, she couldn't believe her baby was the one.

"Sasha baby what's going on with Dennis?" She asked Brea slowed down on her massage on my feet. "Nothing we broke up." I said nonchalantly.

"He came by to see me." I sat up and looked at her. First Hunter now my grandmother? "He was begging me to help him. He misses you like crazy!" She smiled.

"What did you tell him?"

She shrugged, "I told him I needed to talk to you."

"Did he tell you what he did?"

She eyed me; "I know he's not crazy enough to put his hands on you. Richard would lay him out!"

"Worse!" I said

"What's worse than that?"

"He slept with my friend!" Dan-Dan and Brea gasped. "The last time was days ago when I found out. I can't forgive him for hurting me like that. I'm done!"

Dan-Dan started wringing her hands together. "Oh dear! Honey, I didn't know."

My stomach turned, "what did you do?"

"Well he...." She took a deep breath. "I told him we were coming here. He's gonna be outside when we leave."

Dan-Dan apologized over and over again. I took a deep breath, I screamed at the unruly butterflies in my stomach. I straightened my robe and I asked Brea for slippers. When I walked out the door Dennis was there with a big and dramatic bouquet of beautiful flowers. He made sure he looked delicious. He faked scared and said he came in peace. I knew Dennis could not be here without Richard knowing about it. I spotted Bruce by the valet post watching, he waved at me. Dennis attempted to give me the flowers but I refused them. Dennis started apologizing immediately, I looked at the sky then I looked at him. I told him it was already done, and no matter how he apologized it wouldn't change what he did. Dennis told me he loved me and he would do whatever it takes to get me back. He said we still have love and he could see it all over me, and he felt it when we kissed. I told him to let me go, and that I wasn't coming back to him. My comment spread pain all over his face, "since when are you interested in guys with dreadlocks? He's nothing like me."

He assumed I was dating Yussef, but he saw me with El and my parents. I looked away, "maybe that's what I need in order to be happy. Someone who's not like you."

He stared at my face, "I'm so sorry for hurting you Sasha! There's no excuse for how selfish I've been. I can see that now and I want to make it up to you. I'll do whatever it takes."

"Anything?" I asked

"Yes! Anything!" He said hopefully

"Then leave me alone. Stop harassing my family and friends. Let me come to you, if I ever do. You're going about this all wrong. How many laws have you broken just to be standing here right now?"

"I'd do it all over just to look at you right now." He said looking at me with longing in his eyes.

"Leave me alone Dennis please! I'll never come back to you like this. I'm so mad at you! You hurt me! You stole my thunder! You..." I wiped a tear. "I can't! Just leave me alone Dennis! I'd never come back to you like this. You have a son that needs you and a baby momma who thought you loved her. Take care of your family."

Dennis made a wounded sound. "I feel like if I leave you alone, you will forget about me. I can't risk that!"

"So you'd rather risk my anger and disgust?"

"Sasha I'm ready now. I'm ready to give you everything you wanted and needed from me." He took two steps closer. "We can have as many babies as you want."

"I know where to find you." I said backing away. "I have to go!"

"Sasha Please!" He begged

"I have to go!" I said walking back inside. Dan-Dan was in the lobby looking like a mother would. She gave me a big hug while I cried my eyes out in her arms. Dan-Dan rubbed my back and told me I needed more time. She said when you're done with someone it doesn't tear you up like this.

****

Lisa very excitedly introduced me to her other bridesmaids. Everyone said hi at once. But they were all sizing me up. "Ugh!" This is what I can't stand about being with a bunch of females. The party bus arrived and we went to the dress shop in Concord. The other bridesmaids were doing their final fittings, where I was seeing and trying on my dress for the first time. My dress was hanging in the dressing room when I stepped in along with all my accessories and undergarments. My dress was a beautiful Tiffany Blue and it looked like it was made for my body it hugged me perfectly. When I opened my door Lisa sighed and told me I looked beautiful. When I walked out I noticed the other bridesmaids had on taupe colored dresses and none of them were as nice as mine. Lisa read everyone's expressions. She told us that as Hunter's very close friend I was her maid of honor and Clarisa was her Matron of Honor. Clarisa's dress was the same color as mine but a different style. When we stood together my dress was the sexiest of them all. I heard a couple girls asking why they couldn't wear my dress in their color. Lisa told them Hunter picked out my dress specifically for me. Although the bridal party was nice enough, I kept feeling like I was on the outside looking in. Especially after the dresses. At the rehearsal dinner Hunter had me sit next to him and I chatted mostly with the groomsmen. None of this felt new, but I didn't have the thick skin that I used to have to not care about my effect on others anymore. Most of the guys were shooting me wanting looks and the old Sasha would've encouraged all of them to drool knowing that none of them stood a chance with me. But now all I wanted was for this night to be over. I stepped outside to call El. He asked me why I sounded so sad. I told him I felt like a fish out of water. I told him about my dress and the bridesmaid's reactions to me. I know he was trying to cheer me up, but I felt sad and defeated. However, I didn't want to be sad so my patience got short. I kept snapping at El and I could tell he was trying to be patient, but I was pushing him. So he got quiet and sat there listening to me. I apologized for being moody; I decided the best thing for me to do was go back to my room and get in the bed. I told Hunter I was going to catch a cab back. But he wouldn't hear of it, he insisted on taking me to the hotel. In the car, I asked Hunter if he was excited, tomorrow he was going to be a married man. He shrugged and said it was business as usual for him. But their families were really excited. I told him his arrangement shed light on how he was getting married before me. He asked me if I really was going to stick to my guns and leave Dennis hanging? I told Hunter words cannot describe to him how much Dennis hurt me. He said Dennis was wrong but he was breaking his neck to make it up to me. Hunter said Dennis paid for their entire wedding and honeymoon. I exhaled, cause that definitely meant he was going to be here and that El was right. This wedding was all about Dennis. I asked him if Dennis paid for all of my things and Hunter said yes. I sighed, I was tired of fighting. I told Hunter it's been years and Dennis needed to let it go. Hunter looked at me, "he loves you. Why would he stop fighting for you until he wins? He's paid very well to argue for a living. Do you think he's going to give up now? On the one person he loves the most? He might not be a tall black guy with dreadlocks, but who could replace who Dennis has been to you?"

I bowed my head. "He told you about that too?" I felt defeated and like I was fighting a losing battle. El won't move forward with me because of Dennis. And Dennis won't go away! I thanked Hunter for the ride and then I went up to my room. I called El and I apologized through tears for acting so crazy. I told him everything on my heart. I told him how much I loved him. How it hurts that Dennis and Zoila loom over our relationship. He said it worked better this way in his mind. He said a lot of couples hold back what's secretly on their hearts and the other person sits there guessing and wondering why they're stagnant. I told him he was right, and I wished he was with me.

In the morning I got as ready as I could in my room. I had everything together all I needed to do was put on my dress.

When I opened my door Yussef was standing there. "What are you doing here? I thought you were assigned to a regular 9 to 5?"

"Richard's paying me triple time and a half to escort you today. How do I look?" He said modeling his tux. "Hugo Boss!"

"Delicious!" I wasn't kidding. His locs were tied back, his smile was killing me, and oh my! He looked so good, and I was so happy to see him. I called Richard and thanked him for sending reinforcements. In the lobby I introduced Lisa to Yussef, I told her he was escorting me to the wedding. She was so in love with looking at him I don't think she cared. I rode with Yussef to the ceremony and reception site. I tried not to make him uncomfortable by staring at him. I can't explain what my body was feeling every time I looked at Yussef. It's like something inside was telling me that next to him is where I needed to be. I never had this feeling with Dennis or Hubby. Yussef frowned at me and asked me how El was doing, it was like he was reading my thoughts. I exhaled and told myself to focus on El.

Hunter and Lisa were getting married at Heather Farms in Walnut Creek. There was a beautiful garden for the outdoor ceremony and then a small reception hall for the reception. There was a lot of standing around while we waited for Lisa to get ready. I was so happy Yussef was there; I would've felt alone if he wasn't there. The bridesmaids were trying to figure out if we were together as they licked their lips at him. Yussef smiled and said the ladies loved his hair. Hunter shook his head when he saw Yussef but I guess he expected me not to follow instructions. At least that's something the old Sasha would do. Dennis's eyes bounced between Yussef and I. He didn't say anything he went with the groomsmen. I put my dress on just before the ceremony and then we lined up so everything could start. Dennis eagerly extended his arm to me to escort me down the aisle, our first non-traumatic touch since that night at his parent's house. During the ceremony Dennis kept looking at me so I kept looking at Yussef. Yussef blended in with the family as much as a tall black guy with dreadlocks could blend in with a bunch of white people. He was laughing and enjoying himself. After the pictures I stuck to Yussef as much as possible. Dennis still shot me pleading eyes but he stood down. Most likely because he thought Yussef was my man. I relaxed so much, I allowed myself to have a drink or five. I danced with the wedding party and then I danced with Yussef. During the slow song I kept stroking his hair. It was so neat, clean, and soft. I thanked him for coming and saving me from an evening of depression. On the car ride to the hotel I asked him why he never called me. He simply said Drew and it was too close for his comfort. I stroked his hair while he drove, I told him how disappointed I was that he didn't call me. Yussef didn't say anything. He walked me to my room. He called Richard, he told him I was in my room but I was almost drunk. He wrote a number and then they got off the phone. Yussef asked me where my phone was; he said he was going to call El for me so that he and I could talk. I told him I needed to confess something first. Yussef looked at me like he wasn't taking me seriously as he looked for my phone. I got in Yussef's face and I kissed him with everything in me. He kissed me back at first even though he was holding back, and then he broke free. I was ON FIRE! He asked me what I was doing. I explained that he was the first person who ever made me consider leaving Dennis. I told him he was the first real connection I ever had with someone outside of what I thought I had with Dennis. I told him I needed to get him out of my system before I gave all of myself to El. Yussef looked at me like he didn't understand, but he didn't say anything. I asked him why he never called me, and he said Drew again. I told him I wanted him, and as much as the thought pained me I'd walk away from El to be with him. Yussef asked me why would I do that to someone I loved. He told me I was drunk and talking and behaving unlike myself. He was giving me an out, he told me the Sasha he knows me to be loved El and I would never hurt him like this. He touched my face like he was using all of his restraint not to kiss me on his own. I wished he would, I tried to pull him in close in hopes of changing his mind. Alcohol is always a good alibi, but Yussef is a good guy, which made me want him more. I gave him my phone then he called El for me.

****

"I like this Henry, everything looks good!" I said
"Good, now I'm off to the airport." Henry said as he stood. The guy standing in front of me is nothing like the guy who gave me the creeps before. Henry married Head and Shoulders, and then he invested in good haircuts. Stacy gave him style and put him on a diet. Henry dresses like the young guy he is. He has confidence now, I've even seen him ask a couple of ladies out and they gladly accept.
"Have fun," I said
"You like it up here on the fifteenth floor?"

"I do." I said

When he opened the door to my office someone was standing there. My heart sped up when El walked in. I knew it was only a matter of time before he popped up out here. I've been avoiding him, well not avoiding him completely, but definitely holding back. El shut the door then he sat down in the chair in front of my desk and stared at my face. I couldn't place his look so I stared back at him. "Hello," he said without emotion. "Hello" I said in a guilty tone.

He rolled his hands, "so…."

"So?" I said playing dumb.

"Come on Sasha! What's going on?" He was irritated, "why are you avoiding me?"

"I'm not, this job is totally different. You're lucky you caught me at my desk right now. I gotta go meet with a few labels. I have a few contracts to renegotiate based on the numbers that Henry just gave me."

"Sasha!" He said slamming his hands on the desk. I jumped, "I'M NOT GOING TO PLAY THIS GAME WITH YOU! TELL ME WHAT'S GOING ON!"

I got butterflies, "NOTHING'S GOING ON! I'M BUSY!" I snapped back

He stood up and walked around my desk. He pushed my chair back and he looked me up and down. "Stop lying to me! I know you Sasha! You wait this long to start taking steps backwards?"

"I didn't take steps backwards, my head is suspended. It's like I'm on pause and I don't know how to hit play."

"You talk to me that's how. You would die if I did this to you. I need you; I need you to be open and honest with me. No matter what it is come to me with it. Remember we share everything."

I swiveled in my chair then I stood up. "Can you go with me?" He said yes. In the car, I turned the radio off. I told him everything; to me it felt like I was telling the same story over, except this time I was making a distinction between Hubby and Yussef. El didn't say anything he listened quietly taking everything in.

"Your sister's brother, that's what you said when he was standing in your room."

"El I didn't put it all together until the wedding. I thought I told you everything and then there was more. I didn't know if you were going to say this was all too much. I've been shaking in my boots."

"Sasha you always tell me. I tell you, I've needed you. Zoila's been popping up everywhere, crying, begging, and pleading for me to come back to her. She's pulling at my heart, with you avoiding me, things get cloudy."

I looked at him, "what happened?" I prepared myself for the worst.

He looked out the window, "she kissed me. I almost lost it! That's why I'm here." He exhaled, "she doesn't deserve to win. She's pulling at my heart. If I stay out there alone, I don't know what could happen."

"You want to move?" I said in surprise

"I don't know." He exhaled, "would you consider moving to New York?"

"Why would I move to the place she knows like the back of her hand? You don't want to move here?"

He exhaled, "I don't know if that's a good idea either."

"Are we breaking up?" I asked holding my breath.

"Is that what you want? You're the one avoiding me."

"I was scared!"

"After all this time you're scared? What are you afraid of?"

"That I give you everything and then you sleep with my friend. Or you get tired of me and leave me. I don't think we should have to give up everything just to be together."

"Who's asking you to give up everything?"

"You asked me to move. My job, my life, my family is out here. I'm only a car ride away from my momma. My family is always here. New York is too far away to live."

"My family, my life, everything but you is out there. If you can't move you can't move." He looked out the window. "Who were we kidding anyways? Like this was ever gonna really work, right?"

If I thought driving like a crazy person would save me I would've done it. Instead I pulled over and cried. I screamed! El sat there looking at me wide eyed. "Didn't I just say! Didn't I just say this! Men are useless disappointments. I allowed myself to be vulnerable with you. I toned down my personality a lot to suit you. I let you inside like no person has ever been. All for what? Because I won't move it's over? You've got me confused with somebody else! I don't need this! I don't need you! We both know you're looking for an excuse to run back to Zoila anyways. This is just a waste, I can't believe I fell for this!" I looked at him. "And I bet you're gonna hold on to the lie that you only kissed her! Go ahead admit it! You slept with her! You cheated, all men cheat! At least be a man and tell me the truth! Trying to make it seem like my unwillingness to move is the reason. That is so weak!"

"I didn't cheat on you outside of allowing her to kiss me. I'm trying to tell you I need more." He said

"AND I DON'T! I don't even come first with you! I can't believe I let myself take the backseat to another female and still! This is how you do me. This is how he does SASHA! SASHA DOESN'T BEG ANY MAN TO LOVE HER!"

"I'm not asking you to take a backseat, but when I ask you to step up you can't do it!"

"Look El!" I chuckled, and then I started the car. I could feel my wall going up. "You were fun! A good lay, and easy on the eyes. But clearly this isn't going to work. I know better than to put my heart on the line for a fairy tale. I don't get the fairy tale, I knew that. But I let you blow smoke up my butt and actually let my heart want for you. Women like me end up married to the Dennis's of the world. Career, powerful man who cheats on you, and lots and lots of alcohol."

"Sasha...."

"No! Shut up! I'm done talking to you! I'm done with this!" El grabbed the steering wheel I scraped the driver's side of my car on the center divide. "Keep playing! I'll crash this car and try to kill you while I'm at it! I don't even care!" He got madder and grabbed the steering wheel again, and the car crashed into the center divide hard! The air bags deployed and we sat there screaming at each other! "I HATE YOU SO MUCH!" El yelled back that he hated me. We screamed at each other until the tow truck came. The tow truck driver said the car looked totaled to him, but the body shop would have to assess it. I told the driver to take El to the office, but El punked him and made him take us to my house. I thought about sicking my dogs on him, but I knew that was only my hurt talking.

When we walked in the door El snatched me up. I wasn't expecting that, he picked me up by my arms to bring me eye level with him. "Cut it out Sasha!"

"You cut it out! You're the one breaking up with me so you can go back to a female who don't really want you! She misses the love you have for her."

"I don't want to breakup with you!"

"But you give me some weak ultimatum! CRASH UP MY CAR! I bet you, you're replacing my car tomorrow! I WANT A TOP OF THE LINE, SLIDES DOWN THE STREET LIKE BUTTER, WHIP!"

"What is a whip?"

"A car! The best car!" My stomach was going crazy.

"Calm down Sasha! Talk to me!"

"I'm done talking to you! That's all we've been doing is talking and here we are. Get out of my house El! Go run back to Zoila; we both know that's what you're going to do anyways! I'm tired of being vulnerable. I'm tired of caring."

He started shaking me, "you add another guy to this equation and you expect me not to react! Not to feel something about that! The way you tell it, if he would've went for you, you would've gone for him. What do you expect me to do? Especially when you don't come to me, you run! You think it's easy for me to be vulnerable with you like this! I've opened myself up to you unlike any other person. AND I TELL YOU EVERYTHING! I didn't tell Zoila or anyone else half the things I tell you! I've never cheated on you outside of kissing Zoila this one time. Don't forget that I was technically still married to Zoila when I started sleeping with you! I broke all my rules to be with you. I thought I needed to be with you more, but maybe…"

"PUT ME DOWN!" I demanded

He looked up at me and smiled, "or else what?"

"Don't test me El! I'll shoot you!"

He smiled, "tell me you love me first!"

I blew air, "please! I hate you so much right now!"

"Which just means you love me! So just say it!"

"No it doesn't! It means I hate you!"

"Right!" He walked forward and put my back against the wall. He used one hand to hold me up, and the other went under my dress. I was swimming in my panties. "You're a freak!" then he put me down, but he wouldn't let me leave the wall. He unfastened his pants and took my panties off. I was so excited you would've thought I was Niagara Falls. He told me to tell him I loved him and when I said no he down shifted. When I was on the verge of an explosion he pulled out told me to tell him I loved him. I said no, so he waited until I calmed down then he went back in. He kept doing this, playing with my emotions, turning me out! I couldn't win this battle of wills. I heard myself tearfully give in. My body surrendered! I screamed so loud my dogs came to the window to check on me. It seemed like they knew what was happening and they were telling El that he did a job well done! I couldn't stop shaking or crying. I was sprung beyond any love I've ever known.

****

I called my clients and rescheduled my appointments. My legs wouldn't stop shaking; I stopped trying to get off the couch. El laid on the floor next to the couch staring at the ceiling like he was calculating as he was catching his breath. I was too embarrassed to look at him I was acting so ugly. I squished my body as far back on the couch as I could. I didn't want him to look at me just yet. "Sasha?"

"Yeah?" I said sounding like a little girl.

"When was your last period?"

My head popped up, "WHAT!"

"Are you pregnant?"

"WHAT?" I sat up.

He was still lying on the floor staring at the ceiling. "You were so wet!" He didn't look at me.

"El, I'm on the pill."

"Nothing is a hundred percent." He said with his voice trailing off.

"What is it?" I peeked at him

"I can't talk about it right now." He exhaled, "let's get your car in the morning. Where are we going?" He said sounding completely weird.

"Surprise me!"

"You need to take a test. Do you have any?"

"No." Then my phone rang, it was Richard. "Hey."

"WHAT'S GOING ON WITH YOUR CAR? WHAT HAPPENED?"

"I got distracted, I'm fine but the car is jacked though."

"HOW DID YOU GET DISTRACTED?"

"Why are you yelling at me?" I said, El looked at me.

"I'm at the auto body shop!! I'm looking at the car, how did this happen?"

"Richard, I'm fine. I told you I got distracted!" I rolled my eyes at El.

"Sassy were you day dreaming again?"

"Richard, I'm fine."

"Nightmares?"

I exhaled, "a little bit. But I'm ok."

"I'm coming over, you don't sound good."

"You don't have to do that El is here."

Richard was quiet, "when did he get there?"

"Let me call you back, we were in the middle of something." I said

Richard hung up in my face. El got off the floor and sat on the couch next to me. He told me to tell him I loved him. When I hesitated he grabbed my hair and told me again. We were kissing when the doorbell rang. I tensed, I told El it was Richard as he continued to lay in on the doorbell. I told him he probably knows he had something to do with the wreck and it wasn't going to be pretty. El got up to answer the door, but I flew off the couch and ran to the door. I begged him to go sit on the couch and let me calm Richard down. El walked back towards the living room. I opened the door and Richard pushed in. I grabbed his arm; he yanked his arm away and walked deliberately up on El who was standing not too far from me. Richard growled at him and asked him what he had to do with the accident. El told him he caused the accident. Richard pulled his gun on El and put it to his head. He told El he must want to die for ever attempting to cause me any harm. El didn't flinch, he told him he could understand how Richard must be feeling. Watching El's unyielding demeanor had me going all over again. Richard threatened to end his life if I ever suffered a broken fingernail behind him. El didn't say anything he looked at Richard unaffected by his threat.

Chapter 8

I decided that my everyday car should be nice, but not too flashy. When I told El I wanted to go to the Acura dealership he reluctantly agreed. I guess he felt the car should be fancier than that. But I was perfectly fine with my brand new fully loaded whip. This was my first brand new car, and I was loving the new car smell. The sales guy was losing his mind enough when we made the deal for my car. As we were getting ready to walk out of the door, El stopped in his tracks. He told me he should get a car for when he comes out here. I shrugged and told him that was fine if that's what he wanted to do. The sales guy had to take a minute to sit down and gather himself. El picked out a SUV and quickly made the deal. When we drove the cars to my house Bruce and Richard were standing in my driveway talking. Richard told us to leave the cars in the driveway so that he could put the main gate sensor on them, and I figured he wanted to put whatever he had before on my car on these. El told me to go inside so he could talk to my father and clear the air from last night. Richard would not calm down. El said it wasn't that he was unaffected by Richard's anger, he understood it and he said he probably would've reacted the same way if not worse if it were his daughter. Richard was watching El but I could see that fire in his eyes. I always knew Richard loved me, but this over protective daddy thing he was doing was calming to me. I know it's stupid, but you know how you always tell yourself if something happened someone may respond this way or that way. And then when it comes down to it, their lack of response leaves you disappointed. As of today, I don't feel like there's anything lacking in Richard's fatherly love and protection of me. Last night I fell asleep feeling loved and completely satisfied.

I paced in the kitchen for a few minutes, and then I remembered that I needed a pregnancy test so that El could be reassured that I'm not pregnant. Yesterday was system overload! El.... he just... I love that man! Thinking about it right now is exciting me all over again. El popping up on me was a complete surprise. His emotional rage was surprising, intriguing, and orgasmic. The way he handled me was impressive, I knew he was strong, but he held me against the wall with one hand!!! I didn't want to see that every day, but knowing that he's capable of it shoots explosions through me.

I asked Richard for his keys while I ran a couple of errands.
When I turned on my heels, El called me over and then he
kissed me quickly and HARD! I looked at Richard who
still hadn't completely calmed down and he was looking at El
like he was crazy. The butterflies started fluttering in my
stomach even though my body technically needed rest today
after the nightcap El and I had. Bruce couldn't help it he
laughed out loud. He lightened the mood out there a lot; he
told Richard that he liked El. He said El had balls of steel. I
went to the drugstore and bought a few pregnancy tests. I
figured these things were probably going to be a regular way
of living now that there were no condoms between El and I.
Derrick called me while I was walking around the grocery
store trying to decide on dinner. He told me he heard about my
accident, I could hear the smile in his voice.
I couldn't overlook the happiness in his voice. I asked him how
Brooklyn was doing, and his voice lowered a little. He told me
she was fine, but not important at this moment. We talked
business for a few minutes, and then he changed up and told
me he wanted to bring Chantel out soon. He said he was giving
me a heads up cause he'd probably be calling me. I confirmed
that we were talking about the girl from his graduation party
and that used to work for Malcolm. I asked him if that's who
he was complaining about before. I could see the
mind your own business look on his face through the phone. I
asked him why they broke up before, Derrick sucked his teeth.
He debated with himself, and then he told me it was stupid and
that his pride got in the way. He said he was going to be
working remotely a lot and I should contact him primarily on
his cell phone if I needed him.
When I came home, the three of them were sitting outside
drinking and talking with the puppies. I ran upstairs to my
bathroom. I looked at the pregnancy test in disbelief.
I couldn't believe I was taking one. I knew I wasn't pregnant,
but El…. If I was pregnant what would that mean? I don't think
I'm ready to be a mother yet. If I was pregnant and I told El
that I wasn't ready, it would be the end of us. I know it! But
what's worst having a baby when you're not ready? Or doing it
to please the person you're with? I could hear Drew's voice
reminding me that our mothers chose us when they had
choices. I know it would kill Andrew if he ever found out that I
chose not to give my child a chance because of what our
mothers went through for us. Which is why I never understood
him continuing to stick by Toya when she didn't have his baby,

at least one of those was definitely his. If I thought I was lost without Dennis, it would most likely kill me to be without El. Should I get pregnant just to make him happy? He didn't say that he wanted a child with me right now though. Ugh! I stood at the counter forever going over all the questions in my mind over and over. I stood there scared to even think about peeing. I put the box under the sink and then I went downstairs. They were smiling while Richard was talking. "Sassy comes out and says 'Richard! I wanted a pink one not a yellow one!' And I knew I was in trouble!" They all laughed at the story. I could tell they reached some kind of understanding because Richard was normal Richard again. Richard said he wanted to go out to dinner, Bruce said he had to get going. Richard asked where I wanted to go eat. I told him about this spot off Sunset that I wanted to try. El tossed Richard the keys to the SUV and we were off. When we sat down Richard's phone rang. He looked at his phone then his eyes scanned the room. He answered his phone slowly, but I could tell he was irritated. He told the person he was having dinner with his daughter, but they could come over. Ten seconds later a woman was standing at our table. She was gorgeous and had that goofy for Richard look on her face. Richard introduced El and I, he was waiting for me to say if she was invited to sit at our table or not. El told her to join us, and I flashed him a look.

She somewhat nervously sat down, "I'm so happy to finally meet you. I've heard so much about you." She said

"Really, cause I've heard nothing about an Erica." I spit

"Sassy, be nice!"

She looked at Richard, "she really doesn't know about me?"

"I told you it wasn't time. You're the one forcing this right now." He said dryly.

She looked hurt, "I see." She stood up, "it really was nice to finally meet you. Your father is so proud of you!" Then she turned to Richard, "I can't hang on waiting for you any longer. Have a good night!" She said walking away and out of the restaurant.

El and I exchanged looks. "Are you going to go after her?" Richard sat there drumming his fingers like he didn't know what to do. "No," then he sat back in his chair. "It's not like I invited her out with us tonight. She happened to be in the restaurant we came to." In other words he was saying she wasn't my momma so he didn't care. I wondered how long they had been dating for her to feel entitled to speak to me.

That night I gave El keys to the house, and codes for the alarm panel. In the morning, I took the pregnancy test, and when it confirmed that I wasn't pregnant I thought I would feel validated. But I felt empty and disappointed.

****

"Ms. Wallace this is Cleavon Dajean, I take it you got my flowers?"

I frowned, "flowers?" I looked around, "they must be with my secretary. Thank you?"

"The bouncy houses that you donated to our Fall Festival were the biggest money makers."

"That's good to hear... So you thank me by using some of the profit to send me flowers?"

"No," he laughed. "I sent that to you out of my appreciation."

"And you got my number?"

Cleavon laughed, "Busted! It was on the invoice. I wanted to thank you for your support of the school."

"Cleavon the Fall Festival was months ago, what do you need?" I said

"Your little sister is excelling in her science class. I was wondering if you would be attending the science fair?"

I exhaled, "I'm trying to."

"Maybe we can grab a victory sundae after she wins first prize." He inquired.

"We'll see. I have to go." I said as El walked into my office.

"Ok, well I wanted to say thank you, and I hope to see you soon."

"Alright!" I said hanging up. I stood up and hugged El. He's been quiet and thoughtful these past few months since I took that test. I think he was hoping that I was pregnant, but he won't talk to me about it. Whenever he's shirtless I can't help but stare at his tattoo. I wonder what Zohra looked like, what type of baby was she. I don't ask cause I don't know if that's going to put him in a bad place if I ask.

"Who was that?"

"Sabrina's Principal, he's got a taste for some Sasha seasoning." I said nonchalantly as I stood up to kiss him.

I could tell he didn't like that, but it wasn't my fault; and I wasn't encouraging it.

He showed me the latest employee handbook revision from Human Resources a new outline for interoffice dating was stated. El laughed and said it was a good thing we technically didn't work for the same companies anymore. I agreed.

Then he looped back around to Cleavon. He asked how he got my number. I told him what Cleavon told me. He asked me if "we" were going to the science fair. I told him "we" would go. At lunch we went over the plan. One of the labels gave me four tickets to the Alexa Keys concert in New York. El's friend Brody and girlfriend were going to go with us. But Brody had a conflict and couldn't go. I invited Darryl after El invited his sister. I didn't want her to go, but once Darryl agreed to come I knew there was no reason to think about Brielis. Darryl got in this afternoon and then we were flying out together.

El grabbed my hands, his face was very serious. He told me he loved me very much; I was waiting for the but. Instead he kept showering me with affection, which I was not mad at.

We found Darryl at the gate talking to a flight attendant. She was blushing, and he had his "Mister Charming' hat on. I waved at him; he waved back and continued to spit game at the girl. I snuggled into El as we sat and waited. He kissed my cheek, "I know this is the worst timing, but at some point we need to have a plan. When do we want to have a baby?" He kissed me again.

I felt like I burst into flames. "Are you sure we're ready for that? We can't even decide what coast we're gonna live on." He put his mouth on my neck. "I'm not asking for a baby today...." He kissed my neck. "But I think we should have a clear outline of what we're working towards. Our next steps." "Why would we put a baby before marriage?" I asked as gently as I could.

He smiled, "you've got a point." He said putting his hands in my hair. I hated when he messed up my hair like this, but I loved the massage. My hair was gonna be big and wild, I didn't care. "Honestly I'm nervous about getting remarried, but no matter what my clock is ticking. I can't run from that."

I kissed his chin, "honestly. I'm in no hurry to share your attention and affection. I want to be your wife first, and then we can plan it."

"You realize this is the first time you've said you want to be my wife." He smiled real big.

"This is the first time you've painted a picture of our future together." I exhaled, "but I don't know if we're ready."

He tensed, "why?"

"Zoila," I knew I didn't have to say more.

"But if I wait for her to be completely out of my system I'll never have anything. Are you completely over Dennis?"

"I can honestly say yes. The pain still hurts, but I don't have any longings for him anymore."

"Hubby?"

"Come on, he's married and happily married. That's done and over."

His voice got low. "Yussef?"

I felt nervous and like I wanted to deny him. "No".

He squeezed me, "it's not easy huh. To be honest. I wanna say Zoila is over we've been divorced for years. But the pain is still there."

"And you still dream about her. Which only shows how much I love you. I've never in my life played second best."

"You're not second best, you're first." Then he kissed my neck.

I kissed him deeply; I forgot we were in public.

We were lost in each other, and then I heard someone clear their throat. "If you guys don't cut that out I will separate you two on the plane to make sure we have a G rated flight." Darryl said smiling.

"Ooh! On the plane!" I smiled at El.

Darryl's smile dropped. "Sasha!"

Since our plane was a later flight most people were sleeping, and Darryl was a couple rows ahead of us in the first class section chatting with his new friend. El and I gave each other hand jobs under our blankets. El covered my mouth with his free hand as I almost forgot to be quiet. Then Darryl and his friend disappeared to the front of the plane. One guess what he was doing. When he walked back to his seat he had the biggest satisfied grin on his face.

"Brie, this is Sasha's cousin Darryl. Darryl this is my little sister Brielis. This little man is my nephew James." El said holding the baby as he took Darryl around his parent's place to introduce him to everyone. Brielis looked Darryl up and down after he walked away. I could tell she was interested, but she had to know she wasn't getting a nod from me. She walked over to me, "so give me the 411, is he single? Kids? Job?"

I looked around to see who she was talking to. "You're kidding right?"

She sucked her teeth and then she rolled her eyes and walked away. When I heard the men erupt in laughter I knew Darryl was in there being himself. A couple of El's cousins sounded like hyenas laughing so hard and loud. I was talking to Mrs. Parsons and Aunt Hazel when someone rang the doorbell. Brielis opened the door then she immediately yelled for El. All the men came out of the room because of the pitch of Brielis' yell. El was still holding the baby, he paused and looked stuck. Then he looked at me. Mr. Parsons told Brielis to let them in. Zoila walked in the door with two men. Both of them were tall one was skinny and the other was stocky like El. Zoila said they came to her place looking for El, and they wouldn't leave until she did. Mrs. Parsons looked horrified, Zoila stared at the baby in El's arms and she had a pained look on her face. I knew she thought the baby was his. The skinny man said he was here to speak to William, but he nodded his head in El's direction. Darryl came and sat by me. Zoila's eyes followed Darryl probably cause she didn't know who he was, then she locked in on me. She looked at El then back at me, her pain looked bigger.

El asked them why they were here. The skinny man said he was on holiday and he had to see him before he went back. Then the skinny man waved a painful hello to Mrs. Parsons. She sucked her teeth and turned her head. El handed the baby to Brielis. El and his father escorted the men to the back while everyone else stood quiet. Mrs. Parsons reluctantly invited Zoila who was still staring, in to have a seat. Brielis moved in closer. "Sasha this is..."

I cut Mrs. Parsons off, "we've met before. Hello."

"So I guess you're the reason he hasn't come back yet." She spit at me.

I smiled, "guilty."

It was like the more she looked at me the angrier she got. "It's good to know who my competition is."

"Hold on," Darryl said leaning forward. "Who are you?"

"She's El's ex-wife."

"For now, he loves me too much not to come back. Thank you for the baby, now he can get off my back."

"You're definitely talking big talk for someone who just walked uninvited into your ex's parents' house." Darryl said "Who are you?"

"I'm about to be your worst nightmare if you keep talking to Sasha like you've lost your mind!" Forget about his soft and playful nature. Darryl was in all out protect and attack mode. Brielis started laughing. "Who are you laughing at?" Zoila said "You! Neither one of you are good enough for my brother. And it amuses me to watch you try to be."

Darryl leaned over me. "With all due respect I'm begging you to check your daughter. Once I go in on her, I won't be able to stop." He begged Mrs. Parsons

"She's not gonna do nothing. She's weak! Your ex walks in your house and you say nothing! I bet you he wouldn't step foot in my house." Zoila said

Mrs. Parsons looked embarrassed and Darryl looked at me. "There's Toya's EVERYWHERE!"

"I'm sorry Ester, you can't let this little girl sit in your living room and talk to you like this!" Aunt Hazel said. "Get out! You brought them here!"

"If this girl thinks she's going to take my place she should at least know what she's dealing with."

"Why is that supposed to be your place? Anything they need to talk about I'm sure El has it handled." Aunt Hazel said standing up.

"Yeah! You're just mad that he found somebody prettier than you to take your place." Brielis said

That was the first compliment she's ever paid me, even though it was backwards cause she just told me I'm not good enough for her brother. Zoila rolled her eyes, "Sasha is not me! El still wants me! We will be back together!"

"Ick Darryl! She sounds just like Toya!" Then I stood up. "I'm not going to entertain your ridiculous conversation. You got three seconds to get out before I put you out!" Then I moved closer to her. "You might wanna rethink if you could ever keep up with him once he's had me! If you could have him, you'd have him. He's not stupid; hold on to the memories of what you had. The day you walked out of that restaurant was the best day of my life!" Then I laughed, "I don't know what would ever make you that dumb, but thank you!"

Zoila leapt out of her chair. I stuck her in her eye as I moved out her way. "Yeah Sasha!" Darryl cheered me on. I had to restrain myself from tearing into her like I wanted to. She fell on the floor holding her eye. Brielis was looking at me with big eyes.

El came rushing in the room; he gave me a disappointed look. I shook my head at him, "I'm holding back. Don't look at me like that!"

Aunt Hazel helped her up and walked her to the door. Zoila was trying to look as pitiful as she could. She gave El sad eyes and he looked away. "Will please!" She said

El's head almost spun around "GET OUT!" He barked at her. I looked at Darryl who was back in protection mode. I shook my head; she said it to get a reaction to make me ask the question. I was going to ask in private, but I could tell Darryl didn't care. "Who the HELL is Will?" He said looking at El.

El shut the door behind Zoila. "That's my first name, it's a long story." El said looking irritated

"It's not that long. I'll tell it." Brielis offered not looking to see if it was ok with anyone that she spoke. "My mom used to live in London. She was with El's father. He wasn't a good guy. So when my big brother was about six or seven, she ran away to the states. She met my daddy, they fell in love got married had me. Every so often they pop up full of apologies, but Zoila knows he doesn't want to see his father. She brought him here as an excuse to come."

El glared at his sister, " I didn't ask you to speak for me. Why don't you try speaking for your child's father since you seem to be as clueless as the rest of us about who he is!"

Darryl put his head down and shook it; he was trying not to laugh at the dumb look on Brielis' face. "El!"

"I'm so done with you! You have no problem with telling my business and causing me problems! You're just mad because no one treats you like I treat my woman! You don't like Zoila, but you let her talk to your mum like that!" Then he turned to the skinny man. "I can't help you! Please leave!"

The skinny man handed El a card. "In case you change your mind." Then both of them walked out.

"Let's go!" El said to me.

"Son!" Mr. Parsons said trying to calm his son.

"Dad! I need to go! I gotta get out of here! You protect her too much! I'm done with her! I'll visit you and Mum on occasion, but I'm done!"

"El what about James?" Brielis said

"Like Aunt Hazel said, you laid up and made that baby not me. If you had him with the thought that I was going to raise him for you.... I'm gonna have my own children!"

"With who Sasha? She's not gonna mess up her body just so you can have a baby!"

"I love how you choose to speak for me!" I said standing.

"El, please don't go! I'm sorry for upsetting you. I'll be quiet! I won't tell your business no more!"

El kissed his momma, and Aunties goodbye, and then we left. Everyone was quiet in the car, "El I know we were supposed to go to that concert tonight. But I think you and I need to get a drink." Darryl said

"What about me?" I said

"Sorry Sasha I need to have a conversation with my man." Darryl said firmly.

"Fine! I'll go to the concert by myself then."

"Why can't you go home?" Darryl said

"I had plans! You're the one changing them." I said

"I don't want her going by herself." El said to Darryl.

"She won't." Darryl said texting someone. "One of my peeps is out here." I looked at Darryl, and he shot me a look. "She and Sasha should get along just fine."

I knew he meant he was going to send Special Services.

"Right." I said in a defeated tone.

"You gonna be ok?" El asked me.

I could see Darryl shaking his head yes, out the corner of my eye. "Yes, I'll be fine. I'll just have to change what I was gonna wear."

When we got to the condo El and I went in the bedroom. He asked me again if I was going to be ok? I kissed him and told him I was gonna be fine, but we were gonna talk later on when he came home. He agreed.

As I finished my makeup I heard Darryl introducing the person. I exhaled then I grabbed my purse and jacket. Darryl introduced her as Teresa, the way her eyes glided over my outfit, and I shot Darryl a look. Teresa was about the same complexion as me, long hair slicked back into a pony. She looked Latin though and very gay. She said hi and shook my hand. El was trying to read my face, I gave him a kiss and then I left with Teresa. I asked Teresa for her badge and sent a picture of it to Richard. He replied five minutes later "green."

So I told Teresa we were going to the Alexa Keys concert and she got excited. We chatted a little in the car service, her eyes kept roaming and I told her to cut it out. She didn't realize she was shooting me looks so she apologized. We took our seats in the second row. This is the way I like to roll at a concert outside of being backstage. I had passes for backstage, but I wanted to see the show. A few minutes to curtain and a tall and big light skinned guy walked past me with two girls and then they sat in front of me. I smiled and pushed one of the girl's head. She turned around with a lot of attitude and a serious expression like her daddy. I stuck my tongue at her and she screamed and hugged me tightly over the seat. Her sister screamed and hugged me too. I introduced Tiffany and Crystal to Teresa. Dwayne came with his million-dollar smile and a hug. I told the girls Darryl was gonna be mad that he missed them. The girls asked what I was doing after the concert. I shrugged, they asked me to consider joining them. I told them they were on. When they went to their seat Teresa asked me how I knew Dwayne Reed. I told her he used to date my cousin. The show was excellent! Alexa put on a wonderfully artistic show, she even had Comfort the Rapper come out and perform a couple of songs with her.

When the show was over I told the girls I had backstage passes and I asked them if they wanted to go. Teresa told the four of us to go and that she'd meet us back there. The girls were so excited; Dwayne broke out the million-dollar smile when he saw Alexa. She looked tired, but happy to meet her fans. She did a double take when she saw Dwayne smiling at her. The girls and I stood there watching them flirt with their eyes. By the time we were walking away she had given Dwayne her number. Dwayne took us out to dinner at some restaurant that I had never heard of. I thought the food was going to be just ok, but it was actually really good. We laughed so hard telling Teresa story after story of when we were younger and their dad was dating my cousin. Their stories always included tid bits about their favorite big brother Darryl. I told them that Andrew had a baby and they couldn't believe it. Dwayne said, "so Amber's a grandmother. How does she like that?" The girls smirked at him and even I was like un huh he's still in love with my cousin slash auntie slash momma. I wonder if Alexa reminded him of Amber, the more I read him the more it seemed to be that way. The restaurant was pretty empty and we were still talking, drinking, and carrying on having a good time. Dwayne was in the middle of his story when he looked up and smiled.

Darryl and El were walking in with serious faces. Darryl hugged the girls and shook Dwayne's hand. El asked me why I haven't answered my phone in a low tone. I had thirty-two missed calls from El, and two from Darryl. I forgot to turn my ringer back on after the concert, and since my phone was in my purse I didn't feel it vibrate. El looked at Dwayne with jealous eyes and asked what I was doing. I turned his attention to the girls; Darryl introduced them as his little sisters. Darryl told him everybody at the table was related. El's eyes relaxed some, but just so there was no misunderstanding I gave El my seat next to Dwayne and I moved one over when our waiter brought the extra chair. Teresa left once Darryl arrived. Dwayne congratulated Darryl on his new nephew. I introduced Dwayne to El, Dwayne gave El serious eyes. "Word of advice, the women in this family will run from you if you don't chase them!"

"My momma hid from you! She didn't just run! If you gonna tell it, tell it right!" Darryl said swishing his drink around in his hand. Everyone laughed.

"All I know is you were going to propose and then all of a sudden you, were upset, and we didn't see Amber anymore." Crystal said sadly at the memory.

Darryl smirked while cutting his eyes at Dwayne. "D-way! Say it ain't so! No you were not!"

Dwayne nodded his head yes. "Yep, I was going to pick up the ring the next week. I woke up and she left her keys and everything behind. My cousin **_Adrienne_** told me to keep fighting for Amber. I didn't get the impression that Amber wanted me anymore. Before I could think straight I was caught up. I don't regret my kids, but I regret allowing my interpretation of defeat to stop me from fighting." He looked at El, "how many times she shut down on you?"

El laughed and shook his head, "man!"

"Stay on top of your defense! Don't let her call the game at half time."

Tiffany blew air, "daddy use your words. Don't use football talk."

"Let me tell you something about Wallace women, no Wallace's period." Darryl said adjusting in his seat. "We might have our moments like everybody else, but when we decide on someone for forever that's it. That's how it's going down, no matter who comes along. Dwayne you've always been cool with me, D-Rick is a different story." Darryl smiled, "but my father's name is Malcolm! Anyone crazy enough to battle him loses. It wasn't personal, and I know my momma cared a lot for you. No one else ever got as close to her as you did. But she couldn't give you forever, she's in love with my father." El looked at me with a question mark. "Besides, you're too pretty! Who wants to deal with a pretty guy forever?"

We got home after four in the morning. I know El wanted to talk but I passed out as soon as my head hit the pillow. When I opened my eyes El was staring at the ceiling. He said Darryl went out to hang with the girls. I kissed him after I brushed my teeth. I asked him if he was hungry, and he pulled me back into the bed. Then he confirmed that Andrew, Derrick, and Darryl were Amber and Malcolm's sons. Then he asked me why he didn't know after all this time that he was working for my family. I shrugged and told him business was business. At the end of the day, if I didn't do my job I would be fired just like anyone else. I asked him why that mattered, and he said it wasn't it a big deal. But it did make him feel like I was holding back. I apologized, and then I told him to spill it. He exhaled; he said Senior (that's what he called his father) is a pathetic excuse for a man. He said Senior beat his mother, didn't provide for them, and had other children. He said randomly, his mother had the chance to bring them here temporarily. He said his mom met and fell hard for Mr. Parsons. When it was time for them to go back to London his parents decided to marry so that they could stay. He said Mr. Parsons legally adopted him. So even though he was born William Eldridge II, when Mr. Parsons adopted him they changed his name to William Eldridge Parsons. He said he doesn't go by William cause that's Senior's name. I rubbed his back and kissed his cheek. I asked him what Senior wanted. He said Senior needs a kidney and they have a reason to believe he would be a good match. Senior came to buy it. He tried to control his anger, he said he wouldn't give that man the satisfaction of him spitting on him.

Then he asked me if he should look for an apartment in LA. I asked him why he would do that when he already has a home.

****

"You know I love you right?" Ava said laughing at her annoyance

"Yes I do boo-boo!" I said teasing her. El needed closet space and although my uncle created these wonderfully huge closets in each bedroom, my clothes spilled over into the other closets. In my defense they were set up according to seasons though. I kept the summer and spring clothes in my bedroom closet cause I liked to look at them the most. El needs closet space and since we both like to shop something has got to give. I went through my closet and separated all the must keeps first. Ava created a pile of things she wanted to keep for herself. Then the other pile was for donations. Even though I didn't wear half of the things in my closet anymore, I was emotionally attached to everything. I kept coming up with excuse after excuse for most of them. Ava read through my exaggerations and put most of them in the donate pile. Her weakness was my shoes. Even though she took most of them down, I could think of the shoes I wanted to replace them with. My closets were pretty barren when we were done. I couldn't believe how much stuff I was donating. Since I only wear quality items I knew someone was about to come up. We loaded up El's SUV and my car full of bags and bags of clothes. Then we took them to the Goodwill to donate them. I couldn't wait for El to get home tonight and see that I unpacked his suitcases and hung his clothes on his side of the closet. He didn't have a lot of stuff here; he still had a closet in New York full of his things. But at least now he could build his wardrobe out here.

El went to New York to handle Mitigated business as well as finalize the sale of the place he owned with Zoila, sell their furniture, and put a nail in that coffin. I offered to come with him, but he said he needed me to create space for him here. I knew he was talking about the closets.

Living together has been a major adjustment. You never truly know someone until you live with him or her, and living with El was always wonderful during the honeymoon period. Rolling over to his sexiness has always been wonderful and I can't seem to get enough. But the other things started happening. Like whenever we go somewhere I thought he had me drive because he was getting familiar with the area. Until one day I told him I was tired and I wanted to ride instead of drive. We got into the DUMBEST argument ever. He hated that I always put my sun visor down. I told him I needed it for the sun. So he made it a point-to-point out each time I touched the visor. I didn't realize I looked at myself so much in the mirror until he pointed it out. He said he looks to his right to judge traffic and my visor is always in the way. I told him that was a dumb thing to be annoyed about, but that didn't change that I annoyed him when I did that.

El makes a mess when he's cleaning up. Since he can't cook, and can barely boil water. I do most of the cooking when we eat at home and he's in charge of clean up. He gets water everywhere while he's washing dishes, and he doesn't do the dishes like I would. He told me that was a dumb thing to be annoyed about because in the end, my kitchen was clean so he didn't understand my point. But why make a bigger mess and then have to clean it up?

I had to stay on his case about when he trims his beard. I have to constantly remind him to put a towel down and to clip over the towel. When I don't remind him he gets hair everywhere. Until the housekeeper comes I will find little hair surprises everywhere.

I love going shopping with him though. And I have to admit that my expensive taste has only gotten worse since we've been together and I've gotten accustomed to El showering me with pretty much anything I look twice at. He treats me like the Princess I should've always been. Anything I want he gladly provides.

****

"I want to go out tonight." I declared not giving El a chance to say hello or anything.

El was quiet for a minute. "Out?"

"Dinner and dancing." I said matter of factly.

El has been working really hard, not that I haven't. However, I would like to get dressed up and then go out with my FINE man on my arm. El didn't sound overjoyed about it, but he could tell I wasn't going to stop asking until he said yes. I packed up my desk and headed to "The Salon." I called on my way over to let them know I was coming and that they'd have to squeeze me in. When I walked in the door Brea was waiting for me with a big smile. She asked what I had going on tonight as she showed me to her chair. I told her I made El promise to take me out. Brea's eyes got big as she asked me how I did that. Her man has gotten so comfortable that he's forgotten to do things like take her out, make her feel special. I told her to tell him she'd like to go out and if he protests, then she needed to tell him she was going without him. Then she needed to get dressed up extremely sexy and nice and model her outfit for him, as she plays dumb to how she's affecting him. I told her if she makes it out the door alone to go out and have a GOOD time, and to come home late and exhausted. Too exhausted for him to reap the benefits of all of her fun. He should want to go with her especially knowing that she's going out looking good and some guy may try to snatch. Brea sat there thinking about what I was saying. Then she looked embarrassed as she asked me what she should wear to achieve these results. IMMEDIATELY I was irritated that I got rid of all those clothes that she could be using. I told her I would bring clothes by tomorrow for her.

By the time Ava diffused my hair and styled it I had butterflies. One of the things I love about my man is the way he dresses. Dennis always dressed nicely as well. But it's something about chocolate skin in quality clothes. El's bowlegged walk as he glides in and out of rooms.

When I walked in the door El was in the TV room with his feet up. He was dressed and waiting for me. I called out and asked him if we had reservations anywhere. He said reservations were at eight. I ran to the bedroom, I put on my newest little black dress and dressed it up with cream-colored accessories. I took myself in, in the mirror. "Yep! Still got it!" I told myself as I appreciated my reflection. When I walked into the TV room, El nonchalantly glanced at me then he smiled. When I asked him how I looked he said I looked good, but I was missing something. I frowned cause I knew I had everything I needed in this outfit. Then he picked up a gift bag from the floor that he was hiding on the side of his chair. I jumped up and down. I loved gifts just because; I loved it when they were expensive. I loved gifts period. I sat down with the bag and then I pulled out all the tissue paper. There was a box. I opened the box took out more paper and there was another box. I frowned at him cause this went on for a minute. Until I got down to two boxes. They were Tiffany boxes but neither were ring boxes so I knew better than to think this was the proposal. It was a pair of white gold hoop earrings with diamonds sparkling in them. And the other box had a heart pendant with diamonds in it as well. I gave him a huge kiss and then I put them on. We went out to dinner and then we danced the night away.

Monday morning Brea called me in tears. She thanked me for the advice. She said her man got up and went out with her. She said they had so much fun together. She said she thinks it's the start of something good. She said he loved the dress I gave her. I told her one day soon we'd have to go shopping together cause she needed to make sure he remembered that he had a woman worth showing off from time to time.

****

"Sassy thank you for meeting with me. " Richard said
"You sound upset."
Richard took a drink of his wine. His demeanor was tense, he looked beyond stressed. He poured a glass for me and he sat back. "Sassy I don't know what to do. I need to vent and unfortunately you're the only person I could think of. I need you Sassy."
I took a sip of my wine, "what is it?"
"Your momma..."
I cut him off, "Ugh! Richard!"
"I know! I'm tired of hearing myself. Erica wants to be with me. She wants to have a family. I want that but I've always wanted that with your momma. Even now, I want babies with her even though our oldest is grown. Your momma won't come out here."
"Why does she have to? Why can't you go back?"
"I want the space to be us. You came why can't she?"
"She was not happy about me coming out here either. But it sounds like you care about your stand-in."
Richard looked at me then he chuckled. He told me he cared about Erica and he could see being with her. But he will always be in love with my momma no matter what. I told him to let my momma go. He said he's loved her for so long, he doesn't think he can.

****

She was walking towards me and she didn't see me. If I was a snake, I could've bit her. I stood there staring at her waiting for her to see me. She looked rough and sad; her face no longer held it's youthful spirit. I was surprised that she was still out here, when Thea lost her job at Mitigated I assumed she would've gone home to her dad. When Thea saw me guilt was all over her face. My anger was fresh like I just found out about her and Dennis. She debated whether to approach me or not. I opened the freezer and grabbed frozen vegetables. Thea cleared her throat, but that didn't stop her voice from cracking when she said hello to me. I looked at her without responding. She asked me how things were going, and I stood there with a blank stare. She swallowed, she was debating with herself. "He came after me!"

"You went for it! You were supposed to be my friend! You pushed up on my father! Did you push up on my uncle too?"

"JoJo said he has specific taste." She said

"So that's a yes? " I shot her a look. "So that's it? You played the hoe and you don't care? I thought we were friends."

She blew air, "you weren't my friend. You always viewed me as inferior to you. Like I was your sidekick or something. Whenever we went out you always assumed that the guy looking in our direction was looking at you. You NEVER considered that he could've been looking at me. It was always the Sasha show! You didn't even consider that I could've been competition for you!" The thought of it angered her.

"And what did all of that get you?"

She smiled, "lots of passionate rendezvous with your man screaming my name!"

I rammed my cart into her cart pinning her up against the freezer. She continued to smile, she didn't look surprised. Then I had to step outside myself and tell Sasha to calm down. I was about to tear this store up whooping her butt up and down the aisles. "Sasha?" El said walking around the corner with some items in his hands.

Thea's face looked like it wanted to crack. "El baby you remember Althea. Althea you remember my man El!"

El looked at her for a minute like he didn't remember. "Oh yeah! Right! She came out during conversion." Then he looked at our kissing carts and her body being pinned. "What's going on here?"

"She's a nasty hoe and I'm trying to squash her!" I said pushing my cart harder.

El touched my hand, "baby come on. We need to pick out wine for tonight's dinner."

I pushed one more time as hard as I could Thea couldn't pull back the gasp from the pressure. El gently took my hands off the cart then he told me to come on as he took over the cart. Then he looked at Thea. He told her not to be stupid as he pulled the cart back. Thea started laughing as she stood there staring at me. "No matter what you do, it's already done. It already happened, hell it's still happening." She said.

I looked at El like "come on!" He stared at Thea like she was stupid. "If you're smart you'll get out of here!" El said "Whatever!" She said turning her back on me.

As I lunged at her El grabbed me around my waist like he was expecting me to react to her that way. Then he pointed at the camera, he told me to calm down. He put his arm around my shoulders and kissed my cheek. Then he kissed me, he told me to snap out of it. He told me I moved on to bigger and better, and then he kissed me hard. I held on to him cause he made my knees weak.

****

"My plane is boarding, I'll call you once I land." El said kissing me

El and Richard shook hands and then El went to the left and Richard and I went to the right. We were going home for a few days. Darryl put together a baseball game for us at the Oakland Coliseum. He was so excited to bring everyone together for a game, like we used to when we were young. Apparently Darryl and Malcolm have been going back and forth about our ability to squash them. I was excited to meet all the women in my family's lives. Then Andrew informs me that his fiancé Tracy can't make it. This fool has been talking about no one else for the past few years. He finally has her on lock down with a ring, and when I'm coming she's not gonna be there ugh!

Oh well, I figured I'd use this opportunity to make sure Chantel, Derrick's girlfriend, understands where I stand with her friend. When Chantel was in LA they stayed with me a couple of times. Her friend had sneaky eyes; looking in her eyes you could tell she was conflicted about something. But I didn't like her, she's selfish, and her feelings are the most important in the world. I told Derrick Chantel is always welcome, but Caprice couldn't come back.

"Sassy here's your uniform." Richard said holding it like it smelled.

Tanisha and I laughed at him. I waved bye to everyone I told them I'd be back tomorrow then I followed Tanisha out of the door. As soon as we were alone I asked her how she was taking Andrew's engagement. She shrugged and said it was fine. She said although he seems to be excited she would believe he was getting married when he actually gets married. I told her he was so sprung off Tracy, that I believed they were going to get married. She said it didn't matter how sprung he was, we know Drew and we know Toya. She said he was gonna mess it up regardless. Since I hadn't met her, I asked

Tanisha what she was like. What she looked like, did she like her, and was she hiding something.

Tanisha said the first time she met her was at Hubby's anniversary party. That stung a little but I moved past it. She said that Tracy is nice, down to earth. But, she's lived a very sheltered life. She said in her opinion Andrew babies her by keeping her from us. Like we're too much reality or something. I didn't think he kept her from us any more than I kept El away from them. I understand it, there's certain things you don't want to explain. I could hear a little jealousy in her tone. So I asked her point blank if she was jealous. She looked at me while driving. "I'll ask you the same thing when Yussef is getting married and then you tell me!"

I laughed, "I can tell you right now.... Yes! We don't need to see the future for that answer."

Tanisha laughed, then she told me that it would be unrealistic for her to feel nothing about it.

We drove to Berkeley up University Ave. to Shattuck Ave., a couple blocks up we parked. There was a long line outside of "No Words" a poetry club. Carina, Tanisha's girlfriend was going to speak. I hadn't met her yet, but Tanisha is the happiest I've ever seen her since they got together. I honestly thought she'd go back to men. But I guess she's waiting for Andrew in order for that to happen. This place was very dimly lit, with flickering candles on each table. It smelled like fresh baked apple pie in there. There was a full bar and a barista, and tons of fresh pastries and Italian desserts. So I ordered a cappuccino, tiramisu, and Hennessy. Tanisha got us a table pretty close to the front. Carina looked very excited to finally meet me. We hugged like old best friends. Carina told me she was so happy to finally meet me in person. She said she was a little nervous, but excited to perform. We listened to numerous artistic expressions of love and hate. A hour and a half in Carina went up. She was good; she read her poem with passion and enthusiasm. Tanisha sat there so proud of Carina, even though everyone snapped I clapped and stood up. Everyone laughed at my excitement. A few more regulars went up and the MC said, "Last but certainly not least!" Then he turned to the side. "Brotha I didn't even see you walk in!" He smiled, "everybody give up snaps for The Invisible Poet!" My mouth dropped when I saw Yussef walk up to take the stage. I looked at Tanisha and she had no idea as well. I shifted in my seat, after only seconds of being in his presence I couldn't stop my body from responding. I sat forward in my chair waiting for his voice. Yussef winked at me and I melted. I felt like such a groupie. Tanisha touched my arm telling me to calm down. I shook my head letting her know I was cool.

"Darkness surrounds me, am I sleep or am I dead?" *He licked his lips,* "inside I feel numb, searching for confirmation and acceptance, and I must be dead." *He takes one step backwards and then one forward.* "I reached out to her, gave her my everything, when she doesn't feel me, it must mean that I'm dead. Like brothers of a Royal family we have been, my life I risk to protect you, but still you betray me. I know, I know! You weren't in your right mind; your soul was suspended from the pain of your ancestor's tumultuous life. However, why do I pay the price? Applying the good book I put on the Christian cloth of love, brothers we remain. When presented with the chance of a lifetime, a moment to be free and feel alive. I walk away from this ***lady of the court***; my loyalty is to the King. Her touch fades again, my soul screams to live again. The most trusted of the Knights, most highly favored one, I was awarded the primary responsibility to guard your future queen. Now I understand Sir Lancelot, but the question is. How does my story end?"

Forget the snapping everybody was on their feet in thunderous applause! I clapped but I felt sad, who is she? Was he talking about me? The audience demanded an **"ENCORE!"**
As if he was asking for my input he looked at me. I put on a brave smile and clapped harder, when truthfully I was afraid of what I was gonna hear. When everyone was convinced he would give us one more taste, they sat down and anxiously waited for him to speak.

"She walks in the room unsure of herself, ***Intriguing!*** Fake it until you make it, ***Inspiring!*** Her uncertainty is what attracts me, ***Desire!***" He smiled, "Surrounded by the overly confident your uncertainty, ***Refreshing!*** When I talk she listens, only one before her was able to figure me out, ***Yearning!*** He gave me eye contact, "I live in her everyday smell, and peppermint is her biting base, ***Stimulating!*** Watching him disrespect you, ***Infuriating!***" He sounded mad. "Thinking only of your heart I build him up, ***Deception!*** Longing to live in your lap, ***Betrayal!*** Hiding what I feel, ***Fraudulent!*** Speaking what is on my heart to you, ***Freedom!*** Disappointing my brother, ***Growth!*** No longer choosing to be **Invisible** because I know

195

your eyes see. Your sight has resurrected me; given me the
love for my life that I need to set matters straight. No longer
content with being **Invisible**, I demand to be seen. Your love
has done this for me. Without the ability to say it, I read your
mind. Thank you for not being blind, thank you for seeing **me**.
Your Sight has been the cocoon that gave me wings. I know
you love me, although we could never be!"

Then he walked off the stage and hugged Tanisha.
Everyone was applauding again, "The Invisible Poet you
guys!"
He hugged Carina, and then he hugged me. "What are you
guys doing here? This is my honeycomb hideout." He smiled
at me.
As people walked by they patted him on the shoulders or back
to tell him how much they enjoyed his poems. "I came to
support Carina. I wasn't expecting all that. My brain is still
going trying to figure out all that it means."
Yussef patted my hand. "What you drinking?"
"Hennessy"
He smiled, "thug!" Then he walked towards the bar. He came
and then the bartender came with four shots. "1, 2, 3, 4!" We
took our shots. Then we sat back in our chairs relaxing.
"Yussef you're playing with fire! Please don't do this!" Tanisha
said looking really sad.
"So...." I drummed my fingers on the table. "Yussef, we need
to talk once and for all. Clear the air! Everything!"
Yussef sat all the way back in his chair taking me in. Then he
shook his head no, "nope! Can't do it!"
"What?" AGAIN! He's always rejecting me! I can't do like I
used to and push up on someone else to try to make myself feel
desirable.
"You're clouding up this place with pheromones! I know as
soon as one of those things hit my nose I'm a goner!" We
laughed
That made me feel a little better. "Goner?"
"You're always seducing me just being you. You almost got
me killed last time, I didn't want to leave. But it was the right
thing to do."
I started shaking my leg, "can we move over one table for
some privacy then. I'll try my best not to attack you."
He smiled then he agreed. Carina smiled at us, while Tanisha
looked disgusted. He asked me about El, and I told him
honestly. El and I got together before Andrew and Tracy, and

here we are stagnant not able to move forward. I told him how much his being a gentleman has affected me. He said he was glad that I stopped putting physical attributes in the way of everything else. He said there was so much more to me than just being pretty. He said he was happy that I found someone who redirects my attention. I asked him why he didn't want me; I braced myself for his answer. He waited for me to lift my eyes to his. Then he asked me who said that he didn't want me? I told him that he never called, and whenever I saw him he was distant. He touched my hands, "Sasha! I wanted you, but that would've been a disaster. Besides you're only truly single for a matter of days." We laughed. Then he asked again if I loved El. When I said yes, he laughed and shook his head. He said one day he'll get to be first, that hurt. I told him his poetry was really nice. He looked me in my eyes and said it's amazing that I was here tonight to hear both of them. So at some point he was talking about me right? I asked what was going on in his world, and he said a lot of nonsense. I asked him if he was single, and he said it depends. It depends on whether I meant physically, mentally, or emotionally. Cause he had a different answer in each space. I told him he was being vague on purpose and he smiled at me. He told me to be good to El. When the three of us went back to Tanisha and Carina's place it was very nice. I loved how it was decorated definitely Carina's handy work, Tanisha wasn't much of a decorator. We talked for a while, and then I got ready for bed. When I still hadn't started my period I figured my body was changing the schedule again. I brought a pregnancy test with me for the sake of argument. I was getting so used to taking these things that I had my internal clock set to go off when it was time to look for my results. As I folded my clothes in the bathroom I looked at it, and it said positive and I threw it away. I started to walk out the bathroom when it hit me that the test said POSITIVE!

Chapter 9

I called El to tell him my flight was delayed and that Richard would give me a ride home. His voice sounded weird, but I imagined him doing cartwheels when I told him about the test. Richard's nose was completely open from the weekend he spent with my momma. It is refreshing to see a man openly admit that he's sprung. I asked him what was happening with Erica, he exhaled and said he's buying time. He said he still doesn't know what to do. Then he said moving back to The Bay may not be so horrible after all.

We finally got to LAX four hours after we were supposed to be home. We pulled up to the house as the garage door was closing; El was coming home from the gym. I thanked Richard for the ride then I hurried inside. My heart was pounding out of my chest. I finally felt free to give El everything in me. All I kept thinking about was how excited he was going to be and then we could finally plan our next steps. Even though everyone was gearing up for Andrew's wedding, I'm sure I could squeeze my wedding in just before his without a problem. I said an excited hello to El, he replied with a flat hi as he stood in the kitchen drinking water. His lack of enthusiasm couldn't steal my thunder, even though normally when I go away I can barely make it in the door without him being all over me. I asked him what was wrong and he snapped at me saying nothing was wrong. I didn't want to talk to him while he was in a mood, and this mood was so out of nowhere. I went upstairs and he put on music downstairs. Sad depressing I never heard of music. His mood depressed me, which was interesting cause I was so excited before. I made an appointment with my doctor, and then I told myself confirmation from the doctor was a good idea before I told him. When he finally came upstairs he wouldn't look at me. He got in the shower then he slept in the guest room. That hurt my heart, did I do something? Maybe he was tired of me, but he was fine when I left. Amber called me and we chatted for a little bit, her project was wrapping up. She wanted to have lunch and then go to "The Salon" to see Ava for the works. The good part was that all I had to say to Malcolm is Amber wants me and I could have whatever I wanted.

El got up early, but so did I. His mood didn't lighten with sleep so I went my way and left him alone. I tried to shake off the negativity, but this was so unlike him. I cleared my calendar and I told Malcolm I was going with Amber. He told me to have fun.

Amber was so silly and full of energy; I forgot that I was feeling down in the first place. Ava squeezed us in and I had so much fun with them that it wasn't until I was driving home that I remembered how sad I was. I called Amber and I asked her if I could spend the night at her place. Since I didn't have clothes that meant I would have to find something in her closet.

DARN! I LOVED shopping in her closet. She has some of the cutest stuff and the part that I loved is that when I showed that I liked something she'd give it to me. I thought about calling El but I decided against it. I enjoyed the night with Amber eating ice cream and being silly. El didn't call me all night, this is not like him.

In the morning, I stood in front of all of Amber's beautiful clothes. I looked at Malcolm's clothes on his side of the closet. El had way more clothes than he did, and he wasn't as specific as Malcolm. It seemed like his clothes were color coded, etc. everything had its place. I browsed Amber's clothes, I needed something easy to get in and out of at the doctors this morning. I found a cute mocha colored dress that was too cute. Amber said she could kiss this dress goodbye. I smiled at her and thanked her for everything. "Are you ok honey? I keep telling myself to mind my own business, but I see it all over your face and in your eyes." She said holding my hands and looking at me like a mother looks at their child.

"He's acting weird, I don't know what's wrong." I said as tears poured out of my eyes.

She lifted my chin with her finger, "is he worth it?"

"Yes!" I said

"Don't waste time, go to him right away. Stop wasting your energy trying to figure it out. Go talk to him."

"Ok" I said wiping my tears.

I hugged her then I went to the doctor. I went to the lab first for blood work and then as I made my way up to my doctor I stopped at the bathroom. I blinked twice to make sure I was seeing right. There was blood, I went into panic mode. I put on a napkin that I happened to have in my purse. I almost ran to the waiting room. They couldn't call my name fast enough. As soon as I got in the room I was in tears. I told Nurse Jasmine quickly, and she made sure the doctor came in right away. It took her twenty minutes to calm me down. I drank water while she told the lab to process my blood work. While we waited for them I gave a urine sample. The doctor came back with sad eyes. She said the urine and blood work both were negative. It took another twenty minutes to calm me down.

As I walked to the car I called Malcolm. "This is Malcolm"

"Malcolm?"

"Sasha!" His voice had no emotion.

"I need some time off, I can't go into the office today."

He was quiet for a minute, "are you ok?"

"NO!" I mean he hears me crying, what does he think?

"Let me know how long you need."

"Thank you," I said

"I will need your secretary to send me your notes and itinerary."

"Ok, thank you." I wanted him to ask me what was wrong but that isn't Malcolm's style.

I threw myself on the bed and I cried myself to sleep. I heard the garage door close. I buried my face in my pillow and started crying again. At least I didn't have to un-tell him about my false positive.

"Are you sick?" He asked standing in the doorway.

"What's wrong El? We don't behave like this." I said in between sobs. "What happened in Boston?"

He sat on the bed with his back to me. "I ran into my ex. It's been messing with my head. I don't know what we're doing! Everything with us has been a reaction to my past. When I moved here, kids laughed at me and poked fun at the way I spoke. I didn't go for the pretty girl in school that was asking for heartbreak. In college I met Inez. She was not gorgeous, but she was beautiful to me. She started my clothing habits, pretty much everything that makes me who I am today. We promised that as soon as we graduated we were getting married. Was she good to me? No. Sometimes she was nice, but I loved her with everything in me. When she was pregnant I was ready to leave school to support us. I couldn't love her more. I was going to be the father Senior never was. I was going to ask her to marry me after all of the pushing. One problem, when that baby came out it wasn't black. I thought I misunderstood at first and he would darken. Days turned into weeks and months, that baby was not mine. I even tried to convince myself I could raise him anyways but the father came to claim his son. I finished school and got a good job. Then I met Zoila; she wasn't as bad as Inez, and way prettier. Well, you know how that story ends. I'm walking down the street when I see Inez. Her son, I'm assuming her husband and the rest of their kids. I'm wondering what I'm doing with my life.

What are we doing? I'm here showing you that Zoila is my past, I wanna move forward. You're dragging your feet... Your cousin has had a baby and got engaged to someone else and here we are. I don't want to do this anymore Sasha. It kills me to say it."

"Then don't say it!"

"We don't want the same things."

"Yes we do!"

He shook his head, "you're just saying that. No we don't. I don't want you to force yourself to do anything. I want you to want it, and you don't."

"Yes I do!" I said through tears

He took a deep breath, "I talked to Zoila. Knee jerk reaction I guess. We started talking about Zohra. Before I knew it I was back in the city." His eyes were on the floor.

I smacked him hard upside the head. "SO YOU MEAN TO TELL ME! YOU'RE LEAVING ME TO GO BACK TO HER? THE TRICK WHO THREW YOU AWAY! I WANT YOU! I LOVE YOU, AND YOU'RE GOING TO LEAVE ME?"

"I need some space, I need to think this through."

"What's to think about?" My wall started going up. "No one's begging you to be here!" I allowed my bleeding heart to say every mean and hurtful thing I could remember to say. When he tried to hug me I started firing on him. He took the hits while he hugged me.

"I love you Sasha!"

"If you love me why does it have to be all this? You can be a pushover for them, but Sasha gets the man's man who leaves her? YOU'RE NOT A MAN!" Then I went in the closet and got my suitcase.

"Where are you going?" He said sounding tired.

"Out! Away! Doesn't matter you don't care anyways! Just be gone when I come home!"

"Sasha, let's talk about it?"

"Talk about what? You're going back to the woman who can't have babies, until I guess you find a creature from the black lagoon to have your baby. I don't need to stand by to watch this happen! Get out of my house!"

"I'm not leaving until we discuss this!" He said taking my suitcase.

"What is there to discuss? You're over there telling me what I want and how I feel. You don't need me to finish the conversation. Give me my suitcase!"

"No Sasha!"

"Keep it!" I grabbed my purse and hurried out the door. I hit him hard with the door when I snatched it open. I walked out and into the garage. When I opened the garage door he was standing in my way. I put my foot on the gas to tell him I would run him over. When he didn't move I put the car in reverse and I stepped on the gas. He moved just before I hit him, he kicked my car.

I didn't know where I was going, but I needed to feel comforted. I went to the office. I grabbed my laptop and I got in the car and headed towards the North. Five hours later, I walked in my momma's door. My momma and Sabrina were watching TV cuddling on the couch when I walked in. My momma said I almost got shot walking in her door like that, and to call to let her know I was coming next time. Sabrina ran to me and threw her arms around me. I sat on the couch in the middle of them. We didn't say anything I sat there surrounded by love.

****

My momma said I overreacted and that I needed to go back and talk to El. I told her I couldn't do it. I couldn't face him just to watch him leave me. I told her this was so random and out of the blue. Then she pointed out that he always made it clear that he wanted to remarry and have children. She asked me when was the last time he brought it up. I admitted that it had been awhile since he had brought it up. She asked me if I thought his needs had changed just because he stopped asking for them? Feeling like she had me up against the ropes I told her about my false positive, she held her stomach as she waited for me to finish. She exhaled deeply when I explained that the doctor said the test could've been defective or I could've waited too long to read my results which is one of the main reasons why most women get false positives. My momma said she wasn't ready to be a Nana yet. I rolled my eyes at her comment. Then she went back to her point. She said she thinks he was tired of waiting and it was time to put up or shut up. I told her he was saying that we didn't want the same things and that he was pretty much done with me so it was pointless to argue with him or go back to hear him say he was done with me. He pretty much said it all already. I didn't understand what I was supposed to talk to him about. I told her that I told him that we needed to discuss marriage before we talked about babies. He said he was scared to remarry and then that was it. I never said I wasn't open to the idea. Now he's flipping the script, I told her it was making me angry that she was siding with him. She said she was playing devil's advocate, and she wasn't siding with him.

When I logged in on my laptop I had a bunch of emails from El. He wasn't saying too much other than he needed to talk to me. In the end he called the way I left childish, and he knew I ran to The Bay probably using all of this as an excuse to lay up under Yussef. Then my air stopped as I saw an email from Dennis's personal email in my inbox:

From: dennisbarbeau@mytech.net
To: sashawallace@mitigated.com

Subject: Lulu

Sasha,

Lulu is sick. The doctors have given her six months, but it doesn't appear that she's gonna make it that long. I know how you feel about my family and me, I beg you not to hold any ill feelings against Lulu. She has asked me to ask you to come see her. If you can find it in your heart, please go see her. I'll pay for everything, please let me know if you can make it.

Dennis

My eyes filled up with tears. I screamed to my momma that Lulu was dying. I cried on my momma's lap. She called her restaurant manager and told her she wasn't coming in today. I asked my momma what should I do. It wasn't a question of whether I was going or not, it was a question of who went with me. I knew Richard and my Poppa would have a fit if I went by myself. It would've been a no brainer if I had gotten this email a week earlier. El would've come with me and that was that. But now, I looked at my momma and begged her to come with me. Surprise was all over her face. I told her Sabrina could come too before she had the chance to use her as an excuse. I made my eyes as pitiful as possible as I begged. My momma sighed and said ok. I told her I'd have Dennis book our flight to leave Friday and we'd spend the weekend with Lulu, then we'd come back on Monday. She said that was fine. I emailed Dennis back and I told him to book our flight. Sabrina was excited to miss school and to visit New Orleans.

Travis came by that night to get some hugs in with Sabrina before we left. We convinced my momma to go out to dinner with us. It's as clear as day to me that Travis is still in love with her. I could see her doing everything in her power not to see it. I honestly think my parents had their run; they need to let go of each other and move on. Travis is a good guy, and he loves her for who she is today. The only thing is that he hasn't swept her up. He hasn't caught her off guard and demand that she stops lying to herself. If he really wants her back he's gonna have to get her emotionally caught up. And I don't mean some kind of passive emotional outburst. I was always impressed with the way Travis would check my momma when she would get too crazy. He let her be herself, but he had a way of bringing her back in. Besides knowing that Richard's clock was ticking and my momma didn't want any more children, I could foresee the arguments and fights already. They didn't want the same things together that their love interest apart do. I typed up this whole heart felt email to El, honestly telling him how I felt. I poured everything out on my keyboard. When I read it back to myself I couldn't get over how weak and vulnerable I sounded and it made my skin crawl. I played the loving fool for Dennis, I wasn't gonna do it again! No! That fast my wall went back up. I saved that weak email to my drafts folder. Then I typed out a direct message telling him that Lulu was sick and that my momma was coming with me to pay my respects. Then I shut down my laptop.

That night, well that whole week really I kept dreaming about my dad. It seemed like whenever I would get comfortable in his embrace we'd fall, someone would tear us apart, or lastly he ran from me. And no matter how hard I tried I couldn't catch him. I was screaming to the top of my voice begging him not to leave me but he kept running. My momma woke me up holding me like she used to when I was little and crying her own tears. She said she heard me screaming for my dad. We held on to each other crying our eyes out. I asked her why he had to die. My momma said he didn't have to die, but his inability to let the past go is what cost him his life. She started rocking me and I wondered if the caress was soothing her or me more. She said she met my dad in junior high school after he declared his crush on Amber. I gasped and looked at her with wide eyes, "not my dad too!" She asked me what I meant by too? I told her Hubby and his brother Dude had crushes on Amber too. She eyed me and said we'd loop back around to that in a minute. She told me that my dad and Amber were boyfriend and girlfriend for a little while it was PG-13 at best, then Malcolm showed up to reclaim his woman. She said she believes that he honestly thought at some point he and Amber were going to get back together. She said the night he died, he went to Amber's house because he heard that she and David had broken up. I told her he said he was there to see me, but honestly I knew it wasn't true. I hadn't seen him in forever and then he just so happened to pop up. Talking to my momma took a huge weight off my shoulders. I honestly believed he died fighting David cause he was looking for me and David misunderstood.

Then my momma gave me a knowing look and asked when I was gonna come clean about Hubby. I felt like my teenage self as I tried to play dumb. She rubbed my back and laughed, then she asked me if I thought she put me on birth control just because, I really thought she did. We laughed a good laugh, and then I told her everything. Well as much as a daughter can tell her mother without her losing it. She's pretty good at filling in the blanks. I told her I loved her, and then I told her to let Richard go. I told her she's looking backwards just.... It pained me to say his name, but I sucked it up, just like Charles did. She squeezed me tighter.

****

Dennis had the biggest smile when he saw us coming towards him. I couldn't believe my eyes as I looked at the pre-teen version of Jim standing next to him. "Sabrina? Oh my God! You are completely blossoming! Are you driving yet?" Dennis asked her.

"Not legally," she said

"What?" My momma said.

"My daddy takes me driving." She said proudly.

"How are you doing Sophia?" He said as he gave my momma a hug. "This is my son Jim." He said as he looked at me for a reaction.

Jim was looking at me too. I put my arms out to him and he charged me. He hugged me tight picking me up off the ground. Little man was strong, ok. Dennis's face was completely jealous as he watched us. I told Jim I've missed him, and as unemotional as he could he told me he missed me too. Sabrina remembered Jim although Jim did not remember her. Looking at Jim next to Dennis if I ever doubted it before it was so clear now that he was his father's son. I waved hello to Dennis, he gets no hug from me. Dennis took us to our hotel so that we could put our bags down, then he took us to Lulu's house.

Dennis kept staring at me; I didn't feel like rolling my eyes or anything. I accepted his stare and kept it moving. Lulu's house was a big old Plantation styled house. For all I know it could've been a plantation once upon a time. I had only been here a few times before, but I knew that a lot of Dennis's family hung around here. So this is the last place Mrs. Barbeau wanted to be. To have not only her mother but her siblings and family remind her that at the end of the day she's a black woman.

Mr. B was kicking back on the porch swing with some cousins and Lawrence. He got really excited when I got out of the car. He met me on the steps and squeezed the life out of me. He told me I could still come see him, he shouldn't have to lose a daughter because his son's an idiot. Lawrence waved hello from his seat on the rail. I introduced my momma and sister to everyone. Everyone's reaction was the same when I said she was my momma; everyone thought she was my sister. When I walked into the living room Marika gave me the biggest hug then she introduced me to her twin girls, they were beautiful. When I gave her a confused look she said they were adopted. "Hhheeyyy Sasha!" Mrs. Barbeau said with her drink in her hand.

I said hello then I shot Marika a look, she whispered that we would talk about that later. I introduced my momma and sister to everyone then I took one more listen to Mrs. Barbeau speaking in her native down home tongue. Marika and my momma hit it off right away. My momma said she was gonna stay downstairs with Marika. Sabrina was hanging with the teenagers that fast. Dennis told me to follow him. His cousin Rochelle who I hadn't seen in ages was coming down the stairs as we were going up. She gave me the biggest hug and she told me we'd have to catch up before I left. Lulu had so many pictures of all her family all over the walls you could barely see the old school wallpaper behind them. There were so many shades of brown some as light as Dennis and Lawrence to some as dark as Malcolm, and everything in between.

Dennis lightly tapped on the door as he opened it. He gently called out to Lulu and his aunt said she just fell asleep. Then Dennis asked if I wanted to wait with her. I said yes, and then his aunt thanked me stating that she could go grab a bite to eat. I sat in the chair closest to her bed, there were chairs all around the room, like everyone who could fit came and sat in here at one time or another. The heavy curtains were shut which blocked out a lot of the sunlight in the room. The lamp next to her bed was on. Dennis stood by the door; he asked me if it was ok for him to stay. I told him it was, he sat in the third chair away from me. "How have you been?" He asked "Good," I said shaking my head. "And you?" He put his hand out and shook it, "so-so." "I see you and Jim have adjusted to your new rolls." "It's a work in progress, some days are better than others. He's still mad at me for lying to him. I try to explain that I didn't know, but I gotta take the lumps right. If I wasn't self-entitled none of this would've happened." He said sounding defeated. "Yeah, but then he wouldn't be here." I said "Good point, but I know better than to point that out." "He's only mad at you? He's ok with Kelsey?" "No, Jim has enough anger to spread around. Lawrence and my dad are the only ones who can calm him down. I'm still Dennis and Lawrence is still dad." He exhaled, "I made my bed right?" "Right!" I said not feeling sorry for him. Lulu started laughing a deep laugh. She spoke slowly, "that's my Sasha! That's right baby! No sympathy over here!" Then she opened her eyes. "Come and give me some suga!" I gave her a hug and a kiss. "I didn't ask Sasha to come see me for you to Mack. Go find something to do so I can talk to my baby." She ordered Dennis. I could tell he was disappointed thinking he'd have more time with me. When he left she laughed at him and said he's a mess. She thanked me for coming to see her off; she said she wanted to see all her babies one last time. She asked me if I was mad at her for outing her grandson like she did. I assured her that the thought never crossed my mind to feel anything about her other than she was the only one who knew and had my back. I told her Dennis would've lied and her daughter would've gone along with the lie. Lawrence would've been gone, and that would've left the burden on Mr. B and he wouldn't have wanted me to hurt like that. I thanked her over and over for setting the wheels to set me free. She told me that I did look different, I wasn't overly sexy. I laughed caused even Lulu noticed; she said there wasn't anything wrong with me before. But now I look like I know more of who I am. I told her I was still trying to figure myself out. She said she could see it in my eyes that it was a man, and a good man at that. I tearfully told her that El is a good man, but I couldn't stand to hear him say he was done with me so I ran from him. She asked me how I knew he was gonna be done with me. I told her how different he was when I came home. He's never acted like that, she told me to stop running from him. Then she said my disappearing act may cost me though. She said men don't tend to be good chasers when they're going through something emotional. That made me cry more, she rubbed my back and said if it didn't work out with El, that Dennis was waiting on me. That made me cry harder and she laughed. Then she said in all seriousness that she thinks he still sees my friend. I instantly remembered Thea saying that it was still happening when I saw her in the store a long time ago. I told her that I may have heard something like that from the horse's mouth. Lulu and I talked for hours, and then she got tired. Dennis came back as she was dozing off. I told him I'd send his aunt up, I guess he thought I was going to sit in there with him again. When I came downstairs my momma and Marika were cracking up at Mrs. Barbeau and her no rhythm having self as she was dancing in place singing to the music and a drink still in hand. My momma looked at my face and commented on how puffy my eyes were. I told her we talked about a lot of stuff. Marika leaned in, "so you're momma's down to go out tonight, you down to roll?" she whispered.

"What about the kids?"

"Shanna's gonna take the kids to a pizza place that has something for all of them. Dennis is paying for the kids to arrive in style in a limo. Then they're gonna come back to the house."

I shot my momma a look, "Dennis is paying?"

Marika laughed, "you know he set this whole thing up. Your momma told me he doesn't stand a chance. But that don't mean we should go easy on him because of it." Marika winked

I didn't feel much like partying. I wanted to talk to El and apologize for running from him. But I agreed to go. I checked with Sabrina who was in heaven with Dennis's cousins, but she tends to blend in no matter where we go. I love that about her. I told her to call me IMMEDIATELY if she felt even the slightest bit uncomfortable. She promised, and then Dennis took us back to our hotel. I told my momma I didn't bring going out clothes. I brought the clothes I bought for my stay at her house. Nothing to party in, and I didn't feel like partying. My momma gave me a smile; she said she knew I didn't. So she packed a few options, and by a few I mean she brought mega options. Her dresses were nice, but nothing over the top like I used to wear. I picked a grey dress that laid nicely on my body, not too tight or short. While I dressed I kept trying to call El. He kept sending me to voicemail. I sat on the bed and became obsessed with making his phone ring. As long as he was sending me to voicemail, he was interacting with me. My momma came out the bedroom dressed and I was still sitting in the same spot. She took my phone from me and told me to get dressed. I pouted and did as I was told. Marika came to our room dressed and giddy. She said she wished I was gonna be permanently around the family, she really liked me. I told her I liked her too. But unless Mr. B made a specific request she wouldn't see me again. She sighed, and then she told me that I should hear the way Dennis describes me. She said she thought she was gonna find me in some kind of bombshell dress. She said I looked nice, but the way he painted me was like I was always on and I was always a vixen. I told her; we all grow up at some point. I told her I didn't even bring a dress, and I borrowed the one I was wearing from my momma. She gave my momma a high-five and told her she loved her style. Sexy and classy. Then she said the men and cousins were down in the lobby waiting. When we stepped off the elevator the men and the cousins all stood up. Dennis was smiling, but I could see disappointment in his eyes. I stayed next to my momma; Dennis hopped in Lawrence's car at the last minute. We went to a club called La Rue in the French Quarters. We grabbed tables and then Dennis and Lawrence went and got our drinks. Rochelle was sitting at the table with us and we were getting caught up. She said she could tell I wasn't with Dennis even though he wouldn't let the words come across his lips. I told her we haven't been together for years, and the ONLY reason I was out here was for Lulu. A guy asked my momma to dance and she was off. Having a good time and enjoying herself. Rochelle and Marika watched my momma glide on the dance floor. Rochelle asked me if my momma was creole, and I told her no. I told her she grew up in Oakland California; most times she forgets she's white. Rochelle said my momma needed to give Naomi some dancing lessons, as she flapped her arms mimicking Mrs. Barbeau's lack of rhythm. Lawrence came and took his wife out on the dance floor. Lawrence had rhythm; his brother can't dance to save his life. But what I used to love about him is that he would try anyways. Dennis brought our drinks, I thanked him and then I stirred it but I didn't take a drink. When Rochelle cleared her throat like she was thirsty I handed her my drink, I told her I didn't feel up to drinking tonight. Dennis stared at the drink like he lost a bet. A cousin told Rochelle to go dance with him, she told me to tell

Dennis I wanted another one then she went out on the dance floor as well.

Dennis looked me up and down and then he asked me why I was holding back? He asked me if my boyfriend was extremely jealous and that was why I dressed so conservative tonight. I frowned at him and I told him there was nothing wrong with what I was wearing. He said I looked nice, but I wasn't on fire like I usually would be. I squinted at him. I told him he hasn't been in my presence in years; this was how I dressed now. Unless I was going somewhere that absolutely called for it, all my clothes were more modest. He frowned and asked me why. I told him someone showed me that there's more to a person than what they looked like. Then he asked me if I was still dating the predator. I frowned and asked who the predator was supposed to be. He said the fool with the dread locs. I couldn't help it; I had to laugh at that. Then I said I was still dating the same person I've been dating this whole time. I told him marriage was right around the corner even if I had to ask him myself. Dennis got a sneaky look; he reached in his pocket and sat a ring box on the table. He asked me if the ring from the Predator would ever match his. I scooted back in my chair like he sat a virus on the table. My heart was beating so hard. I could feel eyes on me and I looked at my momma who was no longer dancing and looking at us with her mouth hanging open. She looked stuck her own self. Rochelle was extremely drunk off that one drink and enjoying herself. I asked him why he would bring a ring. He said he did a search and there were no records of a marriage for me anywhere. So since he knew I wasn't married it was time for him to ask me a long overdue question. My heart started pounding and my curiosity got the better of me as I reached to open the box. Hearing my momma call my name in that tone that only a mother could, snapped me out of the trance I was in. I put the box down, got up and marched to the dance floor next to my momma. She put one arm around me while she gave Dennis the stank eye. Lawrence was so tickled seeing his brother get rejected like this. I kept looking at Rochelle funny cause she kept going and going off of that one drink. My momma was looking at Rochelle the same way I was. Then we shot Dennis daggers, I couldn't remember if Rochelle was a lightweight or not. But I didn't like the looks of how wasted she was off of one drink. I asked Lawrence if Rochelle was a lightweight, and he said not at all. He said they've been drinking since they got there, and she could hold her liquor. I marched up to Dennis and stuck my finger in his chest. "You tried to slip me something in my drink!" My momma was taking off her shoes cause she was ready to swing on him. Everybody was looking at Dennis as the pathetic joke that he is. He tried to get me to calm down but I wouldn't. I asked him what he put in that drink and then I said we needed to take Rochelle to the hospital to make sure she was ok. He said Rochelle would be fine. That still didn't stop my momma from slapping the mess out of Dennis. Everybody heard it!

In the morning, Momma, Sabrina, and I caught a ride with Marika back to Lulu's house. The doctor was there checking Lulu out. Jim invited us to go horseback riding with him. I don't ride horses, but apparently my momma and Sabrina used to ride with Travis all the time so they were excited and convinced me to go. WHY did I agree to go? It was a twenty-minute walk in the humid New Orleans heat to the neighbor's stables next door. The owners knew Jim already, and he told them to put all of our rides on his father's running tab. Sensing my nervousness they gave me a helmet, and gloves. My momma and Sabrina got on their horses without incident. My horse was HUGE and he looked at me like I needed to get a grip. Everybody was bonding with their horses while I needed help getting on mine horse. After all the laughter, I rubbed my horse who was rightfully named Two-Story and I asked him to forgive my ignorance. I was thoroughly impressed with Sabrina's ability to explain to me how to control the horse, etc. Then we were off, I was the novice rider, so we rode slowly at first. Jim showed us where he's been riding over the past few weeks since they've been out here. It was almost like we were on a talking and walking tour of the beautiful landscape out here. Jim rode next to me while he unloaded and told me how angry he was with his parents. He said he hated Dennis's girlfriend and his momma was always depressed from the guilt of everything. I told Jim I understood where he was coming from. I shared that my parents did something similar with me. His eyes got so big when I explained how it felt to me when everything was explained. I told him about the nightmares I still have sometimes. Then I told him in a way I had to be thankful for it. Jim frowned, I told him if their selfishness wouldn't have taken over completely, I wouldn't be here and neither would he. He held Dennis's expression as he listened. I told him I am thankful to be alive, and thankful that I know the truth. I told him some people are not fortunate enough to find out the truth and we had that. I told him I was happy that he didn't lose Lawrence in all this. He said Lawrence tells him that he didn't do anything wrong and that it wasn't fair to him to lose his dad completely. I told him that was the right way to look at it. I asked him if he could take it easy on Kelsey for me. He couldn't believe I asked him that, but he agreed. I told him she needs a lot of love right now, she lost a husband, a lover, and a son in one big swoop. Jim said he didn't think of it like that. My momma and Sabrina ear hustled a little bit, but for the most part they let us have our conversation. When we got back to the house everyone was up and around. I went up to Lulu's room and I talked to her while I ate. I told her about my conversation with Jim. She thanked me; she said I may be the only person who could reach him on that level. Lulu had a heart to heart with me that had me in tears. She said she was thankful that she had the opportunity to know me. She apologized for the dysfunction of her daughter that she passed down to her children. She assured me that her grandson really does love me, but sometimes love isn't enough to make a relationship work. She said Dennis is too selfish to do completely right by any woman, and he needed someone on that same selfish level. I thanked her for telling me and not keeping it a secret like a lot of families do. I told her about the ring box and his attempt to drug me last night; she rolled her eyes. At first she wanted him to come up so she could go off on him. I told her he was still recovering from Rochelle going completely off on him this morning. She laughed when I told her how Rochelle was punching and kicking him and he had to let it happen. She said he'd most likely give that ring to his girlfriend if I continued to turn it down. She turned her eyes to the ceiling and said she was ready to go to sleep. She was tired of the drama. I felt bad for mentioning it, and she told me she was glad I did. She told me she loved me just as much as her other grandchildren and she hoped when I paid my final respects to her I would be on the man I love's arm.

After that I spent the day blowing El up. Eventually he turned his phone off cause it didn't even ring anymore.

Dennis kept trying to be where I was and I would leave or move. I stuck to my momma, even took her and Sabrina in the room with Lulu. Lulu kept choking cause my momma was cracking her up. Lulu said my momma acts more like one of her own than Mrs. Barbeau ever did.

On the way to the airport Dennis asked if there was any way to reach me. I told him I didn't want him on my phone. He gripped the steering wheel as he tried to control his anger. It was like the kids and my momma weren't even in the car. He went in and so did I. The difference was that this argument did nothing for me. He was passionately enraged and I was annoyed. He accused me of changing everything about myself to fit in with the Predator. I told him I didn't care what his opinion of my self-improvements were. I told him that I stopped being a vixen when he broke my heart. I told him that was exertion of useless energy. I told him that he was so insecure with himself that he had to be surrounded by women who were always on like that. I told him I was young and dumb enough to like living like that before. But I've grown a lot over the past few years without him. When we got out of the car, he kept trying to hug me. I threatened to punch him if he didn't cut it out. Then my momma told him not to make us jump him at the airport. Dennis asked me why I was doing this to him. I screamed at him that he broke my heart! I screamed that if I wanted to do something to him it would be done. I told him that Thea told me that they still see each other. I told him if he has to get married then he needs to marry her cause I'm done with him and I will NEVER get back together with him. Then I grabbed my momma's hand and we walked with Sabrina into the airport.

****

I was an hour outside of LA when my car said that El was calling. My heart sped up. "Where are you?" His voice was angry.

"An hour away."

"Ok, see you in a bit."

My foot got heavier than it already was. I wanted to see him so badly, I hoped we could calmly talk everything out and end up on the same page. El's car wasn't in the garage, which didn't read as a good sign to me. El opened the garage door with a confused look on his face. I was happy to note that he hugged me back when I hugged him. I kept trying to read his eyes and he was doing the same to me. My heart was pounding out of my chest, I have never been more afraid of what could come out of a man's mouth. I had no idea of what he was thinking. As my eyes scanned the room I noticed that his decoration contributions were gone. My heart sank, I knew it. He moved out over the past week. At least he didn't run away, I prepared myself to protect me.

El exhaled and sat in the chair next to the couch. He looked me in my eyes and asked me how things went in The Bay when I went out initially. I was honest and told him that I didn't expect to see Yussef but we got a chance to talk. I told him I couldn't wait to get home to him. He told me since I decided to disappear again he did as he was told and he found a place. I couldn't help it I cried. He said he moved all of his things and he was coming to leave his keys. I sat there crying, then he said there's a message on the machine and I needed to hear it. He put the phone on speaker and then he played the one new message, it was Tanisha. "*Hey Sassy! Can you let El up for air so you can tell me how excited he is about the **baby**?*" She sighed with a smile in her voice. "*I'm so happy for you guys, both of you have wanted this for so long! Call me back! I need information so Carina and I can plan your baby shower, Sassy Style!*" She laughed, "*I'm so excited! I'm gonna be an auntie FINALLY!*" Then she hung up.

El hung up the phone with serious and painful eyes. "A **baby**?" I swallowed, this would not end well. "I took a test while I was there since I was a couple of days late. I was gonna find some cutesy way to tell you but you were in a mood. So I figured I'd tell you after I had the due date and I'd say mark this time off on your calendar or something cheesy like that. But I literally started my period while I was at the hospital. It was a false positive. You didn't even wonder why I was home or why I was upset." When he slouched I could tell he was disappointed. "But I guess it was for the better."

"The better?"

My anger boiled! "How dare you get so pushed out of shape with me because I haven't blessed you with a child yet when you haven't proposed yet!"

"I told you I'm scared to get remarried!" He growled

"But we live like we're married. Fight like we're married and you want a family like we're married. But you are the one holding our progress up not me!"

He sat there with a dumb look on his face. "I didn't think of it like that."

"El I think it's best you moved out." I said wiping my eyes and wall going up. "You're right, we've wasted enough time. If after this time you couldn't put that last part together on your own then obviously I'm not the one for you." I stood up and took my keys out of his hands. "My grandparents anniversary party is coming up and I wanted to introduce you to everybody. But what's the point." I made him stand up, and walk with me to the door. "It's all good, I guess we can say goodbye and cut our losses." I patted his back and opened the front door. I gently pushed him out. "To be so smart you are so dumb!" Then I slammed the door.

****

El is definitely not Dennis; Dennis would've flooded me with apologies and requests for forgiveness. To the point that I had no choice but to take him back. El came up to my office once, and it took everything in me not to smile because I was looking at him. He locked my door and made me stand up. He gave me the biggest hug while he kissed my neck. He told me he loved me, and then he said he needed to figure something's out. When I looked confused he told me that for now I'm free to do whatever I feel I need to do. I frowned, he said if he knows my heart like he thinks he does no one could replace him and he was coming back for me. I rolled my eyes and said that was weak. Then he made me look him in his eyes, which were red and slightly puffy. He told me he was miserable without me, but I deserved a husband who let go of his past enough to appreciate me in his present. He said he knows how beautiful I am inside and out so he doesn't have long, but he needed time and it wouldn't be fair to me to ask me to wait any more than I already have on him. I was ready, I tried to climb him. But he put me down and he walked out the door.

The next day when Malcolm was in the office, I came down to the Mitigated floor for a meeting with Malcolm in his office. El walked by the glass to go to his office. Malcolm looked at him and then he looked at me. He told me I shouldn't have pushed him. When I looked at Malcolm his expression told me that I knew exactly what he was talking about.

****

I could feel eyes on me. When I looked up from my book there he was looking like a model. I told myself not to be affected by him, and to remember why I HATED him. He came and sat at my table I didn't invite him, but Dennis didn't care. "Sasha! You're beautiful!" I didn't say anything I just stared at him. I didn't see the point in him approaching me. He decided to change his approach. Instead of flooding me with apologizes, he overwhelmed me with flattery. I took it in, but I still didn't melt like I used to. He pointed at my book, "So I take it you're single." I looked at my book for a sign to understand why he said that. "Whenever we broke up, that's when you'd start reading those secular books, like you were looking for a story to fill the void." I still didn't say anything, I stared at him. "Does this mean you can finally give me a second chance?"

"Tell me something, who came on to who? Did you approach her like she said? Did she approach you? At what point did you think about how your actions would affect me? Did you ever consider me?" I let my eyes burn a hole in him.

He deflated, "Why do we have to discuss that? We both know what I did and I am forever sorry about it." He said like that was supposed to miraculously change what happened.

"You should know by now that I am so done with you! Single or not I don't want you!"

"I know I messed up, but…."

"YOU HUMILIATED ME! This is beyond hurt, pain, and forgiveness! You could care less about how you affected me. You didn't care! It didn't happen one time and you were riddled with guilt and you came and confessed. NO! You guys were in your own relationship. Meanwhile, you're telling me I'm the reason why we aren't together! Now what? You're supposed to say you're sorry, and I let you back in? NO!"

"Yes, I did all of that and words cannot express how much I wish I could take it back."

"You only want to take it back because you got caught! Look at us! That was YEARS ago! YEARS! And my heart still bleeds like it was five minutes ago. Why would I get back with you Dennis? You're only going to do it again. Then you'll try to convince me that I like an open relationship. I'm not the same person you used to know!"

He sat back and blew air, "clearly." He shook his head. I waited for him to speak. "What are you wearing?"

I looked down at my outfit. I had on dark blue jeans, turquoise flats and cami, Navy blue cardigan, grey cross shoulder bag, a headband and my hair was in a ponytail. I thought I looked fine, but apparently he didn't agree. "Clothes."

"You look like a nerd."

"I am a nerd!"

He rolled his eyes, "well now you look it. If you had on heels, that would spice up the whole look. You don't show off your long legs anymore. You don't, you don't do any of the things I love anymore. When was the last time you straightened your hair?"

I stared at him, "get away from my table. I would like to go back to my coffee and book."

"Just because he's one with nature and has his hair all loc'ed up why do you have to dress down to be with him. What did he do put a spell on you or something? You aren't even together anymore, it's time for you to come back to me. NO ONE

WILL LOVE YOU LIKE I DO! NO ONE COULD MAKE YOU FEEL LIKE I DO! I KNOW YOU MISS ME! Sasha there is no one like you out here. I miss your fire, your spunk. You're the only person who could ever get me to do anything. Jim misses you like you wouldn't believe. Please come back to me. Please!"

I cut my eyes at him, "you humiliated me! I'm not coming back to you."

He stood up, "as long as I have breath in my body it will only be you for me. I'm not giving up on you! I know you love me, and we will be together again. I guess today is not the day."

****

"Yes?" I said looking at the camera

"It's me girl, I'm early." Kai said messing with something on the passenger side of her car.

I buzzed her in, and then I stood in the doorway. My puppies came close by like they normally do whenever anyone comes over. Kai got out the car with the biggest smile. She kept saying thank you, thank you to me for helping her out. Kai met a pilot, she said they've had a bunch of lovely and long phone calls but this was going to be her first time going out on a date with him. She said she didn't feel right about meeting him alone, she said she hopes she's just being paranoid, but in this day and age you just can't tell. I told her I understood and not to worry cause I may need to ask for the same favor in the future. Ava and her boyfriend Nathan were making excellent progress and so she couldn't think of anyone else in this area that could come as well. I didn't mind, I didn't wanna sit in the house and feel sad about El anyways. Kai came inside oohing and awing the new artwork I had purchased.

I got an email invitation to this art show at the Staples Center. I honestly went thinking that I would casually bump into El there, since this is the type of event he always seemed to drag me to. I felt like I was being drawn to this picture. It was a picture of a faceless man and woman and their child. It was titled the American family. The father was brown, the mother was tan, and the baby was somewhere in the middle. I imagined it was a family portrait of my parents and I when I was a baby. The more I looked at it the more I was drawn to it. The artist was there and she completely fit the description of a suffering artist. Wild hair, raggedy clothes, dark makeup to cover up her natural beauty. When she saw me she didn't smile she kind of watched my eyes. She pointed to the faceless people and said it was her mother, father, and her. I shook my head and said it was my mother, my father, and me. She looked at me again, and then she almost smiled. She asked me why we had to identify ourselves. I told her I didn't know what she meant. She said why does she have to be black or white, why couldn't she just be? I told her I'm both, but it doesn't plague me to be me. She asked me if I ever felt like I had to choose. I told her I didn't; I said I didn't have questions about who I am. I told her my momma was a white woman and my daddy was a black man and I was just me. I told her it was that simple and not to let people get in her head. I told her it wasn't complicated, at least not in my book. She stood there nodding like she was digesting what I was saying. When I asked her how much she wanted for her painting she smiled and said it was her most expensive piece. I put my hand up to my ear telling her that didn't name a price. She smiled and said three thousand as if she thought that was going to turn me away. I told her I'd take it and I wanted to see framing options to match my decor. Her mouth fell completely open, she asked me if I was kidding, I looked her in her eyes and I told her I was not. She was stuck for a minute, and then she looked me up and down. Khaki's, flats, white button up, small purse, and blue sweater she decided to judge this book by its cover. She acted like she was humoring me by showing me the different frame options. I picked one perfect for my main walkway. That was another two hundred dollars. She wrote out her receipt with a smile, I gave her my credit card and I told her to charge it. Her hand shook a little as she passed my card through the reader. When my transaction was approved, her eyes were huge. Her friend had to step in and give me a card, and their website information. Her friend said this was the artist's first big ticket sale. I told her I was glad to be her first. I told them that she has talent and to keep me informed about their upcoming shows, etc. Her friend packaged my painting and then I came straight home and placed it on my wall. It was perfect and I loved it! Money well spent.

Kai and I stepped off the elevator onto the rooftop of the hotel. Her friends stood as soon as they spotted us. Kai introduced me to her friend Chris, and Chris introduced both of us to his friend Teddy. Teddy tried not to have a reaction to me, but his eyes showed his approval. Kai and Chris were immediately flirting and in their own world. Teddy was shy and I could see him pushing through to be conversational with me. So I did my best to keep the conversation going. When our conversation slowed down some he asked me what I did for a living. I told him I worked for Latour Enterprises, I told him I did a little of everything. I was vague on purpose, I didn't know this guy. I asked him what he did for a living and he said he was finishing up his residency at the local hospital, then he'd probably continue on there. I told him that was pretty impressive, but I didn't say anything else. I guess that was all he had to say before and a female would flock to him. But it didn't mean anything to me other than if I started choking right at this moment he could help me. Teddy seemed drawn to my lack of a response to his profession. I told him he was weird. When he asked me why I said that, I told him his reaction to my dismissal of his profession turned him on. He smiled an embarrassed smile, and then he said I was weird for not responding to his job. Once we started teasing each other he relaxed and opened up more. He was a better dancer than El, and completely over Dennis. I enjoyed the evening enough to give Teddy my number. I wasn't overly excited about it, but it was nice to have a new something to look forward to while I found myself missing El.

****

"AND THAT'S A WRAP!" Corey yelled through his bullhorn like the man in charge. "GREAT JOB EVERYBODY! This is gonna be EPIC!" I came to the set to go out to dinner with Amber and her director friend. Today was long and very ordinary until Amber called and invited me out to dinner. Since Teddy hadn't called me I knew that meant he was working long hours tonight. I was happy not to be waiting at home for an invitation out. I told Amber the set looked amazing and I couldn't wait to see the finished product. Amber smiled real big and said thank you, we drove to her condo in our separate cars, so she could shower and get dressed. When Amber went in her room to get ready Corey said we needed to raid Malcolm's bar. Every liquor he had in there was top of the line and SO SMOOTH! Corey was telling me the story his wife told him last night about their daughter when the front door opened. Malcolm walked in with a happy but serious face. I hadn't seen him and Amber in the same space in what seemed like forever. I hoped there wasn't going to be any drama. Malcolm said hello but his eyes and demeanor were pointed to the room where Amber was. Corey took out his phone; I thought he was calling the police or something with how quickly he whipped it out. I told him we didn't know that anything was going to jump off in there and he needed to wait a minute. Corey laughed and said he was increasing our reservation from three to four. I told him he didn't know that Malcolm was going to be joining us. Corey laughed at me and called me a little girl. He asked me if I saw the look on Malcolm's face, he said Malcolm was coming out to dinner with us. So we bet five dollars, I couldn't wait to rub his face in it. Malcolm will always have a soft spot for Amber, but I think both of them have finally let the idea go and are moving on with their lives. We laughed when we realized we were trying to hear what was going on in that room. Neither one of them was yelling nor overly quiet so I took that as a good sign. I wondered if she was decent when he walked in there. I imagined if El walked in on me that I would strip and then tell whoever was waiting in the living room that I was sorry and that they didn't have to go home but they had to get out! After a few minutes the bedroom opened a little. "Corey" Amber sang...

"Already done!" He said giving me a "I told you so look." I laughed in defeat as I paid the man.

When Amber emerged from the room in her black and white dress, newspaper boy styled hat black and white shoes and cocktail length red coat I was in love. "You can have it tomorrow." Amber said, already knowing my eyes were pleading. I clapped my hands in excitement.

Corey's limo took us to the restaurant. Malcolm and Corey were talking about some old school movie, while I told Amber about Teddy. I told her how it was weird starting all over again, but this time my head was in the right place. I noticed the way Malcolm kept looking at Amber. For someone who's always so serious, it amazes me how he ALWAYS changes when Amber is around.

When we arrived to the restaurant someone said, "There's Corey Alexander!" and then a camera was on him. "Oh snap! Is that Amber Wallace???" The guy said. "You look AMAZING! You haven't changed one bit!" The camera guy said. Embarrassed, Amber said thank you. Then the guy asked if they hung out on a regular basis, as he completely ignored Malcolm and I. Corey said, "we work hard we play hard!" Then we went inside the restaurant.

"Do people still recognize you a lot?" I asked

"They haven't in a long time, that was weird." Amber said frowning.

"Why are you frowning?" Malcolm asked

"Because tomorrow they'll probably say I'm really a man or that I'm dating Corey. The media circus was a definite a turn off to being in the lime light." You used to see Amber on TV all the time. At first we got a kick out of it, then it became nothing new. In the end Amber hated it, I know a lot of that had to do with her breakup with Dwayne. The media couldn't get enough on the different spins they put on the reasons why, they broke up. But I wouldn't have liked to see my breakup with El all over the place either. I couldn't stop thinking of El and that was driving me crazy!

Dinner was nice; there was never an awkward silence at any point. Corey was telling Malcolm about their last video project. It was for this guy group and very futuristic. Corey told Malcolm he thought Amber would shy away from the project because of all the wires and the direction of the choreography. He told Malcolm they let her loose on those wires for three days and what she came back with was amazing on film. Amber blushed and thanked Corey for the compliment. "Amber can be pretty fearless." Malcolm said smiling at her. "Did she ever tell you how we met?"

"I thought you guys went to school together?" I said

"That's where, but not how." Malcolm said

Corey smiled, "please tell us."

"Some back ground first. Back then most people were scared of me."

"Only then?" I said, "I'm still nervous around you."

"I don't see why, I've been around all of your life. You're like a daughter to me." Malcolm said matter of factly. Then he returned to his story. It nice watching Malcolm and Amber in this space. Malcolm gave Amber compliment after compliment. I felt like my head was going to burst from the system overload, they were too cute.

I decided to mention Teddy to Malcolm to see if he had a reaction to the news. I wondered if he and El ever discussed me, Amber nudged me under the table to stop talking but I kept going. Malcolm was soaking it in, but he didn't say anything. When we were walking out of the restaurant Amber told me I could kiss my relationship goodbye, because Malcolm was gonna hunt him down. When I asked her why, she asked me what part of like a daughter to him didn't I understand? I swallowed hard as the reality of what I did settled in. Then I said oh well and shrugged it off. I was trying to be real with myself about Teddy; I was only passing time with him honestly. I had no plans of sleeping with him or anything deep. Seeing how they were gushing I knew better than to assume we would still have an impromptu sleepover. I got in my car and drove away, I found myself on El's street staring up at his apartment wondering if he was alone in there or if he was thinking about me at all. I wanted to call him, but Malcolm's I told you so kept echoing in my head. So I drove home instead.

****

"Good morning Sasha." El said as his eyes danced all over me. "Good morning," I said watching the elevator doors close. It was quiet for a long time, and then his floor came up, he wished me a good day and then he got off the elevator. I threw a fit when he got out of the elevator I missed him and I wished he missed me just the same. I buried myself in my work and before I realized it my clock said two, and I hadn't stopped to eat. My secretary buzzed my phone twice to tell me El was coming. That was our code. I quickly found my shoes on the floor and then I tried to look nonchalant rather than the stressed and pent up demeanor I held only seconds ago. El knocked on the door as he opened it. I smiled at him. He watched my eyes as he sat down. He asked me if I had plans after work, so I shrugged to say no. He asked if he could interest me in a trip to the Beverly Center for some shopping and then a bite to eat. I told him he was on, and he looked relieved that I agreed so quickly. He said he'd be back up in two and a half hours to pick me up if that was ok. IF THAT WAS OK?? Of course it was ok! I wanted him to pick me up, make love to me and then move back in and we'd spend the weekend wrapped up in each other. But I would settle for a shopping and dinner trip.

Instead of going our separate ways he followed me around the stores. Since I had an audience I figured I needed to make it work for something. I picked up a little black dress, "What do you think?" He shrugged and said it was nice. Then I saw a cream-colored cashmere sweater. The sight of it had me in awe. I picked it up and danced to a slow tune in my head. El smiled then he asked me what I would pair it with. I looked around until I found the perfect brown suede pencil skirt to go with it. El didn't share my vision, so I told him to wait until I tried it on. The neckline on my sweater plunged just enough for me to show off a decent amount of cleavage without looking like I was trying to do it on purpose. What can I say the skirt hugged me just right, I came out of the dressing room and I asked El what he thought. He scanned me and said the outfit looked good. I turned in the mirror looking at myself. I told him I liked it. Then I did a little dance, he got up and

222

joined me in my silly dance. His excuse to get in my space.
OH I SEE! He's missing me! GOOD! NOW! I asked him if
my outfit was a third date kind of outfit or if I should wear
something else? He squinted his eyes at me; he asked me if I
was dating in disbelief. I shrugged and said yes, but it wasn't a
big deal or anything. We weren't serious yet. I asked him if he
was dating anyone. He mimicked me and shrugged and said
yes, but it wasn't a big deal or anything. Ok so I know I started
this game, but instantly I was upset. I stormed back to the
dressing room and all I could see was red. How he gonna break
up with me, to date some random heifer! I was so mad I had to
sit down and take deep calming breaths until I felt a little light
headed. I told myself to be cool, because he invited me out
because he was missing me. Whoever she was didn't matter at
this moment. El was smiling at me when I came out of the
dressing room. He said I was in there for a long time. I rolled
my eyes and then I said I was taking in how good I looked in
the outfit. As we were walking towards the register I saw it. It
was fuchsia and a combination of a sheath and wrap styled
dress. I imagined this dress on me and I had to try it on. I gave
my sweater and skirt to El and then like a moth to a flame I
went towards this dress. I pleaded with my eyes one more
dress and then we can eat. He didn't understand what I saw in
this dress but he agreed. I unzipped the back of the dress and
stepped into it. The fabric was soft and heavy. I zipped it up as
much as I could and I LOVED my reflection. The cream
brown looked nice on me, but this was sizzling! This dress
showed everything, but tastefully. It even showed off my small
waistline and beautiful hips. I now took a deep breath to
compose myself to act like I don't know how good I look in
this dress. Depending on how I stepped in this dress the subtle
split where the dress wrapped to my waistline showed off
major thigh. THIS IS IT! THIS IS THE DRESS! I fanned
myself then I walked out of the dressing room slowly. "El," I
called out before he could see me. "Can you zip this for me?"
Then I stepped around the corner. His mouth started to drop
and he caught himself. He stood up fast and then I walked to
him to zip me. Then I smiled at him, "good huh?" I went back
to that wonderful mirror and turned every which way I could in
the mirror to look at myself from all angles. Then I asked him
if he gave this dress a thumbs up? And he gave me a sarcastic
thumbs up. I called him a hater, and then I asked him to unzip
me. He unzipped me slowly and then I quickly walked away
and did my own silent victory dance in the dressing room. At

the register when the salesgirl told me my total, I flinched a little cause I only had three items and my total was over eight hundred. I had the money; I didn't realize my total ran so high so fast. Before I could give the salesgirl my card, El handed her, his card. He said this shopping spree was on him. I smiled at him and the salesgirl shot me daggers, I frowned back at her. We went down to the restaurant and had dinner. Dinner was nice and almost like old times, but I knew at some point we were going our separate ways. I tried not to let it irritate me, but the later it got the more my temper flared. "El, who does this? Who lives together for YEARS and then goes backwards? What is this? Some kind of seduction scene?"
He smiled, "are you feeling seduced?"
"Frustrated is more like it!"
"I need a little more time Sasha."
"That's not good enough! You've had years, either step up or step down! All this stuff in the middle pisses me off!"
"I…"
I didn't let him say whatever he was going to say next. I picked up my things, thanked him for the clothes then I left. I don't have time for this!

Chapter 10

One thing I like, no, love about this job is that I get to meet
people in power and they're not always obvious. Sometimes I
feel like I'm in a room full El slash Dennis-Type men. Like this
guy in front of me now, he's about mid-forties. Very smooth,
not a wrinkle on even his dollar bills. Everything about him is
on point. The old me would've been on him just based on his
appearance alone. I saw him checking me out and trying to get
a read on me, but then I exhaled as the reality of him crossed
my mind. At his age why isn't he settled? Sounds a mess and
I'd rather bow out now.

We were having lunch at The Vine and going over contracts
for Malcolm's recording studios Silent Chaos. The label he
represents wants to secure the best market rate pricing. I was
showing him the plans for the various locations not only in
California but also across the country, the differences between
the locations, and the plans to upgrade some of them. I was
showing him the newest feature that allows our clients to book
studio time through an automated service, no more calling and
speaking to someone unless they wanted to. I could see
building desire in his eyes the more I stuck to business and did
not address his gaze.

He interrupted me, "are you married?"

I smiled, "no."

"Good, let's go out dancing."

"I'm flattered, but I'm here on business."

"We're gonna sign your contract, that's fine. But I'd like to get
to know you better."

"Where's Jillian? I normally work with her."

"Maternity leave, she'll be back after another six months. So
back to what I was saying."

"I can't, I'm seeing someone."

The paparazzi were just beyond us snapping pictures like crazy
of the celebrity couple at the table next to ours. I was so
thankful it wasn't me they were after they could be pretty
relentless at times.

When we finished our lunch, I went back to my office. I gave
my secretary the minor revisions to make to the contract then
we had them sent over via messenger for signatures etc.
Teddy texted me.

Teddy: r u busy tonight?
Me: what did u have in mind?
Teddy: dinner, drinks, ur lips
Me: sounds good, where?
Teddy: my place
I hesitated; it felt a bit soon to me to be in his place
alone. Although we'd been on a few dates, I still didn't feel
comfortable being "alone" so I wasn't rushing anything.
Me: um... Idk
Teddy: ?
Me: maybe we should meet somewhere instead
Teddy: u don't trust me?
Me: we r still new
Ten minutes passed before he replied.
Teddy: just got called in to work. Rain check.
Me: ok
I couldn't grab whether he was angry or not. You know how
you can't always pick up tone over electronics. But I wasn't
gonna feel bad about not wanting to be alone in his place just
yet. Something says it's too soon.
Clark called me with a smile in his voice. He said we looked
good together. I had no clue of what he was talking about. He
said the paparazzi caught us in their picture. He asked me to at
least meet him for a drink. He said he'd bring my contracts and
then we could grab a cocktail somewhere and then we could go
our separate ways. I agreed to meet him, I told him to come at
four-thirty. Around four-fifteen Richard came up to my office.
He said he was thinking about me and he came to check-in. I
couldn't help but smile at him. My secretary buzzed stating that
Clark Reyes was here. I told her to send him in, and then I told
Richard which label he represents. I introduced Clark to
Richard as I normally would. Clark kept looking at our faces.
He smiled and said he could tell we were siblings cause we
almost looked exactly alike. I smiled, and neither one of us
corrected him. I told Richard that we were going for cocktails
and I invited him to go. I didn't care if Clark had a problem
with that.
Richard got Clark talking. I could tell he wasn't impressed with
him. Eventually Clark left and Richard asked me what the deal
was with El and me. I told him El needed a little time to figure
some things out. Richard asked how I was handling
everything. I told him I'd rather El be moody by himself than
demand that he's around and have him blame me. I told
Richard that I'm tired of the single scene so who knows.

****

"And look at that, in a world where recording studios seem to be a dying business." He exhaled, "the way Malcolm continues to make his businesses thrive is amazing!" JoJo said

"Silent Chaos has been performing really well. But what do we want to do about advertising?" Henry said

I rolled my eyes and looked at JoJo. "What do you mean?"

"I think we could find a less expensive firm if we put feelers out there." Henry said.

I have been telling him for years to backup off of advertising. My cousin Gwen is good at what she does. I always snap when he approaches this conversation so I sat back and looked to JoJo to handle it. "I believe the deal we got is the most competitive for what we get. Do you have a specific firm in mind that you think could compare?"

"I can think of a couple." Henry said with a smile.

"Really?" JoJo said leaning back in his chair and reading Henry. "What's your affiliation to these firms?"

JoJo's question caught him off guard. Henry shifted in his chair as he tried to come up with an answer. "Um!"

JoJo smiled, "Henry you're good at numbers. We appreciate your work, but it would be a conflict of interest for you to strongly suggest your firm or something like that. The firm we have right now does an excellent job fulfilling our needs. Are we good?"

"Good?" Henry asked

"I gather by Sasha's demeanor this is not the first time this topic has come up. I'm making sure you understand that this topic is dead and it will not be discussed again." He stared at Henry's eyes.

"Yes" Henry said looking away.

"Good! Now let's go eat!" JoJo said to me as he punched something into his phone.

As we were on the elevator Malcolm, Richard, and El stepped on. I swallowed and fell to the back behind JoJo. Malcolm asked JoJo where we were going. JoJo told him we were on our way to lunch. Malcolm said they were too and he told us to come with them. I knew better than to write that off as just a suggestion. I screamed inside, clearly Malcolm didn't care about my feelings. Malcolm rode with JoJo and I, while Richard and El followed in El's car. I said nothing when we parked at a restaurant a couple blocks from the hospital. I felt like I was being setup, but I said nothing. El was completely normal, and that irked me. When we sat at our table of course I ended up sitting next to El. He smiled at me and looked at me with so much love in his eyes. Malcolm and Richard were talking and Malcolm sounded stressed. He said there were so many balls in the air right now Toya, Kevin, Phineas, and then business. Richard was very serious although this was supposed to be a casual lunch. Richard said Juan was on top of Toya and Kevin, but the Phineas problem was a whole other problem. Richard kept assuring Malcolm that it was going to be handled. I nudged El and asked him what was going on. He leaned in like he was going to whisper in my ear but he lingered there for a minute. I smiled as butterflies entered my stomach. I playfully touched him again. Then I heard my name, everyone at the table looked up. It looked like Teddy was walking past our table with a colleague when he saw me. I smiled an embarrassed and busted smile. I saw Richard and the colleague exchange glances. This was definitely a set up. Teddy asked me what I was doing all the WAY over by the hospital. I told him we were having an office lunch. JoJo told him and his companion to join us. Teddy tried to decline but JoJo insisted. Teddy's colleague sat down and introduced himself as Doug. Teddy shot him a look like he wasn't feeling the setup either. Everyone was looking at Teddy, I felt so embarrassed. "So, how do you know my niece?" JoJo asked with no expression. Teddy's eyes bounced from person to person. "We're dating..." His voice trailed off.

"Dating?" Richard said sounding surprised and shooting me eyes and then fixing them on Teddy.

"Why is that shocking?" Teddy asked Richard.

"As her father I don't like being surprised like this." I could tell Richard was faking surprise for El's sake even though I didn't talk to him about it.

Teddy chuckled, "her father? Yeah right. And are one of you her grandfather?" He said gesturing towards Malcolm and El. I looked at Malcolm with horrified eyes. Malcolm scanned him; "I'm her Uncle if you need a label. That's her man! You're a waste of time!"

"Whoa! I think we're getting off on the wrong foot. Teddy, they're serious." His friend Doug said.

"What?" Teddy looked around at everyone, then his eyes stopped on El. "You said you were single."

El looked at me waiting for me to answer him.

I exhaled, "it's complicated. I'm free to do what I want." I said flashing El angry eyes.

"Are you dating him?" Teddy asked

I closed my eyes, "no."

"Ok then, I apologize for not taking you seriously. I was caught off guard. My name is Theodore Feller; I'm a doctor at the hospital. I have been spending time with your daughter getting to know her." He said directing his comments to Richard.

"How long have you been dating?" Richard asked me.

"Not long." I said lowly

"Sassy baby, clearly he's just a pawn. Throw that one back." Teddy frowned, JoJo tapped him. "I wish I can say it was nice meeting you." Then he shrugged. "She's spoken for, you understand."

"JoJo wait a minute." I said with my eyes to the floor. "Please don't do him like this. Teddy had no idea. He's a nice guy." I said feeling horrible

"Sasha, how can they tell us what to do?" Teddy asked, his friend shook his head and rested it on his hands like he was embarrassed.

"Mr. Cardell it was nice to see you again. It's been real." Doug said getting up.

"Later Doug!" Richard said, while glaring at Teddy. "You're starting to piss me off. I thought I only didn't like you." He chuckled an angry chuckle.

"Let me understand, you do see the men at this table? You'd honestly tell her to go against her father, uncles, and man for you? You don't even know what could happen to her for doing that! Clearly you have no sense of family honor." JoJo said too calmly.

Teddy frowned, "she's a grown woman. She should be able to choose for herself who she wants to be with. You guys shouldn't bully her into the choice you want for her."

"Bully?" Richard was angry, "he doesn't know you!"

"Teddy please! You're not making this better!"

"I'm just telling you what I see." He said unapologetically.

"Sasha!" Malcolm's voice rumbled the table. "Look at him, he's a Dennis in different clothes. Can I ask you and El to be the drama free relationship of all of my kids? I'm losing my patience with these idiots."

My eyes filled up with tears, "you really do think of me as your daughter?"

Malcolm looked up to the sky and exhaled. "Don't get emotional about it! I told you the other night."

"What happened?" JoJo said with a big smile leaning in. I think he forgot he was mad twenty seconds ago.

"Nothing," Malcolm said flatly.

"Sassy?" Richard asked

"Malcolm told me he's known me all my life and that I was like a daughter to him."

"Aw!" Richard said batting his eyes at Malcolm making fun of him. "Aren't you sweet!" He smiled at Malcolm. Malcolm glared at him.

"The point Sasha!" JoJo said bringing us back in. "He's got to go!"

"JoJo it is my choice in whether I want him to go away or not though." I said

"Sasha! I know you better than this. Heck we all do! Put this poor pawn out of his misery."

"Is he gonna go crazy on me?" I asked Malcolm, not understanding why they were pushing so hard.

Malcolm looked at Richard, Richard looked at Teddy. "You wanna tell us about the restraining order?" I got a knot in my stomach, Teddy's face turned angry. Teddy stood up, "leaving is the smartest thing you've done today! I guess you'll live, but let me catch you around my daughter again and we'll have problems." He growled at Teddy. Then Richard proceeded to go off.

"Daddy!" Richard's mouth fell open and tears came to his eyes as he froze looking at me.

"Yes baby girl?" He said still surprised.

I smiled, "I think we get it! He would die."

Richard started rocking in his chair. "Right! I don't play!" His voice was cracking.

"All she gotta do is call you daddy and you turn into a female?" JoJo said poking fun at Richard.

"Shut up man!" Richard said wiping his face. "You know what we've been going through! Matter of fact, baby girl come here!" I sat in the chair next to him and he put his arms around me while kissing my forehead over and over. Malcolm almost smiled at him while he rolled his eyes.

JoJo turned to El, "ball's in your court. What you gonna do?"

****

I laughed, "Forget it! Forget it!" Ava yelled in defeat.

I told her no matter how hard she tried she couldn't sneak up on me. She gushed over Nathan's proposal; she said it was a complete surprise. Even though she told me the story already in detail. I sat there smiling while I watched her tell me again like it was the first time, she was beaming with love. Ava was so in love with that man, and I was so happy for her. She was always my main cheerleader with El, well she still is. I wanted to think it was only I, but she's just a good person like that. I was completely honored when she asked me to be in her wedding. Cause I was a little annoyed with Andrew that I wasn't in his. Twin cousins! Hello! My momma and my sister are in the wedding, but I'm NOT! I don't even understand that. But I decided to tuck my tail between my legs and get over it. Not my wedding, not my place to say how things should be. At least they remembered to send me an invitation to the shower, but I honestly think that was because Tracy met me at my grandparent's anniversary party FINALLY! She didn't act like she knew all that much about me, but I held Andrew accountable for that. It was a nice party, but when all the couples started dancing I found myself on the side watching and there's no lonelier feeling. Oh well right! Ava snapped her fingers at me asking me where I went. I apologized and I told her I was there. She put the conditioning cap on my head then she told me to stay put. She was gone for a few minutes then she came back smiling as usual, but she was hiding something. When I asked her what it was, she smiled a guilty smile and said nothing. She kept trying to change the subject. I finally let her but I kept my eye on her to let her know I knew she was up to something. She kept talking about her wedding; I always thought she'd want a big wedding. But she frowned at it. She said they were leaning towards a ceremony on a boat, and that would greatly limit the amount of guest she could invite. She said she didn't need a big crowd she just needed the people she was close to there. I smiled at the thought. She said they needed to make decisions fast cause an early date just became available otherwise they'd have to wait too long. She said she thinks they're going to go for it. I thought about how fast we were going to have to move to make this work and I got tired.

When I asked her how come I wasn't processing under the dryer, she told me to shut up and lay back. I shot her a look cause she was up to something. I figured she was cutting my appointment short so she could go lay up under Nathan or something like that. As we walked towards the stations she said she blew a fuse earlier and she was operating on auxiliary power. So it was going to be dim in the shop and the lights might flicker, she said that's why she didn't put me under the dryer. Ava may be a good liar to some, but I can tell when she's lying so I just eyed her. She smiled and pushed the door. The shop was dim and everyone had gone home since I was Ava's last appointment. I sat in her chair, we chatted about her wedding some more. She pretty much knew everything she wanted already which was great. She was diffusing my curls when the lights shut off. Ava sighed pretending to be annoyed. I grabbed her and I asked her what was going on. She kept saying nothing and she needed to go flip the switch. I heard the additional footsteps and I smiled as I released her. I told her she wasn't slick. When she flipped the switch El was sitting in the chair at the station directly next to me. He told me I couldn't let him surprise me. I held on to my smile. His face got serious; he started apologizing for needing time in the first place. He came to ask me for permission to date me exclusively again. I was a little disappointed that it wasn't a marriage proposal, but I loved the idea of not being single anymore. We kissed then Ava excitedly said that he could be my plus one at her wedding.

We met Nathan at a restaurant and the four of us had dinner. El kept shooting me looks, I laughed internally cause I knew I was going to have to explain to him that he wasn't getting none.

I followed El to his apartment; I parked behind his car in his tandem garage beneath his apartment. As soon as I got out of the car he gave me keys and a paper with the alarm and gate codes. As soon as the door closed he was all over me, I forgot how much I loved his touch. To slow him down I told him to give me a tour of his place. He sighed in defeat, and then he quickly led me around his two-bedroom apartment showing me each room. His apartment could fit in my living room, but it didn't look like he planned on staying all that long. As he picked me up and carried me to the bedroom I had to tell my butterflies to shut up and I grabbed the doorframe. He gave me a confused look. I told him he couldn't suddenly take me off of time out and think it was all good. He put me down and then he dropped to his knees begging me. I told him I had to be strong for the both of us. He faked cried and threw his body all over the floor. I asked him to put a movie on; he smiled and said his movies only played in his room. I exhaled cause my butterflies fluttered again at the idea of taking over. He asked me what I wanted to watch, funny how he was naming only chick flicks. I asked him why he had so many, he said when he was going through Sasha withdrawals he'd find himself in the store picking up one of the movies he thought I was torturing him with when I made him watch them. He said they turned out not to be so bad. I smiled at him as I agreed to watch Love

Jones. He gave me a shirt to change into so that I could get comfortable; he sucked his teeth when I went in the bathroom. I asked him for shorts and he refused to give them to me. He didn't even try to give me a reason why, he just flat out said no. When I came out the bathroom he was wearing his shorts only. I swallowed; everything was way more toned than I remembered. He was beautiful, so I turned my eyes. As I approached the bed I heard my phone ringing in my purse. It was Richard's ringtone. When I answered the phone he didn't even say hello, he told me I had been inside too long and it was time for me to go home. I immediately got irritated. Richard softened his tone and he told me if you only wanted the night to stay. But if I wanted something better, then I needed to leave now. I huffed and I told him that I hoped he was right. It took everything in me to tell El we'd have to do the movie another night. El didn't hide his disappointment; he tried everything to get me to stay. I kissed him and told him I loved him and then I left. I tossed and turned all night long. At seven in the morning my intercom was buzzing, El was at the gate. I asked him why he was buzzing and he said Richard deactivated his gate access. I chuckled then I buzzed him in. He had a grocery bag with milk and cereal. He told me he was coming to make me breakfast. I chuckled again. I praised him for his milk pouring skills. As we were eating the doorbell rang. El deflated again, Richard knocked as he opened the door. He smiled at us and walked happily into the kitchen.

"Richard"

"Eldridge" Richard smirked.

"What gives? I thought we were good."

Richard's face turned completely serious. He pointed at me, "this is my baby girl, my only child, my only daughter!"

"For now!" I chimed in with a smile.

That did not amuse Richard. "I like you as long as you're good to her! You think your weak apology is just gonna open the door and let you right back in where you left off?" He waited for an answer.

"Yeah!" El said matter of factly.

I started laughing and Richard smiled a little to control his laughter. "No! You're gonna have to do better than that. So...." He loudly clapped his hands together. "You kiddies finish your cereal then you're gonna meet me in the living room." Then he walked out.

I started laughing, but El was not amused. I never really experienced Richard like this so it was amusing to me. But El was not feeling it. When we went in the living room Richard told me to sit in the chair. "Here are the rules of engagement. If either of you have a problem with it... Well that's tough and I don't care! Cross me and it will be the last thing you do!" Now I frowned, "you're back together. GREAT! THAT'S FANTASTIC! I'm thrilled, even though it may not seem like it Eldridge, I like you. BUT! You will NOT roll over MY daughter! You cannot slide back in like nothing happened. I was very disappointed to see that you weren't together. She's accepted you back and that's good. So now, no hanky panky!"

"What?" El said standing up.

"Sit down Eldridge!" Richard demanded.

"All due respect Richard, Sasha and I are grown!"

"Eldridge sit down or I will shoot you!"

"I guess you gonna have to shoot me then! We are not kids!" El said still standing.

Richard looked at me cause I knew he wasn't joking. Richard shrugged and started reaching for his gun. "Hold on! Hold on!" I yelled putting my hands up as I stood in front of El.

Richard blank stared at me, "you know I'm an excellent marksman! What is standing in front of him supposed to do besides anger me?"

"Can we sit down and discuss this like adults?" I pleaded.

"Sasha why do we have to discuss our relationship with your father? He can't dictate to us how our relationship goes!"

"The HELL I CAN'T! THIS IS MY DAUGHTER! I MADE HER! And she was not created so that you could treat her like this!" Richard said angry with his gun now in his hand.

"Daddy please!"

Richard froze! I'm getting a kick out of seeing my kryptonite like effect on him when I call him that. Richard melted then he looked at me with soft eyes and exhaled. "Ok" El smiled at me, Richard grumbled as he put his gun away. "You better be happy, I was about to shoot you!"

We went to the dining room and sat at the table. We sat there for hours. Richard and El would argue cause El wasn't backing down to him. Then I had to remind Richard that this is why he moved away from The Bay. Richard deflated again. He held back a lot better at that point. And our communication improved. El agreed to never disrespect me again, and Richard agreed to hurt him if he ever did.

Chapter 11

"That's pretty good, but come look at mine. This is how you hit
a target." I pulled him by the hand to look over at mine.
El's mouth dropped, Richard smiled at him. I told him I was a
good shot, but seeing is always believing. El said he could do
better. So we put new targets up and went again. He did a lot
better, and mine were the same. Of course Richard had to show
him that he always hits his target no matter how far away. I
guess that was meant to scare El, but he didn't seem to care and
I appreciated that. After our drills we went out to lunch. We
stopped at Gussie's, a little but nice restaurant in Inglewood not
too far from the firing range we usually go to. The
environment was family oriented and lots of open windows all
around. You could watch the cars drive by on the busy street.
Some people sat outside at the tables and enjoyed the sunshine.
This place has the best burgers and sandwiches. I LOVE their
garlic fries but I had to convince El to get them too or he
wouldn't want to kiss me the rest of the day. I looked over the
menu with my mouth watering anticipating whatever thick and
juicy burger I picked. There were so many options I was taking
longer than normal to decide. Richard had Erica meet us at
Gussie's. When he asked me if it was ok if she came to the
restaurant, I wanted to ask him what that meant, but I decided
to let it go. She was extremely excited; she kept talking and
talking fast. All three of us stared at her, as her mouth shot off
rapid fire faster than I had ever seen a person's mouth go. And
it wasn't like she was saying anything important, it was just her
nerves. When she paused to take a drink of her water Richard
told her he didn't know there was a fifth gear on her mouth.
Even Erica laughed at his comment; I touched her hand and
told her it was ok. She exhaled and tried to relax. I realized that
I might've been a little cold the last time we met, and I felt bad
for her. I wish I understood what Richard was doing here. Was
he gonna move on or was he going to get back with my
momma? I don't think he even knew what he was going to do.
Then the debate between Richard and El began. El told
Richard he was not old enough to be his father, technically he
wasn't old enough to be mine. El is four years older than me
that would've made Richard ten turning eleven when he was
born. Richard said it didn't matter, since he was my father he
was right to receive elderly respect from El. El says he will
give him elderly respect by making sure his walker is ready

when he needs it, but that's as far as it was going to go. They go back and forth and I look at them like brothers debating over power. Richard pretends like he gets mad, but I know he gets a kick out of El standing his ground with him.

I was so busy staring at them that Erica had to ask me who the guy was that was staring at us, as I took a big bite of my delicious burger. It was Dennis. He looked so hurt! All this time he thought it was Yussef, he forgot he saw El with my parents before. Richard and El were having a good time too; I don't know what part of this scene hurt worse for him. I told Erica he was my ex, I told her to be cool cause Richard would lose it if he saw him. He couldn't have been sitting there when we came in, Richard would've lost it immediately. I wondered how long he had been sitting there watching. Then Thea sat at the table and Erica's mouth dropped as my stomach turned. Dennis looked embarrassed to be sitting next to her. Nothing like the proud man that used to sit next to me. I could tell he was trying to tell her they had to go. After all they were probably in Inglewood so that there wouldn't be these kinds of run ins in LA. With her age starting to show on her face, Thea wasn't wearing her dress all that well. Her body was still tight; She was just starting to look a little too old to be wearing that dress. After all she was two years older than El. Sure enough she was wearing the ring he tried to give me. She cut all of her hair off. Her short style actually suited her a lot better than long hair did. El was laughing at Richard when he noticed Dennis. He did a double take while I kept my eyes on my plate. El bumped me under the table and I nodded my head yes without looking. I was hoping he would be cool so that Richard wouldn't turn around. But of course Richard noticed El's subtle change up, he looked around and then he turned around. There was fire in Richard's eyes; I tried to calm him by explaining that his life was miserable enough having to live without me. And Richard had to know that when he saw Richard and El happy together that had to hurt more. Richard nodded as if the thought of that calmed him a little but then his body jerked and he was out of his seat. El smiled a big smile as he leaned back in his chair to watch. Dennis's eyes were sad already and seeing Richard coming at him wasn't going to make him any happier. Thea's eyes got big; she hadn't seen any of us. She was too busy being excited about Dennis. Even though we were trying, we couldn't hear what they were saying. Richard was barking at them and they were submissively standing down, at least they weren't stupid. El and I kept popping French fries while we watched the show. Thea peeked at our table, when she saw Erica she got mad and wiggled her neck when she said something. Richard barked and she backed down. I asked Erica what that was about, she said Thea introduced them, but not in a hey hook up kind of way. She said she could tell Thea was feeling Richard, but he wasn't feeling her. She said that she and Thea weren't acquaintances. She said she'd see her around from time to time cause Rodell's momma worked for her at the hotel she manages. I leaned in and asked if she knew if Thea still saw Rodell, and she said as far as she knew they were still dating. Then she said Thea was pregnant one day not too long ago, and then the next day she wasn't. I asked by whom and she said she assumed by Rodell, she didn't know about Dennis. Thea's eyes were burning a hole in us cause she knew we were talking about her. Plus I kept looking at her while Erica was talking just to be evil. So I had Erica back up to the introduction. I asked her if Richard and Thea were on a date. She said they were working but it was clear as day that she was feeling him. I rolled my eyes and asked whom she wasn't feeling. Then El chimed in and said Henry. We laughed; I told him she could've wanted him. El said if she wanted Henry she would've had him and we saw the way he changed once he got some. El and I laughed loudly while Erica smiled politely cause she didn't know who we were talking about. As El and I described how Henry used to be Erica frowned in disgust. Thea couldn't take it anymore. Richard was mid-sentence when she stood up. I watched her walk over, and the whole time I'm thinking she can't be this dumb. She's seen me in action, she has to have something otherwise I couldn't understand her actions. Maybe she felt today was a good day for a beat down. "Erica you need to keep your mouth shut!" Thea stated. I put my elbow on the table and I rested my face in my hand. I sighed loudly, "you can't be this stupid!" Thea frowned at me. "Go sit down Thea!"

"You mean go sit with the man you couldn't satisfy!" She said like that was something for her to be proud of.

I exhaled, "do you even realize how dumb you sound? Dennis and I are not together because I refused to get back with him. Don't you see who I'm sitting next to!" I smiled at El, and he smiled back. "Why would I care that he's settled on you. Giving you the ring I refused. At least he was proposing marriage, I'm sure he gave that to you because he couldn't return it. Oh and does that mean he's been begging me to come back to him the whole time he's been putting miles in your coochie? I guess so! If I came back what would that mean for you? I don't want Dennis, been there done that! I hope you guys end up married cause it seems like you guys don't deserve to do any better."

Thea started to wiggle her neck, "you're just mad...."

I cut her off. "Yes! Yes! Yes! I'm mad cause I used to be in love with Dennis. Whoopty-Doo! Thea you need to grow up, you got him and now what? You get married then what? You think there won't be another Thea to come along? Your future is very sad to me and what's worse is that you're too dumb to see that he's still in love with me. I left him, he was never gonna leave me. If you were his secret why would he ever make you his Queen? Even when you think you've won, you'll constantly be looking over your shoulder wondering who's coming for your lover. Who you're competing with, your gonna drive yourself crazy and haggard worrying about it. While me..." I looked at El and smiled again. "I'll be unbelievably happy on the arm of a good man who only has eyes for me."

"Well, as long as you're out of the way I won't need to be worried about anyone else."

I smiled, "have you met his momma yet?"

Thea looked like she wanted to explode. Dennis called Thea back to their table, as he signaled their waiter. Dennis had turned red and he was thoroughly upset. Richard came back to our table and he took an angry bite out of his sandwich. Richard texted someone while he chewed very angrily. Dennis paid for whatever they had and then we watched them walk out of the restaurant. They were parked in the parking lot next to the restaurant so we watched them get in their car. Thea was driving, I could tell by her demeanor that she was upset and fussing. As she was pulling out of her space she almost ran over a family who were coming into the restaurant and almost hit a car as it was coming in. I was about to say she needed to calm down when she pulled out on the busy street, cutting a car off which plowed into them because they were coming too fast to stop. I blinked a couple times to make sure my eyes just saw what I thought I just saw. People in the restaurant screamed and someone yelled to call 911! One of the waiters ran to the car and people outside were running to the car as well. El and Richard went outside, I couldn't move. It seemed like everything went silent, my heart sped up when no one was getting out of their cars. The fire department got there first, then the police and the paramedics. Erica grabbed my hand as I sat there, I couldn't figure out how to tell my legs to take me outside. Richard and El stood by on the sidewalk and watched as everything was happening. I noticed only two ambulances came and then tow trucks came. They took Thea and Dennis to the hospital but I couldn't tell who was driving the car that hit them. I heard a waiter telling someone no one knows what happened to the other driver, it was like they disappeared into thin air. El and Richard returned, we had our food wrapped up to go. Richard asked me if I was ok, and I didn't say anything. I was still processing what happened. He said from what he could tell they were going to be ok, but they were pretty banged up. When I looked at El he read my eyes and said I wanted to go to the hospital as if he was translating for me. Richard didn't look happy but he didn't argue with me. The hospital wouldn't tell me anything because I wasn't family. I called Thea's father and Mr. B, Mr. B said they were coming and that he would call the hospital. Thea's dad and sister came to the hospital an hour and a half later. Mr. B and Mrs. Barbeau got there more like four hours later. Mr. B said they got lost. Then they went directly to the back as well. We left once their families were there. Mr. B called me and told me that Dennis had a concussion, broken arm, and he was banged up from the deployment of the airbag but he was going to be ok. I asked him about Thea and he asked me who was she. I told him she was his girlfriend she was driving. Mr. B was quiet he said he's never met her. I was confused cause Lulu mentioned a girlfriend before she died. Mr. B said that Thea wasn't the girlfriend they met before. I exhaled cause that just meant there were more and I was so happy not to be involved in all that drama. Mr. B thanked me for calling them, and then he went to find out about Thea.

****

"Ava! That's it! That's the dress!" Kai said dabbing her eyes and holding onto Ava's mother. Ava twirled in the mirror getting emotional at the sight of herself in her wedding gown. She told us all of a sudden this whole thing got real! When Ava said she knew what she wanted she meant it. She wanted a dress that would flow on the ocean air. She came in with a design in mind and pictures, the consultant pulled dresses along those lines. The third dress she tried on was the dress for her. Then we went to the bridesmaid section. She was only having Kai and I in her wedding. Her sisters were not happy that they weren't in the wedding, but Ava cut them off by saying she didn't want the fuss or the stress of them in her wedding. She told her mom that if they fought her on this they wouldn't be invited to the wedding at all. Ava's wedding was in Spring and she wanted nice spring colors. The consultant took her to the pastel section, but Ava wanted a little more electric but not dark. She picked out this pretty turquoise blue. Then she picked a dress for each of us according to our body type. I told her she was bringing out the vixen in me in the dress she chose and we laughed. The dress was tasteful, and I loved the way it hugged me. Since we were buying off the rack, we took our dresses to alterations and got that started right away. Ava's things were happening in order liked she planned and I was so happy for her. We spent the day doing wedding things, picking out flowers, music for the DJ, table set up. Her wedding was going to be eighty people max.

****

Ava couldn't stop crying and smiling. She said she was so excited that her day was finally here. She kept hugging Kai and I and thanking us for helping her with everything. We made this wedding happen in a tiny window of time, with as little drama as possible. The consultant assigned to our event came to let us know it was time for us to make our way to the boat; all of the guests were boarded. Ava gave a nervous laugh, she said she was excited. Our bouquets were a pretty orange and green and they popped rather nicely against our turquoise dresses. I followed Kai, and the consultant walked with Ava behind me. Once we were on the boat we started moving out of the dock. Once we were out in the middle of the water we marched out to the front and Nathan and Ava were wed with the Sunset on the Ocean as their backdrop. I knew those pictures were going to be amazing. El couldn't take his eyes off of me, which made me blush so hard. During dinner, Ava and Nathan thanked everyone for coming. And then various ones in the room took turns wishing the couple well. I relayed how I met and fell in love with Ava, and how happy Nathan instantly made her. I told her I was so happy she didn't settle for less than she deserved. Ava's Mom spoke, and Nathan's parents spoke. You could tell he was closer to his stepmom than he was to his biological. His family was from The Bay Area as well. The microphone was making its way around the room when Ava signaled for the mic to come back to our table. The DJ gave the microphone to El. "I'm Eldridge and I have the honor to be the escort of this beautiful woman sitting here." He motioned to me, "I don't know about you guys. But when I was growing up the beautiful girls were the worst! They would be wrapped in a beautiful package and then you'd get to know them, and they would be horrible people. No heart or soul, they didn't care about how they affected the world around them. And sometimes they acted like the world was their stage. I've gotten so used to horrible beautiful ones that I automatically turn a blind eye to them. But this one," he smiled at me. "Despite being the most beautiful woman I've seen in my life, had the nerve to have a big heart. Within days of meeting her, it was clear to me that she only wanted to be loved just like anyone else. Even though she's gorgeous she EATS!" Everybody laughed. "And she makes sure you're fed. She quickly became my soul mate when I just about gave up on the idea of such an existence. She's my best friend and I can share everything with her. Thank you!" Then he looked at Ava and Nathan. "When I met Ava, I liked her immediately. I could tell that she and my lady were good friends. In a world where it's hard to remember who you are sometimes, I was amazed that two beautiful women could be such good friends." Everyone chuckled, "you guys know what I mean. It takes two women who are very secure with themselves to be as equally beautiful and good friends to each other. But somehow these two made it work. And people had the nerve to tell me that California was only full of the superficial." He exhaled and looked at me. "Ava and Nathan are a beautiful couple and I wish you guys all the happiness in the world. Thank you for allowing me to come and be a voyeur on your special day." Then he gave me an evil smile. "Sasha, we've been plotting on you." My heart dropped into my toes. "The three of us have had a plan since that day when the lights went out in the shop, you just didn't know it." Then he dropped to one knee and pulled a ring box out of his jacket pocket. "I apologize for taking so long to get around to asking you this VERY important question to our life plan together. Sasha Wallace my best friend and soul mate will you marry me?"

"YES!" I said throwing my arms around his neck and almost knocking him over. I didn't care what the ring looked like; I was so excited that FINALLY he asked me! Ava and Kai came over and hugged us too. I couldn't even be surprised that Richard was there, he congratulated us. But I could tell he was thinking about my momma even though Erica was on his arm. It took Richard asking to see the ring for me to remember to open the box. When I started crying El told me Ava helped him pick it out. I told her I couldn't believe she found time to

Carey Anderson

do any of that amongst her planning. Richard eyed the ring
then he told El he did a good job. El put the ring on my finger
and now I felt so complete. The DJ opened the dance floor and
El took me out on the floor. I kept kissing him and telling him
how much I loved him. Even though Richard told me not to, I
couldn't help it. That night I was filled with so much love I
went back to El's and I finally spent the night with him since
we've been back together. I felt like I was going to explode if I
wasn't with him, I needed him and I wasn't sorry about it
either. In the morning I called my momma with the good news.
She screamed into the phone, she was so excited her mouth
was going a mile a minute. I laid there smiling and staring at
El. Sabrina heard all the noise and when my momma shared
the news Sabrina was excited as well. My momma said when
El comes out with me for Andrew's wedding he could meet my
Poppa and Nana, and my Uncle Jeff who he hadn't met yet.
El said he liked Ava and Nathan's small wedding and that he
wanted something along those lines. I told him my family was
too big to have such a small wedding. He said his family was
good sized as well, but he didn't care. He said he didn't want to
waste all of that money on a big show. I told him he wouldn't
have to spend a dime, I told him I was sure that Richard would
foot the bill and whatever he didn't cover my Poppa would. El
acted like he was putting his foot down to say that he had
spoken. Irritated I got up, put my clothes on and left.
In tears I called my momma from the car. She exhaled; she
said that El and I were going to figure out the compromise in
this situation. She said our family is huge and we don't ever
really do anything small, but the wedding day would be his as
well. She said El had to be as happy with the final result as I
was. I told her I've always wanted a big wedding with all of
my family there. She said he may be over the idea of a big
wedding since this will be his second marriage. I hadn't
thought of that. I made a U-turn and I went back to El's place.
He was standing in the kitchen when I walked in the door. He
looked like he was trying to figure out breakfast. I told him he
was going to have to learn how to make breakfast at least so
that he could make me breakfast in bed. He slightly smiled, but
he was watching me. I exhaled and I said I didn't take into
consideration that he may feel the way he does because this
would be his second marriage. He didn't say anything he just
watched me. I asked what our compromise would be. I wanted
a big wedding with all of our families there. I wanted his
family to celebrate with us just as much as my family had to be

there. I liked Ava's wedding, but in all my years of dreaming I never dreamed of anything that small and intimate. I wanted big HUGE and wonderful! I told him this is my first and only wedding. He kissed me and thanked me for coming back. He laughed when I said I noticed he didn't chase after me. He said I wasn't crazy, it was a wonder I had the strength to walk out of here this morning. Then he said he really didn't want to do the big wedding again. He said it was more fuss than it was enjoyable. To keep the peace we decided to let it rest for now.

****

"How's the baby?' I asked excited to see Jillian

"He's so delicious! I dreaded coming back to work. What's new…" She screamed as she noticed my ring. "Oh my goodness! Princess cut, one and a half karat center stone, almost a full carat past and future stones on either side, platinum setting." She drooled, "they look flawless! This man loves you!"

"Who loves who?" Clark said walking in the room and shutting the door behind him.

"Sasha's engaged!" She said holding my hand up giddy with excitement.

Clark flashed me an irritated look. "Why does everybody want to get married? Marriage is ridiculous and I've seen it ruin too many good people." He said taking his seat.

"Clark since when have you been so cynical?" Jillian asked

"Since my cover girl said yes to another man. Sasha we look good together."

Jillian and I looked at each other like this man was completely off his rocker. "That's interesting, your cover girl? Well I hope you find someone one day that makes you change your mind."

"I doubt it! Marriage is only ideal if you…." he looked at me with a horrified look. "Please tell me you're not going to ruin your body by having a baby!"

Jillian was not amused, "what do you mean ruin?"

"It won't be the same! Things will shift and deflate or get bigger. Sasha your body is perfect right now. I bet your breast still sit up perky and at attention when you take your bra off. A baby will ruin all of that. Not to mention the stretch marks, the skin that doesn't snap back." He made his face look sick at the thought of it all. "Please tell me you're not going to do this to the work of art you call a body."

Jillian looked like she wanted to stab him. "My mother has two kids. And while she had me when she was very young. She had my sister around my age now. My mother looks exactly the same as she did in high school. My cousin, oh you should know her. Amber Wallace, yeah she has three kids and she doesn't look like she's had one. You are such a pig. That's why the man I'm marrying has promised to love me through the fatness and then the sagging. Beauty fades Clark. I'm marrying a man who sees me past the cover girl exterior and will want me even if I get fat or my body is ruined as you call it."

"AMBER WALLACE HAS THREE KIDS???" His face was pale like the thought of it made him sick.

I looked at Jillian, "that's all he heard me say." I shook my head. "Clark you need help. Jillian let's conference Joseph and Cyrus in to get this meeting going."

"Ok," she said visibly still upset with Clark's comments.

"Congratulations Sasha, I'm happy for you even if no one else is."

Chapter 12

"What's happening with the planning? When should I bust out the checkbook?" Richard asked as he walked into my office.

I smiled, "hello. How are you?" As I stood to hug him.

"I need to know how broke I'm going to be after this is all said and done. Are you guys going to have babies right away? I think I'm a bit too sexy to be a grandfather just yet." He smiled

"You want to pay for my wedding?"

He looked at me like that was the dumbest question ever. "I'm paying for it, and I'm giving you away. Well I'm not giving you away, but you know what I mean." He took a seat in front of my desk.

I could tell something was up with him. "Ok, so... what's up?"

"Your wedding."

"Besides that, I can see that there's something else."

He was going back and forth in his mind. "What do you think of Erica?"

"You love her, why do you try to fight it?"

"I love your mother more!" He said like it pained him. "I feel so torn."

"Erica loves you. She wants to have babies with you. Our Kids will grow up together." I smiled, "isn't that the American way?"

He rolled his eyes, "your mother won't give me a straight answer. But I don't think she wants to have any more kids."

I knew she didn't want any more kids, but it wasn't my place to tell him if she hasn't. "Kids are the deal breaker?"

"You were never supposed to be an only child."

"I'm not, I have a little sister you know."

He frowned, "she had Sabrina to hurt me."

"No she didn't! She fell in love with her man, they wanted a living expression of that love."

He looked at me, "if they were so in love. Why didn't they get married?"

"She doesn't want to get remarried. You see how well she did the first time."

Richard shook his head, "Sassy baby you don't know your momma like I know her." Then he exhaled, "I think I want to give it a real go with Erica. My clock is ticking and I don't have time to convince someone to get on board. Either she is or she isn't. I love your momma! I don't think I could ever love someone like I've loved her. She was my first everything! Erica knows about your momma. She can't know me without knowing everything about me. I just don't want you to hate me."

"Why would I hate you?"

"This situation is messed up! I'm always gonna be in love with your momma, but I'm gonna have a family here."

I let his words swish around my brain for a minute. "Is Erica pregnant?"

He watched my face, "yes."

"Daddy!" I smiled, "how you gonna tell me not to put out and you're over there raw-dogging with your girlfriend."

He looked embarrassed and touched all at the same time. "Are you mad?"

"Why would I be mad?"

"I just explained all of that to you."

"No, I'm not mad. I'm happy for you."

"Please let me tell your mother." He said with sad eyes.

We talked for a long time. Eventually he started showing how excited he was about the baby. He said she just got confirmation from the doctor and she was due early next year. I told him when we came back from the wedding we'd have to all go out to celebrate. He reminded me not to tell Dan-Dan either, he wanted to at least have them meet when he told her. When I met El for lunch, I made him promise not to say anything until Richard told him and he had to act like he was surprised when he found out. Then I told him about the baby, he said that was going to be weird to have a brother or sister in-law around the same age as our children. I smiled and asked him how many kids did he want to have. He said it didn't matter to him, but he wanted more than one. So we made a plan to start with two and then see how we felt at that point. Our plan would be for four though, two and two. At least we could agree on that much, but we still weren't agreeing on the size of the wedding.

That night I called Tanisha and I told her about the debate with El and I. She said we should find a way to have lunch next week when we came out. She said if the fuss of the wedding is the major turn off, maybe we could sell him on the advantages of having a wedding planner like Carina. She said maybe even have Tracy give a testimonial of how Carina has saved her life. I told her I loved that she was thinking. I couldn't wait to bring El out to meet a lot of my family.

****

"What's up Sasha!" Darryl said surprising me by being at the gate when I walked off the plane. I gave him the biggest hug. Then he pulled my left hand, "what is this?" His eyes were big. "I know finally huh." I said with a big smile.

He looked at me in disbelief. "Where is El? Clearly he forgot what we discussed." He said in an angry tone. I was confused. He pulled out his phone and called El. I didn't know they talked on the phone like that, but ok. "El! MAN! What did we discuss?...." Darryl rolled his eyes and looked at me. "Look at the caller ID again you know who this is! And you know why I'm UPSET!" Darryl said taking my bag from me and starting to walk. I was completely confused, I thought he liked El. "Didn't we discuss that I was gonna hand you the ring and say something perfect to set the moment off just right! Didn't we? Didn't we?" When I started laughing he shot me evil eyes. "I'm glad my pain amuses the both of you, but I don't appreciate being cut out of the process like this. To make it up to me, I will settle for being your best man!" I laughed again, "WHAT! El you're messing up man! I called myself liking you. I'm over here talking you up to everybody. Setting you up so you could slide right in and dazzle everyone. And what are you doing? You're pissing off your wingman, you're messing up!" He stopped walking behind something that El said. "Oh! Ok! Well that's why your woman is going to see strippers tonight! Big strippers! The kind that pick your woman up and turn her out! Yeah, and I'm not gonna stop her! Nope! Nope! And you know how wild Sasha is! Yep all your fault...." He smiled at me, "so you're going to rethink the best man thing. Yeah! That's what I thought!" He laughed. "The ring is cool though, good pick." Darryl caught the shuttle to the airport so that he could tag along with me. We drove out to my momma's house to put my bags in the door then I grabbed my overnight bag for Tracy's Girl's Night. Darryl had me cracking, I was happy he was driving my rental car and not me. I couldn't breathe I was laughing so hard. We went to Drew's loft in Emeryville; on the way there he told me he was taking it over after the wedding. Andre gave me the biggest hug, I was afraid he might've forgotten me. You know how kids easily forget you. But he was an exception to that rule thank goodness. They were getting ready for Drew's bachelor party. I had no idea how raw and uncut that was going to be, so I was happy not to be invited. As I was leaving to head a few blocks over to the hotel for Tracy's party Hubby was walking up. I hadn't laid eyes on him in years, and I don't know why I didn't think about the fact

that I would see him at Drew's wedding. We said hello and
hugged each other, but it was the courtesy hug. Nothing that
would ever let on that we had a past. We were too awkward to
get our first sentences out. Drew walked up and put his arm
around my shoulders, he asked when El was coming. I told
him he was coming Monday night after work.
"El? The singer?" Hubby asked looking confused
Drew blank stared at him and then he said yes and all his
siblings too. Then he said El was my fiancé as he pointed to
my engagement ring. Hubby whistled and said my ring was
nice. Then Drew got the evil look, "and wait until you see him.
I mean I'm not gay, but he's a NICE looking cat too!" Drew
smiled real big rubbing it in. "How tall are you?" He asked
Hubby.
"Six foot."
"Even?"
"Yes!" Hubby said annoyed with his friend.
"How tall is El?" He asked me
"He's almost 6' 3"." I said
"Ooh! You hear that? He's even taller than you!"
Hubby blank stared at his friend, "you play too much!"
"Whatever man! You're always out gunned! You better hope
Nicole don't catch on that there's something better too." He
said laughing and leading me to my car.
I wondered if Andrew would be this tickled if he knew
everything that happened between Hubby and I. I wondered if
Drew's words had any effect on him. Everybody says how
happily married he is, but you know how you still wonder if
that person ever thinks about you from time to time. When I
got to the hotel Amber's party bus was already there, thank
goodness, I forgot that Hubby's wife was Tracy's good friend,
and she's the reason Tracy and Andrew met. I didn't know if
she knew about me. I was going to be cool for my cousin's
sake regardless. But I was happy I was going to have backup.
My cousin Sharon was in the lobby coming from the
bathroom. She gave me a hug; she said Amber and my momma
just went up to the room to tell Tracy to come down. She said
they were on the tenth floor and to follow the noise. When I
stepped off the elevator she wasn't lying. They were laughing
about something with the door cracked. When I pushed the
door open everyone jumped, no one realized the door was
open. Amber and my momma were on their knees on either
side of the coffee table with their arms behind their backs.
They were hovering over shot glasses that had liquor and then

whip cream on the top. A girl said go and they bent over, put their mouths around the glasses and then they turned their heads up and took the shot to the head. Everyone was cheering them on. My momma and Amber were cracking up laughing. Gwen was snapping pictures, and then she asked me if I wanted to do a blowjob with her. Everyone was looking at me. I told them I wasn't used to performing for an audience but I'd do it. Everyone erupted into excited energy. I gave Tracy a hug hello and my momma, and then Gwen and I got down and did them just like we just saw. The shot was delicious and it had to have some cinnamon schnapps in it cause that taste was dominate with the creaminess behind it. Since it appeared they hadn't just started I stayed down there taking shots with whomever until I felt my buzz start to kick in. Tracy introduced me to her sisters who were twins and identical, her friend Joy, and…. her friend Nicole. I could tell by her eyes that Nicole had no idea who I was other than I was Drew's cousin. I guess that was for the best. And I relaxed at that point; at least there wouldn't be any cattiness. We went down to a conference room for the pleasure party. I was so excited about all the toys, gadgets, oils, and creams I ordered. On our honeymoon, El was going to think he died and went to heaven. Our presenter couldn't believe how big our orders were. Amber and Gwen convinced our presenter to stay for the strippers. Before the strippers came in the room, Nicole gave a disclaimer to everyone. She said the weak at heart should leave now, and anyone who suffers from loose lip syndrome should leave as well. She said what happened from this point onward was not to be discussed with anyone outside of this room, and no one should be judged for how they conduct themselves cause no one in here was a wife, mother, girlfriend, or anything else. Tracy was the only bride to be which meant all eyes on her. Everyone applauded her little speech, with drinks from the bar in hand, and then they came in. Three scoops of hotness, chocolate, caramel, and white chocolate. Gwen was always the first to volunteer for anything, she was hilarious! By the end of the night, I was thoroughly entertained and so happy I came. A small group of us went back up to the room. Tracy asked me personally to sleepover and I was glad I did. I had a good time listening to their stories and finally getting to know my new cousin.

****

"Mr. B, I'd like you to meet my fiancé Eldridge." I said with the proudest smile.

249

"You were at the hospital weren't you?" Mr. B asked
"Yes, I was. It's nice to meet you." El said shaking his hand,
"this is very nice." El said looking around.
"Hospital?" Dan-Dan asked.
"Dennis and a friend were in a car accident not too long ago.
Everyone is ok now, but you know that's the phone call no
parent wants to ever get." Mr. B said
Kelsey was sitting behind the counter trying not to stare in our
direction. I asked Mr. B to wait a minute before he took us on a
tour of the grounds. Kelsey looked nervous about me
approaching her. I'm sure she didn't know how I was going to
respond to her. "Hi" I said
"Hi," she said looking down at the counter.
It was silent for a minute; I was giving her a chance to
apologize to me for sleeping with my man. All those times I
defended her against Lawrence and she repaid me by sleeping
with my man, and then playing innocent in my face. Or even
my pep talk with her son, she could've thanked me cause I
could've told him to give her hell, it's not like she didn't
deserve it. But the silence said maybe she hadn't put all those
dots together. "How's Jim?"
"He's good. He'll be back with Naomi in a minute. I'm sure
he'll be happy to see you." Then she exhaled, "Sasha I'm mad
at you!" She didn't yell, but I wasn't expecting that to come out
of her mouth. I waited for her to explain, "I keep telling myself
it's not your fault. But every man that I love in my life prefers
you first!" She put her fingers up, "Jim, Dennis, and even
Lawrence!" Then she paused like I was supposed to have
something to say to that.
"Are you waiting for me to apologize for something?" I looked
at her like she had to be kidding.
"You don't see where you should?"
"Uh! Clearly you've gotten Sasha Wallace confused with
someone else. I don't owe you diddlysquat! Dennis was my
man; he was supposed to prefer me first! I never encouraged
Lawrence and I did my best to stay out of his way. I guess
when he figured you guys out is when he stopped caring. I'll
tell you, the way he treated you, Marika would have his head
for even thinking of acting like that with her. And your son has
always had a little crush on me. I don't know why the crush of
a child would bother his mother to the point of pure ignorance.
You slept with my man, had his baby, and kept messing
around with him and smiling in my face. I guess feeling
remorse about something like that would be too much like

right. AND I still told your son to go easy on you! Kelsey you are stupid and easily manipulated. I still feel sorry for you."
She rolled her eyes then she stood up and showed me her very pregnant belly. She smiled and put her hand on it, "Dennis junior!"
I stumbled backwards, "WHAT?" Mr. B said from across the room. There was fire in his eyes.
Kelsey's smile dropped. Then Mrs. Barbeau and Jim walked in the door. Mrs. Barbeau was wondering what was going on cause she heard her husband's voice all the way outside. "What's going on?"
"Naomi! She's been giving us the run around about the father of her child all this time. Then she tells Sasha it's Dennis's baby!"
Ignoring everyone Jim came to me giving me the biggest hug. He told me he misses me; I kept my arms around him while I stared at his mother. "Baby, can we discuss this off the floor? Customers!" She said with the most plastic smile. Mr. B, very angrily walked out the door with Mrs. Barbeau in tow. She turned around and shot Kelsey an evil look. Jim looked at El and Dan-Dan. He asked me who was with my grandmother, when I told him it was my fiancé he looked like he blanked out for a minute. I told him he will always be the first man who wanted to marry me. Then I introduced him to El. He looked mad then he looked at his mother, "why would you say something right now? You made me promise not to tell Grandpa, and then you tell him?"
"I was talking to Sasha and he overheard." She said in her defense
"Why would you tell Sasha?" She opened her mouth and then she closed it. "You see why it's hard to go easy on her?" He said to me. "I'm sorry Sasha!" You could tell it didn't embarrass her until her son thought to apologize.
"Baby, never apologize for your parents. One day they'll grow up and be as mature as you. We're going to go. Please give Mr. B my regards." I said hugging Jim again. I felt sorry for him and Mr. B.

****

"Let me see it again." Randi said reaching for my hand. "It's beautiful! Congratulations Sasha!" I said thank you but my eyes were glued to the backyard. I was watching El talk to my Poppa, and my Uncles. El's back was to me while my Poppa, JoJo and Jeff had serious faces while they talked to him. My Nana told me to come in the kitchen with her. She told me no matter how much I stared it wasn't going to change the outcome of their conversation. She told me to make the salad while she put the finishing touches on dinner. I was worried because if anyone thought Richard was bad, my Poppa was the ultimate. But I was the only girl until Sabrina came. Everyone was already set in their over protective ways, so now was not the time to try to turn it around. Randi asked if we wanted a large wedding, I told her we hadn't decided yet. My Nana told me not to EVER do like Randi and Jeff and elope. Randi put her eyes on the counter. She apologized for the umpteenth time. She said they got caught up in the moment, and so on and so forth. My Nana told her to stop apologizing. She said every time she voiced her irritation with it Randi didn't have to apologize. Randi was really sweet and not used to standing up for herself. She's gotten so much better than she used to be, but she still has a long way to go. Dan-Dan and my momma were in the living room having a good time chatting up a storm. I gave the salad to Sabrina to put outside. My Nana looked out in the yard, then she said it was time to end the boy's party. We took dinner out back with us, and Nana called the men to the table. When I saw the smiles on everyone's faces I sighed a sigh of relief. My Poppa said he liked El, he said he doesn't scare easily. I looked at El and he smiled at me, I told my Poppa Richard has been trying to scare him this whole time and he's still here. I said proudly. As we finished our delicious meal, my Poppa asked if it was stepping on Richard's toes to offer to pay for everything. I told him Richard was already waiting with his checkbook out so they needed to discuss who's paying for what and then let me know.

On the car ride back to Dan-Dan's house we had a nice conversation about love and relationships. Dan-Dan told El she enjoyed spending the day with us. She said she really liked him and she couldn't wait for him to meet the rest of my family. She said hopefully that would happen before our wedding otherwise he needed to be prepared to meet a gang of people at the wedding. I looked at El and smiled, I dared him to tell my Dan-Dan he didn't want a big wedding just because he's done it before.

****

"I'm not gonna beat around the bush with you. Where do you stand with the big wedding?" Tanisha asked

El chuckled, "you too?"

"Me too what?"

"As he's meeting more and more family they're all automatically assuming that we're having a big wedding like Andrew. I don't have the heart to tell them that the guest list is going to be really small."

El rolled his eyes at me. "Big weddings are nightmares!"

"Yes, but that's why you hire a wedding planner. And guess what, you've got one built in. Carina could take care of everything for you." Tanisha said

"That doesn't take away from the fact that Sasha's gonna be stressed and impossible."

"Me impossible? No more than usual!" I said

"Let me show you what I've done for Andrew and Tracy." Carina took out all of her notes. She showed El how she met with Tracy and Andrew to find out what they wanted. Then she selected venues that fit what they were looking for. She explained her process, and I could see El's resolve melting. I got excited!

****

El and I said "WHOA!" When we arrived at the Ritz-Carlton in San Francisco. The bellhop came and loaded our luggage while the valet took our rental car. Andrew definitely wasn't pinching pennies for his wedding. The lobby looked like something out of a movie. It was very fancy and now I felt very confident in my very fancy dress that I bought. Sabrina found us in the lobby. She walked with us, El whistled as we stepped into our room. Everything was plush and top of the line. I ran my hand over the bedding and it was completely soft and crisp.

"What's with the goofy look?" I asked Sabrina

She put her arm around mine and told me to walk with her. I told El I would be right back. She told me she didn't know how to feel right now, but she was really confused. She said she had dinner last night with her dad and he was in a mood during their entire dinner. She said she thinks he and his fiancé had gotten into it or something. She said when they got to the house he opted to come in and she didn't expect him to but whatever. She said her friend called her so she went in her room to take the call. She said momma didn't come to take the phone and she lost track of time. She said when she went in the living room the TV was on and everything looked like momma had gone to the bathroom. She said the top lock wasn't on the door, and then she noticed her dad's car was still outside. I put my hands over my mouth. Sabrina turned red, she said she went to momma's door and she heard something. Both of us

253

gagged! Then we cracked up laughing. I told her at least she didn't walk in on them. I gagged at the memory. She said in the middle of the night, she checked and his car was still outside. She said she didn't know what to do, so she stayed in her room until she knew he was gone in the morning. She said momma's been acting weird all day. Then she said she was confused cause she thought momma was in love with my dad. I told her I really hoped they got it together this time. Sabrina asked me what she should do. I told her she didn't have to do anything. I told her my dad was coming in a little bit, and we just needed to sit back and be the kids mixed up in their love triangle. We went back to the room got El, then we delivered Sabrina to Tracy's room and El and I went to Andrew's room. Darryl and my cousin Ryder together was system overload. They had everybody in stitches. When it was time for the rehearsal, El and I got on the Party Bus to go to the rehearsal dinner. El put his arm around me; he said he loved my family. I smiled it was working. El recognized my Uncle Dale and my cousin Sharon from the remodel of my house. We met a bunch of Tracy's family as well. Andrew and Tracy looked so happy.

Richard and I made eye contact while my momma was talking to someone else. He looked so guilty; it was only a matter of time before my momma picked up on it if she hadn't already. I wondered where her head was with the information Sabrina gave me earlier.

When we got back to the hotel El and I hung out with Darryl, Ryder, Jeff, JoJo, and a bunch of other cousins. We had such a good time and one by one each one who still owed me a nod, gave it. They liked El, but I wondered if that would continue if he stuck to his guns about the small wedding.

In the morning, El and I went down to the restaurant for breakfast. Right after we sat down Andrew, Andre, and Andre's friend AJ joined us. El asked Andrew how he was feeling. Andrew was full of smiles and excited energy. He said he was so happy that today was finally here! Andrew reminded me that he's been pretty much sprung off Tracy since the beginning. "Are you happy to have the planning drama over?" El asked Drew.

Andrew leaned back and put his arms up on top of the cushions. "Planning wasn't the dramatic part. Once we got over the guest list hurdle planning has been pretty smooth. I know we owe that to Carina."

El looked at me, "hurdle?"

"Yeah, Tracy was concerned about cost. Where I wanted everyone I love here, I mean stuff like this is what my family does. We come together to show love and support. This is a monumental moment for me, for us. Anyone willing to come celebrate with us is welcome! I went through a lot to be here with the woman I love!"

"She tell you to say this?"

"Who?" Andrew's eyes bounced between us. Then he smiled, "I had no idea. Is our twin connection still working?" He winked at me.

"Obviously not enough!" Andrew dropped his smile. "I told myself to let it go, but I can't! How is EVERYBODY else in your wedding except for me?" He exhaled, Andre started laughing. I looked at Andre's friend. "Are you in the wedding too?"

"I knew you were gonna feel some kind of way about that. Honestly, I thought you would call me going off about it." Then he exhaled, "so much has been happening the brief moments when I could breathe I didn't want to think about anything. It's my fault and no one else's. I apologize for leaving you out. I'll pay for whatever you say for yours."

"Whatever I want?" I said tapping my chin.

He swallowed, "whatever you want." He said like he was nervous.

"What should I ask for?" I asked the boys. Andre shrugged. "I'll have to think about it and then discuss it with El. But you're gonna pay!" I gave him an evil grin.

Hubby and Nicole walked into the restaurant. Andrew sat up straight and he asked El if it was ok with him if he invited Hubby and Nicole to come sit with us. El looked at me to see if I was ok, and I told Andrew not to try to be cute. I told him I could tell Nicole doesn't know. He agreed and then Andrew waved them over. Andrew introduced Hubby and Nicole. Nicole gave me a thumbs up as she walked behind Hubby to sit on the same side of the table with her man and Andrew. Hubby tried not to, but I saw him sizing El up. Kind of the same way I did Nicole initially, but I like her. And it was so long ago why care. Andrew was watching the way El handled the situation. El didn't change up and pretty soon it was like the boys club. Nicole drank tea with us then she had to go to Tracy. Nicole very lovingly said bye to her man, then she told us she'd see us after four.

At three-forty-five El and I took our seats amongst the tons of family who were all eagerly awaiting the ceremony. We sat next to one of Tracy's aunts. She said she and her husband drove up from past Stockton, which is an almost two hour drive one-way for them. She was telling us how excited she was for Tracy. She was gushing over how much she loved her niece and how proud she was to be there. El was quiet and taking it all in. The ceremony was short and sweet! In the banquet hall, Richard, Chantel, and her brother and sister in law sat at the same table as us. I asked Richard if he talked to my momma last night. He said stuff kept happening, and he didn't think this weekend was the right time.

When the dance floor opened El invited me out to dance. "I can see how much this means to you. As long as it doesn't turn into some overrated business expense and the focus is on family and close friends, I give in. We can have your dream wedding." I hugged him, but I knew he would cave. "This is huge, but it's all about the wedding I like this."

"Thank you baby!" I kissed him. "I love you so much!" I said "I love you!" He said

MORE FROM THE AUTHOR

Thank you for allowing me to entertain you. I hope you have enjoyed reading my current release. If you have not read Volumes I – VIII of the Wallace Family Affairs series, please do so. Click here for a list of all the background stories. Once you have read the background stories, please checkout the current date series Together We Are Strong. Stay tune for more to come shortly.

Wallace Family Affairs

At Last (Click here)
Tracy's Complications (Click here)
Distorted Mirrors (Click here)
Sometimes Love Isn't Enough (Click here)
Love Is Just Enough (Click here)
Just A Friend (Click here)
Invisible (Click here)
Look Beyond Your Eyes
No Regrets (Click here)
First You Laugh Then You Cry (Click here)
A Heart That's Taken (Click here)
Abandoned (Click here)
Last Words (Click here)

Together We Are Strong

Season 1 Present (Click here)
Beyond The Wallace's ~ I Knew You When (**TBD**)
Season 2 What Comes Next (Release **TBD**)

Standalones

Secrets & Lies ~ (**TBD late 2016 release**)
Anthology **Short** Story (Where Love May Find You Collection)
~ (Click here)
Waiting (**TBD**)

Hopefully you've enjoyed all of the background stories for our lovely Wallace's and Latour's. Please tune in for more from the "Together We Are Strong" Wallace & Latour Family Episodes on Amazon.